SECOND TEAR

EMMANUELLE

USA TODAY BESTSELLING AUTHOR

SNOW

Smart Lily
Publishing

Second Tear
Emmanuelle Snow

Copyright © 2022 by Emmanuelle SNOW

All rights reserved.

No part of this book may be reproduced in any form or by any electronic or mechanical means, including information storage and retrieval systems, without written permission from the author, except for the use of brief quotations in a book review. No part of this book may be used to train, educate or otherwise inform any Artificial Intelligence including but not limited to those operating as large language models for any reason without prior written consent from the copyright holder.

First edition - April 2022 (V_1) (2025 update)

ISBN eBook: 978-1-990429-01-9

ISBN paperback: 978-1-990429-67-5

Contained Cruel Destiny (part 1) and Beautiful Salvation (part 2).

This book is a work of fiction. Any references to historical events, real people, or real places are used fictitiously. Names, characters, places, and incidents are products of the author's imagination. Any resemblance to actual events, locales, organizations, or persons, living or dead, is coincidental.

The publisher and author acknowledge the trademark status and trademark ownership of all trademarks, service marks, and word marks mentioned in this book.

Editors: Shalini G. and SLE

Cover: SMART Lily publishing inc.

Published by SMART Lily Publishing inc.

———

Emmanuelle Snow
www.emmanuellesnow.com

CARTER HILLS BAND UNIVERSE
(SUGGESTED READING ORDER)

Carter Hills Band series
False Promises

HEART SONG DUET
Blindsided
Forevermore

Whiskey Melody series
Sweet Agony

SECOND TEAR DUET
Cruel Destiny
Beautiful Salvation

BREATHLESS DUET
Wild Encounter
Brittle Scars

Upon A Star series
Last Hope

Midnight Sparks

Love Song For Two series
<u>Lonesome Heart Duet</u>
Fallen Legend
Rising Star

<u>Two of Us Duet</u>
Snowbound

Wicked Love

All titles available at
emmanuellesnow.com

For the best experience, read in the order as shown above

WHAT THE REVIEWS SAY

- "The journey these two needed to take I order to find happiness again was worth every page of this book." **(Tanja, OMGreads)**

- "A book that made me smile through my tears... Read the book with your heart as only Ms. Snow can break it as well as glue it back together. Emotions are her forte. And she get me every single time." **(Book Reviews by Shalini)**

- "Emmanuelle Snow wrote a perfect strangers-to-lovers realistic love story. But it is so much more than a romance book. It's a journey, it's a second chance at love and at aiming for your dreams, no matter how big or small they are." **(Goodreads)**

- "This is a novel with so much depth, so much heart and so much love. There is steam, there is loss and there are moments of shock." **(Book.ish Julie)**

- "Emmanuelle Snow is very talented with her words and getting them just right so her readers are feeling what her characters are feeling." **(Jennifer, Goodreads)**

- "I have a new favorite Emmanuelle Snow book. This story had it all, it was full of emotion and heartbreak but also just so heartwarming and wonderful." **(Sarah, Goodreads)**

- "Wow. Just wow. If that could be my review, that is all I would write." **(Reba, Goodreads)**

- "Emmanuelle has a way with words, making you feel like you're part of the story, going through the rollercoaster of emotions with her characters." **(Amanda, Goodreads)**

TRIGGER WARNINGS

Disclaimer

My books are realistic and emotional romance love stories.

I'm an advocate for mental health, and some topics could be sensitive for certain readers since they are portrayed as close to real life as possible.

I've listed the potential trigger warnings for each title on my website.

Be advised that those trigger warnings could potentially be spoiler alerts for the storylines.

Those sensitive topics have been written with the utmost care and respect. Please reach out if you have questions or comments.

All books contain sexuality, mature content, and language not intended for people under 18 years of age.
For other readers' sake, please avoid spoilers in your reviews.

Thank you and have a wonderful day!

Emmanuelle

emmanuellesnow.com

When everything goes sideways, stop, think, roll up your sleeves, and start over.

To my family, who've always stood by my side, even when the storm seemed too big to be contained by all of us.

I love you guys xx

BECOME A VIP

TO NEVER MISS A THING

Snow's VIP

Join **Emmanuelle Snow's VIP newsletter**

Be the first to know about new releases, giveaways, sales, and special events. And step into a space where big emotions are celebrated, love is messy and beautiful, and stories linger long after the last page.

emmanuellesnow.com

Snow's Soulmates

Join Emmanuelle Snow's Facebook VIP group, **Snow's Soulmates**, to chat with her and other readers, get updates, and more bonus content.

facebook.com/groups/snowvip

YOU AND ME

THE SONG

Oh, oh, oooh, you walked into
    the room
And suddenly I couldn't breathe
You looked at me with those eyes
And suddenly nothing existed
    but you
You took my hand in yours
And suddenly my entire world
    became you

[CHORUS]

I've never believed a love like ours
    could exist
But you came my way, and all my
    silly thoughts flew away
You came my way, baby, and I
    couldn't look away
I've never believed I had a place in
    this world

But you came to me as if you'd
    walked out of a dream
You came to me and made me
    believe we could be that team
I prayed for so many times in
    the dark
So many times I lost count

Without a warning, you made your
    way to my heart
Without a warning, you made your
    way to my head
Even if I wanted to chase you out of
    my bed
My heart belonged to you since the
    day you walked in, baby, oh, oh
The day you walked in, you gave
    me hope
The day you walked in, I started
    living again

[CHORUS]
Now I can't remember my life
    before you
No, I can't remember a time when I
    was alone and sad
Now every day I wake up with a
    smile
And every day I choose happiness
Because you've made me remember
    that's how things should be
Oh, baby, this is how our lives
    together should always be

[CHORUS]
You and me, that's how the story
    should be
You and me, forever it will be
Oh baby, you and me, forever it
    will be

Music and lyrics by Carter Hills and Dahlia Ellis

1

NICHOLAS

I rapped on the ajar door with my knuckles, pushing it open when the words "Come on in" resonated from inside the room. Murielle, Derek's mom, gestured for me to join them.

"Nick," the boy exclaimed, a permanent smile etched on his face, as if his life was fucking fantastic.

"How are you doing, big guy?" I asked, quirking an eyebrow at him, pulling my lips into a warm smile when we fist-bumped.

"Amazing. Look at this," my little friend said, pulling a red jersey from the side, pride gushing out from every pore of his being. "Barry Hamilton came over this morning."

"The hockey player?" I asked.

"Yeah. He's so huge. Cory Black and Rory Dupont came too."

I smoothed the polyester fabric of the shirt between my fingers, taking in all the signatures written in black ink.

"Man, this is awesome. The entire team signed this?"

Derek bobbed his head, stars twinkling in his eyes, his

grin stretching to both ears. "And we took pictures too. Show Nick, Mom. Show him."

Murielle handed me her phone, and I swept through the dozens of pictures with the pad of my thumb. My heart frizzled in my chest. I blinked, pushing my emotions down. Derek didn't deserve my being an emotional mess beside him. He needed my strength. And my unconditional optimism.

"Man, this is pretty cool." I lifted the paper bag I'd dropped on the edge of the bed when I walked in. "Thought you and I could have lunch together, you know, just us guys. I've had a shitty week—oops, sorry," I said, wrinkling my face and offering Murielle an apologetic smile.

Derek let out a heartfelt laugh. "I'm not six anymore, Nick. It's okay, I won't repeat it."

His mother rose to her feet. "Since Nick is here, I'll take an hour or two to run some errands. You boys be good, okay?" She turned to face her twelve-year-old. "You all right, baby?"

Derek nodded, the smile still anchored to his face as if every day was the most amazing one in his short life.

"Make sure you keep Nick out of trouble."

The boy's laughter reverberated through the small room and multiplied when I shrugged. Murielle gave a head shake and spun to face me. "Can you stay until I'm back?"

"Sure. My entire Sunday afternoon is dedicated to my friend here. I'm not going anywhere."

She squeezed my upper arm and bowed her head before walking out of the room, her lips pressed together in a thin line. I knew the look. Something was going on. It was in the air. Thick and barbed. With a grin plastered across my face, I tried my best to avoid bringing the subject up while Derek could hear us. It could wait. *Later*, I reiterated to myself.

With a soft thud, I landed my ass on the chair Murielle had vacated seconds ago and fished the food out of the bag. Greasy cheeseburgers, seasoned fries, extra-large sodas —root beer with no ice for my young friend, just the way he liked it. I knew Derek wasn't supposed to eat junk food, but I'd asked his doctors a few months ago, and they agreed he could use some fun in his life. And if it meant eating burgers or tacos with me once a week, then so be it. Even Murielle concurred.

Derek lifted his cup and clinked it against mine. "Thanks for the burger, bro."

I coughed, almost choking on the pieces of fries in my mouth. "Bro?" I repeated, taking a sip to alleviate the itchy feeling in my throat.

Derek shrugged and ended up giggling. Like a kid should always do. "Saw it in a movie last night. Sounded nice. Since we're best friends, I thought it was fitting."

I swallowed hard. Sometimes I forgot I was the closest thing Derek had to a friend. His peers from school had stopped visiting him a year ago. Kids his age ought to be running around on a soccer field or riding bikes, chasing frogs or going to camp, not stuck in a hospital bed, bald, skinny, alone all year round. It wasn't fair. None of this was how childhood should be.

My eyes found a picture of us by his bed, back when I coached his Little League team, before cancer, smiling on the field with matching golden jerseys and unruly blond hair. A mixture of emotions swirled inside me. I remembered that day as if it were yesterday. When we used to be carefree.

I shifted my gaze to my friend and mirrored his smile.

"I'm fine with bro if that's what you want. What do I call you from now on then?"

Derek sighed. Like the pre-teen he was. "*Bro*. C'mon. If I call you *bro*, you call me *bro*. That's how it works, no?"

I nodded. "I guess." Bro wasn't a word I used with Tucker and Jace. We usually called each other *man*. "Bro's fine, *bro*."

After a game of chess, which Derek won, as always—this kid was smart beyond words—he asked in a small voice, needing the reassurance of my presence, "If I take a nap, will you be there when I wake up?"

I nodded.

There was no other place I'd rather be. In all the years we'd known each other, this kid had touched my heart in countless ways. I didn't have it in me to refuse him anything. Minutes later, the sound of his steady breathing filled the air, and my heartbeat kicked up. A nagging feeling clawed at my spine, crushing each vertebra. Derek could bring much-required sunshine to this world in the way he beamed and left a permanent mark on those he blessed with his presence rather than being stuck in this room, glued to a bed, too weak to get up. A dark cloud hovered over me each time the thoughts ran freely in my head. With a deep inhale, I scanned the room, pushing all my gloomy reflections as far as I could. Over the last year, Murielle had decorated the walls with her paintings and framed family pictures. The hospital allowed it. Since cancer hit Derek five years ago, this room had become a second home to him. Between surgeries, radiation, chemo, and an endless list of infections, he now lived here full time.

My gaze lingered on his taut face as he slept. Pain dodged his footsteps and won most days. Purple rings shadowed his eyes. In the last year, they had lost their vibrant blue color and were now more a dull shade of gray after everything his body had been through. A baseball cap covered his bald head. My eyes drifted to a picture on the wall. A six-year-old Derek blowing candles on his birthday cake, the same smile he bore earlier today, lighting up his healthy little boy's face. A weight grew in my chest, pressing against my lungs, suffocating me. Nowadays Derek's skin looked pasty white—almost translucent—having lost its rosy tone.

The boy was dying. I could feel it. My soul recognized the signs as my body ached at the realization. Chills ran through me, involuntary tremors shaking me. The sight of him brought back the memories of watching my father fight cancer when I was fifteen. But my father survived. Derek wouldn't.

I put the remnants of our lunch back in the paper bag and took everything to the trash can next to the bed.

My gaze lingered on the boy I'd got attached to over the years. Each time I had time off, I swung by the hospital to spend a few hours with him. It felt important. Filling my lungs with quivering inhales, I pinched the bridge of my nose, fighting the emotional storm spiraling inside me that threatened to shatter the facade I usually wore in his presence.

Memories of my time spent with him resurfaced. A tiny smile tugged at my lips.

I was barely seventeen when I'd met him on the field before one of our Little League games for the first time. From that day on, I'd stuck by his side. His passion for the game, his cheerfulness, the glow within him drew me in. He was always eager to learn more, always giving his best. We connected big time during those games. Soon, Derek had felt like a little brother to me. Murielle, being a single mom, would often run late to pick him up after practice.

He and I started hanging out together while we waited for her, eating ice cream from the truck parked next to the baseball field, chatting about school and his friends. In more ways than one, from that moment, Murielle and Derek had become my second family.

I would watch him on the nights Murielle had to work double shifts at the restaurant.

Sometimes I'd invite him to throw the ball with Tucker, Jace, and me.

Once a week, Murielle would have me over for dinner after my parents left town so I wouldn't feel left out. Because four months after I'd turned eighteen, my folks had moved to Italy. A dream they both cherished. One they had been caressing for years. But also, one I didn't share. They'd asked me to come with them. My younger sister, Jessica, had. I refused. My life was in Chicago. My friends were here. And as much as living in Europe sounded awesome, just the idea of going away would knot my stomach in a tight bundle back then.

This was my home. I loved it here. Instead of chasing other people's dreams, I chose to cherish mine. I only had one shot at this life, and I wanted to make mine count. On my own terms. So, I got a job, worked my ass off to get experience, showed my commitment and integrity, and secured my own money. So far, my plan had worked great.

Two years after we met, Derek began chemotherapy. All his hair—including his eyebrows—fell off, and he kept fighting. Thinner and frailer through the battle, he never lost that mischievous spark shining in him.

Still on that bed, his breathing shallow and his frame delicate, I could picture the healthy boy he had been, because no matter how the illness had changed his appearance, it had never altered his essence. It shone bright like the scintillating gem he was.

A long huff escaped my tight lips as my eyes stayed anchored to Derek's figure.

Murielle came back at the exact moment. She touched my side, her tiny hand feather-light against my muscles. "Thank you for spending time with him," she whispered, her loving eyes resting on her son's recumbent form, so small under the covers I'd adjusted around him.

I shoved my hands into my pockets, my shoulders sagging forward. "What's the prognosis?" A lump grew in my throat, and I pushed it down to even out my breathing. I could do this. I had to know. I deserved to know. No matter how bad the truth would hurt.

Murielle cast a glance down and took a wheezing breath before meeting my eyes. "Not good. A few weeks at, huh, the most… If at all… His body can't… His body can't take it anymore. His white blood cell count is too low… He's tired. The last infection drained all the energy reserves in him. He doesn't want to fight anymore. We talked about it… He-he says he's ready to go."

I wiped the tears building in my eyes with my thumb. "It's unfair. I'm so sorry…" I shifted around to wrap a defeated Murielle in my arms, rocking her back and forth. I'd do anything to stop the heartbreaking, silent sobs coming out of her. Her shoulders heaved in my embrace. Nothing I could say would make this moment less painful, so I kept my mouth shut, my throat constricting painfully with unshed tears.

————

Hours later, after I promised Derek to visit the next day, I slouched my ass on a bar stool, my fingers knitted together on my nape, my elbows anchored to the worn ebony counter as I tried to wrap my brain around all the jumbled-up emotions swirling in my head. And my heart.

Tucker, my best friend since we were five, lightly punched my arm and slid onto the stool next to mine. "I knew I'd find you here. Bad day?"

I huffed before turning my head to stare at him. "Derek. He's dying. For real this time. Nothing the doctors can do. It's over. He's done fighting."

"How long?" he asked, motioning the bartender over with a flick of his hand. "We'll have two more of those," he said to the man, pointing to the empty tumbler before me.

"Weeks. A month or two at the most."

"Sorry, man. I know how much you love that kid. Life is fucking unfair. In which world do children have to fight for their lives? It's a freaking joke." Tucker shook his head and guzzled half the drink the bartender brought over.

"He asked me if I would look after his mom." Moisture welled up behind my eyes, stinging the already raw emotions lingering there.

Tucker glided his finger into his shirt collar and cracked his neck before loosening the navy tie. "Fuck," was all he said. Yeah, no other powerful word could translate the feeling we both shared.

In silence, we sipped our drinks while my best friend signaled the bartender for another round.

"Make them double this time."

The bartender nodded and turned to grab the whiskey bottle we'd surely empty tonight.

After another minute of silence, where we each ruminated over the unsaid words floating between us, Tucker cleared his throat and fixated his somber eyes on mine. "How's Murielle?"

The lining of my throat hurt as if a million needles

prickled the flesh. It wasn't from the liquor we'd been drinking. I blinked fast, pleading my emotions to settle and prevent the tears from blinding me. If Derek could be strong facing a death sentence, then I had to be too. Only then could I support his mother when she'd need me the most. My gaze drifted to a table where a group of women was celebrating one of their milestone birthdays. Big silver balloons, a two and a five, were attached to the back of a chair, and a dozen cherry-red shot glasses were spread across the table. The birthday girl rocked a white top and a teal crown, her smile huge and expectant for the years to come. As if nothing could shadow this moment. I used to be that guy. Years ago. Before I understood life was a flimsy line that could fray at any moment and shatter everything in its wake. With a shake of my head, I swigged down half my drink in one go and focused my attention back on my friend.

"A wreck. The worst part is I couldn't say anything to lessen the pain. For once, I-I couldn't find the words…" I sank my face into my hands and dropped my shoulders with a loud sigh. "What are you supposed to tell a mother who's about to lose her only child?"

"Nothing, I guess."

I brought the whiskey to my lips, enjoying the trail of fire down my throat, reminding me I was still alive.

And about to get wasted.

2

NICHOLAS

I spread the blueprints across the makeshift table on the twentieth floor of the condo we were building, trying to figure out a solution for the missing twelve inches on the twenty-fifth floor. The elevator couldn't open, lacking the required clearing, which rendered the floor useless unless we found a great idea. Kevin, the concrete guy, had worked with us on numerous projects before, and the last thing I wanted was to fire him over this. Not a moment of recrimination, the next couple of hours demanded new ideas, something I could pitch to the promoter and architect by the next morning to save face— and my job.

Kevin scrunched up his face, his expression apologetic. "I messed up, Nick. I'll understand if you tell me to get the hell out of here. My head has been all over the place lately. I know it's not an excuse. I appreciate you not screaming at me right now or telling me to gather my stuff and fuck off. If I were in your shoes, I'd be furious. I can take your wrath. I know this is your shot…your chance to get in Cody's good graces and prove yourself."

I breathed out my ire and shut my eyes, a groan leaving my throat. "Throwing you out will not change anything, man. You messed up. Big time. I can't believe you didn't realize you were using the preliminary plans. Believe me, I'm pissed. But let's work together and engineer it to play in our favor. If we use our collective brains, we'll find a way to convince the guys this fuck-up is a good thing after all. Stop chastising yourself and put that head of yours to good use."

He nodded, inching closer, studying the blueprints next to me.

Jace, the electrician contractor on the project and my other best friend, joined us. "Hey, what happened? You both have this look on your faces."

I pushed the table with both hands, tilting my head back in slow motion.

"The second to last floor misses twelve inches in height. The elevator can't open, which makes the floor useless. And redoing the structure will cost too much and put us three weeks behind schedule. Kevin and I are trying to find a way to make it work somehow."

"Oh shit. Don't want to be there when Cody learns about it." Cody, my boss, wasn't the most reasonable guy. If you failed him, you were put on his shit list forever. No second chances granted. Ever. I was lucky he let me supervise this project. Younger than most other foremen in the company, he offered me the job, hinting that if I surpassed myself—which meant keeping the costs to a minimum and delivering the building without any delays—I'd supervise much bigger projects in the near future. The idea sat well with me. Chicago being a booming city, I could see myself managing high-rise buildings in a few years. But first, I had to deal with the concrete flooring predicament.

"Did you hear about the guys showing up at the

hospital yesterday?" Jace asked, positioning himself between Kevin and me, studying the plans over our shoulders.

"Derek was ecstatic. You should have seen the stars in his eyes when he told me. Please tell Barry I owe him one."

Jace tapped my shoulder. "No worries. He was happy to do it. When I told him he was one of Derek's idols and what he's been going through, he didn't even hesitate. I'm glad the boy liked it."

"You're kidding? He *loved* it."

"How is he doing? Any news?"

I shook my head, swallowing hard, avoiding his inquisitive gaze. "I'm not sure he'll still be here next month."

Jace bowed his head. "Sorry, man. I know how much you care about him."

I offered him a tight-lipped smile, bringing my attention back to the construction fuck-up instead, chasing the reality of Derek dying as far as I possibly could, scared I'd tear at the seams or implode from inside if I let myself think about it for a second too long.

An idea flashed through my mind. "What if the penthouse had two floors instead of one? Maybe we could—"

"Man, you're a genius," my friend praised, his face lighting up like those high-wattage bulbs—the ones we used on every site in the early stages of construction. Finding a possible solution to the present problem flushed out the fragments of tension inside me, loosening the knots in my back and shoulders, as Jace continued, "You know Ted Duffy?"

"The goalie from New Jersey?" I asked.

"Yeah. Anyway, he signed with the team and is looking for a place in the city. Barry mentioned it the other night. He has two kids and doesn't want a place downtown, but somewhere close. I know for a fact he doesn't want a house. Let me make a call. See if he'd be interested in taking a look." Jace stepped away, his phone already glued to his ear. "Hey, Barry. Listen…"

His voice got drowned by the noises surrounding us as he spoke to his sister's friend from college. Barry Hamilton, the number one center and captain of the professional hockey team, the Chicago's Busters, had spent many holidays and summer vacations at my friend's house, and the two had stayed close over the years.

Jace came back ten minutes later with a beaming smile stretching his face. "Got Duffy on a conference call. Hasn't found a place to stay yet. He'll meet with us tomorrow. He said if he can use his own designer team to look at the blueprints and work with us, he'd be interested in getting both top floors for added privacy. His kids are attending a school fifteen minutes from here. I told him the view of the city from the twenty-fifth floor was one to die for."

The three of us angled our heads in the direction of where the panoramic windows would be installed soon.

I blinked. Once. Twice. Yeah, the view from here was spectacular.

Reality hit back, and I spun to stare at my friend.

"Are you messing with me? I'm not in the mood for some stupid joke."

Jace shrugged. "No. The guy's filthy rich and doesn't want to live in a fifty-floor high rise or a house. I think this could work out. All you have to do is sell him the project. Once he's on board, Cody won't be able to chew your ass off."

I pulled my friend into a hug. "Thanks, man. You know you just saved my life, right? Or rather, my job."

"You would've done the same. No worries. Now that the puck is yours, you better score this goal." He winked as I glared. Not truly. But in jest.

"Hockey pun? Really?"

Jace let out a warm laugh, his head falling back. "Couldn't help it. The guy is a fucking god behind the net. You need to be better."

Kevin huffed, his shoulders sagging, putting a stop to our well-deserved minute of fun. "Thank you, guys. Once again, I'm sorry, Nick. And if Cody wants to fire you, just know I'll take all the blame. It wasn't your fault. I screwed up. If it works out, I'll never be able to thank you enough."

"Let's brainstorm, man. We're not done. We must find a way to make this two-floor-penthouse idea work. I might be good at solving problems and being creative, but it's not a done deal until it's signed."

And just like that, we spent three hours after everybody left the site, studying the plans so we could present something amazing to Ted Duffy the next day.

———

A week later, Jace and I sat in Tucker's high-end condo overlooking Lake Michigan, playing poker, as we did every Wednesday night. I looked at them, and my heart swelled with gratitude for our friendship. Something had been prickling at me all day, though, nothing perceivable, just blunt thorns under my skin, making me want to scratch them out.

Tucker's voice brought me back to the present. "I can't believe you guys sold your condo fuck-up to Duffy," he said, sipping his beer.

"It was Jace's idea. He saved the day. It turned out the promoter made half a million extra in profit with that sale only. It could have turned out much worse. We were lucky this time."

"You did all the work. Don't shy away from your success," Jace said.

Tucker nodded in agreement. "You'll get that promotion, Nick. Now it's certain. No way Cody will let you go after this. If I were him, I'd even promote you to partner."

I shook my head and let out a snarky laugh. "Forget it. He'll never agree to sell shares of his business. The guy is territorial. And greedy as fuck. Anyway, I just did my job. Anybody could have done it."

"Man, you're too humble. Take the recognition for once. You killed it."

Tucker and Jace raised their bottles to mine.

"Tuck is right. You're the one who sold the project to Duffy. You know, scored that goal," Jace added with a wink.

Fucker. I threw a beer cap square at his chest. "I'm right. He could have said no. All I did—"

Jace's phone vibrated on the table, and he flipped it over with a deep scowl before jumping to his feet. "Gimme a sec, guys." He stepped away from us, clutching the device in a white-knuckled grip.

"I bet a twenty it's Pam," Tucker mocked with a disapproving twist of his lips. "Tell me again why he married her?"

"No idea. I can't believe I devoted one year of my life to her. Guess they have the chemistry we missed."

"She's a control freak, man. You're way better off."

"Well, I wasn't in love with her. We just happened to enjoy sex together…on occasions. Other than that, we had nothing in common. She wasn't even that nice. I hope she treats Jace better." I scratched my temple. "I still can't believe she went after him the moment we broke up, though. He said she's his true love. Let's hope he's right—" I swallowed the last words as Jace came back.

"Sorry, guys. Need to bail. You know Pam. She's not a fan of our Wednesday poker nights." He gave us an apologetic, timid smile before leaving as if the building was on fire and he had to save his life.

Tucker stared at me when the door clicked after Jace's exit. "It's messy. Pam owns his balls. I'll repeat what I said earlier. Why the hell did he elope with her? Worst decision of his life."

I bowed my head.

Pam moved on to date one of my two best friends after we decided not to see each other again, and I wasn't even upset about it. Rather, I hated that she had dug her claws into Jace's soft heart. He deserved so much better. But he'd made his bed, and now had to sleep in it every night.

"I'm glad you got an out. Your romantic heart could have put you in his shoes. You're a sucker for love. L.O.V.E."

"I'm not." Tucker harrumphed, and I had to agree, "Okay, I totally am. What's wrong with that? Not all of us want fuck buddies. I tried. It ended badly. We fought because she wanted more than I was willing to give her. Now she despises me. Never again. My folks are still in love after thirty years. I'm aiming for that. Life is too short to spend time with people you don't genuinely care about." Tucker opened his mouth to say something, but I rushed on, "Before you object, there's nothing wrong with it. I don't want to spend my life fucking random chicks. That's your thing. And if you're fine with it, then good for you. It's just not my way."

I drained my whiskey, slamming the empty tumbler with a thud on the poker table.

My phone chimed with an incoming call, and something coiled around my stomach. Nobody except my friends ever called me at this late hour, and they were all accounted for, except for my youngest one. My breathing hitched on its way out as if it didn't want to know the truth. I recognized the number. My fingers hesitated to accept the call, knowing I wasn't ready—and would never be—for the words that could sink everything I hold dear in my life.

I eyed the screen warily as if it could explode any second.

"You're not getting that?" Tucker asked, snapping me out of my daze as my fingers curled around the device.

I cleared my throat, braced my shoulders, and answered, digging deep inside me to search for the flecks of courage I knew I'd need. Courage I feared I didn't possess in that instant.

"Mu—Murielle." I stammered a greeting, my voice low and uneven. My tongue couldn't seem to formulate the words.

The woman on the other end of the line said nothing, her sobs filling the silence and making their way to my heart, piercing through its wall like thousands of sharp swords. My chest deflated. My shoulders slumped. No matter how much I tried to stay strong, her sobs broke my strength. Since Derek's final prognosis, I'd been anticipating the call that would change my life, but deep down I still carried hope this wasn't the end. Murielle's sobs froze my blood and rattled every bone in my body. Slivers of my soul where hope resided withered to ashes. My knees lost their strength to stay upright. I clamped my fingers around the edge of the poker table, the nerve to utter a word—any word—disappearing with each passing second.

"Murielle?" I closed my eyes as grief warped my heart, its bindings tight, making a single tear flow down my cheek. I whispered, my voice sounding hollow even to my ears, "Talk to me. Wh…what happened?"

A weird gasp followed by a low, keening moan that made my hair stand on end resonated through the phone. Murielle's heart was breaking, shattering to dust on the other end of the line, and all I could do was stand there, listening to the cries of her empty womb. The cleaving of her soul. Her child. The blood of her blood.

I waited, my words stuck in my throat, my body slowly turning to concrete, one cell after the other.

She inhaled loudly and stuttered, "C-co…co-coma. He's on life support. My baby will… he…huh…will never wake up….they said. How could they say that?"

I stopped breathing the moment my brain processed what she was saying. I tried to move but couldn't. I looked down at my legs. They were there, but I couldn't feel them. They seemed paralyzed. Hot, then cold, then ice and burning fire. My body didn't know how to react to grief. Murielle's words sounded surreal, coming from a far-off place.

A hard mass grew in my chest, compressing my heart.

"I'll…I'll be right there," I said, speaking through the lump in my throat. "I'll be there. In…huh…ten. I'm coming. I'll be there." I hung up, the sensations twirling inside me, strange and alien, as I scanned the room around me. I blinked. Where was I?

Tucker stepped next to me and squeezed my arm. "Nick?"

I looked at him with unseeing eyes. Why was he here? A fog seemed to envelop my brain, blurring my thoughts. I had to be somewhere, but where? I blinked again, praying for my brain to take over. To get me out of this fugue.

Was I dreaming, or was I awake? It all seemed so tangible, and so unreal at the same time.

Tucker shook me—hard—both hands clamping my upper arms. Maybe I wasn't dreaming after all. "Nick.

C'mon, man. Talk to me. What's going on? Is it Derek?" His voice sounded as if coming from a dark tunnel.

I nodded, unable to get a word out.

My friend closed his eyes and sighed.

I watched him, but it was like we weren't in the same room. As if a glass wall stood between us. Still, he hadn't released my arms.

I rubbed my eyes with the heels of my hands and inhaled. "I-I need to be there. With him… With Murielle… He's on a ventilator. The doctors say he won't wake up…" Tears flowed freely down my cheeks, escaping to their freedom. My heart fractured in my chest, and any fragments of hope I had left free-fell to my feet. My lips quivered, and my palms turned clammy. And cold.

A wave of nausea hit me. I shut my eyes to calm the earthquake rising from the void inside me.

"Nick, I'm sorry—" He dragged a hand over his face. "Man, you gotta pull yourself together. Be strong for Murielle. I'm there whenever you need me. Whatever the time, okay?"

I nodded. "Thanks." I cleared my throat. "I appreciate it."

"Want me to drive you?"

I shook my head. Acid filled my mouth. I prayed for fresh air.

"No. I'll walk. Better to tame some of my emotions before I get there. It'll take me only, huh, five minutes. I can manage. Else, I'll implode. The night air will cool me down."

Without another word, I strode out in the inky darkness toward the hospital, my insides knotted so tight they hurt, desperate to get my emotions under control before entering the room and facing Murielle and her dying son. They needed me. My courage. And my strength. A light breeze tickled my cheeks, cooling my burning eyes. "You can do this, Nick," I said out loud. "Be brave." My voice cracked.

Over the last few years, I'd seen Derek at his best moments—well, the best he could have, considering the illness—and his lowest. But, somehow, he hung in there, always awakening hope in me that he'd pull through this. Now I knew better. The brain tumor had won the battle. I'd felt it ten days ago when I visited him, and Murielle confirmed it. The creepy feeling had been clinging to me since that day. When I went to see him yesterday after work, Derek was already asleep. I spent three hours at his side, hoping he'd open his eyes. In vain. Finally, Murielle had pushed me out of the room at ten when I promised to come back on Thursday after work, both our hearts hemorrhaging with dreadful trepidation.

And now I would never get a chance to say a proper goodbye to my little friend. To hear him call me *bro* one last time or fist-bump me over cheeseburgers and sodas.

My legs grew heavier when the hospital came into view. I could do this. Time to be strong. Time to be there for those who'd welcomed me into their lives and shown me what strength was. I straightened my back, sucked in a breath, and approached the building, the feeling of dread growing stronger.

3

NICHOLAS

In the doorway, I ground my molars together. Derek lay in his hospital bed, and if it weren't for the steady beeping of the monitor next to his head, I'd think he was already dead. His face—usually a mix of gray and white—had lost all traces of color. All the spark. All life. I studied the rise and fall of his chest, thanks to the ventilator.

A nurse spoke to him as she adjusted the pillow underneath his frail frame. Did he lose even more weight in the last twenty-four hours?

Murielle cocked her head, and our eyes met. My feet turned to lead as I stumbled forward and enveloped her in my arms, her tiny figure trembling, her tears soaking my clothes. No words were needed as grief poured out of us, creating a lifelong bond.

"Thanks for coming, Nick. I-I know he'd want y-you to…to be here. I believe he can feel us. I-I feel my baby. He isn't gone."

"Derek is the best. A good kid. You did well. I'm so

sorry it's happening to you two…" Emotions drowned my words. I blinked to get a slice of composure back.

Murielle hugged my midsection. "You're one of the… the good ones, Nick Peterson. Derek is lucky to have you in his life. You make him happy. You…you brighten his days. He looks up to…he looks up to you… You'll never understand how much you mean to him."

I rested my chin on the top of her head, watching Derek as he lay there peacefully, not knowing the rubble he was leaving behind. My gaze zeroed in on the equipment keeping him alive. So many tubes. And cords. And machines. Drips and pumps everywhere. Each one of them splintered my heart a little more. A firm clamp tightened around my chest. My friend was a trooper, took everything head-on. My eyes followed the ventilator as it pumped air into his lungs through the tube. No expression marred his face. The lines had smoothed out. No sign of pain. He seemed to be almost at peace. After life had put him through a wringer. Deep down, I already missed him, his cheerful grin and sparkling eyes. And liveliness. Everything that made him—well, him. A big chunk of my heart died at the sight.

The room looked like a scene from a sci-fi movie, but this wasn't fiction. It was real life. Derek's life. Ending too soon. Way too soon. I wrinkled my face, not ready to give up hope as burning tears cascaded down my cheeks. People often talked about out-of-body experiences. Now I got it. Nothing felt factual right now. As if I was living someone else's surreal existence and this wasn't my life.

In silence, Murielle and I broke apart and sat on the opposite edges of the bed, each of us holding one of his hands.

"Hey, bro. It's me and your mom. Listen, we'd like you to fight this. Come back to us. It's selfish…but can we have more time together? We're so not ready to let you go. But only if you can, okay? We miss you… I-I miss you… And I…huh…promise I'll learn to play chess better so that I can be more of a challenge. And…we still have that game to go to. With the guys. Come back to us, bro. I-I promise I will buy the front row seats, okay? I don't want to say goodbye just yet. I can't… I need…" My voice fell to a whisper as my words echoed through the room, strained. My trembling chin pointed to the ceiling, my tears soaking the short stubble covering my jaw. I squeezed Derek's hand, relishing the warmth in his. My voice cracked as I forced the next words out. "Come back to me, bro. I am not…I am not ready to say goodbye." I bent my head down to watch our clutched hands as tears covered his.

Then it happened. Derek squeezed my hand. My breathing halted. I blinked, wondering if I'd dreamed it. My eyes landed on our connected hands, begging him to do it again. After a few seconds, his hand jerked. A tiny, barely perceptible movement of his fingers against mine. A ghost of a smile grazed my lips.

"He moved. Derek is still in there."

Murielle straightened. Eyes round and full of confusion, she pressed the emergency red button, and two nurses rushed into the room.

Still perched on Derek's bedside, I urged him to shift his hand again. "Come on, bro. Show them. Move. Derek, I'm asking you to move your hand. Please. Once. Just do it. Show them." I wrapped my fingers around his, pressing harder. Nothing. Not even a tiny flicker.

Stephen, the oncologist, walked in. Over the years, we'd gotten to know each other pretty well. He had always treated me with respect. Almost like a son. He examined the boy and joined me by the side of the bed, clapping my shoulder with his large hand. "Nick, what you witnessed is called spontaneous movements from the muscles. They spasm sporadically… spinal reflexes. Nothing more. It has nothing to do with Derek's brain activity."

"But he moved. I felt it. He squeezed my hand. I swear."

"Son, I know. It's quite common. He suffered an intracranial bleed due to his metastases. Hence, we put him on the ventilator. We've run tests and scans. No neural activity. We will be repeating them in the next twenty-four hours, do another EEG, but I'm not expecting a different outcome."

I folded my arms on each side of my head, curled on myself, shielding my body from the pain—and the harsh words.

"What do we do, huh, now?" Murielle asked, her usual soft voice gravelly and shaky, imprinted with a cocktail of emotions that should be illegal to feel as a parent.

"We wait."

And so, we waited.

———

For the next few days, our vigilance by Derek's bedside never stopped. Either Murielle or I would speak to him, holding his hand, praying for a sign. Any sign. My heart broke a little more as she related the story of his birth, the first time she held her newborn baby close to her heart. Happy milestones in her child's short life. His first smile. His first crawl. His first steps. Every story enveloped in a mother's love and wrenched in her tears as she probably realized with each word that they were all she had left. Memories.

My friends kept in touch. Jace even offered to deal with Cody, smoothing out things with my boss since I was in no mind to heed the five times he called to coax me back to work. All my focus was on this friend of mine. The brother of my heart. The light of my soul.

Murielle read stories to him, and I told him all about my friends' antics. Tales from my own childhood. My work. Our Little League days. Anything that struck my mind at this time. I wasn't completely aware of the words I spoke, but I knew they were memories of my good times. Minutes became hours as Derek was wheeled out of the room for his scans, then wheeled back in. Each time, I held my breath, bracing myself for some news. Any news. Nurses drew blood, specialists came in, then walked back out with a grim demeanor. Even as the tears of our hearts deepened, we refused to let go of the tiny bursts of hope we held on to. Derek still had the good fight in him. Didn't he? In silence, I prayed for it.

Night overpowered the light of the day. Murielle took the mattress provided for her. I paced the corridors. The hospital, which was so busy during the day, turned into a grave town where only the machines made their beeps and nurses spoke in hushed tones at night. The respectful silence accentuated the emotions floating in the air, knowing someone was leaving and someone else was being welcomed in this cycle of life.

A sudden series of high-pitched beeps followed by an alarm pierced the heavy silence, and nurses ran toward Derek's room. My steps carried me inside. *Code blue.* A crash cart was rolled in, along with a defibrillator. Murielle and I hunched in the corner of the room, clutching each other for support, taking the whole scene in with widened eyes and hitched breaths.

My blood turned to ice, firing chills through my entire being. A rock grew in my chest, pushing against my lungs.

Derek's heart had stopped.

The scene played before me in slow motion.

Doctors bustled into the room. Injections were given. Pulse was searched for. The faces of comfort became tighter as tensions ran high. More medicines were loaded while buttons were pressed. Nothing. Paddles were placed on his chest. The defibrillator was cranked, and his heart was shocked. Derek's limp body arced, then thumped back on the bed. I blinked. Was I dreaming all this? How could any of this be real? Air jammed in my throat. Holding our breaths, we all waited for the beep that would tell us he was still fighting. Seconds passed. Nothing. Murielle's prayers sounded louder than usual, calling all the saints above. The doctors shocked Derek a second time. Nothing. They increased the power and shocked him for the third time. Nothing.

Beside me, Murielle wailed, slouching forward. Through the tension floating high in the air, a faint beep resonated, becoming louder with each second. Derek's pulse. A shared sigh of relief echoed through the room. Derek—or someone above—had heard our prayers.

Oxygen struggled to reach my brain. Dizziness, some emotional hurricane coming from a chasm inside me, sent black spots dancing before my eyes. I breathed in. And out. In and out. My heart fought to wander out of my chest. To go on a strike instead of having to go through all this aching pain. I didn't want to feel so much. I looked at Murielle, who was slumped in my arms. I had promised Derek I'd be there for her. Even if my composure was only held by a flimsy thread, I couldn't be the one breaking down.

Stephen came in.

He gave extra orders, and the nurses busied themselves, administering injections through the intravenous line in Derek's arm and pressing more buttons. All this time, I stayed frozen, unable to even twitch a finger. Stephen turned to look at Murielle and me and tilted his head. In a trance, we followed him out, leaving Derek in the care of the nursing staff.

The oncologist cleared his throat. "Okay, here's the situation. Like we discussed, we did some scans and an EEG to check out the electrical activity of Derek's brain. I'm sorry, but there's nothing." He paused. "This cardiac arrest isn't a good sign. Derek's heart is unable to pump blood. His organs are starting to fail. Now it's up to you. Your call. Derek won't wake up."

"Will his heart stop again?" Murielle asked in a hoarse voice.

"Yes. Our medicines are trying to maintain his vitals, but eventually, it will stop again."

"How long does my baby have?"

"We can't tell. Every time his body suffers an insult, we'll have to shock him to try to bring him back. He is weak, so I don't know, could be hours or days. We'll give you some time to think about it. To discuss Derek's final moments." His eyes traveled between the two of us. "When you're ready to turn off the ventilator, let us know. It will be the hardest thing both of you will ever do, but it will also be the kindest thing you can do for him. Derek fought a long and hard battle. Now he's tired. Remember, we're here for you, okay? Every step of the way."

Murielle's sobs punctured another wall around my heart, her tears soaking her shirt. The nurses walked out, and she rushed into the room. I leaned against the wall in the corridor, hoping… What was I even hoping for? It wasn't fair to let a child be shocked to life. My emotions twined in my throat and stayed there.

My phone vibrated inside my pocket. With trembling

fingers, I dug it out and rubbed my fist over my eyes to clear the fog clouding my vision.

TUCKER

You okay, man? Any news?

ME

Heart stopped. They shocked him. Vitals down.

Dots bounced at the bottom of my screen, then disappeared. They reappeared. Only to vanish again seconds later. A telltale sign that my friend had no clue what to say to ease the pain, raw and unbearable, growing in my chest, crushing all my organs.

ME

You don't have to say anything. I know you understand.

TUCKER

I'm so sorry. Call me if you need anything.

ME

Will do.

I waited for a few minutes to compose myself, then slowly dragged my weary body back to Derek's room. My heart skipped a beat, aching at the sight that faced me. Murielle was lying beside her little boy, whispering into his ear, stroking his arm, a loving expression painted on her face.

I slumped against the wall, its vertical surface the only thing keeping my body upright, my fingertips pressed together under my chin, my vocal cords frozen.

"Baby, you came back for me. I hope you can hear me. 'Cause Mommy loves you. And…and will always love you. You are…you are a fighter, but it's time for you to rest. I understand it now. You can't tell me with your words, but your body is, and I'll…I'll respect your wishes. Mommy's heart knows what you're asking for. I'm sorry I'm the one keeping you in this life just because I wasn't ready to let you go… While you told me multiple times you were. Just know I hear you loud and clear. Now I get it. Please keep smiling. And be happy, okay?"

She kissed his forehead.

Lying by his side, her arms around the still body of her son, she started the song that she hummed every night during Derek's chemo and radiotherapy treatments to help him fall asleep. When she stared at me, tears shone in her eyes, along with knowledge. Resignation. Surrender. And love. My throat worked. She didn't have to speak the words.

With a slight nod, I straightened and exited the room to get the staff.

Minutes later, Stephen walked back into the room along with his residents. We all waited for Murielle to finish her final lullaby, a haunted expression shadowing every-one's faces.

With a finger, she beckoned me. On weakened legs, I approached the bed and sat down, holding Derek's hand.

My chest ripped in two, and the raw suffering poured out, as if the dam broke and no one possessed the required skills to fix it. Silent tears slid down my cheeks.

"Bro, it's time. Your mom is right. We must do this. Honor your wishes. You wouldn't want to be stuck to a machine." I sucked in a scorching breath. One that fed the blazing flames down my larynx. "We'll set you free. Wher-ever you are next, I hope you're happy. And healthy. And safe. That you'll run around or fly a helicopter or some-thing. Or maybe play ball like we used to. Heaven's Little League could really use your talent. And your leadership.

That's all I hope for you, bro." I sobbed, the back of my eyes burning from crying too much. "We'll set you free," I repeated. "Shine up there, okay? Shine brighter than you did here, which is kinda hard since you were everybody's light." A tiny smile curled my lips, happy memories flooding in. "Watch over your mom. I will too. Like…like you asked me. The sky is lucky to have another star. I love you."

Murielle's last words permeated the eerie silence of the room. "I love you, baby. I'll love you forever."

The air tensed. Goose bumps spread across my nape.

Only the whoosh of the ventilator and the beeping of Derek's heart could be heard.

Stephen cleared his throat, and Murielle nodded to me. I moved to her side and supported her up as we watched the scene, helpless. Her attention drifted to the switch of the ventilator, inches away. Her face wrenched in pure agony as her hand reached for it, then withdrew.

She retreated to his bed and brushed Derek's bald head with her hand as if to push his hair back. The same way she always did when he was just a little boy with a headful of golden locks.

Shrills of pain filled the room. "My baby. My baby… No. I-I can't say goodbye. *Noooo—*"

Standing close, I pulled her into my embrace, rocking her, wishing I had a magical way to soothe her distress through this heart-wrenching moment.

With a long quivering huff, I braced myself, squaring my shoulders. "Do you want me…to…. huh…you know? I can… if-if you want…" No matter how hard I tried, those words refused to pass my lips.

Murielle studied me, her face a broken roadmap of bleakness and a thousand more emotions I refused to dig into but could feel down to the marrow of my bones.

A slow nod confirmed it.

In the semi-lit room, I did the one thing I'd never imagined myself doing in my life. I turned Derek's ventilator off.

The heart rate slowed down with each second. Lost in my own grief, I zoned out.

My mind went numb, and even if I tried, I couldn't seem to draw a full breath.

Murielle hugged her son and whispered the words over and over. "Baby, Mommy loves you. Now and forever. In every lifetime. You are a true fighter, the best amongst us. Now you're free. Free to run, free to live, not bound to a bed. Be safe up there. Make friends. You deserve it. Nothing will come in your way anymore. You're allowed to be a child. Go now. Please remember… I love you."

I love you too, bro. And I always will. I'll never forget you. You'll be in my heart forever.

I kissed my fingers and saluted the sky.

4

NICHOLAS

A week ago

"When will you get a girlfriend?" Derek teased me. "You never meet anyone because you're too busy working. Do you want to turn into Cody?"

A heartfelt laugh broke free. "You're twelve, bro. Since when do you have this much interest in my love and professional lives?"

The boy shrugged. "We're best friends. It's my job to make sure you don't miss out on important things in life." He flipped his hands so as to say, *Come on.* "Tucker is always hitting the clubs. I'm sure he can help you if you're too shy to ask a girl out yourself."

I blinked. "Since when did you turn into a mini version of him?" I asked.

Derek's contagious laughter filled the room. "We talk, you know. Me and Tuck. And Jace too."

I blinked again. "About me?"

Derek bobbed his head, his mischievous grin never faltering.

"And Tuck told you about his dating life?"

"And the lack of yours," he continued.

Wow, this was a conversation I never thought I'd have with a twelve-year-old—my little brother in so many ways. Sometimes it seemed as if the boy had lived ten lives, smarter and wiser than all of us united.

Derek rocked his head from side to side, his shoulders mimicking the movement. "I asked him questions. Because I don't want you to end up like my mom. Alone. She thinks I don't notice, but I know she's lonely and could use a nice man in her life. Some love. To help share the burden of the pain."

How could these words come from a child?

"She has me—"

Derek giggled, the sound warming my heart. "It's not the same. Unless you tell me you're in love with her." He tipped one invisible brow, and I burst into a fit of laughter.

"Fine. You're right. It's not the same."

The air in the room shifted, the lightness replaced by a suffocating tightness.

"When I'm gone, will you make sure she's okay? My mom, I mean. She'll need a best friend too. Maybe you could be hers. Until she finds one of her own."

My throat closed.

No air or sound could pass through the rock sitting there and taking permanent residence.

"Bro—" I began.

Derek raised his hands between us. "I'm serious, Nick. You know it will happen. One day. And I don't want any of you to be too sad. Crying is okay. But don't stop being happy because I won't be there."

Tears rushed to my eyes. Everything in the room blurred.

Derek moved to his knees and wrapped his arms around me, steel bands keeping me in one piece and preventing my heart from being ripped apart on hearing his words.

I returned his embrace.

"I'm glad you won't be alone," he spoke into my chest. "You have Tucker and Jace. I'm sorry I won't be there to watch games with you anymore."

I'm sorry too.

"I'll miss you," I said, my voice low and rickety. "Let's enjoy the time we have together." Those sounded like sensible words to say because I wasn't ready to admit the unavoidable out loud. Not yet, at least.

"You know that song from Carter Hills Band about monkeys that makes me laugh?"

I nodded.

"Once I'm gone, if you hear it, please turn on the volume so I can hear it too."

The heartache enveloping my throat tightened until my voice resembled a whistle. "I will."

Derek straightened. "Can I show you something?" he asked, leaning back.

I cleared my throat to chase the strangling emotions lodged there, sounding more confident than I did inside. "Sure."

He fished a piece of paper out from under his pillow. "Do you remember that movie we watched together? The guy was making a bucket list, and you explained what it was. Well, I made my own. It's not done, and I hope I'll be able to finish it by the time I need to go to heaven. It's hard choosing only ten things when there's so much of the world I haven't experienced yet. I know I won't be able to fulfill it, but I like the idea I might get another chance in some other life if that really exists. This will be my *I wish I had experienced in my life* list instead."

I read Derek's list, schooling my expressions to hide my emotional overload.

"You should make one too," the boy said.

I released the breath I had been holding for far too long and didn't even notice I had.

"What would you write on yours?"

My eyes met his. Sharp and guileless, revealing his maturity and ability to accept the truth. I smiled at the way Derek glanced at me. With love. Honesty. Trust. Adulation or something close to it.

I rubbed my jaw with my fingers. "I never thought about it," I said, genuinely surprised. Many ideas swirled in my head. "Yeah, you're right. Choosing only ten things is hard." I paused. "Let's see. First, I'd like to do something different. Try something new."

"Like bungee jumping?"

I rolled my jaw back and forth. "Maybe. But no… Something bigger. Like an adventure. Can I have time to think about this?"

Derek nodded. "Sure. It took me many days to write mine. This is serious stuff."

We exchanged a smile, the air loaded with unsaid emotions evaporated.

"Chess?" Derek straightened and asked, his glee back.

"What? You know I'm about to get crushed once again. I'm starting to think you enjoy watching me getting checkmated every time."

He chuckled. "How would our friendship be if you didn't lose to me?" He rested his hand on mine. "Don't worry, bro, you have other talents."

He poked his tongue out, and I did too.

We both laughed.

This time, the tears pooling in my eyes weren't from sadness.

5

NICHOLAS

Present

This morning, I called in sick. For the first time ever. And I really was sick. I'd been throwing up all night, in between drinking whiskey straight from the bottle.

Deadly combination.

But necessary after what I did. I fucking pushed that button.

A flame of pain licked my spine, crushing my vertebrae, pooling in my neck and shoulders. Tension extended to the length of my back.

In my mind, images of the previous night flashed in a loop, haunting my dreams. Even the ones where I lay awake on my couch, staring at the ceiling, relishing the sensation of the room spiraling around me, making it harder for me to notice the spins in my head.

"Nick, there are no sick days on this job. You either show up, or you don't. If you choose the second option, don't bother stepping a foot on one of my sites again. You already missed a few days last week without my consent. No second chances granted either. You know the drill," Cody yapped on the other end of the line.

I sealed my lids, wishing for the room to settle. If only for a minute.

Grief, hangover, and the sound of my boss's raspy voice were an awful mix. One I didn't need at five in the morning.

To erase my annoyance, I moved to a reclining position and took a gulp of the amber liquid, the fire soothing the pain of my heartache and the squeaky voice of my boss.

"Some…someone died…in my family…" I covered my mouth with my hand to silence a hiccup. "I-I need another day to deal with it… I spent the entire night up." *Don't need you to chew me one in addition to everything else,* I had the decency to speak only in my mind—or I wished I did. When he didn't reply to my insolence, I knew my wish had been granted. Never in my life had I argued with my boss, and I didn't want to start now. But today all I craved was a break. To fucking mourn in peace.

And erase those images so I could sleep peacefully later.

Fight left Cody's voice. "How long do you need? I have no one else to replace you on the condo project on such short notice." His annoyance spilled from each syllable he spoke.

I huffed a jagged breath. "A day. I'll keep my phone next to me. Tell my guys they can reach me in case of an emergency."

The man on the other end of the line sighed, what sounded to be a relief, a tiny reprieve from his ire for the next few hours.

I took another sip, congratulating myself for avoiding a near-certain fight with the man I half-respected and half-feared who had started his business more than twenty years ago from scratch—down the way, he had forgotten to be fair and humane. And furthermore, fully grateful for not losing my job.

No matter the reason, he'd never grant me any more sick days. That I knew as much as I was aware that being hungover wasn't a cure for sadness. Yeah, Cody could be an insensitive jerk most of the time.

On unsteady legs, I stumbled to my bedroom, bottle in hand, chasing some darkness. The sun coming through the small windows of my living room could shine on me some other day. Now all I wanted was to be left the fuck alone. In my bed, I tossed and turned, unable to find a comfortable position. Derek was gone. I still couldn't wrap my head around it. An invisible hand strangled my heart, crushing it so tight, it prevented the blood from reaching it.

Later, a knock on the door brought me out of my slumber. My fingers tapped the bed until they connected with my phone—the one I kept close in case of work-related emergencies. I peeled my lids off, one at a time, my eyes dry and prickling. With the crook of my elbow, I rubbed the sleep away from them. My gaze adjusted to the screen. *Six.* Was it morning already? From the early darkness outside, I guessed not. My heart sank. For a beat, I almost fancied I'd slept for an entire day. I pushed on my hands to sit up, but the room waltzed around me. Geez, how much did I drink that I was still wasted? Through my foggy mind, I did the math, trying to assess how long I'd passed out. The simple calculation turned out to be much harder to do in my intoxicated state. My brain took over after a full minute as more poundings resonated on the door. Squinting at my hand, I counted my fingers. Well, I'd slept for four—no, five hours. Yeah, five. I desisted the urge to pump my fist.

Lumbering toward the door, I unlocked it.

Tucker almost ripped it from its hinges as he yanked it open. His face creased with concern as his eyes moved up and down my body with a worried frown. He raked his fingers through his hair and shook his head in despair. "Fuck, man. Jace called and asked if I could come check on you since you weren't at the work site today. Not that we hoped you'd be… But fuck."

In one stride, my friend erased the gap between us, resting one palm on my shoulder. Without a word, he studied me. A mixture of empathy, worry, and fear flashed in his brown irises.

In my head, I thanked him for holding me still, not sure my legs would support my weight on their own. The room spun.

A bitter taste had taken my tongue hostage, the after-taste of whiskey persistent.

My body rocked to the side, and I closed my eyes, certain I could fall back to sleep even while standing. A constant buzz filled my ears.

The pain that had been haunting my mind, soul, and body had numbed out, and I relished the feeling. Because now I couldn't feel a thing.

I pushed that button. I caused a life to end.

Right now, nothing mattered, except burying myself back in bed.

"Shower. Now." Tucker's tone brought my attention back to him. Oh yes, he was here. In my apartment. A man who never went unnoticed, yet somehow, my mind had turned him into a figment of my imagination.

He spoke, but I caught nothing.

"Nick, focus. Shower. You reek of booze, puke, and sweat. It's disgusting. Gosh, I should have come earlier…or taken the day off."

One at a time, I pried my eyelids open, their weight making it a challenge. I could only zoom in with my right eye, the left too lazy to focus. I wiggled a finger in his face. "I'm *alll* right, *Tuckkk*."

A loud hiccup followed, and a smug grin stretched one side of my lips.

Tucker's face stayed impassive.

I was doomed. I recognized the look. He wouldn't leave—or leave me alone.

Through slit eyelids, I studied him while he kept talking. As if I were seeing him for the very first time. Somehow, his brown skin looked darker right now. I blinked. It became shinier. Was I hallucinating now? Nope. His black crew-cut hair and skin tone seemed to be a kaleidoscope of alternating colors. No kidding. My lips bent at the thought he had magical skin.

"Nick. Shower," he barked, pausing my flow of thoughts.

Geez, why did he have to be so bossy?

With my hands up to silence him, I leaned back and stumbled toward the bathroom, Tucker hot on my heels.

Twenty minutes later, with a black towel draped around my hips, my chest still drenched from the shower, I teetered on wobbly legs to the kitchen, my throat and mouth resembling the Sahara. Right now, I was so thirsty I could have drunk the entire Atlantic Ocean…if only it weren't so salty. Maybe Lake Michigan would be a better option. Was it, though? Pollution. Factories. Weird species of fish. Damn.

As if he could read my mind, Tucker uncapped a bottle of water and pushed it into my hand, stopping my random thoughts.

"Thanks," I mumbled, sipping the water, worried my stomach would turn if I wasn't gentle.

Drops of water rolled down my torso, and a chill ran through me. As I retraced my steps to the bathroom, I took in the wet path I was leaving behind. Great.

Tucker brought me a pair of sweatpants and a T-shirt. Unbalanced, I sat on the edge of the bathtub, like a child dressing on his own for the first time, struggling to fit my limbs into the pant legs.

Before I exited the bathroom, I caught sight of my reflection in the semi-foggy mirror. Oh, shit.

My face, usually tanned, was blotchy. My golden eyes were now bloodshot and rimmed with dark circles, my lips cracked, my shaggy jaw unruly. Even my blond tousled hair looked dull. My shoulders, wide and muscular from years of working in construction, appeared narrower than usual. And my back was slumped as if layers of weight had lumbered it. I barely recognized the image the mirror reflected.

Reality hit me. Grief had turned me into a zombified version of myself. Derek wouldn't want that. Shit, I had let myself go even when I'd promised him to take better care of myself. This was bad.

Shaky on my feet, I reached the kitchen, where Tucker stood at the sink, cleaning the mess I had made. Food containers were now stacked on the island beside the empty beer and liquor bottles. In the last two weeks, since I came to know about Derek's fate, I had let myself turn into a slob.

I shoved my hands into my pockets, now sober than I had been in hours.

"Man, how hard did I fall last night?"

Last night.

Time had no meaning anymore. Hours. Days. Somehow, it felt time had stopped the moment Derek passed away, and no one was in a hurry to restart it and fix the broken clock. Every hour that had ticked by since then felt like a year of my life forfeited.

I watched Tucker when he said, "Bad."

Minutes later, Jace joined us, bags of food and a bottle of alcohol in his arms.

My stomach heaved at the sight.

The smell of food attacked my nostrils. Nausea hit me. I waited for the waves to die down, replaced by the rumbling of my stomach. Traitor. Maybe I was hungry after all.

"We're worried about you." He paused. His silence spoke volumes as I realized I wasn't alone in my grief.

Derek had befriended both of them over the years. They too had lost someone they loved. None of us said anything for a long beat. My eyes filmed with unshed tears as the three of us stood for a moment, reminiscing the one who was no longer there but whose essence would always touch us.

My voice turned ragged as I whispered the truth. "I unplugged him, guys. I'll have to… I'll have to live with this for the rest of my life… I-I, huh, I ended his life, for God's sake…pushed that button. I. Fucking. Killed. Him. I-I killed Derek."

My head bent low with each word as if my neck couldn't take its weight.

Tucker rounded the island, grabbed my arm, and forced me to level my gaze with his. "You're a hero, man. You freed that boy from further suffering. Remember that part. He was already brain dead. Nothing you could have done more for him… You just put an end to *his* hell. We also knew Derek. He wouldn't want you to be miserable. He would want you happy. Not ha-ha happy right now, but happy. And thriving. If he could tell you himself, he'd be grateful for the courage you showed him in the last seconds of his life."

Some of Derek's words came back to me.

I don't want any of you to be too sad. Crying is okay. But don't stop being happy because I won't be there.

I cocked my head to avoid looking at my friend, a new batch of scorching tears stinging the back of my eyes, the wave of pain turning into a tsunami. How many tears could I still cry? I thought that well had emptied a long time ago.

Jace neared us with shot glasses. "Drink this. Today you're allowed to mourn—and get shit-faced—but only under our watch. No more lone drinking spree. Starting tomorrow, you'll start living again. It's unfair. It's stupid. It's heartbreaking. But it's life. You can't throw your future away. We won't let you." Jace had lost his cousin when we were ten. If someone knew how I felt, it was him.

He offered me a taco as we sat around the kitchen counter and poured me another shot.

Even if I had drunk my weight in whiskey already, I enjoyed the effect the booze provided. Knowing this time around, it wouldn't make me sick. Just numb. To pain. And everything that ached inside.

After dinner, I slouched on the sofa between my friends and downed the other shot Tucker handed me. My lids weighed tons. And so was the invisible burden on my shoulders.

"Thanks, guys."

Unable to sit straight, I lay down, not even bothering to go to my room.

"Your alarm is set for six in the morning," one of my friends said. My brain was a blurry bliss, and I had a hard time pinpointing who said those words. "Just sleep."

"Thank you," I muttered when someone covered me

with a blanket as sleep claimed me and made me forget my pain—again. Only for the moment.

Seven hours and four coffees later, I drove to the condo work site, my spirits undefinable. Needing a clear head-space to go through my day, I pushed all my feelings and angst down and locked them up for good measure.

"Glad you're feeling better," Sammy, the plumber, told me when we crossed paths after I climbed down my truck.

I nodded, not ready to speak, fearing I might break down if I did, my throat tight with emotions.

With a deep inhale and a roll of my shoulders, I met my men for our morning meeting. The one I was in charge of. The one I led every single day. Minus the last few days.

I had no word of advice to give them today, my usual leadership missing. If they noticed, they said nothing. Not in the mood to talk to anyone, I retreated into the trailer, working on administrative shit, far from the noisy commotion outside.

My day passed in a blur.

And the next one too.

Keeping myself busy had become my main objective.

My nights were more agitated, though.

Images, memories, conversations with Derek took center stage in my mind, preventing me from sleeping all through the night.

———

In the hallway, I glanced at my reflection in the mirror and fumbled with my tie. I hated these things. In my teen years, I'd decided I'd never work in an office. Just the idea of putting a suit on every day was enough to make me hyperventilate. Tucker loved those, obsessed over them even. If he could, he'd probably sleep in one.

Cufflinks? They were the worst.

Tucker let himself in and neared me, wolf-whistling, while he scanned me from head to toe.

"Stop being a dick and help me out. I'm about to rip this tie to shreds and forgo the whole thing."

My friend came up to me, smiling like a loon. He expertly handled the tie. "Stop squirming. It'll only take a minute. Let the expert deal with this."

With a loud huff, I lowered my shaky hands to my sides. "Fine. But hurry up. I don't wanna be late."

The front door opened and closed, and I spotted Jace from the corner of my eye.

"Hey, man," I told him. "We'll be ready in a minute. If Tuck can hasten up."

"I brought reinforcement," Jace said, raising a bottle of whiskey.

"Pour us two shots each," Tucker told Jace. "Nick here needs to calm his nerves. Trust me. He's about to turn into a wreck any minute if we don't do something. Time for an intervention...a boozy intervention."

I backhanded his chest with as much strength as I could muster, and he faked being hurt for a second.

It had been ten days since I'd drunk myself into oblivion. From that day on, I had reduced my alcohol intake to two shots a day. In my entire life, I'd never tanked that much alcohol in my life, and it took me days to recover from my twenty-four hours slip-up.

Tucker growled. "Stop moving. Geez. Even a toddler can stay still better than you."

I rolled my eyes and let him do what he did best, making me look sharp—and put together. Tucker adjusted the lapel of my jacket and fixed my hair next.

"There," he said. "You clean up well. Now let's drink

those shots before we get going. A little liquid courage never hurt anyone."

"Whiskey can't fix things. Soon I'll turn into an alcoholic," I complained as I slumped on a bar stool opposite my friends. Not in the mood for a drink, but knowing there was some truth to their words, I prayed my stomach could withstand the booze better this time around.

"No, you won't. The days will get better. Promise," Jace stated.

"To Derek," Tucker said as we each brought our shot glasses to our mouths.

"To Derek," Jace and I repeated.

"Fuck, what's that?" Jace asked, going through the copy of the contract Cody had given me last Wednesday that I'd thrown on the counter and forgotten all about.

I shrugged. "Work stuff. Cody wants me on board for a project starting in the fall. It's a renewable five-year contract to make sure I won't leave the company in the middle of it. He gave it to me a couple of days ago."

"And he's offering to pay you that much money to oversee the job?" Jace asked.

"I guess." I scratched the top of my head. "It won't be a seven-to-four job. I'll need to put in extra hours on most days and work on the weekends when necessary. It's big."

"Gimme that," Tucker said, stealing the paper from Jace's hands, the hedge fund banker in him already analyzing the offer. Tucker was gifted. With numbers. And stats. And everything business-related. He wasn't even twenty-five and was already earning a mid-high six-figure salary. Yeah, the guy had it in him. A natural talent, as one of his college professors had once said.

"Okay. This is big, Nick. If you sign this, you won't have an out. For five years. But you'll be making a lot of money. Even if you work one hundred hours a week, you'll still be plenty rewarded for your hard work. And you know I'll help you invest it wisely. Why didn't you sign it yet?"

I sighed and buried my face in my hands. "I don't know. Something doesn't feel right. Maybe it's the lack of sleep. Or the drinks or something else, but I need time to think it over." I took the contract from his hand and put it back on the countertop. "Let's not think about this for now. We should go. I don't want Murielle to be alone. Not today."

I pinched the bridge of my nose and straightened my back, and swallowing the gigantic lump blocking my airways, I rose to my feet.

"Let's go."

In the front row, sitting next to Derek's mom, holding her hand in mine, I listened to the pastor talking, not registering a word he said. Only the sound of Murielle's sobs made their way to my conscious mind.

Someone tapped my shoulder from behind.

I turned my head and gave Tucker a *deer in the headlight* kind of stare.

"Man, it's your turn."

I watched him, blinking.

"Speech, Nick. Can you do this?"

I nodded in a daze, no words coming out.

"You sure? You don't look so fine."

I swallowed as I tried to reboot my frozen brain. My gaze drifted to Murielle, looking at me with expectant eyes.

"I am," I said, moving to my feet, using the back of the chair to keep my balance, my limbs heavy.

In the front of the small room, I glanced around,

taking in each face who came here today to say goodbye to my young friend, whom I already missed so damn much.

With my eyes closed, I cleared my throat while I fastened my fingers around the folded sheet of paper in my jacket pocket.

You can do this, man, I repeated to myself. Over and over. Until I started believing it.

"Thank you all for joining us today." I sighed, putting to rest the frayed nerves bouncing around in my chest cavity. "Derek was more than just my friend. He-he was a brother to me…or my best friend, as he used to say. From the moment we met, we..huh…shared a special bond. He had a way to brighten everyone's days, always smiling and full of optimism as if nothing could go wrong… And God only knows his life wasn't just rainbows and unicorns. I-I would like to think those qualities have rubbed off on me, and somehow, he has made me a better person. Just by being himself till the end."

I dried my moist hands on my trousers and sucked in a cleansing breath.

"It's not… It's not every day you have to face courage, but Derek did, and I'll forever be grateful for everything he taught me in his short life. He was always the smartest guy in the room. It's ironic when you think about it. His brain had so much potential, and it was the same organ that failed him and cost him his life… I'll never understand why he needed to leave this one so fast. Life is tricky and unfair. The only thing that keeps me going is…is the thought he is now finally free to be a child. To laugh. And play. And run around. And eat candies. And ride a bike. And hopefully, lead Heaven's Little League to the championship he'd dreamed about years ago when he had to retire from the game."

I pushed a hand through my hair while my eyes drifted to Murielle.

She smiled and bowed her head, encouraging me to continue.

"Derek, you will forever be missed. I'm sorry we didn't…we didn't get more time with each other. That will be one of my biggest heartaches. But I'll always be thankful for the time we spent together. You'll be with me every day for the rest of my life…and I'll never forget you. Thank you for being you, bro. Hope they have root beer up there. With no ice."

Tucker gave me a thumbs-up, and I nodded. He fumbled on his phone and through the small portable speaker he brought, one of Derek's favorite country songs about monkeys from Carter Hills Band filled the room.

How many times did Derek play this when we hung out together? So much I knew each line by heart. It always brought a smile to his young face. And just for that, it became one of my favorite songs too. Because it reminded me of him.

Tears flew down my face, and I did nothing to stop them or to wipe them off as the silent room listened to the funny lyrics and catchy melody.

As much as I craved air to survive, I needed those tears to purge my pain. To free my heart from all the aches filling it.

Those tears reminded me I was alive.

That I had no choice but to keep going.

For Derek.

And for myself.

6

NICHOLAS

A week later, I was in my apartment with Tucker, watching a hockey game on TV, while he cursed nonstop at the defensemen for doing a shitty job. "C'mon, Jonas," he screamed at number forty-two. "If you keep playing like this, Jace will win this year's fantasy hockey. Damn it. Two of my players are off for the season, and my star defenseman is playing like he's never been on the ice before," Tucker whined. "No way I'll let pussy-whipped Jace win. I'll never hear the end of it." He downed the beer in his hand.

"Next year, maybe you'll listen to me for once. My team is doing pretty good so far. I still have faith I'll beat Jace," I said with a wink.

"Jace has insider information. I bet Hamilton filled out his form. Do you think he's in on it?"

"Oh, someone's jealous," I teased. "Be a good sport, man"

Tucker nudged me in the ribs as I laughed at his defeated demeanor."Glad you've got some of your sense of humor back, man," he said, halfway ready to jump at the

TV screen and shake some sense into the players himself. "I've missed this side of you. The one not taking himself too seriously."

"Pushing that button changed me. Forever."

"I know. Still, your old self is seeping through. You've changed. It's hard to explain. As if you are more adult now. It's not a bad thing…just different. Nobody said you had to choose only one or the other. Perhaps you can find a way for those two sides to coexist."

I sighed. "Yeah. It's been a rocky road. Some days are better than others."

"What did you decide about that promotion?"

"Nothing. Cody has given me one more week to agree to it." I peeled the label from the beer bottle in my hand, my eyes fixed on nothing. "My gut tells me I shouldn't, and I have no idea why. I've been dreaming about an opportunity like this since I was a teen. Everything I have done in my career so far has been toward this goal. I guess my priorities aren't the same anymore. That's the only explanation I can give you."

"What are you gonna do if you decline?"

I shook my head, meeting my friend's worried gaze. "No idea. Money and a seat at the table just seem silly now. There's more to life than this. It's like I'm re-living the same day over and over. The world is spinning, but I'm still, stagnant, stuck at the same hour of the clock. I need to break the cycle, to find happiness again…my balance. To redefine my place in life."

Tucker cleared his throat. "What about a vacation? Could do you some good. Do something different for a while. Go places. Fresh air. And—" A mischievous glint flashed in his brown irises. "You should get laid. It's been a while. Could bring you some peace of mind and relax that body. Get the angst out. Daisy, the girl I'm fucking these days, has a friend. Long legs, great tits, red hair. Everything you have a boner for. Anyway, let me know if you're interested. I can put in a good word for you."

"Damn it, Tuck. Casual fucks aren't my thing anymore. Already told you. And a pussy isn't a magic wand. I'll pass. But thanks for offering. I prefer the vacation idea."

Tucker chugged the rest of his beer. "If you change your mind, let me know. In case I—"

The doorbell rang, cutting my friend short, and I rose to my feet, grateful for the interruption.

"Did the pizza delivery guy teleport himself here? I called fifteen minutes ago," I wondered with a shrug as I grabbed the two twenties on the counter.

"*Noooo*. Not again. Please, someone get Jonas off the ice," Tucker hollered from behind me, his eyes throwing daggers at the TV. I breathed out a laugh as I yanked the door open.

On the threshold stood an older man, probably in his late sixties, studying me with a frown and a no-nonsense expression on his grave face.

He held a large manila envelope and a box in his wrinkled hands.

"Huh, can I help you?" I asked as his eyes scanned the length of me.

"Nicholas Peterson?"

"Yeah, it would be me. What can I do for you?"

He pushed the envelope and box into my hands. "My name is Thomas Jefferson—"

I cocked a brow, waiting for him to continue. Was he kidding me? Thomas Jefferson, yeah right. He must have seen my reservation because he made a business card appear and shoved it between my fingers. I studied the white rectangle. *Thomas Jefferson. Lawyer.* Whoa, his parents must have had a blast when they named him.

Maybe they were high. Or they lost a bet. I pushed the thoughts away.

"Don't be sorry. I get that look a lot. My parents were a bit too patriotic. Anyway, I was mandated by Mr. Derek himself to deliver this to you in person." He averted his gaze and nodded. "I'll let you to it. Mr. Derek was a nice boy. He told me great things about you. Have a nice night, Nicholas."

The words jammed in my throat. I mimicked Mr. Jefferson's nod as I held out my hand to shake his. My eyes followed him as he walked to the elevator, never looking back. What the fuck.

He said Derek sent this. That made no sense. I shook the box, but no sound emerged from it. Once I clamped my jaw shut, I joined Tucker in the living room.

He zoomed in on the package in my hand. "Where's the pizza, man?"

I blinked and shrugged. "Huh, yeah. About that. It wasn't the delivery guy. The food isn't here yet."

He pointed at my hands. "What's this? Man, you look like you've been hit by a truck. Did you see a ghost? You okay?"

I bowed my head, not knowing what to say.

"You all right?" my friend asked, springing to his feet to join me.

I snapped out of it. "Yeah. Fine. Some lawyer dropped this off. Said it was from Derek."

"What are you waiting for? Open it."

We sat around the square kitchen table as I tore open the flap of the envelope and pulled the sheaf of papers out.

I recognized Derek's handwriting and artistic abilities when a DIY card, made of orange construction paper, caught my sight. I studied the drawing on the top for a long minute. Derek had drawn both of us, me and him, with matching grins, eating our weekly cheeseburgers, a baseball game playing on TV in the background. How many nights just like this one did we spend together? I lost count a long time ago.

To Nick,
I love you.
Forever.

Derek

My throat closed. My heart slammed against my ribcage. A million thoughts ran around in my head. How? When? Why did Derek send me this? At that moment, I longed to ask him. I wished I could hear his voice, breathless with excitement, filled with his contagious sunshine cheer, telling me everything would be okay.

Next to me, Tucker studied me in silence. I felt the weight of his stare on me. With my gaze down, I handed him the card.

He read it over and loosened the tie around his neck.

My insides trussed into a barbed coil. A fresh surge of emotions washed over me. I scrunched up my face and inhaled through my mouth until my lungs were on the verge of bursting, then exhaled a long, painful breath.

Beside me, a low *fuck* left my friend's lips. "This is sick. You fine?"

I nodded, not sure I could muster the courage to speak right now, everything inside me fickly.

With my fingertips, I rubbed my temples. "Mm-hmm."

With glossy eyes, I scanned a letter Murielle wrote and pinned on the top of the pile of paper.

Dear Nick,

Thank you for everything you did to brighten Derek's life. All of this was his idea. He put everything together himself.

Nick, don't let life pass you by. You and I know how precious it is. Grip every bit of it with both hands. Enjoy every moment. Seize the chances.

Be wild (a little at least). And be brave.

I'm going to Greece for a while. As you know, I have family there. A change of scenery will be good for me. Being home is too painful. And Derek made me promise I would finally go on that trip after putting it back for years. And because I need to live again. Those were his exact words.

Yes, he would've never taken no for an answer. My boy was special.
But so are you. Never stop yourself from following your heart.

Please stay in touch. And I wish you the best.

Murielle

The lining of my throat itched. The spiked sphere heaving in my chest doubled in size.

With trembling fingers, I unfolded the next sheet of

paper filled with Derek's scribbling. I dug my elbows into the wooden tabletop and rested my chin on my closed fists.

The pizza delivery guy rang the doorbell—or I hoped it was him this time. No way could I handle another surprise.

Tucker got up and sauntered to the door, his hand squeezing my shoulder when he passed me. From the tone of the conversation, it seemed this time it really was the pizza guy.

I brought my attention back to the papers still in my hands, my grip on them too tight.

Tucker returned and put the box on the countertop. "I'll run a quick errand. Give you some space."

I nodded, unable to get a word out.

My friend hadn't voiced it out loud, too busy making sure I was all right, but I knew Derek's passing had been hard on him too. How couldn't it be?

I swallowed hard and blew out a quick breath. Firming my back, I read the last letter I would ever get from the boy who had touched my heart in a million different ways and who had showed me what true heroes were made of.

Hello bro

I'm happy you agreed we should call each other this because it sounds like a grown-up friendship. Like you have with Tucker and Jace.

Mom is helping me put my gift to you together. She smiles under her tears as she watches me, telling me over and over how she's proud of me. She keeps kissing my cheek, and it's annoying, but I know she's heartbroken because I won't be here for long.

They explained it to me yesterday. I didn't cry, bro. You will think I'm crazy, but I knew about it before they told me. It's okay, I guess. I don't know what to say. This makes me sad because I know you and Mom are sad. Living in the hospital sucks. Except for you, I don't have any real friends anymore. I'm all right with it because you're the best.

I'm sorry we won't be able to go to that hockey game you and I talked about so many times.

I don't know when you'll receive the package. I asked Mom's lawyer to give it to you as soon as Mom was ready. It's not much, but I wanted you to remember me forever.

Don't be sad that I'm gone. I'll never be one of your best men after all, but I'll cheer for you from a cloud when you finally find a girl to share your life with. Don't be lonely. (You'll never guess. This morning, I heard two nurses discussing how they thought you were cute. Seems girls like that scruffy jaw look you've been wearing lately. One wanted to ask you out. Fingers crossed).

All those dreams of yours you shared with me, make them happen. You never know when it'll be too late. You deserve happiness. And a bucket load of joy, as Mom always says. I'll never be able to do everything I wished for, so don't miss your chance. In the box, I have included something to help you get started. In case you need a little push from me.

Fist-bumping you from heaven. Or that cloud.

Your other best friend,
Derek

My shoulders dropped as I re-read Derek's last words once again.

"What the hell, bro," I said, looking up, "even your exit is phenomenal." I smiled through my tears and shook my head. "You wrecked me. How could you think I'll ever forget you? You and I are best buddies. Forever."

Every fragment of my heart turned to dust. My stomach churned at the whiff of pizza just a few feet away. I clamped my hands together to stop the quivers.

Once my breathing steadied, I opened the box Derek had sent me.

Lightness mixed with the jitters twirling inside me, because I had no doubt whatever it contained, it would have his colors. And just that thought calmed my racing heart.

7

NICHOLAS

On the top lay a sheet of paper that seemed to have been folded and unfolded dozens of times. I put it on the table next to the box. Underneath it was the framed picture of Derek and me in our matching baseball jerseys. The one he kept on his bedside table at the hospital. With my fingertip, I traced his face over the glass. A post-it had been stuck to the back.

Remember me like this. Happy and healthy. D.

A hint of a smile graced my lips. Yes, I would. I loved this picture of ours.

Carefully, I put the frame aside and returned to the box. My breath came out as a wheeze when my fingers grazed the fabric inside. My heart flipped and entangled within itself.

Slowly, with gentle and measured strokes, I skimmed the fabric between my forefinger and thumb again. My lips stretched wider, glee replacing my heavy heart as I recognized what it was.

My pulse thumped harder—this time with excitement. I could picture Derek in my head that day, pride brightening his face when he showed me the present he had received from his idol.

The images repaired the fractured pieces of my heart, the scent of the memory binding them close.

While I unfolded the jersey, Rex, Derek's favorite stuffed dinosaur—the one his dad had given him on his second birthday before abandoning him—fell to the floor. I leaned over to pick it up. "Hey you, what are you doing here?" I asked the stuffed animal. My gaze lingered over two of Derek's most precious possessions.

Now I couldn't contain my smile because the boy knew I would hold on to these. Forever. He was damn right.

I cast a glance down at the letter, excited to see what it was about.

With a long exhale, I unfolded the sheet of paper.

Derek's ~~Bucket List~~ I wish I had experienced in my life List + Nick's Bucket List

1. **Go to a hockey game with Nick and the guys**
2. **Make ~~1 new~~…no, 3 new best friends**
3. **Kiss a girl until my heart beats fast**
4. **Go camping and sleep under the stars**
5. **Watch the sunrise every morning**
6. **Dip my toes into the ocean even if jellyfish are gross**
7. **Go to a Carter Hills concert because duh, he's the best**
8. **Do something deemed impossible**
9. **Build something with my own hands that I'll keep forever or gift someone**

10. **Nick: Go on an adventure (now you must pick one)**

I love you, Nick. You're my bestest friend in the entire world. Please take care of Rex for me. I want you to have it. You'll have each other. He'll need a new best friend too.

We never jotted down your bucket list, as you were too busy being here for Mom and me, but I've got your back. In case you need inspiration, you can use mine. I left spaces for you but already added the one we talked about. It's time for your adventure. Don't wait, life is too short. Be happy, okay? I am. I promise. And don't cheat because I'll be watching you, you know, from that cloud.

With love,
Derek

P.S. #1 If you ever encounter a jellyfish, you know how to relieve the sting. At least I hope you remember. (I'm laughing right now because I'm imagining your face doing it!) You gotta let me know if it really works.

P.S. #2 Now go out and order a deep-dish pizza with sausages. Extra mushrooms. You always order your pizza without, even though you like them, because you know how much I hate their taste. I was aware all along. Thank you for this. For your huge heart.

The piece of paper fell from my hands and landed on the table as I sat there, unable to breathe. Unable to move. Unable to think.

This time it wasn't from sadness, but more from shock. As if Derek had opened a door to the life I never gave myself permission to explore until now. And knowing it could change everything if I agreed to cross the threshold.

I didn't even budge when Tucker came back, sat on the chair to my left, and poured me a tall glass of amber liquor. Who served booze in a water glass? Tucker. That's who.

I shook my head, with what could pass as a smile tugging at my lips.

"Drink this," he ordered, oblivious to the confusion and opportunities tangling in my mind. The seed a twelve-year-old had planted. Tucker put a slice of cheesy pizza before me and stared at Rex for a second. "Is it—?" I nodded. He took the picture in his hands. "That's a good shot of you two. You look like you're related. I never noticed it until now." He rose to his feet and placed the picture on a shelf by the TV. When he sat down again, he asked, "Can I?" indicating the letter half-folded on the tabletop.

"Yes."

I rubbed my palms over my eyes while Tucker read the list. A throaty noise left his mouth. "Wow, I'm speechless. This is…wow. Derek's my man. We're spirit brothers. He told you to go on an adventure. I told you to go on a vacation. See? We think alike. You should listen to us, man."

"Oh God. I'll never hear the end of it. You're terrible…but part right." I pushed on the tabletop with both palms and moved to stand up. "Let's go out."

"And waste that perfectly good-looking pizza?"

"Yep."

"Something changed in your eyes while I was gone," Tucker stated, furrowing his thick eyebrows.

"Derek set me free. In his own way. I'll tell you all about it. Let me figure out what it means."

"Should I worry?"

"Nope. All good. I just need time to process it. And make choices. You'll be the first one to know once I understand the meaning of it."

My friend eyed me for a long moment and shrugged. "I trust you, man."

Without touching our food, we made our way outside.

"Deep dish?" Tucker asked.

"Fuck, yeah."

Tucker got in step with me. "Fine by me."

We sat at our favorite pizza place, in the basement of an office building a few blocks from my apartment. It was considered a landmark, according to people in the neighborhood, since it had been here for over half a century.

The lights were dim. Red leather booths filled the eatery. With a dark carpet and low ceiling. Over the years, the owners had maintained the retro-charm vibe.

Tucker leaned over after we ordered. "I'm curious about what's next for you, man. A glint you had lost over the years is back, and I wanna know how Derek's letter brought it home."

I ruffled my hair with my fingers. "It's more a gut feeling than anything. Like he gave me permission to think big. And outside the box. Reach for goals I never thought possible before. When all I expected from this life was to climb the ladder of Cody's business. And now"—I scratched the side of my head—"Derek's bucket list. It meant something to him. As it does to me. I don't wanna settle down without living first. I gotta do something to honor his short life."

I waved a hand around me.

"Nothing here really matters when you think about it. You were right too. A change of air is what I need. Perhaps Derek has a pull on me from where he is. Maybe he's the one who prevented me from signing this contract. I don't know. I sound delusional, but I swear I'm not. I feel it. There's something else for me out there."

"Never thought I would hear you say this one day. You have Chicago tattooed on your heart."

"Things change."

"I suppose. What's the plan? You always have one."

I sipped my water, ordering my thoughts. "Man, for once, I have none. Told you I need to figure out what it all means…but I'm excited to discover what's next…to get out there and see what could be." I blew out a long breath. "What if I follow his lead? Go away for some time and complete the list? You know, do the things Derek never got a chance to accomplish and find my true purpose along the way. I have no idea. Being Cody's perfect employee isn't important anymore. He treats people like shit. Why would I want to link myself to him for five years with no way out? That's crazier than going on an adventure, no?"

I put my glass back on the table and lifted my eyes to my friend.

He watched me with interest. "I'm not sure what to say. It reminds me of when you were sixteen and carefree. When you thought the sky was the limit, and you could do anything if you put your mind to it."

The chaotic thoughts swimming in my head lined up somehow.

Something woke up deep inside me. I felt it. It ignited my soul.

Could I do this? Leave? Chase down some dreams that

weren't mine? Or could be if I shaped them to fit my own life?

"Murielle moved forward. When I talked to her last night, she sounded at peace. Sad, but hopeful. Perhaps that's what I need too."

My last words lingered between us for a long minute. Neither of us said anything.

Tucker sipped his drink, a hundred thoughts filling his eyes along with awareness of the change. Tingles of thrill spread inside me.

My chest inflated. So many possibilities could come my way if I let them. Squeezing Tucker's corded forearm, I asked, "What do you think?"

He lowered his glass to the white-clothed table. "How long would you be gone?"

I sighed. "Weeks. Months. Nobody is waiting for me here. I have no woman in my life. No kids. My family is abroad, and my parents are too busy at that winery to care. My sister is somewhere in Australia, living her best life with her surfer boyfriend. If I want to do this, it's now or never."

Tucker rubbed his flexed jaw. "What about your apartment? Your job? Are you sure you're willing to start over once you come back?"

I released a slow breath, the puzzle pieces shifting into place in my head. "It's just a job, Tuck. Sure, I love it and I'm good at it, but I can find something else. Somewhere else. Chicago isn't everything. There's so much out there I've never explored. What if I'm missing out on something? What if Derek's right? I've never done half the things on his list, and I'm twice his age. Don't you think I should try? For him…for me…" My gaze descended to my joined hands. "I wanna do this. No, scratch that. I need to do this. This is my calling. Right now. Right here. To find the person I am. Deep inside. I thought I had everything in my life figured out, but I was wrong. I know nothing. I could go fishing in the ocean or travel the west coast in a van and learn how to surf. Maybe I could build a house… or work on a farm. Learn to play the guitar. Or how to fly a plane."

"Damn, you're serious about it," Tucker stated, his eyes wide.

"Well, I'll never know unless I try."

"Listen, we gotta talk logistics. Are you gonna go on your own?"

"Yeah. I should do this by myself. On my own terms. In my own timeline."

Tucker raised his glass. "To new adventures. Cody is gonna lose it. I bet a twenty he'll throw a fit. God, I wish I could see his face when you tell him."

A small smile tugged at the corner of my lips. "I'll give him a month before taking my leave of absence, then I'm outta here. If he really wants me on his team and he's serious about that promotion, he can wait until I return. If not, then it wasn't meant to be."

"Whoa, my friend is back. Finally." He lifted his arms over his head as if to praise a god somewhere. "Get the hell out of here. Go find yourself. The one you lost along the way. The one with the easy smile, who joked around and messed with me, always up for a good time. I've missed that version of you lately." Tucker's throat worked, and emotions flashed in his dark eyes.

"I'm doing it," I said, my voice laced with conviction.

"You're doing this," my friend echoed. "One thing is sure, though. I'll miss you, man. A whole lot."

"I will too. But this is for the best."

Tucker winked. "And thanks to your amazing best friend who invested your capital wisely over the years, you don't have to worry about money for a while. That big fat bonus check you got last summer from Cody has made some great interest. No doubt the one from the penthouse sale will too."

"Thanks, man. What would my life be without you?"

He shook his head. "I really don't know," he said, his deep baritone laughter resonating through the small eatery.

We ate in silence, both our minds busy with what we discussed.

"What about your place?" Tucker asked, pushing his plate aside. My apartment was small and modestly furnished, nothing like Tucker's condo in a high-rise down-town with extravagant furniture and decor.

"I'll put my stuff in a storage unit. Don't worry about me."

He nodded. Something shifted in his gaze. An emotional battle passed through it. His cheerfulness dissipated a little, giving way to concern.

"Hey, you're really doing this?"

"Yeah. A fresh start. A second chance. Derek was way wiser than his twelve years of age. I have to give it to him."

Tucker raised his glass once more. "To you, man. You're the most selfless person I know. You deserve to be happy and fulfill your own dreams. And get your groove back."

———

I weaved through the crowd, trying to get to my seat, maneuvering four hot dogs and two large cups of soda in my hands. It'd been a week since I gave my one-month notice to Cody. Things had been tense between us since, but he still needed me on that condo building project until he found a replacement, and so he had kept his wrath mostly to himself.

I could still hear his harsh words in my head, calling me stupid for walking away from the *chance of a lifetime,* as he had said. That no one my age was a foreman to big development projects in Chicago and that I was bailing on him like a coward. The final nail in his coffin was when he argued I was leaving to honor some dead kid's life. What Cody ignored was that the cruelty of his words only strengthened my desire to take off and live my best life.

Now I had the certitude Derek had been watching over me, and that all the pieces had aligned so I could be free from things tying me to Chicago—except for my friends. But our friendship could resist almost anything. That I knew for sure.

A week ago, while Cody had delivered his angry tirade, I'd stuffed my hands into my pockets, nodded, and kept my mouth shut the entire time. He didn't get it. Anyway, I had more important things to do than try to make him see things from my perspective.

The same night, I'd called my parents. We usually chatted once or twice a month. They rarely came to see me anymore. Last winter, I'd visited them for a week. We were close but not that close, if it made sense. Over the past few years, Tucker and Jace, along with Murielle and Derek, had become more of a family to me than the one I shared blood with.

As I had predicted, my parents weren't ecstatic about the idea of quitting my job to go on a road trip leading me to wherever. Luckily for me, since they lived in Italy, there wasn't much they could do from their end of the globe to convince me otherwise. They were clueless about my life, and they had never witnessed my bond with Derek with their own eyes.

Since I'd decided to go on this journey, the sun shone brighter, and the air smelled fresher. Yes, I was doing the right thing. I felt it in the marrow of my bones. In the deep end of my soul. In every fiber of my being.

In the crowded arena, I sat next to Jace. "These seats are sick, man. Your connection with Hamilton is once again very much appreciated."

Jace tilted his head and studied me for a beat. "Are you going to tell me who's joining us? I've never bought four tickets before. Did Tucker finally meet someone, or did he get a woman pregnant and now feels like it's his duty to bring her along? Someday, his flavor-of-the-week, no-strings-attached ways will catch up to him." His brows furrowed as he stared at me longer than required. "What's the catch? I'm pretty sure the woman isn't yours. You wouldn't go away if you had met someone and it was serious. I know you, man."

I swallowed at the mention of the fourth seat and shifted in mine, balancing my food between my thighs. "It's Derek's seat."

Jace's eyebrows shot up.

"Remember, he was supposed to come to a game with us. We made him a promise… The three of us. On his eleventh birthday. Well, I'm fulfilling that promise today. It sounds silly but—"

Jace broke out into a smile. "Oh. It's not stupid." His eyes drifted from my face to the food. "Are you having a growth spurt? Since when do you eat this much junk? You know I already got food for myself, right?"

I fought an eye roll. "Derek deserves the full experience. For once, just pretend he's here, okay? I need this. I have to keep my word, do something. And this is it."

Jace cleared his throat. "What about that trip?"

I shook my head, avoiding his eyes, his stare sharp as a

laser beam. "The trip is for me. But this"—I moved my chin around—"is for him."

I rolled my shoulders back and looked at the crowd. The ambiance. The joy. The enthusiasm. Derek would have loved it. My lips curled up at the thought.

Jace nodded and returned my smile as Tucker joined us, a pile of hot dogs stacked in a cardboard tray. Jace gave him a quizzical glance.

"We're here for Derek. So, we better give him the best possible experience. It starts with greasy food. I've even traded my usual beer for a soda. Kids prefer this shit."

A loud laugh bubbled out. Only one Tucker Philips existed on this Earth. "Thanks, man. It means a lot."

We all raised our cups—except Jace, who raised a beer can because, for some reason, he didn't get the game memo—as the players lined up on the rink.

The crowd erupted in a loud cheer when Chicago scored its first goal, and I brought two fingers to my lips, kissed them, and saluted the sky. "This one is for you, bro," I muttered, emotions wrapping my heart in tight knots and healing bands. "Hope you are witnessing it."

Jace elbowed me, snapping me out of the moment.

My eyes landed on the LED ribbon panel opposite us. The words *To Derek, we will miss you* appeared.

I blinked. A new emotion blossomed in my heart… something nearing pride. Because Derek would have gone crazy if he had seen it himself. "Did you do this?" I asked my friend.

Jace shook his head, looking as surprised as I did. "I didn't think of it."

I angled my body toward Tucker, silent in his seat, when he usually cheered and screamed at the referees for nothing and everything. His face had turned a shade paler

—which said a lot, considering his dark skin—and his eyes shone under the arena's white lights.

"Tuck? You did this?" I asked as goose bumps appeared across my arms.

"Maybe. Derek was a great kid. We're here to celebrate him….huh…to celebrate his life. It seemed appropriate."

The word stuck in my throat for a brief second. "Wow. This means so much. Thanks. I know he'd appreciate it. A lot."

"Yeah. Well, I'm not some insensitive jerk. I have a soft side, you know," Tucker said.

Jace and I failed to contain our laughter. "I know you do, man," Jace said. "You're just that good at hiding it most of the time. Don't worry, your secret is safe with us. We wouldn't want Chicago's number one player to be unmasked in front of the ladies."

"Shut up now and watch the game, dickhead," Tucker said, nudging our friend's arm.

Derek's Bucket List —1. Go to a hockey game with Nick and the guys

8

NICHOLAS

Jace and I walked into the crowded building, skipping the line of people on the sidewalk. After exchanging a few words with the bouncer, a guy we knew from high school, I pushed through the crowd to reach the bar, hoping Tucker had already ordered us a round. One of his special lady friends had been working as a bartender here for a couple of months, so he'd spent a lot of his free time in this establishment.

The deafening music throbbed in my skull.

These days, we only frequented bars whenever Tucker was on the prowl. For all I knew, this week, he wasn't. He was seeing someone. Not that it would last, because Tucker Philips didn't do relationships, but he never dated more than one girl at a time. He had principles. Those were his exact same words.

Just when I was about to round the corner, Jace clutched my elbow and pulled me back. I turned my head to watch him with questioning eyes.

"What?" I yelled, to be heard over the music.

"We're not going there."

I scanned the dark space around me, not quite understanding. When I returned my gaze to my friend, he was pointing to the staircase blocked by a velvet cord. "There?" I asked, following his line of sight.

Jace nodded, adjusting his shirt cuffs. "Come on, man. Let's go."

He motioned me forward, then halted and exchanged a few words with the security guarding the stairwell.

"How? What's going on?" I asked. We weren't the type of guys usually invited to the VIP section of the hottest bars in town for no reason.

Jace prodded me between the shoulder blades as we made our way upstairs.

The room above, a mezzanine opening to the dance floor underneath, was bathed in low light. A semi-circled bar stood in the middle of the room, surrounded by velvet plum couches and booths, leather chairs, and artworks in shades of purple and violet hanging over black walls. Thick dark curtains were pinned back, in case added privacy was requested. The eclectic decor, almost seizure-worthy due to flashing pink and white beams of lights coming from the DJ booth below, worked—for some reason.

Beside me, Jace shrugged, answering my silent question.

From where we stood, we had a perfect elevated view of the DJ on the first floor as she mixed songs, the patrons intoxicated with the upbeat and rhythmic music.

Too busy taking in the VIP section of the bar, I failed to notice the people sitting around in a booth, a server nearing them with a tray full of shot glasses and beer bottles.

Before I noticed him, Tucker jumped up from his seat

to meet us. "You made it." His grin was wide as he pulled me into a hug. "Don't make the guys wait."

Thanks to the padded booths and curtain panels, the music from downstairs was muffled enough for us to hear each other. Even when it reverberated through my skull, the effect from up here wasn't too crippling.

I frowned. "The guys?"

"Yep. Jace invited the team. Well, some of them. We haven't spent time with the Busters players in a long time. Since it's your last night in town, we thought this called for a celebration."

I tilted my head to face Jace. "You did that?"

"Hamilton asked to join when I called him last month for the tickets. I thought it could be fun. And he invited the team, so—"

Tucker harrumphed. "What did you have to sell to rip the leash? A kidney? Or your soul?" he teased Jace.

Our friend shook his head. Tucker would never let it go. I refused to get in the middle of whatever this was. "Nothing. Pam's sister is in town. She was more than happy to have me out of the house for the night."

"No woman tonight?" I asked, watching Tucker, who had clearly caught the eyes of the bartender. He never spent his Saturday nights by himself. Rarely ever.

He moved behind us and swung his arms over our shoulders. "Bros before hoes. Always."

Barry Hamilton stood up when we neared one of the booths. "Nick," he greeted me with a handshake. "Glad we were in town for your last night. Grab a seat. We ordered booze, shots, snacks, plenty for everyone. More people are coming soon."

The five other guys around the table, all about Tucker's size—which meant over six feet tall with broad shoulders—

extended their fists to bump mine. Most of them I already knew because we had met on other occasions.

Ted Duffy, the goalie who had bought the two-story condo unit, was last. "How's it going, man? Can't wait to move into that building of yours. I'll be honest and say I was upset when Jace told me you wouldn't oversee the construction anymore. Hamilton vouched for you, and it was enough for me. The first time we met, I loved your guts. I trust you, man."

I swallowed hard. "Yeah, well. It wasn't the plan. Things happened."

"No worries, man. Jace told us everything. Sorry about that kid. I'm a single dad. If anything ever happened to my kids, I'd leave too. Get the hell away. Change of scenery. Change of life."

"Thanks," I said with a stiff nod.

That was how I spent my final night in Chicago with a bunch of professional hockey players and their guests, goofing around and having a good time, the pressure of the last couple of weeks dissolving with every passing hour.

A little before midnight, Jace came to me and pulled me aside. "Nick, I gotta go."

I fished my phone out of my back pocket to look at the time. "Everything all right? It's still early. You sure?"

My friend sighed and looked down. "Yeah, you know Pam, she's pretty—"

"Fuck, you have a curfew?" Tucker asked, joining us, busy zipping his fly and adjusting his shirt. Where the hell did he come from? I pushed the thought away. I didn't need those images in my head. He shook Jace, holding both of his shoulders. "Tell me you're shitting me. Please. I need to hear those words. I'm begging you. For once."

Jace's face flushed, and he jerked away from Tucker's grip, his shoulders slumping. "Sorry, guys. Married life.

One day you'll understand. We both compromise. That's the way it works."

"Pussy-whipped," Tucker said under the guise of a cough.

"It's okay," I told Jace. No, I wouldn't get in the middle of this. "Thanks for getting all these guys to join tonight. It was fun. I'll miss this," I said, flicking my hand around the room.

"We will too. Miss you, I mean," Jace said. With his thumb, he traced the length of his eyebrow. "Well…huh… I should get going. I'll try to see you tomorrow before you leave, okay?"

I nodded. "Sure."

Silence fell between us—loaded and unsaid.

The three of us had been friends for over two decades. We grew up together. Messed up together. Experimented life together. And right now, neither of us could certify if we'd live in the same city ever again. Now that Jace—hopefully—was happily married and I was going away for only God knew how long, nothing would ever be the same.

I felt the change in the air, and I bet my friends did too.

"You sure about leaving?" Jace asked.

"Yep. Still going. Everything is set."

He swallowed a couple of times before he could speak again. "It will be weird…not having you around, but"—a smile spread across his lips—"I hope you have the time of your life. I mean it. You deserve to enjoy your journey. Or whatever it is. Hey, you turned down a fucking load of cash for this. It better be worth it."

"I hope so… It will… It sounds crazy, but I'm supposed to do this."

The same way he did earlier, Tucker moved behind us and slung his arms over our shoulders, pulling us to him. "Motherfuckers, it was an honor to spend Nick's last night in town together. Now he and I will return to those gentlemen while you crawl back to your executioner," he said to Jace, who let out a soft laugh.

"See you, guys." Jace walked away, waving at us as he reached the staircase.

Tucker's chuckle vibrated through me, his arm still around my neck. "Jace marrying that bitch is the best thing that could ever happen to you," he added, poking my chest with his finger.

"Is it?" I teased.

"Don't mess with me. Let's get some shots to forget you ever said that."

Derek's Bucket List — ~~11. Nick. Knowing I can always count on my friends~~

9

NICHOLAS

"That's the last one," I said as Tucker took the box from my arms and locked the storage unit door behind us. "The rest of my stuff is either in my truck or I gave it away." I swiveled to face him. "Thanks for the help, man."

"Are you kidding? This is the least I could do." His face turned serious, the lightness in his voice gone. "You know…" He scratched his nape. "It's weird thinking you won't be around for a while."

"Come on. You have all these women to keep you fully busy—and warm at night. You don't need me," I deadpanned with a chuckle.

"Nick, there's more to a man's life than a buffet of pussies," my friend stated resolutely, counting on his fingers. "There's beer. And whiskey. And hockey. And poker nights."

I pulled him into a side hug. "I think you'll be okay. Jace's still here, and you could get a steady girlfriend if you want full-time company."

He stepped away, smoothing his designer shirt with his

hands while shaking his head. "Jace is Pam's slave, and no way I'm settling down. Look where it got my old man. Not gonna end up with the same fate. I'm all in for the fun part, not the relationship and love complications, though. You should know it by now."

I looked up at the sky in despair, then grinned. "I wouldn't recognize you if your speech was different. Sometimes it's like I'm having a talk with your sixteen-year-old self. Glad this lifestyle suits you, Tuck, but I want more. Someday… I want what my folks have." I dug my phone out to check the time. "Guess I should hit the road."

Tucker nodded. "Yeah. I've got something for you. Wanna give it to you before you go. Something on the… huh…list." He raised a finger and ran to his car. A minute later, he came back with a white envelope.

"What's this?" I asked with a frown.

Tucker handed me the envelope and pushed his sleeves up his forearms, his eyes flickering back and forth. Was he nervous? Tucker Philips didn't do nervous.

Angst filled me. What did he do? With care, I opened the flap and pulled two tickets out. Whoa. Tickets to Carter Hills's show in Nashville next fall. My gaze sprang to my best friend, rocking on his heels, watching me. A million thoughts rushed to my head.

Tucker offered me a lopsided smile, his usual confidence gone. "Thought you could use those. You know… since he was one of Derek's idols and shit. You get the point—"

I stared at him. My voice got lost on its way out. The back of my eyes prickled. With my free hand, I rubbed the column of my throat, trying to ease the tightness rendering me speechless.

Tucker shrugged, and I pulled him into my arms. We

hugged like we'd never done before. After a beat, I moved to study his face.

"Two tickets. Does it mean you're coming with me?"

My best friend shook his head, his legendary smug smirk fully back on. "Nope. Don't get your hopes too high, man. No way I'm going. Only girls gush over tickets like these. I wouldn't recognize one of his songs, even if my life depended on it."

I glanced at them—*fifth row*—and blinked.

"Okay, you went all in for this. You would miss seeing Carter Hills up close for some principle? Now I see it. You're afraid you'll turn into a groupie. Or a die-hard fan. That makes sense. You're right then. Yep. You should probably avoid going. Just in case," I teased. "You can't be too careful about fangirling. I heard it's super contagious."

"I'm just not a fan."

I offered him a pointed look.

We stared at each other, and Tucker sighed with a head shake.

"Okay. Fine. If you insist and only if you haven't found anyone to go with you by then, I might consider it. Unless you want to keep the second ticket as if it were Derek's. Your call. Do as you want, but promise me I'll be your last choice, okay? I'm not ready to transform into a Carter Hills follower, but I prefer sacrificing my ego than letting you go to that show alone like a loser who got dumped at the last minute. Are we clear?"

I drew my friend into my arms again. "You're just jealous because the guy is hotter than you. But I love you, man. You know I'll miss your sorry face, right?"

Tucker pushed me back with both hands. "You better, and if you don't, I will find you. I have my ways. Now go. Find your destiny or happiness or whatever. Find the old *you*. Make Derek proud."

He averted his eyes.

My throat worked as a curtain of emotions wrapped around me.

Tucker stepped forward, and we fist-bumped. "See you, man. If you ever change your mind, you can always come back and crash on my couch, now that you're officially homeless. I wouldn't say no to having you as a roommate. You clean after yourself, and you can cook."

"Thanks. Very noble of you." With a half-smile, I hauled myself behind the wheel of my pickup truck, pulled out of the driveway, and rolled down the window. "Don't do stupid shit while I'm not there to watch your back," I told my friend.

"Will you come running back if I do?" he asked, a cocky grin now curving his lips.

"Nice try, man."

He waved at me as I drove away. My heart did a funny flip in my chest. For a second, I wondered if going on this trip was truly my purpose. But then my fingertips grazed Derek's bucket list I'd clipped to the sun visor, and liquid warmth filled my heart to the brim, knowing I wasn't alone on this journey.

A few miles west of Cleveland, I took an exit, parked my truck on the side of the road, and studied the piece of paper. I had no idea what to aim for first. With my eyes closed, I tried to picture Derek beside me. "What do you wanna do, bro?" I asked out loud. Yeah, as if he'd answer me. After a moment, my phone vibrated in the center console. With an exhale, I picked it up.

JACE

You left already? Sorry I missed you. Be safe. Sea you in a few weeks. Or months, I suppose.

*see, not sea. Obviously.

Something in me sparked, and my whole being surged to life.

My heart leaped in my chest.

I breathed easier once the shock subsided.

Jace just gave me the answer I'd been waiting for without even knowing it. I kissed my two fingers and saluted the sky. "To the beach then. Let's go see the ocean. I haven't been there in a long time."

ME

Near Cleveland. Going to the ocean first. I'll keep you posted.

JACE

Have fun. Call if you need anything.

ME

Thanks, man.

Never. Jace didn't need to know that, though. Pamela would kill me if I asked my friend for anything. Why she hated me that much, I had no clue. Somehow, I always thought she slept with my friend, hoping I'd run after her and tell her she was the one. Things were clear between us from the start. We saw each other on occasions. It suited us both. Until it didn't and she went all crazy on me. Now Jace was stuck in the middle.

Never would I have thought Pamela White was marriage material, though. I was wrong—or I wished I was —for my friend's sake.

My grumbling stomach cut my thoughts short. A quarter of a mile to my left, I spotted a truckers' diner. Perfect timing. I'd been on the road for five hours, munching on snacks. I could use a real meal just about now.

I parked next to an eighteen-wheeler and got out. The driver, a man sporting a gray beard and a forest-green cap, bowed his head as I rounded my truck, giving me a front view of his crooked smile. "Lost, young man?" he asked.

"No. Just hungry."

"Ask Betsy for today's special. Tell her Dick sent you."

I offered Dick a smile and nodded my acknowledgment. "Thanks."

After hesitating for a moment, I slid into a cracked old vinyl seat next to the wide window.

Betsy, according to her name tag, neared my table, a glass of water in hand. Placing it on the table, she pointed to the plastic-covered menu stacked behind the metallic napkin holder.

She stood there, watching me as I studied the dishes, her fists on her large hips. "Need more time?"

I cleared my throat. "Still serving today's special? Dick told me to ask for it."

A wide grin spread across her face, and she pushed a white curl away from her forehead with one thick finger. "Oh, you know Dick? One special for you then." She winked. "We only serve it to our *special* customers."

"Thanks." I ordered black coffee before Betsy could walk away. After she retreated, I opened the map app on my phone, wondering where I should head to first. Following the roads that led out from this diner, I found my destination.

Medora Beach.

It was a long ride from here, but somehow, it appealed to me.

After my late lunch, I drove four more hours and

stopped at a motel for the night, craving a more-than-welcome shower and a few hours of sleep.

The persistent ringing of my phone shook me out of my slumber the next morning. With my eyes closed, I patted the bed and nightstand to silence the noisy device. I hadn't slept this well in a long time. Right now, I could've used a couple of more hours of sleep. Since I left Chicago yesterday, a piece of my heart had been slotted back into place. I couldn't explain it in words, but I felt it, deep in my bones. In my everyday life, I used to have plans. Nothing was done randomly. Never. Which served me in my job. That was how I got away with the penthouse fuck-up two months ago. But now that I'd decided to check every item on Derek's list, I wanted to be more spontaneous. To live and let live. To let life show me the way.

This freedom, even if scary when I thought too much about it, appealed to me.

No expectations. No obligations. No nothing.

Tucker's face flashed on the screen. *Seven a.m.* Yeah, two or three additional hours of sleep would have been amazing.

His cheerful voice contrasted with my sleepy state. "You up?" he asked.

I grumbled something, rubbing my eyes with my fists to wake up a little more.

"Just came back from a run. Thought you could use some morning cheer. Back on the road yet?"

I swept my legs over the edge of the bed and sat with my elbows propped up on my knees. "Slept like a baby. Didn't put an alarm because I figured I'd toss and turn all night like I've been doing for months. But you're right. I should go on a run too. Clear my mind for the d—" Whispers on the other end of the line stopped me mid-sentence. "Why did you call me if you're not alone, man?"

"Bros before hoes. Remember?"

I stretched my arms over my head, got up, and slid my bare ass into a pair of black jogging shorts.

"Go back to your booty call. I'll ring you later when I hit the road."

"Have you decided on your next stop?" Tucker asked.

"Medora Beach. Seems like a quiet, small town. It's not Chicago, but it looks cozy."

"Wait for me in the shower," Tucker said to someone who wasn't me. The sound of a hand smacking naked flesh and a high-pitched laugh replaced the silence next. I shook my head. Some things would never change. "Sorry, where were we? Oh yes, that beach. I think I have what you need to continue your journey. You'd have to be there in about a month. I don't have all the details yet. Let me know when you're tired of the ocean breeze and the shining sun so I can run it by you."

"Let's talk later. You'll tell me all about it then."

We hung up, and I ran for the next forty-five minutes—until my lungs burned and my knees wobbled. On my way back to the motel, I accepted a call from my mother. "Hey, Mom."

"Oh, Nicholas. How are you? Have you left town already?"

I nodded, even though she couldn't see me. "I did. In Havertown now. Some small town in Maryland. Just finishing a run."

"Nicholas, I'm worried about you. Are you sure this entire trip is a good idea? I know you always plan everything out, so this doesn't sound like you."

"Mom, I'm fine. I'm actually more than fine. Can we talk later? I gotta go. Tell Dad I said hello, okay?"

"I will. Be careful out there."

"Always. Bye, Mom."

My parents were pretty clueless about my life. I had no idea why they acted all parent-y now. It made no sense. Murielle had been much more of a maternal figure to me over the last few years.

After a quick shower, I grabbed breakfast and got on the road again.

Tucker called me back before I could merge left on the interstate. "Uncle Mike," he said as soon as I accepted the call instead of his usual "Hey man" or "What's up?"

My jaw clenched around the bagel I was about to bite into.

"What if I told you that you could cross numbers four and five in one go?"

"Wait. What? You know Derek's list by heart?"

"No. I took a picture of it with my phone the other day. Thought it would come in handy along the way. Keep tabs on you. Anyway, Uncle Mike is looking to hire a foreman for the next six months for this residential development he's building. None of his employees are qualified enough for the job. I told him all about you, and if you're interested, the position is yours. It would be a new experience, and you'd earn great money. Kind of a sweet deal, if you ask me. It's not Chicago high-rises or Cody's big fat contract, but it's a start."

My friend didn't have to say he was worried about me. I could tell in the way he tried to watch out for me, even from hundreds of miles away. Tucker and I were like brothers. Always had been. Jace was more like our annoying little cousin. We loved him very much, but we weren't as close.

"O-okay. I didn't think I'd make definitive plans so quickly. I left less than twenty-four hours ago. Can I think about it? The offer is nice, though. But it's a long-term commitment. Where is Uncle Mike living?"

"Green Mountain, Tennessee. The Smoky Mountains, you know? It's not that far from where you're heading. It's close to big cities. Nashville, Atlanta, Cincinnati, Louisville. There is plenty all around to keep you busy on the week-ends. The job starts next month. Think about it. Uncle Mike needs an answer by the end of the week."

I sighed. I hadn't even reached my first destination, and my plans were already changing. I emptied my lungs. *Let it go, man. Don't fight this. No plans. Everything happens for a reason. Life will show you the way. Just this one time.* Yeah, I could do this. Or I'd at least try to.

"Gimme forty-eight hours."

———

Excitement jitters traveled through me, so much that I skipped booking a motel room for the night and parked my truck along the wooden boardwalk running the length of the beach. With a baseball cap over my head and dressed in washed-out jeans and a long-sleeved white T-shirt, I ran a hand over my face, chasing the sleepiness that had taken over my mind and body in the last hour. I had one goal: dip my toes into the ocean. There was no other reason I drove here. The warm spring breeze swept across my face. Adjusting my shades over my eyes, I tilted my head back, taking a moment to admire the azure sky and enjoying the sun's warm rays grazing my skin.

Why didn't I come to the beach more often?

I hadn't been here for more than a couple of minutes, and already I felt more at ease than I'd been in a long time.

I forgot how good the hot sand felt between my toes as I removed my shoes and rolled my jeans up to my knees. How I loved to look at the horizon and imagine life had no beginning, and no end. No limits. With my fists on my hips, I inhaled the salty air, burning the memory to my senses.

My exhaustion left me as if the Atlantic Ocean breeze had a mysterious rejuvenating power while I walked along the shore, the waves washing my feet every few seconds. A sense of peace invaded me. For the first time, I realized how tense my back had been. Dead weights I'd been carrying around for far too long vanished.

"Thank you, Derek," I said, kissing my fingers and giving my friend up there a sign. "I'm happy to be here. How you guessed it, I'll never know, but you were right."

Emotions I'd pushed down in the last month swirled inside me, and I blinked them away. With my legs folded and my arms wrapped around them, I rested my chin on my knees, throwing broken pieces of shell into the waves. All the while keeping an eye on the two fishing rods I'd set up by the water, my ass buried in the now-cold sand.

I'd been sitting here for hours, waiting for a fish to nibble the bait I changed every ten minutes or so.

On my right, a girl, about seven or eight years old, ran my way, curiosity bubbling in her eyes. Dressed in pink shorts and a mint-green T-shirt with her blonde hair sweeping her shoulders in a ponytail, all frizzy from the ocean air, she stopped in front of me. Crossing her arms over her chest, she studied me with one arched brow, her cheeks reddened by a day spent under the sun.

"What's your name?" she asked, whistling her words, her two front upper teeth missing.

"Nick," I said, mirroring her smile. "What's yours?"

"Kelly. What are you doing?"

I shrugged. "Fishing."

She stepped closer. "Alone?"

"Yeah. Why not?"

"Because you have two rods. Are you waiting for someone?"

I rolled my shoulders back, fighting the new tension trying to settle in.

"No." *My friend is not really here. I can't see him. I can't talk to him. But imagining we're doing this together makes me feel better, so I brought two rods.* In my head, I sounded like a lunatic, so I kept my thoughts to myself.

"Can I sit with you?"

"Sure. Where are your parents?"

The girl pointed to a woman dressed in a maxi white floral dress, her brown hair dancing in the ocean breeze. Even from a distance, I could tell she was pretty.

"My mom is arguing with my dad. Over some child support thingy. They divorced last year. Now that Dad has a new wife and a new baby, he doesn't visit anymore."

Kelly looked in the distance. "Are you from out of town? I've never seen you before, and we come here a lot. Like a *lottt*."

"I'm from Chicago. It's up north. I'm just passing through town…for a vacation."

"You will love it here. I'm telling you. Did you know that my great-great-great-grandpa helped to build this town a long time ago?"

I shook my head as a smile bent my lips. "No, I didn't. That's pretty cool."

"Yeah. They named a street after him."

I let out a heartfelt chuckle. "Wow, that's even cooler. You're a lucky girl."

"Have you caught any fish?"

I lowered my shoulders. "Nah. No luck so far today."

Kelly's mom neared us, her attention fully on her daughter, a scowl painting her face. "Baby, you can't leave my sight and run to strangers. We've talked about it a million times before." The woman turned around and eyed me. "Ohmygod. I'm sorry if my daughter has been bothering you. She's not supposed to venture away on her own and talk to people she doesn't know."

I was right. The woman was beautiful. Big caramel eyes, high cheekbones. But she bore sadness in her eyes—and wariness.

"Actually, your daughter is sweet. She's the first person I've spoken to since I got here earlier today."

The woman glared at me, all trace of friendliness gone.

I offered her a hint of a smile.

"I'm sorry, Mama," Kelly chimed in, breaking the awkward silence that had settled between us.

Softness soothed her mother's frown. "I know, baby." She switched her attention back to me and shook her head. "She has a tendency to forget personal boundaries," she said with a sigh. "I'm scared one day she'll get herself into trouble. She trusts everybody she meets."

"I knew a child like this. The world would be a better place with more kids like them. Contagiously happy. And fearless."

The woman's shoulders dropped, and she returned my smile. "I don't know about that. With Kelly, I feel like I should get another pair of eyes sometimes. She's always in exploration mode."

We both watched the little girl as she played with seashells.

"I know what you mean," I said.

"You have kids?" the woman asked, toying with the flip-flop on her left foot, a light flush coloring her cheeks. I had no idea if the sun put it there or if she was shy.

I shook my head at her. "No. Not yet."

A wall seemed to lower around her. "Sorry about that," she said, motioning to her little girl. She gave me a slow once-over. "She obviously disturbed your fishing time. Kelly has to stop doing this. Last week, she gave our phone number to a man, and he's been texting me, thinking I was interested." The pink hue on her face darkened. "Embarrassing." She extended her hand. "I'm Amanda, by the way."

"Nick."

She smiled, and the curve brightened her face. "We took enough of your time. We should go. Come on, Kelly," she said, inviting her daughter to follow her with a hand.

The girl scooted closer to me. "I don't wanna go."

Amanda kneeled in front of her, lowering her voice. "We have to. It's already dinner time. We've been here all afternoon. It's time to go."

"Do you wanna come?" the girl asked me.

I failed to hide my amusement.

Before I could say something, Amanda jumped in. "Personal boundaries, Kelly." She lifted her eyes and offered me an apologetic half-smile. "Again, I'm sorry."

I rose to my feet. "I'll get going too. I gotta book a motel room anyway before it's too late and there's no vacancy."

I reeled the fishing lines in.

"Can I help?" Kelly asked.

I handed her the second rod. "Sure. Here, place your hands like this." She executed herself. "Yes. Like that. Now reel in."

She did as I instructed, focused on her task.

"Wow, look at you. You're a natural."

"Where are you staying?" Amanda asked while I removed the hooks.

"No idea. I haven't decided yet. Any place you recommend?"

Kelly jumped to her feet and turned to face her

mother. "Mama, you should let him stay in the garage apartment."

Surprise passed through the woman's eyes. She seemed to consider the suggestion for a beat. "You know what? It's actually not a bad idea. It's not a five-star penthouse, but it's located on a dead-end street, and it's fully furnished. How long will you be in town?"

"A week. Maybe two. Not sure yet."

Amanda clasped her hands in front of her. "Well, if you want it, it's yours."

"Huh, I don't want to intrude."

"I'm the one offering. The rent is cheap and honestly, I could really use the money. I have to fix the roof, and those things are pretty expensive."

"Say yes, say yes," Kelly chimed in, bouncing around, flapping her arms at her sides.

"You sure?"

Both mother and daughter bobbed their heads with enthusiasm.

Should I worry? They didn't know me. How could they be so trusting with a stranger and invite me to stay over? People in small towns had to be less fearful than those living in big cities. No woman in Chicago—even less a single mom—would invite a man they'd just met to stay in their garage apartment.

Grins lit up their happy faces, and I lost the fight.

"Okay then. Also, I'll look at the roof while I'm there. I'm a carpenter, so it's no big deal," I said with a one-shoulder shrug.

"No. You're a guest. Just enjoy your time in Medora Beach," Amanda said. "Now let's go. I'm starving. We're going to eat at Barry's." Barry's? What is another sign? She gestured toward the boardwalk with her thumb, and I brought my attention back to her. "If you're hungry, you can join us. Only if you're free…" The pink flush on her cheeks turned crimson. "This is so embarrassing. You must think I'm asking you out. Ohmygod, I'm not good at this. This is not a date. Rather, a friendly dinner. Okay, that doesn't sound better. You must think I'm lame. I'm making a fool of myself. For God's sake, I—"

I placed a hand over hers. "I'd love to. If you're okay with it." I lifted my hands in surrender. "It's not a date. If you prefer eating alone with your daughter, I won't object. Don't feel obligated to invite me."

Amanda cupped her mouth with both hands. "I was rambling, wasn't I?"

I nodded, not hiding my grin.

"You must think I'm such a weirdo. I'm not used to asking men out, but…huh…you probably can tell…" She exhaled, firming her back, and extended her hand. "Let's start over. I'm Amanda. This is my daughter, Kelly. We're having dinner at Barry's. If you want to join us, you're more than welcome. There, I said it."

I shook her hand, her palm warm and soft as it slid into mine.

"Well, Amanda, I'm Nick. I'm from Chicago, and I don't know anybody in this town. I came here to see the ocean, and I'm famished. I'd love to eat with you guys."

Without another word, Kelly gripped my index finger and led me away.

"Are you here on a vacation?" Amanda asked, once Barry, the owner, brought us our food.

"Not really." I closed my eyes for half a second to settle my emotion each time memories of Derek or why I was on this trip resurfaced. "One of my friends died almost two months ago. He made a list of things he wished he could have done before passing. Some sort of bucket list. I guess I'm trying to fulfill it for him. While making it mine in a way." I glanced down and winced. "It sounds weird when I say it like that."

Amanda leaned back in her chair and brought the wineglass to her lips. "No. It sounds quite the opposite. That's very sweet of you. Your friend must have been someone wonderful if you're doing this to honor him."

I sipped my beer, my heart rate picking up. Once it decreased, I cleared my throat. "Yeah. He was. I hope I'll find out a lot about myself in the process. What I want, where I'm heading to. In every aspect of my life. I've never lived one day at a time before. It's my first try. Honestly, it gets me a little antsy."

Amanda's warm laughter bounced against the walls of the small restaurant. "Being a parent kind of does that to you. Every day is a brand-new adventure you're never prepared for… It keeps you on your toes."

She flashed me a smile, but the fog in her irises betrayed her fake sense of calm. Wrinkles around her eyes deepened, and her lips tightened. I recognized the signs. Something, or someone, had hardened her. I wondered what—or who—it was.

Our conversation had turned heavy. As if she sensed it, Kelly barged in and entertained us for the next hour.

After dinner, I followed Amanda to her house. Once she put a sleepy Kelly to bed, she showed me around the garage apartment. In the semi-darkness, under a golden light, the only source of lighting, we shared a moment. Amanda flashed me a coy smile, standing a foot from me.

Right there, I could have kissed her. I bet she wouldn't have objected, but never would I be able to take advantage of this woman, not even for a night. Even though comfort and company were what we both seemed to crave—or need. I could tell she'd been through a lot. The last thing Amanda deserved was a one-night stand with a guy who wouldn't stick around or promise her anything. A guy who would disappear in a week or two, chasing a dream he didn't yet understand.

When she leaned in, my lips connected with her cheek instead. I breathed in her lavender perfume.

"Good night," I whispered into her ear, my cheek brushing hers. "Thank you for tonight. And thanks for letting me crash here."

She nodded and stepped back, and I walked her to her front door.

"Are you gonna be okay?" I asked.

She nodded again. "Thanks for reminding me there are good men out there, Nick. I forgot for a while."

I bowed my head. "Night," I said before she closed the door behind her. I stood on the front porch, watching the house as lights switched on, one by one, on the second floor. With my thumbs hooked to my pockets, I strode back to the garage apartment that would be mine for as long as I was in town.

After a well-deserved shower, I turned my phone back on.

I had three missed calls and five text messages.

Three of them from my friends.

> **TUCKER**
>
> Did you think about Uncle Mike's offer?
>
> **JACE**
>
> What are you wearing?
>
> Can't wait to undress you later. Did you try the red thong I sent you?

A loud chuckle tumbled out of my mouth. This was hilarious. Who knew Jace and Pam had a kinky side? They seemed so *missionary* together.

My thumbs typed fast.

ME

> The thong is too tight at the front. Not sure you picked the right size. Love the lace, though. Red looks fabulous with my skin tone. You won't have to undress me. I'm already halfway there myself.

I could imagine my friend's face in my head. Unlike Tucker, Jace had never been the one to brag about his sexual conquests in the past.

I slapped my thigh and doubled over with laughter as the three bouncing dots appeared in the corner of the screen.

And waited.

They disappeared. And never returned.

With a long sigh and a head shake, I turned the light off, my lips curling upward.

Did Pam intercept our exchange? I hoped not. If she did, she would castrate her husband. No doubt.

In the dark apartment, I fell face first on the comfy bed and yawned, exhausted, but hopeful.

Derek's Bucket List — 6. Dip my toes into the ocean, even if jellyfish are gross

Derek's Bucket List — 10. Nick: Go on an adventure (now you must pick one)

10

NICHOLAS

I woke up to the sound of a knock on the door. For a moment, I wondered where I was. Canary-yellow walls, a quilt that had, for sure, been sewed by hand, a two-seat wooden kitchen table, a floral loveseat along the wall. In the daylight, the apartment was cute and welcoming. A soft voice spoke from the other side of the door. "Nick, are you awake? It's Kelly. I've made pancakes. With homemade peach jam my granny taught me to make."

I yawned, stretching my arms above my head. The night had been restful. "I'll be right there, Kelly. Can you gimme…huh…about ten minutes?"

"Yes. Meet us in the kitchen when you're ready. Mama said you don't need to knock."

"Awesome. See you in a bit."

What did I do to deserve so much hospitality from Amanda and her daughter? A grin took over my lips. Today would be a good day. I could sense it. The sun shone high in the sky, flooding the entire apartment with light once I opened the curtains. At the sight, the fog around my heart lessened—a tad more.

Dressed in dark jeans and a hoodie, I joined my hosts.

"Good morning, Nick," Kelly singsonged, placing a mountain of pancakes before me on the table.

"Wow. All for me?" I asked.

The girl bobbed her head. "Yes. Mama said grownup men eat a *lottt*."

Amanda and I shared a stare, and she shrugged.

"Coffee?" she asked, holding a mug in her hand, barely hiding the curve of her lips.

"Sure. Black."

The girls sat on the opposite side of the table, and once Kelly's chitchat lessened, I attacked my breakfast, my mouth watering at the sweet smell tickling my nostrils.

"These are amazing, Kelly. You should be a cook when you grow up."

"You think?"

"I'm certain. You gotta share your recipe with me. I promise to keep it a secret. But it's that good, I'm telling you."

The girl giggled, and the sound, innocent and warm, fixed more pieces of my broken heart. "You're funny, Nick."

Amanda mouthed a *Thank you* my way, sipping her caffeine, her stare locked on mine.

My heart frizzled in my chest. I hadn't imagined the connection we shared last night.

"About this roof leak? Where should I start?" I asked, putting my dish into the sink once I finished my breakfast. "I'll stop by the hardware store but gotta assess what must be done first."

Amanda stepped closer to me, her arm brushing mine. "Nick, you're not fixing it. Already told you. You're on vacation. Wouldn't you prefer visiting the town or doing something fun instead?"

"I don't know what is there to do around here."

"Well, if you agree to have some company, Kelly and I are free to give you a tour. It's Sunday after all."

"You sure about that?"

"Affirmative. This could be fun."

"In that case, I'm ready when you are, ladies."

The three of us spent the day walking along the streets of the old town, eating lunch in a park not far from a taco shack belonging to Kelly's aunt, and visiting the petting zoo and the fair, where I won Kelly a pink stuffed elephant so big she had to use both hands to carry it around. The distinctive whiff of pretzels and corn dogs permeated my nose, and, for an afternoon, I went back to being the ten-year-old version of myself. The boy whose parents took him to the carnival every summer.

The next day, I woke up early and was finishing my morning run when Amanda drove past me.

I stopped and jogged in place when she lowered her window. "Good morning, Nick."

"Hey, Nick," Kelly chimed in from the backseat. I waved at her, and she offered me a wide smile, full of mischief—and missing teeth.

"Listen, I'm driving Kelly to school and going to work afterward. Message me if you need anything." She rolled her window back up but stopped midway. "Enjoy your day."

"I will. See you later."

We exchanged a smile, and they drove away while I resumed my run.

My phone rang. *Tucker.*

"Hey man, how's it going?" I asked when I connected the call through my earbuds.

"You sound happier. These vacations are good for you.

Anyway, I'm calling about that job. Did you think about it? Are you in?"

I reduced my pace, going from a run to a light jog.

"About that…" I slid my arm across my forehead, wiping the pearls of sweat with my sleeve. "I looked it up. Green Mountain doesn't sound so bad."

Tucker made a funny sound, and I pictured him pumping his fist.

I stifled my laughter. "Do you think Uncle Mike could point me to a place to stay? Since I'll be living there for at least six months, I'd like to avoid motel rooms. A semi-permanent place would be great."

"Still in Medora Beach or you hit the road to elsewhere already?"

"Yeah," I said, walking to cool down. "Still here."

"I thought it was a one-night kind of destination. See the ocean and get going. What are you doing while you're there? Getting your suntan in check? I don't want to piss on your parade, but I'll always win at this contest."

I let out a heartfelt laugh. "Finally, something you're better at than me."

"You wish, man."

"Good to know you didn't lose your sense of humor since I left." An idea popped into my head. "No, no suntan. I'll fix the roof leak at my landlord's." I had nothing better to do, anyway, and I loved my job, so why not?

"Landlord? What the fuck, man? I thought you were staying at a motel or a B&B."

"Nah. Change of plan. Met this woman and her little girl. Staying in their garage apartment…" I grimaced the moment the words flew out of my mouth. Damn it. I wouldn't hear the last of it.

Tucker's loud chuckle resonated through the line. His

amusement tinted every word escaping his mouth. "You're messing with me on purpose, right?"

I reached the house without even noticing and had to walk back to get to the alley leading to the garage.

"Are you fucking her? The mom, I mean. Is she hot? How old is she? Thirty? Forty? You could use a woman with more experience than you to help perfect your technique."

I pinched my eyebrows. "Damn, Tuck. Yes, she's hot. No, I'm not sleeping with her. Her daughter told me she was twenty-nine. Anything else you wanna know?"

"Can I visit? I want to see with my own eyes."

Despite myself, I smiled at my friend's enthusiasm. "No. Leaving for Green Mountain in a few days. Your idea, remember? You can meet me there, though."

"Be serious, man. Is *roof leak* a code for blowjob or something?"

I spluttered into a loud laugh, unable to contain it anymore. "Roof leak means exactly what it is. I'll fix the roof, then get going. Let's talk later."

Tucker sighed. "Fine. I gotta get to work, anyway. Don't do anything I wouldn't do, man."

I shook my head. "Tuck. You do about anything and everything. That's a shitty piece of advice."

"Yeah, so you're entitled to some fun. Just wanted to put it out there in case you change your mind. Or forgot. Blowjob or whatever. Gotta go. Bye."

We hung up, and after a quick shower, I climbed on the roof to assess the damage left by the last tropical storm.

Two days later, I was in the garage apartment, ready to go to bed, when loud voices erupted outside. I recognized the first one but couldn't place the second, a deep male voice.

"Stop asking me for money. You and I are done," the man barked.

"I'm not asking for money. I'm only asking you to be there and provide for your daughter. I thought we'd settled everything in court. You just never kept your end of the deal. Remember Kelly? The girl you used to call your princess but forgot all about, then flushed from your life the day you married that woman you met on a train. She needs you. She needs her daddy. She asks for you. All the freaking time."

"Mandy, don't tell me what I should or shouldn't do."

"Let go of me. You're hurting my arm."

I'd heard enough. By the window in less than five seconds, I pushed the curtains to the side and watched Amanda being manhandled by a man who I supposed was her ex-husband. The one Kelly told me all about.

With disheveled dark hair and a few-days-old scrub spotting his jaw, he looked threatening even from up here.

I put shorts on and slid a T-shirt over my head as I hurried down the stairs.

"Let go," I warned, inching closer to them. "I believe she asked you to let go of her."

The man twisted Amanda's arm, and she winced, trying to free it. In vain.

"Oh, Mandy. You've got yourself a boy toy. Real nice. How long have you two been fucking under my roof?"

Tears glistened in Amanda's eyes. "This isn't your home anymore. I bought your share of the mortgage way over the market value. You have no right to come here unannounced anymore."

"We'll see about that." With his free hand, Dickhead clamped Amanda's jaw, pushing her backward. "I can do whatever I want, Mandy. Why should I even listen to you?

I'm tired of you calling my phone at any time of the day to whine about your problems."

Enough. The wires in my head short-circuited, and liquid rage ran through my bloodstream. A split second later, I had Dickhead's hands off the woman, who wrapped her arms around herself. "Don't you ever touch her again."

Dickhead took a step back and charged at me. I dodged the fist about to connect with my jaw, and it ended up hitting the wall behind me.

Born and raised in Chicago, I'd seen and been in my share of fights growing up. Tucker got himself into many of them, always stealing other guys' girlfriends—a dumb habit of his. I often ended up jumping into fist rumbles to save his ass. If Dickhead thought he could scare me, he should do a better job.

A train of curses left his mouth, and he nursed the probably broken fist with his other hand. "You jerk," he spewed, venom coating his words. "You did this."

As a precaution, I pushed him back and stood between him and Amanda. "You did this to yourself. You should get your hand checked. By the way, I'm nobody's boy toy. I'm just helping your ex-wife out. There was a leak in the roof that needed fixing. Since you're too selfish to help her out and your sweet daughter, I took it upon myself to repair the roof because I happened to be around. Now leave. And don't bother coming back if you have no intention of saying you're sorry."

Dickhead mumbled something I didn't bother to catch and drove away in his red sports car, tires screeching.

I whirled around, and Amanda buried herself in my chest, her shoulders heaving. "Thank you, Nick. Y-you didn't have to but…thank you."

I wound an arm around her. "You shouldn't have to deal with him on your own. Did he ever hurt you before?"

She shook her head. "He has a temper…a bad one, but he usually breaks stuff or screams. This is the first time he's put his hands on me. I swear. Sorry you had to witness that."

I swept her hair away from her forehead with a finger. "I'm just glad I was around this time." I perused her face, making sure he hadn't hurt her in any way.

We stood like that for a while, the sweet scent of Amanda's perfume penetrating my nostrils.

Without a word, she leaned back, and lifting herself onto her tiptoes, she brought her mouth up, her lips soft and warm against mine. Our mouths fused gently, and we took our time tasting each other. She tasted like apple and cinnamon and something exclusively her. With one hand entangled in her hair, I deepened the kiss, relishing all the sensations swirling inside me. It'd been a while since I kissed a woman, and now, I felt alive.

Amanda slid her hands under my shirt, tracing the planes of my abs. My pulse kicked up. Goose bumps blossomed along the length of my spine. I held her hips with both hands, but when our tongues tangled together, I leaned back. Amanda watched me, panting, her lips red, a light flush covering her cheeks.

"We shouldn't," I said, hating myself for speaking the words out loud.

"Sorry, it's my fault," she said, spinning around to walk away.

I grabbed her wrist before she could leave, resting the pad of my thumb against her racing pulse point.

Her heart rate matched mine. Strong and bounding.

I inhaled through my mouth to even my breathing. "It's not you. I-I'm not good at keeping it casual."

Amanda avoided my eyes when she spoke. "You know you don't have to move out. You could stay longer. From what you told me, you have nowhere to be…for now. Medora Beach is kinda nice."

I tipped her chin up with my finger and locked my eyes on her glimmering ones. "I can't. I'm starting a new job soon. I just agreed earlier this week. They're expecting me by the end of the month. Medora Beach is not where I'm supposed to be. I can't explain it, but deep inside, I'm certain…" I paused. "Amanda, you're an amazing woman. You deserve better than a quick romp between the sheets. You need to be wooed and treated like a queen. I-I can't be that guy for you. Also, a short-term relationship…a fling… isn't good enough for you. You deserve forever."

She nodded, and I let go of her as she turned around and went inside. Before closing the door behind her, she watched me over her shoulder. Understanding and regret passed through her eyes. "Good night, Nick. I hope one day you'll find what you're looking for."

I rubbed the nape of my neck and offered her a lopsided smile, waiting until I heard the locks, then returned to my apartment.

The next morning, I woke up early and went for my daily run, desperate to relieve the angst bubbling inside me. My dreams had been filled with images of my hostess. Sometimes, I wished I could be like Tucker and abandon myself to pleasure without overthinking everything.

Armed with my tools and building materials bought from the hardwood store, I worked on the roof for hours. The sun rested high in the sky. The gentle breeze from the sea swept across my skin. At that moment, a thousand miles away from home, I could say, in all honesty, that I was at peace. That every day, every new experience, made me feel more alive than the previous one. Sitting on the shingle, my legs stretched before me, I watched the horizon, sipping water. Sunlight danced across the ocean's surface, turning it into an infinite mirror.

The view burned itself into my memory.

I grabbed my phone and snapped a picture. To remember what freedom, optimism, and happiness looked like—felt like. Nature was healing the breaches of my heart, its vastness and constancy dampening the sharpest of my pain.

Without Derek's bucket list, I wouldn't be here enjoying this moment.

"Thank you, bro. I'm grateful." I kissed two fingers and saluted the sky.

At the end of the day, I met Amanda and Kelly in the backyard for a barbecue.

"Let me," I said, exchanging the flipper in the woman's hand for a glass of wine.

Amanda studied me. "Nick. You don't have to. You've already done enough. I can't believe you patched the roof." She returned my smile.

"It was nothing. I told you I'd take a look at it. You don't have to worry about it anymore. You should really trust me with dinner. You never know, perhaps I'm Chicago's Grill Master. Are you ready to take a chance and miss out on great food if you don't let me work the grill?"

Amanda's smooth laughter warmed my heart. "Oh, you could be." She arched a brow. "I'm not a risk-taker. The grill is yours, Grill Master."

I nudged her shoulder with mine. "Now that's the spirit. Sit and relax. I know how hard single parenting is. Enjoy yourself for once."

We stared at each other for a long minute, my eyes

traveling to her pink lips. Neither of us said anything, our gazes lingering on one another. Amanda's chest rose and fell quickly.

The images of last night's kiss played back in my head. My lower body tensed. Right now, I wished I'd never stopped our make-out session. Amanda possessed every-thing I loved in a woman. A sense of humor, natural inner beauty, enticing lips, intelligence, and a caring soul. I relished the desire simmering between us, but somehow, it lacked the heat of lust I craved so badly.

Her lips parted, but before she could utter a word, I cupped the back of her neck and pulled her into my chest. I pressed a kiss to the top of her head. "You deserve a great man. I'm sorry he can't be me."

She tipped her head to gaze at me. "I'm sorry too. You also deserve your own great love story."

Unable to resist her, I kissed her, taking delight in the feel of her warmth one last time.

Amanda fisted my shirt with both hands.

I lost myself in the comfort of her. Until Kelly exited the house, her contagious cheerfulness reaching us. Amanda and I broke apart, and I wondered if my cheeks were blushing like hers. With one hand, I pushed her hair away from her face and drew the length of her lower lip with my thumb, erasing all traces of the kiss as I righted her lipstick.

"I'll go set the table," she whispered, breathless.

I pointed to the grill. "I better start on those patties, or I'll lose my Grill Master title."

Amanda giggled, the sound packing my heart with newfound joy. "Impress me, Nick," she said with a wink as she joined her enthusiastic daughter.

Two days later, I stood by my truck, my heart knotted tightly, as Kelly ran my way.

Her voice quivered, and she batted her eyelashes fast. "Nick, do you really have to go?"

I squatted before her, tugging on her pigtails. "Yes, I do. My time here is over. Remember, I told you I was only passing through town."

The girl fastened her tiny arms around my neck. "Oh, but I'm sad you're going. Because I'll miss you."

"I know, Kelly. Because I'll miss you too. Be good to your Mama."

She bobbed her head.

Amanda neared us, and I slid an envelope into her hand. She bunched her brows as she looked inside. "Nick, I can't accept this. You've already covered the rent. And repaired the roof. That's much more than what we talked about."

I enveloped her hand with mine, closing it over the envelope containing a few hundred dollars. "Our deal didn't include meals and laundry. You need this. It's not much, but I want you two to have it. I was broken when I came here. Your hospitality and generosity made a huge impact on me. Now I don't feel like as much of a mess as I was, thanks to you two."

A fat tear sloped down her cheek, and Amanda swiped it with her hand. "Nick, I don't know why you appeared in our lives that day, but you made an impression on us too and showed me how a man should be. I'll never settle for anything less. You raised the bar pretty high for anyone entering my life from now on. I'll forever be grateful. Thank you." Moving closer, Amanda rose to her toes and kissed my lips. "I'll never forget what you did for us…for me," she added in a hushed tone.

She stepped back with a hand pressed against her heart, her eyes teary.

With a lump growing in my throat, I climbed behind the wheel when Kelly's voice startled me.

"Nick, wait. Wait. Wait for me," she yelled, hurrying my way.

I opened the door, and she almost ran into me. "The recipe. I wrote it down for you. So, you'll remember me forever."

Waves of emotions rushed through me, leaving behind memories as flotsam on the tide. Soon, though, they were replaced by a smile. The innocence of this kid. She had a special way of reaching my heart. Derek would have agreed because she reminded me of him in so many ways.

You'll remember me forever. They were the same words he wrote in his letter.

For a second, I felt like Derek put us on each other's path. Because in some crazy way, we could help one another to move on. To sew back rips in our hearts.

Mine warmed up when I took the card, a folded white sheet of paper with a drawing of me and her fishing on the shore. "This is beautiful, Kelly. Thank you so much."

Inside, the girl had written the recipe and:

From your friend, Kelly.

She had also drawn a multicolored unicorn on the other side. My lips tipped into a smile, and I pulled her into my arms.

"Thank you. I'm lucky to count you as one of my precious friends. I'll keep this forever."

Her mother tugged her hand, and they waved at me as

I drove away, my heart searing with a mix of joy, sadness, and hope.

Derek's Bucket List — ~~42. Nick. Be a knight to a damsel in distress, not that the damsel truly needed me~~

11

NICHOLAS

I left Medora Beach with a lighter heart than when I arrived, though not without a pang of pain at leaving Amanda and Kelly behind. In the short amount of time we'd known one another, they had injected my life—and my entire being—with new doses of love and compassion. Nobody had asked them to strike up a conversation with a stranger or invite him over that day, but they did, and somehow our encounter had patched some of the wounds I carried around.

"If you made it happen, bro, thank you. I needed that."

An hour later, I took an exit when I crossed a sign announcing a distilleries and breweries tour. It was something Jace, Tucker, and I had talked about doing for years. Since I had almost three weeks to spare before arriving in Green Mountain, I could make pit stops wherever the opportunity presented itself along the way.

To grasp as much as possible from my journey.

On the country road, I rolled the windows down,

cranked up the volume of the radio, and sped off, following the road signs to a small town. No, tiny would be a better word to describe it.

I parked my truck in front of what resembled a century-old brick building. The early spring breeze swept across my face. From the backseat, I fetched a hoodie and made my way to the main building. After paying for the tour, I joined the crowd of people as they left for the hour-long visit.

After lunch, I walked to the site announcing the bourbon trail and embarked on a bus trip to two distilleries. In front of a wall of wooden barrels with a tray of samples, I snapped a picture of myself and sent it to my friends back home.

JACE

You didn't.

TUCKER

Fucker

ME

I did. *winking emoji*

JACE

I hope you liked the practice tour because we'll do that again sometime. All three of us.

ME

Wasn't a practice tour. Just awesome. Tasting great stuff. You should be jealous. You have a right to be.

TUCKER

I may choose to stop talking to you for a while.

ME

Haha. I'd like to see you try. You won't last a day.

TUCKER

...

ME

I got each of you a nice bottle. Stop being babies about it, or I'll drink them myself.

We'll do the Kentucky bourbon trail together. When you guys are ready.

JACE

Awesome. Thanks for the bottle, man.

TUCKER

Okay. Fine. You win.

I grinned at my phone. My best friend was predictable. Whatever he said, or chose to believe, whiskey, designer shit, and women were his weaknesses.

JACE

I'll ask Pam if I can get away for a weekend

TUCKER

Jace! Balls, man. GET. THEM. BACK.

JACE

My balls are doing just fine. Thank you for checking up on them.

ME

And they prefer red lace.

JACE

Need to go.

TUCKER

Red lace? What does that even mean? How
do you know what his balls like?

Lace? Really? What did I miss?

Guys?

Answer me before I get the wrong images
in my head.

Too late.

It's etched in there forever.

Not funny.

Come on, guys. What did I miss?

JACE

Nick. Shut up.

ME

My lips are sealed. Talk later, guys. They're
waiting for me to sample a single-barrel
bourbon that hasn't hit the market yet.

TUCKER

That bottle better be good because I'm
hating you right now.

And don't think you're off the hook. I'll get
to the bottom of this lacy-balls thing. Be
warned.

I stifled a laugh and followed the tour guide outside as
we boarded the bus to our next destination.

For the rest of the afternoon, I strolled around town
and grabbed a bite to eat from a local sandwich shop.

Sitting on a park bench, I checked the options for my
next stop. A town about thirty miles from here was hosting
a rodeo next weekend. I'd never been to one of those. It

sounded fun. Chicago wasn't big on the cowboy vibe. Well, it was pretty non-existent if truth be told.

According to the app on my phone, all hotels and B&B had no vacancy for that weekend, so I decided to drive out there and see for myself if I could find anything once I arrived. Perhaps they could recommend a place to stay outside of town, but still nearby.

The sun hung low in the sky, replacing its usual blue color with orange and pink streaks. In my life, I never took the time to just admire everything around me and to savor the beauty this world had to offer. Nature was the true artist if you paid attention.

Now that I had the time and the will, I considered myself lucky to be able to enjoy this moment as the bright day ceded its place to the upcoming darkness.

Lost in my contemplation, I passed a pickup truck hauling what looked like a livestock trailer parked on the side of the road. I slowed down and caught sight of an elderly couple arguing while poking at a deflated tire. A few yards away, I stopped my truck and got out.

"Barb, are you going to help me or not?" the man asked.

The woman rested her closed fists on her wide hips. "I'm past the age where you get to tell me what to do, Harold."

The man lifted a spare tire from the back of the pickup. "I'm too old for this."

"See, I told you," the woman replied.

I pinched my lips together to avoid smiling at their dispute. From the way they bickered, I bet they were an old married couple.

"Careful with your back, Harold. These things are heavy."

The man huffed. "Had you brought that phone Rupert gifted us last Christmas, we could have called in for help."

I inched closer. "Hey," I hailed them, waving. "I'm Nick. Maybe I could give you a hand."

Their stares drifted to me, but soon their argument resumed.

"Harold, your pants. Don't ruin them. It took me hours to fix the hem the other day," the woman said.

"Barb, it's you who wanted me to dress nice for a livestock auction. That makes no sense. I should have worn my usual work clothes."

I stepped between them. "If you let me, I could change that tire for you."

Both their gazes shifted to me, studying me with matching frowns.

"Oh, you heard the boy, Harold? He could help you out. You're too old to do this yourself."

The man growled. "That's what I said. If you would've listened to me."

Barb added, "It is the ranch hand's job to pick up the animals."

The man continued. "I know, but we're short one right now, so we need to do it ourselves in the meantime."

Without a word, I picked up the jack from the compartment in the open bed of their pickup truck and after disconnecting the trailer, I got their vehicle lifted, ready to remove the flat tire.

"Wow, you're strong," the woman remarked with an appreciative nod.

"I used to be strong too," the man grumbled with a sigh.

"Yes. You were the strongest man I knew. It's okay if you're not so strong anymore." Love passed between them as they stopped arguing. The man leaned forward to kiss his wife's—now I was sure—forehead. The way they smiled at each other made me yearn for a connection like theirs. One day.

After I re-attached the trailer, I wiped my hands on the rag cloth Harold handed me and accepted the bottle of water from Barb.

"Thank you so much, son. You really saved the day," the old man said.

"I'm happy I could help."

"How can we thank you?" Barb asked.

I raised my hands. "No need. It was my pleasure."

"You have an accent. Where are you from?"

"Illinois." I paused. "Chicago."

"What are you doing on this deserted road all by yourself at this hour? Chicago is far from here. Are you lost?" the woman questioned with arched eyebrows.

"On my way to Green Mountain. I wanted to spend the weekend in town for the rodeo. I have some free time —about three weeks, to be exact—before I gotta reach my destination. I don't have any plans, so we'll see."

"Oh," was all Barb said.

"Are you okay to drive?" I asked them before moving on with my day. Semi-darkness had descended upon us, the sky now a darker shade of orange as the last sun's rays lit up the horizon.

"Yes. I might be old, but my sight is still good," Harold said.

I laughed with him. "What do you have in there?" I asked, pointing to the trailer.

"That? This is Roseanne, our new reproductive sow."

"You guys are farmers?"

A proud smile stretched Harold's lips. "Ranchers. For the last forty-six years. Our son is in charge of operations now, but we're still overseeing some of it. One of our ranch hands quit yesterday. Met a girl, moved to Arizona. This means we're short-handed, so we offered to pick up our newest resident ourselves. Like we did back in the day when we ran the ranch together."

The couple exchanged a loving gaze.

"Wow, I've never been to a ranch before. It sure seems like a lot of work."

Barb rested her hand on my forearm. "If we offer you a place to stay and three meals a day, would you like to spend a few days with us? You'll never find a hotel for next weekend at the last minute. All rooms have been booked for months. It would be our way of thanking you. Also, we could show you around. If you like it, you could be our ranch hand until you have to go. See for yourself if it's as much work as you think it is."

I let out a deep, heartfelt laugh. "I'm not sure I would be a big help. I've been living in the city all my life and working in construction since I was eighteen. Not sure how to care for farm animals, though."

"Oh, we have the stable doors that need to be repaired, a part of the sheep's hurdle to fix so coyotes can stay away at night, and a hundred more such tasks around the almost two-thousand acres. You would be more of a handyman than a ranch hand. Would that work? We would pay you for your time. Plus, meals and lodging. This could be good for all of us. What do you say?"

Me, a ranch handyman? I pondered the idea for a minute.

Why not?

It could fit into my new philosophy of surfing life's wave for a while.

"Okay. I'll do it."

We shook hands to seal the deal.

"Follow us, son," Harold said. "We'll show you the way."

———

Geez. I woke up at the crack of dawn to roosters crowing. All my life, I'd thought that was an old wives' tale. A story to make them interesting. Guess not.

The high-pitched sound made my skin prickle. I buried my head under the pillow. Nope. It didn't work. I was wide awake and knew I would have a hard time going back to sleep. I used to get up around six when I worked construction back home, and right now, I could tell those two additional hours made a huge difference.

Rubbing the heels of my hands over my eyes, I sat on the edge of the mattress after turning the bedside table lamp on. The one-room wooden cabin looked cozier than I remembered in the golden light.

Wooden walls, floors, and ceilings. A lighter shade of wood cabinets. A two-place white table and a queen bed in a corner. The masonry fireplace created a screen between the kitchen and the bedroom area.

A small bathroom with a shower, sink, and a toilet was hidden behind a curtain in the opposite corner.

The place was small but perfect for a single person. It reminded me of those industrial loft apartments back home, but the country version of them.

When we arrived at the ranch last night, Harold gave me a short tour of the property as his wife helped Roseanne settle in her new environment.

I even spotted a trail I could run in the morning that circled the pond.

How I found myself living at a ranch, I had no idea, but here I was.

I slid my legs into a pair of joggers and grabbed my sneakers and a long-sleeved T-shirt, my phone, and earbuds and made my way into the crisp early morning spring air.

Relishing the icy burn from the cold air flooding my lungs, I ran as if I had all the time in the world. My eyes and ears took everything in. The birds chirping in the trees, the sunrise as it cast a twinkle from behind the mountains far away, the sound of the stream as I crossed a wooden bridge. I was alive, and the reminder filled me to the brim with a warm and fuzzy feeling.

Being one with nature around me quietened the voices in my head. My fears. My doubts. My painful memories. It only left me with calmness. And hope that everything would be okay.

I ran with my arms open. As if I could imprint this peace in my soul forever and lock it in my heart. To remember it every time my spirits failed to lift me.

I ran up a hill and stopped at the top, bent forward, my hands propped on my knees as I caught my breath, admiring the scenery around me.

Once my breathing returned to normal, I spun around slowly, taking in the vastness of the blue sky.

"Bro, this is amazing. Can you see it from your cloud? This view? How did you know? I have no clue what I'm doing here, to be honest…or how I really ended up here. Circumstances made it happen, but it's like it was planned all along." I scratched the side of my head. "I won't pretend I understand how fate works, but every day, I can feel you around me, pointing me in the right direction… Toward my destiny." I tilted my head back, inhaled, and screamed at the top of my lungs, "Thank you."

Shards maintaining my heart in a semi-permanent state of agony turned to dust.

A loud laugh bubbled out. I shook my head and exhaled.

At a slow pace, taking my time to etch each tree, plain, fence into my memory, I returned to the ranch's main building. They asked me to show up at seven after everyone had started their workday to really take the time to explain what was expected of me and what my job would entail.

Commotion by the main house caught my attention, and instead of going to my cabin to shower before breakfast, curiosity pushed me to follow the people hurrying in the direction of the barn.

"What's going on?" I asked a man wearing denim overalls over a white shirt and a cowboy hat.

"The twins are coming," he said.

My brows shot up. *Twins?* "Oh. What twins?"

The guy halted and turned to face me. "Oh, you're the new guy. I'm Russ." He held out his hand, and I shook it.

"I'm Nick."

"Well, Nick, Felicity, that's one of the ewes, is lambing right now. She's having twins. It calls for a celebration. When she was a lamb, she got strained from the flock and almost drowned during a storm. She's a bit special to all of us. A fighter." I could read the pride shining in his eyes.

"Can I come?" I asked, not knowing if I should or not.

"Sure. You don't wanna miss that. Felicity is the ranch icon. It used to be Butterscotch, Harold's horse, but he died, and the ewe took his prestigious spot."

For the next hour, I watched the vet and a man I assumed to be Rupert, Harold and Barb's son, caring for the lambing sheep as she delivered her twins.

"A boy and a girl," someone shouted, and all the people around cheered.

My throat worked. I watched this miracle of nature

occurring before my eyes, and I was grateful for every second of it.

"Hey, new guy," Russ called, snapping me out of my amazement. "Any idea for names?"

All eyes converged in my direction.

I blinked, not sure Russ was talking to me, and pointed to my chest with my thumb. "Me?"

"Yes, you. Pick a name. It's a tradition. The new guys always get the first choice."

"Any name?"

"Yep."

Before I could think about it, I said, "Barry."

If I could've ever gotten Derek a dog, that was the name he had picked. In honor of Barry Hamilton, his favorite hockey player. The one who had visited him in his hospital room and gifted him the jersey.

"Barry it is," Russ said.

They all voted for the other name. Too absorbed in my own head, I didn't really register anything. Busy, my brain replayed the last twelve hours since I'd met Harold and Barb on the side of the road.

A small hand tapped mine, and I came face to face with Barb. "Nicholas, I'm glad you're here and that you didn't miss the twins' birth. Now come with me. We'll get you settled."

Flickers of joy spread inside me. I'd witnessed a life ending, and now I saw two lives beginning. The animals weren't Derek, and they would never be, but somehow, they were a reminder that life goes on. That the cycle never stops.

For the next twelve days, I worked from dawn to dusk on the ranch, doing any work that seemed fit. I painted more fence pickets than I thought possible, fixed doors, pens, and floors, set hurdles, fed the livestock, and even learned how to ride a horse under Harold's watchful eyes. The man had turned into a mentor. He took me under his wing and explained each tool and piece of equipment to me. He coached me every time we moved cattle around.

"Nicholas, can I ask you something?" Barb asked one afternoon, meeting me by the piglet pen, her voice soft and her brows furrowed.

"Sure. What can I do for you?" I asked as I stuffed my gloves into my back pocket.

With a swipe of my sleeve, I dried the sweat pearling on my forehead, the spring sun blazing above me. A smile stretched my lips as she offered me a cold, refreshing glass of iced tea. I nodded my appreciation and took a big gulp.

"As you know, Rupert is about to be a daddy. The doctor said yesterday the baby could come early." Wonderment lit up her round face, pride radiating from every feature, as her eyes glazed in the sunlight. "He's working long hours. Has been since he was just a kid. Always there for us. Ready to help. Deals with 'bout anything going on here so that Harold and I can enjoy some free time. The thing is, we've been renovating the two-story cabin on the south side of the ranch—a surprise before the baby's born. Nobody knows about it. We thought Rupert and Maureen could use it to jumpstart their new life as a family. They are high school sweethearts, you know. Nice girl. Her Mama is my hairdresser." She sighed, cupping her heart. "Until now, they've been living on the upper floor of the stable we converted into an apartment a while back." She paused to catch her breath. "Anyway, we have a problem."

I waited for her to continue.

"All the furniture for the nursery arrived this morning." Barb pushed her hands together, glee radiating from her. "But the rocking chair we got them—it's the finest thing you can get on the market, I'm tellin' ya—doesn't fit through the door opening. I can't fathom how much work it would take to widen the doorway. It would mean drywall, paint, a new frame. And most importantly, the time we lack. Maureen could go into labor any day now. Little Romy is ready."

In one swift jump, I hoisted myself over the pen. "Show me the way. Let's see if we can brainstorm something. I'm sure I can help."

Barb patted my hand. "Thank you, Nicholas."

In the kitchen of what would be Rupert and Maureen's family nest, I spread a piece of paper on the countertop and drew a freehand plan of the nursery.

"Whatever we do, except sewing it in two, this chair won't go in. The opening is two inches too small."

A loud gasp left Barb's mouth, a horrified expression taking over her face.

"What we could do is enlarge the opening." Before she could object, I raised my hands. "I know, I know. That's what I wanna show you right here," I said, tapping the paper with the tip of my pen. "Some verifications are required, but if there's no electrical wiring nearby, we could widen the doorway. Now, instead of a regular hinged door, since two additional inches in width will prevent the door from clearing completely and would push into the crib when opened, we'll be creative." I drew a layout just to prove my point. "The drywall and paint jobs will be minimal once I reframe the door opening. Also, I saw old wooden barn doors in the garage when I grabbed tools earlier. What if we sanded, trimmed, and stained them the same shade as the flooring and hang them to a rail system —which I'm sure we can find at the local hardware store? There are only three rooms on this floor, so we could swap out all three doors to give the bedrooms a cohesive look. What do you say?"

I stepped back as Barb studied my drawing, her attention riveted to the paper as she bobbed her head, gears already turning in her head.

On my phone, I searched the web until I found a picture of the design I was going for. Flipping my screen toward her, I watched her expression change—lips curling, eyes bright, joy unfurling across her face—when she took it in.

"Beautiful. How long will it take? We can afford to delay the surprise another week. Are you sure it's not too much work?"

"No, it's really not a big deal, and I'm almost done with the piglet pen. If you give me the green light, I can do almost all the work tonight. The paint touchups will be done tomorrow to give the wall putty enough time to dry. It'll all be ready by the end of the day tomorrow. You won't have to worry about anything. I'll make sure of it. Also, I can also finish installing the banister while I'm at it."

Barb's eyes flared. "Nicholas, you'd do that?"

"It would be my pleasure."

The woman squeezed me tight in her arms. "Whoever put you on our road, Nicholas, should be blessed." She let go of me. "I like the idea. Make me a list, and I'll get everything ready while you finish with the pen."

The next afternoon, I presented an enthused Barb with the finished nursery. I had put the chair in the spot she had shown me the day before and even hung the paper birds she'd mentioned on the wall over the crib. The new door looked great, even better than what they had before.

Her eyes brimmed with tears as she cupped her heart, sniffling, her cheeks rosy.

I grinned because her happiness and gratitude bled on to me.

———

I shoved my bag onto the backseat of my truck with a heavy heart.

My stay here had come to an end.

Leaving the ranch felt like leaving a family behind. People I grew to admire and respect over the three weeks we worked together.

"I've prepared you a lunch basket. And this," Barb said, offering me a pale yellow knitted blanket next.

"For me? You made this?" I asked, emotions swirling inside me.

"Yes," she added with a proud smile, pulling me into a warm hug. "For you. It'll keep you warm." She paused, leaning back to watch me. "You'll be missed, Nicholas Peterson. It was fun to have you around. Our next ranch hand, who's starting in a few days, will have big shoes to fill."

Her words found their way straight to my heart.

"I'll miss you guys," I said, extending a hand to shake Harold's.

The man inched closer and drew me into a hug too. "You take care of yourself, son."

I nodded and grabbed the basket—she wasn't kidding, it was a real basket, not a plastic container—Barb handed me, plus her gift, and dropped them onto the passenger seat.

"If you ever come back to Beddingford, please stop by. You'll always be welcome here. And if that job of yours doesn't work out, I'm sure we can find you a permanent position here. The head of maintenance or something. You did a great job. We're proud of you, Nicholas."

Wow. Those words, right there. They reverberated through me.

"Thank you. For the opportunity. And everything."

Barb hugged me one last time before I climbed behind the wheel.

With my heart lurching in my throat, I waved at the people who had not only been my friends but also my family over the last few weeks.

"Thank you, bro." I kissed two fingers and saluted the vast sky I was leaving behind. "What's next?" I asked nobody but me as I watched the ranch sign getting smaller and smaller through the rearview mirror.

Derek's Bucket List — ~~43. Nick. Work on a ranch (why not?)~~

12

NICHOLAS

A few miles outside of Beddingford, I stopped to fuel the truck and studied the map app on my phone.

Green Mountain.

Would it be where the list was supposed to bring me? Or was I forcing fate by accepting Tucker's offer to work for his uncle?

Hundreds of unanswered questions popped into my mind.

Parked on the side of the road, with a bag of takeout on my lap and two soda cups in the center console—because Derek would've liked this road trip—I called my best friend.

"Are you heading toward Green Mountain?" he asked as a greeting.

"About that—"

"Did you change your mind? Are you still at the ranch?"

"No," I said, pushing a handful of fries into my mouth.

"Where are you now?"

"By the side of the road, eating my weight in fries."

Tucker's tone turned serious. "Not what I meant, man."

I chuckled and washed the food down with a sip of soda. "Fine. On my way. Should be there by the end of the afternoon."

"Yes," Tucker screamed. "Are you okay? You sound a bit off."

I pondered what to reply for a long second. "Yes. No. Medora Beach, the ranch, they just happened. Green Mountain…" I searched for the right words.

"Nick, it just happened too. Don't overthink it. What are the chances that a job, in your field, close to where you were heading, got available at the same time you were around? None. I barely ever talk to my uncle, and one morning, out of the blue, he called to chat about his investments because he wants to retire within a year and confided he couldn't find a qualified person to lead his new project. It's fate, man. Nothing else can explain it. Serendipity. Luck. Aligned stars. Call it what you want."

I closed my eyes. Tucker's words hit me hard in the chest—they made sense—and goose bumps blossomed all over my arms.

"You can't argue because you know it's true," my friend said.

"Maybe."

Tucker's confidence in my destiny shook me to the core. My eyes traveled to the two soda cups, and the air around me lightened.

"You're right. It's too many coincidences to just be all by accident." My zest returned. I dragged a hand over my face. So many things in my life hadn't been making sense lately, but they all interweaved, one thread at a time, as if I had planned them perfectly.

"Let me call Uncle Mike right away. He'll meet you there. For what it's worth, I'm glad you're committing to something. I know this whole trip is about being free and going with the flow, but I'm not sure you would've thrived in the long run. You're happier when there's structure involved, always have, and with this lifestyle, you would've been miserable in no time, not knowing what to do next at some point."

"Have you talked to my mom? She said the same exact thing."

"No, Mrs. Peterson and I haven't talked in a long time. I'm thrilled we agree on this, though. Should I call her? Or send her flowers?"

"Why?"

Tucker sighed. "To thank her. For drilling some sense into you, man."

I shook my head. "Forget it. She didn't. I listen to you more, to tell you the truth."

"Haha. I've always suspected I was your voice of reason," Tucker bragged.

"I'll deny it in court."

He chuckled, and it chased all the remnants of doubt in the air.

"I'll let you know when I get there, okay?" I sighed. "Thanks, man. For everything. Including your trust in me."

"Always. I'll send you the info. Talk soon. And Nick? You're doing great. I'm glad you're getting your groove back."

"Thanks."

We hung up, and I finished my meal.

When I left Chicago, I had no real plans. Nothing tying me to anything.

Now I had something to look forward to.

A destination. And goals.

No matter how much I tried to convince myself I could do impulsive shit, having a plan soothed the storm inside me. It loosened every knot and calmed the heavy spiral of nerves in my chest. Tucker knew me too well, that I couldn't deny.

I looked up and cleared my throat. "I don't know where this will bring me, bro. I have no idea what I'm doing. Or if you can influence my journey, but it feels right….somehow. Thanks for opening my eyes because I wouldn't have done it if it weren't for you."

And Tucker, I muttered to myself.

Lost in my mind, I drove for the next four hours in silence.

When "Monkey Business," the Carter Hills Band's song that Derek loved so much, started playing on the radio, I cranked up the volume.

> **…I thought there was a hippo**
>   **in your closet**
> **A monkey hidden under**
>   **your bed**
> **I thought I saw a lion in your**
>   **kitchen**
> **And a snake hanging from the**
>   **chandelier**
> **Because that's what your love**
>   **does to me, baby**
> **You turn my world**
>   **upside down**
> **My imagination runs wild**
> **I can become a pirate, a ghost**
>   **hunter, or even an**
>   **astronaut**
> **There's nothing I can't do**

No, nothing I can't do
As long as you're beside me...

I sang so loud I had to soothe the itchiness in my throat with a sip of water once it was over. I'd heard those lyrics a hundred times before, but now they meant something else, something deeper. They spoke of resilience.

With my phone in hand, I looked at the address displayed on the screen twice. Yeah, that was it. Beaver Line. Squeezed between Falcon Avenue and Steep Valley Crescent.

For someone from the city like me, those silly street names made no sense.

It felt like I'd landed in another dimension. Another universe. Green Mountain, Tennessee, was everything it promised to be. Green. And lodged in mountains with miles and miles of lush landscapes.

Sure, I looked it up, but deep down, after spending weeks on a ranch, I bore hopes there'd be some city vibes so I'd feel more at home.

I should've known better, though. *Green Mountain*. The name said it all.

I sighed, straightened my shoulders, and turned left.

Tucker's uncle had found me a place to stay. A friend of his had left town after her husband passed away a while back, and she had decided to put her property on the market. It required a lot of fixing up, so Tucker told me I could live there rent-free in exchange for work around the house to make it ready to sell. It was a pretty awesome deal. Nothing like keeping my mind occupied and my hands busy in a new town until I made some friends.

Parked in front of a two-story farmhouse, way too big for one person and which had seen better days, I studied the place. The banister could use a bit of restoration and the front lawn, mowing. The gutters needed a good clean-up, with plants now growing in them, and the siding called for a fresh coat of white paint.

I exited the truck and rounded it, staring at the house before me. A cracked window on the second floor. A broken stair leading to the front door. Most of the planks on the wrap-around porch had to be replaced. From here, this place looked like a serious case of a safety hazard.

I had no doubt that back in the day, it had been a beautiful house. There was a sturdiness in its frame, a quiet strength, and an untapped potential. Plus, it sat on a big piece of land, something my hometown missed.

Would the inside match the outside, or had the owners put more love into its maintenance? I hoped so because it'd be sad to see a house like this turn to ruin.

I walked around the property. The land was flat—about the size of two football fields—with huge mature trees lining each side and a weary green lawn, thirsty for a little love and care. A garage, also requiring major restoration, stood right behind the house. I could picture a barn in its place. All white—like the main house—with matching black shutters.

I pivoted around to study the back porch, noting every critical repair in my head, already making calculations in my mind about material costs and work hours required to give the place its grandeur back.

With my hands shoved into my pockets, I stood still, the fresh mountain air flooding my lungs as I watched the valley in the distance. That view. I bet the sunrises were to die for from here. The thought sewed together another lost fragment of my heart.

"Wow. Bro, I'm convinced you sent me here on purpose. Great job."

For a reason out of my understanding, right now, I felt

as if I had always been meant to end up not only in Green Mountain but exactly here, where I stood.

Like I belonged in this place.

This house appealed to me, more than just for the work it required, as if I already knew every corner of it. Inside and out.

In some crazy way, it felt like coming home after being away for so long.

The breeze brushed across my face, its crispness addictive. With my eyes closed, I etched this new episode of my journey into my memory.

"Thanks, Tuck. For this chance. And Derek, for making it happen."

With purpose in my steps, I made it back to my vehicle when a deep-green pickup truck halted beside me, and a man in his sixties with white hair and a salt-and-pepper beard climbed out.

"Howdy. You must be Nick," he greeted, getting closer.

"Yes, sir."

"You've gotten all man over the years. Last time I saw you, Tucker and you were about"— he placed his palm down at his hip level, pretending to measure a child—"that tall."

I chuckled. "It's sure been a long time."

"Yeah, tell me about it. Tucker couldn't stop bragging. God, I miss that bratty kid. He claimed you were Chicago's best and that I'd be a fool not to hire you." Uncle Mike held out his hand to shake mine.

I mirrored his smile and met his palm with mine. "Tuck says a lot of things."

Uncle Mike let out a loud belly laugh. "Yeah." He locked his eyes on mine, and his playfulness vanished. "So? Tell me. Are you really Chicago's best?"

I firmed my back. "I'm quite competent at my job, sir.

Ran a few big condo building projects back home. I know what I'm doing. Tucker's right. You'd be a fool not to hire me," I said with a half-smile, trying not to sound too presumptuous even though I knew my worth and what I could bring to the project.

The man nodded. "I like that. Confidence. And being able to tell things the way they are. We'll get along just fine, you and I." He nodded some more.

"Thanks for the chance, sir."

Uncle Mike flicked his hand. "Call me Mike. Don't go all *sir* on me, son. We're practically family." His eyes drifted to the house, standing there, waiting for another opportunity to shine and show its own value. "Jeanine Rutherford, the owner, moved out of town to stay with her son and his family two years ago. She hasn't been back home since. Gosh, she loved this house. Many good times here." He sighed as old memories danced in his dark irises. "She agreed to let you live here for free if you helped her fix this place up. Give the grand lady its youth back. All it requires is a few hours of your time every week to get it back into shape before putting it on the market by the end of the year. She wanted to welcome you herself but couldn't handle the drive. Her daughter-in-law came yesterday to clean up the place, and she stocked the refrigerator. You'll have everything you need until you're settled in. Jeanine is paying for all the expenses. All you'll provide is the labor force and expertise."

"That's pretty generous of Mrs. Jeanine," I said, wondering what I did to earn so much trust from all these people I knew nothing about. "I can still pay a rent—"

Mike stopped me with a raised hand. "Nah. She's grateful to have someone taking care of her home. Don't worry about it. Anyway, we'll meet on Friday to sign your contract and go over your employment. Everything you need to get going is in the garage. The key is hung by the door." The man fished something out of his pocket—a business card—and handed it to me. "Here. Call my assistant first thing tomorrow morning, and she'll schedule an appointment. See you around, son."

As fast as he came, Mike left, the engine roaring and his tires leaving a cloud of dust behind.

With hesitant steps, I climbed the four steps leading to the front door, the planks cracking under my weight. Perhaps this should be my priority.

With a straight back and puffed chest, I opened the front door, wondering how bad it'd be inside. Standing on the doorstep, I scanned my surroundings and blinked. My heart raced in my chest, and most of the knots coiling my stomach slackened. The entire place looked amazing. Nothing like my apartment in Chicago, but once again, it felt like home. Yeah, I could get used to living here.

Soft cream-colored cabinets lined the kitchen walls. The ceiling soared overhead, its wooden planks a pale, weathered brown. The windows were huge and offered the best view of the mountains and valley. A gray-stoned open masonry fireplace with a large wooden beam mantle, flanked by a set of matching gray couches, stood majestically in the living room.

It reminded me of cozy winter nights when I was a child, playing board games and sipping hot chocolate.

How could this place appeal so much to me? As if it had been built from my dreams…the ones I'd never stopped to think about.

As if, somehow, I'd been here before.

On the southern side was a large den with wrap-around floor-to-ceiling windows, housing a piano and a small bar.

The place wasn't just farmhouse chic, it was inviting

and could only be described as a home. A true home. Not a place you only passed by, but a place where you grow old and create lasting memories.

Once I sanded and repainted the cabinets and hardwood floors, changed the countertops, and applied a fresh coat of paint on the walls, this place would sell in no time.

I climbed the staircase which was in the same condition as the floors. Upstairs, the house required a bit more love and care. The master bedroom wallpaper looked straight out of another decade and was peeling at the corners. The bathroom begged for a complete makeover. Outdated, awful green color fixtures, leaking pipes, chipped paint. Even the tiled floor had to be removed, leveled, and redone. The broken window I'd seen earlier belonged to one of the bedrooms. The entire second floor screamed for a fresh coat of paint and some drywall patching. Nothing I couldn't tackle.

This new project excited me. If I were being honest, it sparked my excitement even more than my new job. The joy of this newfound freedom seeped its magic into me, and I relished the feeling.

Was it wrong to feel so happy when someone I knew and loved had just died? What was I doing here? Caught in a six-month contract. Why did I agree to that? My breath hitched, and suddenly the Earth seemed to be spinning too fast around its axis. I had attached myself to this place. What if I wanted to leave this town and continue my journey elsewhere? Or discover new places? What did I do? Being hooked to one place felt all wrong—deeply wrong.

My thoughts bumped into the bones of my skull, my worries clamping around my heart.

The sound of a tinkling bell startled me and put a stop to my panicked state. I turned around and came face to face with an old bloodhound. He stared at me for a long second before moving closer, butting my hand, asking to be petted.

I squatted before him, a new wave of calm invading my senses. "Hey, buddy. What's your name?" I rubbed him behind the ears with one hand and reached for his tag with the other. *Buddy*. "Oh, I guessed it right then. You live here?"

Buddy made some sort of yapping sound and waggled his tail.

"You like that, don't you? You thirsty?"

Rummaging through the kitchen cupboards, I found a stainless-steel bowl, filled it with fresh water, and placed it on the floor. After the dog gulped half the bowl, I moved toward the door.

"Come on. Let's get my stuff from the truck."

The dog watched over me for the next hour as I carried boxes inside and stacked them in the corner of one of the bedrooms upstairs.

I went back to my truck to pick up the last few things when a woman's voice with a southern drawl called out behind me. "Hey there, are you the new tenant?"

I wiped the sweat across my forehead with the hem of my T-shirt and turned around. "Yep. That would be me."

In her late thirties, with brown hair and hazel eyes, dressed in a long steel-blue dress with buttons down the front, she offered me a huge smile. "I'm Greta. The neighbor."

I held out a hand. "Nick. Nice to meet you."

She met my palm with hers. "Seems like this old fellow has adopted you."

I nodded, patting his head. "Buddy and I are now best friends."

My own words settled inside me, appeasing the panic

that had risen earlier. *Best friends.* Had Derek sent this dog to watch over me because he knew I would need someone to rely on in a town I knew nothing about—and no one?

I refrained from smiling because even if it made no sense, I now believed Buddy appearing on my doorstep was bound to happen. That it wasn't just a coincidence.

"Then you must be a nice guy because Buddy isn't the most social dog. He's half-blind, and it wouldn't surprise me if he was half-deaf too. Let's just say his hearing has seen better days."

Buddy sat next to me, his back firm and chin high. Yeah, no coincidence.

I grinned. "He looks like a youngster to me. I'm sure you've mistaken him for another dog."

The woman chuckled and pushed her hair behind her shoulder."When did you get here?"

"An hour ago. I've just finished unloading my truck, thanks to Buddy here."

She smiled again. "Well, I'm sure you could use a home-cooked meal after that. How about you meet us for dinner later?" Why were all the people here so welcoming? No way a neighbor would have invited a stranger to dinner back in Chicago. Our doors had three locks, and we kept mostly to ourselves. All the time.

"You sure?"

Greta bobbed her head. "Come knocking at six. Brett, my husband, and Chaz, my son, will be ecstatic to have some male company over." She beckoned Buddy to follow her, but he kept his stance next to me, eyeing me sideways to make sure I wasn't throwing him out. She sighed, a small grin stretching her lips. "Well, just bring the dog with you when you come over."

"I will."

Greta crossed a line of trees, and from where I stood, I

could see hints of a white house on the other side. I leaned forward to talk to my new friend. "We gotta make ourselves presentable, Buddy."

The house came fully furnished, so I only had my clothes to hang in the closet, my toiletries to put in the bathroom, and my tools to store in the garage. Everything else was already there, so I was settled in before I knew it.

With a bottle of beer in hand, I sat on an Adirondack chair on the back deck, the late afternoon sun warming my skin. The view of the mountains from here was spectacular. It seemed like the world had no end, as if I could see miles ahead.

At this exact moment, I didn't miss the city. The noises. The smog. The parking hassles. And the concrete buildings.

Green Mountain was peaceful.

Buddy curled under the chair, his snores the only sound breaking the silence.

"You know," I told him, "before you, I had a best friend. His name was Derek. He passed away not so long ago. I'm here because of him. If he's watching us from somewhere up there, from his cloud like he used to say, and now I'm pretty sure he is"—I raised my beer toward the sky—"I think he'd like to hang out with us. He…well, he loved animals but never got a chance to have one of his own. I would have gotten him a dog if he ever went into remission." Unshed tears constricted my throat. Swallowing hard, I had to force myself to breathe. "It…it, huh, never happened… One day he was there and the next… he…he was gone. You would have liked him. A lot. I'm glad we found each other. Let me tell you a secret. I think he put us on each other's road. Anyway, I could use the company…if you agree to become my friend."

A growl left the dog's mouth.

"I'll take that as a yes. Funny, because I have no idea how this friendship is supposed to go. You're not a big talker, huh? Guess I'll do all the talking then. Perhaps you could come visit every day or so. That way, we could get to know each other better… Except for Uncle Mike—and truthfully, I don't know him either—I know nobody in this town."

My phone vibrated.

"It was nice talking to you, Buddy. At least you're a great listener," I said, picking it up. *Tucker.* He'd never called me as often as he had since Derek died. We usually messaged each other instead. "Hey man. How is it going?" I asked, pressing the speaker button after placing the device on the armrest and stretching my legs before me.

"Good. I was about to ask you the same thing. Did you make it to Green Mountain?"

"Yep. Met Uncle Mike. Somehow, he remembered me. All set here. Even got a new friend."

"Already?"

A lopsided smile peeked out. "Yeah, his name is Buddy."

"Buddy? What kind of name is that?"

"Someone with four legs and shiny fur."

"You already replaced me. Man, that was fast."

"Sorry. This friend doesn't argue or leave me for booty calls, so it's a win-win friendship."

"I'll see it for myself 'cause I'm coming down in a few weeks. I need to witness you turning into a mountain man. Do you think you'll become a lumberjack? Women like that manly-woody vibe, you know."

"Damn, you're impossible," I said between chuckles. "Not everything in life is about sex."

Tucker whistled. "Yes. It. Is. You're turning into a monk. You need some action down there. Got a question for you. When you said the other day you were sore from riding that mare, were you talking about the actual animal, or was it the ranch secret code for a cowgirl with a great set of tits and a greedy tongue?"

"My ass cheeks were killing me, man. She gave me the ride of my life. It was wild. I'm telling you."

"Oh, she was naughty then. Good for you."

"You wish."

We talked some more until I noticed it was almost five thirty.

"I have to go. The neighbors are having me over for dinner, and I have to shower and change."

"You keep mentioning new friends. When did you find time to meet people? You've been there, like what? Two hours?"

"Thank the dog. He's a real matchmaker. Talk to you later."

———

"You drove away from Chicago and ended up in Green Mountain. How is that even possible?" Brett, my neighbor, asked me as we sat around the kitchen table, eating the cannelloni Greta made from scratch.

"I can't wait to get out of this hole," Chaz barged in. "College life will be awesome next year."

"Wait until you're stuck in traffic. I lived in Houston for ten years, and as much as I liked it there, I'd never go back. Nothing equals the mountain air, son," Brett said as he sipped his beer.

"Do you miss Chicago?" the teen asked me.

"It's too soon to tell. I really love the city, but I hope I'll like it here as much. I never lived in a small town before. It's all new to me."

"We're glad you moved next door," Greta chimed in. "Mrs. Rutherford really needs help if she wants to sell the house. It's been vacant for a while, and that's a shame. It's such a beautiful property."

"Are you looking for a job? They're hiring at the firm," Brett asked next.

I shook my head. "Already have this covered."

"You don't waste any time, do you?"

"No. That's the main reason I moved here."

"If you need anything, even if it's just sugar, let us know. We'll be happy to help and show you around."

After dinner, I walked back home through the line of trees with a light heart.

In a very short span of time—more like hours—Green Mountain had made a mark on me. People I didn't know were happy to have me around. It was too soon to call them friends, but they made me feel welcome.

The next morning, I woke up around seven and made my way to the garage to find everything I needed to fix the front porch stairs.

Chaz and Buddy met me after lunch.

"Can I give you a hand?" the teen asked.

Buddy curled under a lilac tree and sighed as he made himself comfortable.

"Sure. You can mow the lawn. Then we'll paint the borders. They're not so white anymore."

"Great. I'll go change and be right back."

Chaz and I worked side by side for the next two hours. Greta brought us sweet tea, and we took a break, sitting on the front steps I'd repaired earlier. Glancing around, I felt proud of what we'd accomplished in just a day. I kept looking at the porch, feeling like it lacked something. Yes, I should get a swing. They looked homey, and I'd always wanted one of those. It would fit perfectly here.

Reality hit me.

Homey.

Since when did I start thinking about this house as my own? Again, the thought seemed ridiculous, but it didn't unsettle me as much as it probably should have.

"You really want to get out of here?" I asked Chaz, changing the topic.

He nodded.

"Where would you go?"

"I'm moving to Columbus soon. It isn't Chicago or New York, but it's a start. I've been dreaming of leaving this place for a long time. I can't believe someone like you would want to move here." He shrugged. "You look sane. I'm telling you it's boring as hell. You'll realize it soon enough. Also, I've known all the girls here since I was a toddler."

"No girlfriend then?" I asked, taking a gulp, enjoying the cold beverage as it slid down my throat.

"There was this girl. She used to date my best friend." The boy shook his head with a frown. "She's off-limits now."

"Does she like you back?"

He sighed, looking past my shoulder. "Not sure. Anyway, I won't date my friend's ex...that wouldn't be right. Bro code and shit."

"Sure." I hid my smile behind my glass. Been there. Chaz should have had this talk with Jace.

"Mama wanted me to tell you we're having a barbecue with some friends on Friday night. You're welcome to join us."

The invitations kept pouring, and soon, this town wouldn't feel so lonely anymore.

"Sure. I'd like that. Count me in."

"Great. I gotta go. I'm on dinner duty tonight. See you

tomorrow, Nick."

"Bye, Chaz. And thanks for your help."

———

On Friday morning, I woke up at seven and repaired the banister leading to the back deck of the farmhouse. I also used the time I had left before meeting with Mike to weed the flower beds.

Buddy joined me mid-task, nudging my hand with his nose and waiting for me to pat his head.

"You like that?" I asked, more to myself than to him. "I wish you could talk back, but hey, that's not how this relationship goes. I get it."

The sun was hot and high for a spring day, so I showered and changed before my meeting.

"White or black shirt?" I asked Buddy as I dug clothes from my wardrobe. I caught my reflection in the mirror above the dresser. The dark circles around my eyes had receded, and the days spent working under the sun in the last few weeks had brought back some color to my skin. I looked better…and almost rested. I had no idea how to describe it, but the shadows of grief had left my face— most of them, at least.

This new life suited me. Even my body agreed.

Buddy head-butted the black shirt hanging from my fingers.

"This one? Okay then."

I walked the dog back to his home before getting into my truck. My pulse quickened as I settled behind the wheel. This new adventure had me excited and energized all at once. Some parts of me longed to return to the job I loved and adored, while others questioned if it was the right choice.

So far, since I'd left my hometown, all the pieces of my life had fallen into place, so I trusted life to push me in the right direction once again.

To make sure I'd find a parking spot near Hilton and Sons and because I hadn't ventured to the town center yet, I left a bit early. Not used to small towns, my eyes flared as I realized there was no shortage of parking around here, and they were all free. I checked twice to make sure there was no meter hiding somewhere. Nope. All good. Chicago could use a tip or two.

To settle my nerves, I people-watched from the comfort of my vehicle.

Town Square seemed like the place where everyone in Green Mountain gathered. The coffee shop terraces were bustling. People looked joyful here. Relaxed and friendly too.

A mother, pushing a stroller with one hand, kissed the head of a little boy with long blond hair while tugging at his hand.

A man, in his late eighties, walked hand in hand with a woman about his age, exchanging grins.

A group of women, dressed in yoga gear, attended a class on the patch of grass next to the gazebo in the middle of the square. Tucker would like it here. Or rather, he'd like the view. I chuckled into my fist at the thought of his joining a yoga class just to meet women.

I surveyed the people around me again. Had I landed in Happy Town?

I'd never seen so many people smiling for no apparent reason, and it fascinated me. How could those people seem so easygoing and laid-back?

My gaze followed two teens riding skateboards and halted on a redhead standing on the sidewalk. She had the most magnificent smile as she waved at a little boy with dark hair. She tilted her head back as if to embrace the rays of sunlight on her pale skin.

From the cab of my truck, I studied her. She looked like a mythical princess, her hair bright and shiny in the light like a halo of fire.

She scanned the street around her before walking inside. The number on the door she held open caught my attention. *Forty-six.* I grabbed the piece of paper in the center console to double-check the address where I was supposed to meet Mike. *Forty-six.* Working for Hilton and Sons now seemed even more enjoyable, knowing I'd see this woman every time I came to the office.

With a renewed sense of purpose, I exited my truck and strolled in the direction of the building, my eyes trained on where her silhouette had just disappeared inside.

My attention stayed on the street number, my field of vision confined to the two digits painted in black on the door. With a deep inhale, I straightened my back. My insides clenched. I wasn't sure if I was desperate to meet with the woman or if I hoped she wouldn't be around once I entered.

A bell chimed over my head as I stepped in.

"Hey, Cart. Did you forget something?" the woman asked, hanging the gown in her hands before turning around to face me.

We stared at each other for a beat.

Her gaze burned my skin. The air lodged in my lungs couldn't get out.

The woman's floral scent enveloped me and held hostage all my senses.

Her lips parted, but no sound came out.

"Hey," I said, breaking the awkward silence that had settled between us.

She ran her tongue over her lips. I wasn't at Hilton and Sons, but I was stapled to the floor, unable to move.

"Hey," she echoed in a silken voice. One I could listen to every night before going to sleep. One that could soothe all my worries away.

Our eyes locked.

Fireworks erupted inside me.

This woman had cast a spell on me, and I had no intention of breaking it.

She could've asked me anything right now, and I would've agreed.

My heart drummed in my chest, its beating deafening.

I blinked twice.

What was going on with me? What was I doing here? Oh, yeah. Hilton and Sons.

I cleared my throat and found my voice. "I'm sorry to bother you. I just moved here, and I'm not really familiar with the town yet." I scanned the room—it looked like a bridal shop, with gowns in every corner and a glittering pile of shoes on display—and brought my attention to the piece of paper in my hand, trying to escape the woman's probing glance. "So, I guess you're not Hilton and Sons, the construction business?" I raised one eyebrow. I wasn't used to being speechless in front of a woman, or anyone else, for that matter. I folded the paper and stuffed it into my pocket. Why was I so nervous? I was being silly. I raked my fingers through my hair, unable to decide what to do with my hands.

I must've looked stupid right now.

The column of the woman's alluring throat worked as she swallowed, and my eyes followed the movement. Did I just tell myself her throat was alluring? Damn it. I was drawn to her far more than I'd first thought I would be.

"Hilton is on Elk Road, not Main Street," she said, her southern drawl now clear in her voice.

I scratched the side of my head. "And where is Elk Road? I'm a bit lost."

She smiled at me, and I almost melted into a puddle right there on the floor of the store.

"Give me a minute. I'll lock the shop and walk you down. It's not that far."

My pulse raced. "Are you sure? I don't want to be a bother." *Please let me be a bother.*

She shrugged, and now I found even her shoulders alluring.

"I insist. Fresh air will do me good. And it's a shame to be stuck inside when the weather is that great outside. I've been in the store fifteen hours a day for the last month. I'm in dire need of some vitamin C." She laughed, the most beautiful sound I'd ever heard.

I snickered behind my hand. "I think you mean vitamin D."

She flustered, and her level of beauty multiplied. A strand of her hair fell over her forehead, and I would've given anything to be able to tuck it away.

"Yeah. Vitamin D. You're right."

We walked for about a minute before I tilted my head to the side to watch her, breaking the silence. "I'm Nick, by the way."

"I'm Dahlia." Even her name sounded divine. "We're here," she said, stopping in front of a two-story building.

Already? I wasn't ready to let her go just yet. I hadn't felt an instant connection with anyone in…in like forever.

Dahlia smiled at me, and I knew, in this moment, that I would carry the curve of her lips into my dreams for a long time.

My entire body reacted to her closeness, as if her

warmth could spread to my skin even as we stood three feet apart.

I shut my eyes and breathed out. I only had one chance at this.

My pulse raced, and before she could walk away, I spoke the words that had been lingering on the tip of my tongue. "I just have to sign a few documents. I'm starting here as a carpenter next week. It'll only take a couple of minutes. Would you care to wait for me? We could grab a coffee or something. I'm starving, and the sights and smells of all those restaurants on Main Street did nothing to tame my hunger." I smiled, pretty sure I looked like a fool. "Unless you're too busy at the store and having lunch with me would make you late."

Please say no. Please say yes. No. Yes. No. I was so bad at this.

Dahlia tipped her head up until she stared into my eyes. "I'd like that."

I blew out a breath. Did I really ask the first woman I met on a date? My heart thundered in my chest, the pummeling of my organ vibrating all the way down to my toes. Dahlia wasn't any woman. She had the power to capture my heart. I had no idea how she could do this, but I knew I was right. Her power over me resided in the moss-green depths of her irises, in her smile, in her voice. Next to her, my body pulsed in a way it had never done before and I barely recognized.

It tensed and relaxed in all the right places. Even her energy field enticed me. It felt, in a strange way, as though we had met before.

"Great." I touched her arm, and something shifted inside me. A wave of heat washed over my entire self. A million tingles lined my spine. I jerked my hand away, trying to keep my composure intact. "Wait for me. I won't be long."

Our eyes met again, as if unable to look elsewhere. As if everything around us had vanished and only we existed.

I sucked in a breath that reverberated through me and walked in, my mind on the woman waiting for me on the sidewalk.

"Can I help you, sir?" a woman with cat-eye glasses and red lipstick asked me from behind a chestnut counter. She could have been twenty-five or fifty, naked or sporting a snowsuit, I had no clue. All I could see in my head was Dahlia.

It took me a few seconds to snap out of my daze.

I cleared my throat. "Sure. I'm Nick Peterson. I'm starting next week, and I'm here to sign some papers."

Linda, according to her nameplate, grinned. "Sure. We were waiting for you." She stood up and beckoned me with a finger to follow her. "Everything you gotta fill out is in the conference room." She led me to a small room with a large black table taking most of the space, a stack of papers kept on one end. "Take your time. If you have any questions, come get me. You should be done within five minutes."

I nodded and thanked her as I got to work.

I was signing the last form when Mike joined me. "Ready to start on Monday?" he asked in his rough voice.

"Yes, I am."

"Great. Meet me here at six-thirty, and we'll go over everything. See you then," he said, turning on his heel.

I capped the pen and took the stack of paper to Linda, ready to get the hell out of there.

Dahlia grinned at me as I joined her outside, the loose tendrils of her hair framing her porcelain face, like flames in the sunlight.

Her beauty stole my breath away.

Side by side, we strolled down the sidewalk in comfortable silence. I used the time to peruse my surrounding. Main Street looked like it came straight from a Christmas movie, minus the snow. A hairdresser, a little library, a baby gear store, and a bakery—amongst other businesses—had taken up residence on one side of the bustling main shopping street in town.

"Follow me," Dahlia said as we reached the crosswalk, two vehicles stopping when we stepped onto the pavement.

My eyes traveled between them.

Dahlia must have sensed my silent hesitation because she rested her palm on my forearm—jolts of current shot from where we touched—and said with a smile, "You'll get used to this. It's surprising at first, but cars in small towns usually yield the road to pedestrians. They'd even get into a fender-bender to let you go first."

I blinked. My breathing idled, the heat from her hand messing with my composure. "You joking, right?"

"Fairly. They always insist you go first."

She removed her hand, and the tenseness inside me decreased.

My breathing returned to normal.

What had just happened?

If someone had told me I had just gone under hypnosis right about then, I would have believed them.

"Okay"—her voice brought me out of my trance, or whatever it was—"over there is the best place to grab breakfast on the weekend."

I followed her finger as she pointed to a small restaurant on the opposite side of the town square.

"And next to it is the movie theater. It only has two screens, so you gotta get there early if you want a good seat. Behind the red building is…"

And just like that, Dahlia gave me my first express tour of Green Mountain.

A minute later, we stopped in front of a café. White-washed walls, white shutters, and a matching canopy over the entrance. A wooden deck full of people stretched out to the left.

"Here we are," Dahlia announced. "My favorite lunch spot in town. Still hungry?"

"Famished." I cleared my throat, my voice sounding rough.

My hand skimmed her back as I gestured to Dahlia to go first, and a sudden jolt of electricity where our bodies touched caught me off guard. She watched me over her shoulder, her smile disarming, and I wondered if she felt it too. Jitters took root inside me at the possibility, and I had no rational reason to explain the way I felt.

With an exhale, I removed my hand and scratched the side of my head to busy my fingers.

Guess I should be careful around Dahlia and avoid touching her, or I'd be in big trouble.

And fast.

13

DAHLIA

With my hands locked in front of me, I stood there on the sidewalk, wondering why I'd agreed to have lunch with a perfect stranger. I knew nothing about Nick. Sure, he seemed nice and every-thing, but I was so rusty in the relationship department that I feared I wasn't the best judge of character. And I'd never really gone out with guys before.

All my life, there had only ever been Jeff.

No one else.

He had been my first everything. And up to now, my last too.

Carter was my best friend, but we never dated, so that didn't count.

I had no idea how to do this. Dates. Friendship with other men. New relationships.

My heart banged in my chest.

Was I excited or scared? I couldn't tell right now. I just knew that the idea of having lunch with Nick made me all jittery. Hopefully, in a good way.

Nick stepped outside Hilton and Sons, and my breath

halted on its way out. Oh God, he looked so handsome. It just wasn't fair. He smiled at me, and every molecule in me sat up and vibrated at a higher frequency. Maybe he was married. Or gay. Or whatever. But right now, I didn't care. I wanted to spend more time with him. Get to know him. Be on the receiving end of the warmth of his smile.

Side by side, we walked back to Main Street. Silence had felt upon us—comfortable yet prickly. I chewed on my lower lip, debating what to say. Nick's proximity did funny things to my body I could only describe as burning awareness, and I relished the sensation of standing in his orbit. His arm rested at his side, and for a second, I wondered if touching his fingers would bring back the tingles that had spread through me when our skin had connected earlier.

With his eyes busy taking everything in, I glanced at him, enjoying the curiosity animating his features.

An idea popped into my head. "Follow me," I said as I stepped off the curb to cross the street.

Nick stood there, unmoving. Oh yes, I'd forgotten that city people weren't used to stepping into the street until the cars had come to a stop. My hand found his forearm, and at the contact, I swore I couldn't swallow, my body too attuned to him, sparks of electricity traveling through me in every direction. I removed my hand, sucking in a quick breath. Okay, that was intense. I hadn't dreamed it earlier. Those tingles were real. A warm sensation pirouetted inside me, settling in my stomach.

Hoping Nick couldn't notice my body's reaction to his closeness, I decided to give him a tour of the square as we walked toward my favorite eatery. As long as I kept busy, I could keep the attraction—and all the sensations inside me —in check.

Nick gave me his full attention, his gaze fixed on me as

I introduced him to everything I loved about the town center.

The conversation now flowed easily between us as we reached Ivy's Café.

"Still hungry?" I asked.

"Famished."

Ohmygod, his husky voice, smooth as whiskey, sent a zing to my ovaries. A dull throb started in the deepest part of me. How was it possible? We didn't even know each other. Nick's hand brushed my lower back when we climbed the five stairs leading to the entrance. By now, I believed I could melt at the slightest brush of his fleeting touch.

Feeling the intensity of his eyes on my back, I swallowed hard and exhaled. Every cell in my body spasmed with a desire to be touched. As if he too had been shocked, Nick removed his hand, and the air going to my lungs froze midway for a split second.

Nick's palm returned to my lower back as we approached a table on the terrace, a short distance from Dahlia's Bridal Shop. A shiver skated up the length of my spine. Barely managing to ignore the stir his hand evoked in me, I glanced toward my latest project, and waves of pride rippled through me. I'd done it, cementing the belief Jeff had in me.

Since his passing away, life hadn't always been easy but the nickname he had given me all these years ago, *Princess*, had held me in good fortitude to stand strong when winds of destruction ravaged me. Calling on all my inner reserves, I had taken the reins of my life back—for my sake and my son Jack's—and carved out my own dreams. A flicker of an idea, a vague conversation I'd had with Jeff after our wedding, and Dahlia's Bridal Shop had taken root in my mind. Three years later, I had finally made that dream a reality. Something that resembled me, born from my passion to *design beautiful creations and turn boring, ugly things into pretty ones*, as Carter used to say when we were kids. Proud of what I had accomplished, I intended to make the most of it. If he were here, Jeff would be cheering me on—and maybe he was, from wherever he was—because he had always believed in me, in my abilities, and in my dreams.

Nick's hand brushed my arm as he pulled out a chair for me, and my thoughts swam back to him.

More jolts of electricity traveled through me, once again, disturbing my ability to remain indifferent to him.

My heart, which had remained dormant for so many years, did a tiny flip in my chest. Until that instant, I thought it had forgotten how to feel—or be alive.

The owner handed us the menus. "I'll be right back to take your order."

"Thanks, Ivy," I said as Nick took them and passed me one.

"You're a regular here?" he asked.

I nodded with a smile. "Everybody knows everybody in Green Mountain. I have been visiting this town since my teen years, so I've made some friends long before I moved here three years ago."

Nick studied me for a moment. "Okay. I'm not crazy, I swear, and this may sound weird, but I feel like I've seen you before. As if I already know you from somewhere." He shrugged. "Must be one of those *déjà vu* feelings…hard to explain."

I shut my eyes for a few seconds, debating if I should be honest about who I was or not. When my gaze drifted back to Nick, he watched me with a mix of interest and sweetness. A warm sensation I hadn't felt in years filled my belly.

Before I could say anything else, Ivy came back, a notepad in her hand.

"I'll have the turkey wrap, extra lettuce, please," I said.

"That sounds good. I'll have the same," Nick said, taking my menu and returning them both to Ivy. "With water."

"Anything else?" Ivy asked.

Nick's eyes searched my face for a split second before returning to Ivy. He pointed at something on the menu, flashing her a smile that caused a wisp of envy in me. "Avocados crostini. As an appetizer."

Ivy smiled back. "Okay then." She brought her focus on me. "You're always ordering meat when Carter's not around," she said in a teasing tone.

"Yeah. I've decided to treat myself."

"I've missed you guys. Where is he? Still traveling the world one stadium at a time?"

"He's actually in town. Got here last night. He's with Jack right now. They had some catching up to do."

"Tell him to stop by the next time you see him. I have a new recipe I want him to try before I put it on the menu. His feedbacks are always welcome."

Ivy had been running her little restaurant forever. When Carter and I had a band together years ago, we used to come here to eat every time we were in town. Over the years, Ivy's Café had become one of our favorite spots in Green Mountain.

"I will."

Ivy offered Nick a smile. "You two enjoy your lunch. I'll be back with your food in a few minutes."

Nick rose to his feet. "Can you excuse me?" he asked as he motioned to where Ivy had disappeared.

"Sure. I'll be right here." I watched him as he entered the café. Muscled back. Firm ass. Long legs. My insides ignited at the sight of him, all male and every shade of handsome.

I sipped my water, urging my hyperactive hormones, and my thoughts, to cool down.

For the first time since Jeff passed away, I wondered what it would be like to be kissed by another man. How it would feel to have someone else's hands on me.

Shivers ran through me as images formed in my mind. More thoughts settled in my head, rent-free, and goose bumps prickled my skin.

I'd just met Nick and knew nothing about him. I couldn't think about him this way. It was too intense, too soon, right? And who knew? Maybe all he hoped for was to make some friends in town, and I wasn't even on his radar.

And now I was talking to myself, trying to calm the tumult inside me, like a madwoman. My inner voice fell silent when he pulled back his chair to sit.

His face had blanched, and he studied me with a frown.

"You okay?" I asked, snapping out of my dirty thoughts about the man I'd met just an hour ago.

Nick cleared his throat, the wrinkles across his forehead deepening. "Listen, I'll ask you something. Don't freak out, okay?" He swallowed, and my eyes followed the movement of his throat. "And you don't have to answer either, but something clicked in my head, and well, I'm curious. Are you Dahlia Ellis, the famous country music star?"

I cringed—well, sort of. I walked away from fame because I hated being recognized. In my everyday life, I rarely told people about my past. That life seemed like a lifetime ago. It happened before everything. Before my heart shattered. Before Jack's birth. Before I had to reinvent myself and move here in order to survive.

Nick eyed me, one finger wiping away the condensation around his glass.

"You want the truth or a tale I can come up with?" I asked, trying to get out of spilling my life story.

His expression shifted, shadowed by something unspoken. A memory flickered in his whiskey-colored eyes. Hurt. Defeat. Sadness. They swirled quietly beneath the surface. "The truth. Always. But if you want to warn me off, then I think it would be better to come up with an unbelievable story instead."

His eyes glinted under the noon sun, and a mischievous smile bent one side of his lips.

I couldn't refrain from laughing at the sight of him. "Nah, none of that, I promise. I love the truth too." I shook my head and pressed both palms onto the white linen covering our table, gathering what little courage I had. "The truth it is then." I inhaled, then dropped my shoulders. "Most people around here know parts of what happened to me, so they're pretty shy about asking questions. Wait. How did you find out?"

"Ivy showed me the wall with pictures of you guys. She thought I was aware. I had no idea. I swear. And I'm not some sort of sick fan. Call it curiosity…or a deep quench to know you better. I don't wanna start our friendship on half-truths."

"Oh, you want us to be friends?" I asked in a hushed tone.

Warmth pooled in my cheeks. I used to turn crimson with embarrassment as a teen, and I thought I had outgrown it. Apparently not. Right now, I felt like I was back in time, experiencing attraction for the very first time.

Nick shrugged. "Yeah. I might even consider you my first official friend in town." A boyish smirk spread across his face, and I couldn't help but think he looked even more attractive.

"Okay. I'm Dahlia Ellis, founding member of the Carter Hills Band. Fun fact, it used to be called Ellis and Hills back in the day. Anyway, Carter Hills is my best friend. The one person I can't live without—other than my son. My husband died when I was pregnant, so my baby has never known his daddy. Carter is the closest thing to a father my son has. We're family—the three of us." I breathed out. There. I said it all. Well, most of it. The important parts at least. "You know my secret now. Please don't let it change the way you perceive me."

Nick's smile softened. "I won't. Thank you for being honest with me. It means a lot."

A server brought Nick's appetizer, and after thanking him, he moved the plate to the center of the table. "Here, help yourself."

I blinked then reached for a crostini, my smile growing. "Thanks," I said as I savored the avocado delicacy. "What about you? What's your secret? Why did you move here? You're not wanted by the police or anything, right? No psycho tendencies?"

His eyes dropped to his folded hands, turning somber. No smile graced his lips at my quip. Instead, he inhaled sharply before bringing his attention back to me. A steel grip clenched my stomach as I caught the pain masking his features.

"I've just moved from Chicago. Someone I really cared about died not so long ago and…it, huh…it affected me… a lot… In many ways. He never had the chance to reach for his dreams…" His throat worked, and he looked away for a second, blinking hard. "I had a great job, amazing friends, but after he passed, I felt like…like I was missing something…" He blew a long breath. "Anyway, I-I thought

I could follow his advice and reach for my dreams too… you know… And that a change of air could do me good."

"Oh shit."

"Yeah." He downed half his glass of water in one gulp. "I packed my stuff, drove to the beach first, spent a week there, worked on a ranch for three, and then landed here. It's been a great journey so far."

My eyes flared of their own volition. "Wow. That's quite an adventure. Also…I'm sorry for your loss."

"Don't be. Some days are rough, but most are brighter."

Ivy brought our plates, and we each took a bite before I spoke again.

"How do you like Green Mountain so far?"

Nick's lips widened. "Better than expected. To be honest, I thought I'd wanna drive away within a day. Somehow, it's growing on me. But tell me something. Why does everyone smile here?"

"Everyone does, huh? We are just laid-back and happy. It's the mountain air. It makes us feel peaceful and content. You tell me now. There are like a million small towns in this country. Why here?"

He took another bite of his wrap and swallowed before speaking again. "My best friend's uncle is Hilton and Sons' owner. He got me the job."

"You know Mike?" He nodded as I continued. "He's a nice man. Honest and hardworking. He helped me with the store renovation."

Nick studied me for a moment. "Somehow, I wish I could've been the one doing all the work there." His eyes, honey-gold in daylight, locked on mine. His loaded stare stole every ounce of air from my lungs. For a reason I didn't quite understand, I loved being on the receiving end of such intensity. As if Nick could read me, and my soul begged to reveal all its secrets to him. As if we already knew each other, long before today.

A heated wave swallowed me.

Tickles rattled my spine, lighting up all my senses until we were in sync. I lacked words to explain the ardent buzz.

My body overheated, and I bet my face had turned tomato-red.

Why were Nick's words making me feel giddy? It defied logic. I was imagining things—had to be. Besides Carter, I hadn't spent time with another man in so long. Nick wasn't flirting with me, just making conversation.

Still, the sizzle in my body couldn't be ignored and told me otherwise.

The sound of his voice—dark and addictive, smooth and layered, just like his eyes—enveloped me. Like whiskey, I wished I could drink every word.

Nick continued, and I forced myself out of his energetic field.

"So? How was it? Fame, I mean. Touring the world? Being chased by loony fans? Having people reporting your every move?"

I let out a heartfelt laugh. Okay, I could do this. We were just talking.

"Fun. Exhausting. Weird. Exciting. It's hard to define it in just one word." I twisted the wedding ring hanging from the chain around my neck. "I loved it…at first, but it complicated my relationship with Jeff, my late husband…in many ways. Being famous is Carter's thing. From the start, he was destined to make it big. I just loved doing it by his side for a while. We were awesome together."

"You said you two are family. Jeff was his brother, no?"

I nodded, looking away for a flash second. "Yes. And his best friend too."

"Dahlia, I'm sorry you had to go through this. If you

don't mind me asking, did you leave the band before or because you had to?"

I toyed with the paper napkin in my hands. "Before. Things got messy, and at that point, our lifestyle—being on the road all the time and waking up in a different bed every morning—didn't suit me anymore. I craved stability and a normal life away from the limelight."

"And you came here to escape the madness?"

"Pretty much." I gave Nick a raised brow.

As if he sensed my silent question, he grinned. "I knew someone who was a huge fan. I think he secretly had a crush on you. And my sister was a die-hard fan too. She followed the band and had posters of you, Carter, and that other guy on her bedroom walls as a teen. Shit, now that I say it out loud, it sounds creepy. Anyway, I assure you I'm not a weird, obsessed groupie. I just remembered now she'd told me all about it."

"It's okay. I've met crazy fans, and you don't fit the profile. You're safe. My psycho-meter isn't picking up anything suspicious." Nick's grin held, while mine wavered briefly—a ghost of the past catching me off guard—before I pulled it back. Even if heartbreaking, I valued those memories. "Jeff, Carter, and I, we were this everlasting trio. Our relationship wasn't perfect, but it was precious. I'm telling you, the younger Hills brothers were crazy in their own way, but I wouldn't change any of it. Carter and I have been best friends since we were babies."

Nick's eyes rounded.

"Yep, we go way back. After everything we've experienced together, our friendship is stronger than ever. If we didn't have each other, I'm not sure either of us would have survived Jeff's death. When I left Nashville to come here, to escape the media circus my life had turned into, it took me almost a year to start living again. For months,

Jack was my only source of happiness. Slowly, with Carter's support and love, I built myself up again. Now I'm in a happy place. I'm thriving." I paused. "Carter is my rock, and I like to believe I'm his too."

Nick lowered his sandwich to his plate. "I'm sorry, Dahlia. That it happened to you. Life is tough sometimes. For all of us."

His shoulders hunched over the table, and he stared at me. With intensity. As if to commit my strength to his memory or something. Or as if he could understand me and that part of my life.

Nick's aura allayed my doubts, inviting me to share with him. To be honest—and real. For once, it felt right to just tell the story as it was. To someone who didn't have a pre-conceived opinion about it. Who wouldn't judge me.

I nodded, appreciating his compassion. "I'm just not used to talking about my journey—at least not on the first meeting. That's all."

He bent his lips, and the air lightened as his smile brought attraction to the forefront.

We finished eating, our conversation effortless, stealing quick glances and smiles. Fascination purled between us.

Now I was certain it wasn't my imagination playing tricks on me.

"Where are you living?" I asked, relishing the friendly atmosphere we basked in.

"A farmhouse on Beaver Lane. The lady who owns it is letting me stay there for rent-free as long as I put the place back in order so she can sell it by the end of the year." He shrugged. "I love working with my hands. It's my first resi-dential renovation project, but I can already tell I'll enjoy pouring love back into this stately house. I'm good at what I do, and this deal feels like a perfect trade-off."

Nick's words sent a jolt racing through my heart.

"Oh, I love all fixer-uppers. Except for the shop, I haven't done any in a while. I miss it. I used to be good with a saw and a nail gun, and even better with interior design. It's something only a few people know about me. Consider yourself lucky. You know my other secret now," I said with a wink and a grin.

Nick blinked. "You do? I mean, you love home renovation?"

I nodded, now enthusiastic about the idea of fixing an old house and turning it into a gem. "If you're ever at a loss for ideas or need an opinion on something, I'm your woman. I won't have a lot of free time once the shop opens, but I can still give you a hand, even if it's just with what to hang on your walls or picking paint samples."

"Whoa. Duly noted. I might actually take you up on your offer. I'm skilled when it comes to woodwork, tiles, or tools, but I lack serious talent in the decoration department and color matching."

My smile grew so big, probably about to split my face in two. "Nick. You and I will have to talk business then."

14

NICHOLAS

"I'm expected for dinner," Dahlia said, a light flush coloring her cheeks, her silver bracelets tinkling as she squeezed my finger in regret.

"Yeah. I'd stay here all night talking to you if I could. But I gotta go too."

Her eyes, enticing moss-green abysses, darted back to mine. As if my words had roused them, making them come alive. The color on Dahlia's cheeks darkened.

"You do?"

I nodded. "A barbecue. At my neighbors' place."

"Oh, you already made friends." She frowned. "I'm sad. I thought I was your first one in town." She let out a warm laugh. "It shatters the idea I'd woven about us in my head."

I studied her, trying to hide my amusement. "You've already woven ideas about us?"

Dahlia's eyes brightened up, and the red shade on her cheeks deepened. She was beautiful, and even more irresistible when a blush colored her cheeks in response to my words.

"Well. To be honest, I did, but I'm heartbroken they don't meet my expectations."

"They don't?"

She shook her head, staring at me, twinkles dancing around her green irises. "No. They surpass them."

I threw my head back in laughter, failing to hold my glee in.

This thing between us could catch fire any second now.

It was powerful, easy, and intoxicating all at once.

Dahlia's eyes never looked away.

I cleared my throat to relieve the tightness in my airways. "Since I've been invited to a barbecue my neighbors are hosting, I think the 'first friend' title still applies to you," I said, using my fingers as quotation marks.

"Why?"

"Because they're living next door. It doesn't mean we're friends by default. Only good neighborhood practices here. Your title is safe."

Dahlia's face dazzled. Her full lips curled up, happiness reaching her eyes. "Fine. You and I are now officially friends."

She held out her hand, and we shook on it.

Warm tingles transferred from her palm to mine. Something deep inside me woke up as if it had seen the sun for the first time.

Not sure what to think of it, I tugged my hand gently away, using it to raise my glass to my lips, hoping to hide my uneasiness.

After I paid the check, I walked Dahlia back to her store.

"This day is really not what I expected it to be," Dahlia rambled with a nervous chuckle. "It's much better. I'm glad we met. This is new and exciting. When do we meet up again? I could give you a tour of the town, a real one this time, or we could do something else. I'm a bit rusty. Most of the time, I hang out with a toddler."

"To be honest, my two best friends are guys. Our time together usually involves poker nights and whiskey. Pretty straightforward. But somehow, I feel like we need to up the game here." I paused and mirrored her smile. "If we were kids, I'd propose a day at the park or a—" The word *sleep-over* almost tumbled out, but I caught it in time. "Huh, a playdate," I said instead, feeling all shades of stupid.

Dahlia giggled, the sound wrapping around my heart like a warm blanket. "Yeah, kids have it easy."

I puffed my chest out and pushed all my angst down. "Since we're not five anymore, I could ask you on a real date. As friends. We could get to know each other better. Like friends do. Plus, I'm not letting a stranger work construction on a house with me if I haven't conducted a complete interview beforehand."

"Oh, this would be a job interview? Interesting," Dahlia teased, one brow tipped up to her hairline, her full smile directed at me, sending heat to my core.

"Yep. Something like that. What do you think?" I asked, hiding my hands in my pockets to avoid touching her flaming cheeks.

"Sounds fun. I've never been interviewed for a job before."

"You kidding?"

"Nah. Back when I was a teenager, I met with a restaurant owner who offered us a weekly spot to perform. Later on, I also met with Riley, our manager, but that's about it. No real interview."

"Well, I'll be your first." Oh, how I loved the sound of this. Dahlia flustered, and I was pretty sure I did too. "Interviewer, I mean," I added quickly. "Okay, I'll go before I embarrass myself further."

This enticing, fiery woman nodded, still grinning.

I was about to tread away when she spoke again.

"Hey, Nick. Wouldn't it be easier if we exchange phone numbers? Isn't that what friends usually do?"

I spun around, face-palming myself, feeling sheepish. "Yeah." I traced my eyebrow with a finger. "Huh, you're right. That's what friends do."

I fished my phone out of my pocket and handed it to her.

Why did everything about Dahlia Ellis turn me into a fool?

———

The next morning, I woke up early and went for a morning run. The air was crisp, and each inhale prickling my lungs reminded me I was really doing this. That I was alive and could take the world by storm if I decided to.

With each step forward, I contemplated the scenery around me. Green pastures. Green valleys. Green mountains. Cabins. Farmhouses. Streams. Woods. Nothing here resembled my hometown in any way.

I trained my gaze on two women power-walking with a large gray-and-white dog on a leash and a young couple running while pushing a double stroller. I returned their waves and continued my jog. The first rays of sunshine warmed my skin as they climbed higher in the sky. When I returned home, slowing down my pace, I noticed my neighbors on their front porch, sipping coffee, still in their robes.

"Hey, Nick," Greta said. "You're up early."

I removed my earbuds and let them hang around my neck while I smoothed out my breathing. "Yes. Had to get rid of all the angst before starting the day." I rested my hands on my hips and looked up, admiring the sun now shining whole, not a cloud ruining the blue sea above.

"Coffee?" Brett asked.

"Come, sit with us," Greta added. "You've earned yourself a little rest."

I shrugged. "Why not? Thanks, guys."

"Where do you get your burst of energy after a late night? We were up too last night, but look at us, still in our nightclothes. Did you enjoy the barbecue?"

"Yes. Thanks for having me. I had fun. Now I've met six other people in town."

Greta waved her hand. "Oh, we're happy you're settling in. I'm sure you'll feel at home in no time."

"People are pretty nice here."

"It's the southern hospitality. It runs in our blood."

"Well, it's working. Let me just say it makes a great impression on us, tourists and newbies. Now I wanna say hi to everyone I meet."

Greta's lips extended. "I'm glad it's rubbing off on you."

"Cream and sugar?" Brett asked.

"Black," I said.

He disappeared inside and came back a minute later, handing me a mug, before retreating into their home.

"Thanks." I took a sip and almost coughed the scorching-hot caffeine all over Greta when I took in the inscription etched on the side: *Live your best life, bro.*

Were my neighbors in on it? Derek seemed to be everywhere, sending me messages wherever I went.

Greta, oblivious to my thoughts, asked, "How is the house? Inside, I mean?"

"Beautiful. It mostly just needs some freshening up—a new paint job, sanding the floors, and a few updates in the kitchen. The second floor requires more work, though, but nothing too extensive. I can't wait to really get started."

"Breakfast is ready," Brett called from behind us.

The woman grabbed the plate of freshly baked croissants her husband handed her and held it out in front of her. "Want one?"

"Sure."

The three of us moved to sit around the small table on the back deck.

"Can I ask you something?"

They both nodded.

"I'm going on a date later next week, and I'd appreciate some pointers since I know nothing about this town yet. Someplace nice."

Brett's eyes widened. "Okay, you've not been here a week and yet, you've got yourself a job and scored a date. Wow, I'm impressed. You wasted no time. Good for you, man."

I chuckled and shook my head when Greta slapped her husband's arm and growled through clenched teeth, "Brett. Where are your manners? Let Nick be." She brought her focus back to me with a huge smile. "I know a few places. Trendy and loud or quiet and remote?"

I considered my options for about two seconds. "Quiet and remote." I had no idea if people around here had a thing for fame, and I didn't want to take any chances. Dahlia Ellis didn't seem like the kind of woman who'd be bothered by a public date, but even so, I wouldn't put her on the spot without her approval first.

"Perfect." Greta opened her palm, silently asking for my phone. "I'll send myself a text message so I can send you all the info later."

"Thanks. I really appreciate it."

She shrugged. "Anytime. What are neighbors for, if not to help each other out, right?"

I nodded as I pocketed my device.

For the rest of the day, I took measurements and notes as I inspected every corner of the house.

In the middle of the kitchen, I surveyed the area around me. If this house were mine, I'd put in a little more work than what was requested to bring it to its full potential—like rearranging some of the rooms to make the most of the view. Yes, I could see it all so clearly in my mind.

This house was beautiful, but with the right owner, the right vision, and the right budget, it could become exceptional.

Buddy trotted over while I was busy replacing the worn wood planks on the porch with new ones.

"Hey you," I said, stopping to pet his head. "You had a lazy morning. I didn't see you when I went over to your place earlier."

The bloodhound inched closer so I could pet him with both hands.

"Okay then."

I sat on the floor and laughed as I scratched the dog behind his ears, and he let out a growling whistle.

"I met someone yesterday. Someone special. We got along fine. More than fine, actually. And you know what? She agreed to go on a date with me. I never do that…ask women I've just met on a date. But Dahlia… I don't know. I can't explain it." I sighed. "She had a pull on me. I feel like a fifteen-year-old having a crush for the first time."

Buddy watched me with interest.

"I'm telling you. I never saw it coming. I didn't expect to meet someone on this journey. It wasn't the plan, but I guess we'll see how it goes. Can I tell you a secret, though? She is really hot. And sexy. She's beautiful and smart too.

It's a compelling combination. How's your love life going? Any Mrs. Buddy out there?"

The dog huffed and recoiled into a ball next to me.

"Fine. Sorry I went there."

I chuckled as the dog ignored me and fell asleep, snoring within a minute.

"Enjoy your nap, Buddy."

My phone chimed with a message, and I failed to contain my smile as I saw the name flashing on the screen.

———

"Okay, so I think we went through all the basics," Mike said after we looked over the blueprints for the new residential project a second time. A new mountain lot had been bought and cleared to welcome a twenty-cabin gated community with a covered pool and playground area.

I'd have a team of eight to bring this project to life within a six-month timeline. The delays were tight but with hard work and dedication, doable.

Adrenaline rushed into my veins. I rubbed my hands together. This building site would be my second home for the next few months. It was different from the ventures I'd led in Chicago, but just as exciting because it was all-new and would provide homes for twenty families.

I scanned the plans once more, taking in every little architectural detail.

Yeah, I was at the right place. Green Mountain was where I was supposed to be.

"Too big for you, son?" Mike teased with a side grin.

"Nah. Perfect. Can't wait to get started. I can already picture it in my mind and see what it'll look like once it's done." I closed my eyes for a minute, mapping it all out in my head. "When can I begin?"

Mike let out one of his belly laughs. "Not so fast, son. Next week. Take a few days to meet the guys. Survey the building site. Check the order forms we've already placed to make sure you don't miss anything. If all is good, you'll be ready to roll by next Monday."

"How about weekends and nights? Do I need to ask permission to have the guys work longer shifts?"

Mike's lips stretched bigger, and he clamped my shoulder. "Nick, Green Mountain isn't some big shot city with short deadlines and high stress levels. Here, we work regular-hour days. Unless, and I repeat, unless there's some sort of emergency or a big fuck-up we can't deal with otherwise. You're not here to burn yourself—or my guys—out. You're here to enjoy life, to work, and to find a healthy balance between the two."

"Huh, okay then." Mike's words were the opposite of everything that had ever come out of Cody's mouth. "Whoa, that's all new to me. I'm not used to this slower pace."

Mike chuckled. "Guess you'll have to learn how to live then."

He wasn't wrong. Back home, I used to put in so many overtime hours that some weeks I forgot what day it was, because my weekends and nights were nonexistent and often blurred together.

"Hear me out," he said. "I agree it's early to talk about this, but I'm pretty sure Tucker already opened his big mouth." Mike winked. "Anyway, I'm thinking about retiring next year. Or selling shares of the business until I'm ready to let it go fully. If you like it here and you can see yourself living in this town full time, maybe we could discuss it over a drink someday. None of the guys are interested in running big projects, even less running a business. You have the drive and that sparkle in your eyes when you study blueprints. Anyway, I'm putting it out here—in case… Sorry, I should have waited to dump all this on you. I just see so much of my younger self in you."

I stared at the man. "Wow, I'm flattered. You haven't even seen me at work yet, but I'm really excited to be here. Who knows? I might just fall in love with the town"—or a certain redhead—"and end up staying for good. Gimme a month to get my bearings, and we'll have that drink. Deal?"

Mike's palm met mine. "You and I will get along just fine, son."

I mirrored my boss's easy grin and followed him to his truck.

Opening my phone to message Tucker, my attention drifted to Dahlia's name, and I caught myself re-reading our first conversation, smiling at the memory.

DAHLIA

Hi friend. Just making sure I had your contact right.

ME

All good. Glad it's settled.

While we're at it. I made a reservation for our date. I'll send you the details later.

DAHLIA

Can't wait. Hope you're having a great day.

ME

You too. See you soon.

The exchange was a balm to my heart. Yes, date night couldn't come fast enough.

We'd messaged each other every few days since then, and somehow it felt like I was talking to a friend I'd known for years—not a girl I'd just met. With a newfound lightness waltzing inside me, I climbed into my car and drove away.

The next few days passed quickly. I was so busy familiarizing myself with Hilton and Sons' procedures, my new work team, the purchase orders, and scheduling and sequencing every other trade to make sure no one steps on anyone else's toes that I didn't see the time come and go.

DAHLIA

Still on for tonight?

ME

Yes. Six okay for you?

My heart throbbed a little faster in my chest while I waited for the three dots to stop bouncing.

DAHLIA

Absolutely. I'll be ready *happy face emoji*

My heart swelled in my chest. This woman. I couldn't wait to see her again.

ME

I'll pick you up. Send me your address.

I was about to put my phone away when it went off again.

DAHLIA

Hey Nick?

I'm happy we're doing this.

I exhaled, a stupid grin now overtaking my face.

ME

Me too.

It was late afternoon when I spotted a few minor mistakes on the blueprints and half a dozen extras that had to be dealt with before we began construction the following Monday. It couldn't wait. I crossed my fingers, hoping it wouldn't take hours to find a solution. No way I could be late tonight. After an hour-long discussion with the architect and concrete guy, we reached a compromise that pleased everyone and only required a few minor tweaks to the original blueprints. I had done these last-minute meetings countless times before, and right now, it felt like being back in familiar territory. When I finished, a surge of excitement invaded me. Yeah, it felt good to be back.

Sideways, I glanced at the time and jumped to my feet.

Damn. I had to hurry home, freshen up, and change, or I'd be late to meet the woman who had the power to transform the course of my life.

Derek's Bucket List — ~~44. Nick: Having a meaningful encounter and finding something that makes you truly feel alive~~

15

NICHOLAS

It's just a friendly date, I repeated to myself an hour later for the hundredth time. Why was I so nervous? I wasn't really a date person, and the last woman I kind of dated turned out to be crazy in her own way.

I had a good feeling about Dahlia, though. Over the years, I'd fine-tuned my crazy-radar, and hopefully, it should work fine now.

But still, I didn't want to screw things up with her. For some reason, it made me nervous. I wanted everything to be perfect. We'd gotten along great last week, but a formal date sounded more official—like the real deal. Like I had no room to mess up. Not that I had a track record of bad dates, but still. Dahlia Ellis wasn't the kind of woman you let down.

In a swift movement, I discarded the towel wrapped around my midsection and rummaged through my wardrobe to find something decent to wear.

Casual, but not too casual. Dressed, but not too dressed.

Those were the words Greta had used when she sent me the link to the restaurant.

That sounded easy, right? It should, but right now, her dress code tip confused me instead of helping me.

I scanned every piece of clothing I owned, trying to come up with the best outfit possible, and yet, nothing seemed nice enough. I ended up picking a pair of dark jeans and a black shirt. I couldn't go wrong with that.

Buddy, who'd been spending all his time over at my place, neared me and sniffed around. "It's called after-shave, old pal." I patted his head, and he snuggled at my feet. "You know you'll have to move out by the time I go, right?"

He snored as a reply. Great.

Half an hour later, after I had fixed my hair away from my face and grabbed the bouquet of daisies I'd bought earlier, I made my way to my truck. Jitters invaded my belly. I sucked in a cleansing breath. Dahlia and I had hit it off the other day. There was nothing to worry about. Except, I hadn't been on a date in a while. How did Tucker do this all the time? I hoped, for his sake, that it got easier with practice, because right now, it totally freaked me out.

My stomach tightened in a chain of knots at the idea that Dahlia and I could be much more than friends some-day. No matter how hard I tried to ignore it, the chemistry between us was undeniable last Friday, and I'd been thinking about it nonstop ever since. No, I hadn't imagined the connection and the attraction we shared.

There was no point in lying to myself. Every conclusion I came to carried the same hope: that we might grow into something more.

"Okay, bro. Wish me luck. I still can't believe tonight is happening," I said, glancing at the sky. "I'm going on a date with one of your idols. Or rather, his best friend. Maybe you have something to do with it…or not. In either case, if you do, thank you for watching over me. Now go play and let the adults be." I winked, kissed two fingers, and raised my hand above my head.

I parked my truck and looked twice—just to be sure—at the numbers on the door. Yes, this was the right address. I sucked in a calming breath, gathered some courage, and walked up to the front porch. The door opened, and Dahlia stood on the other side, radiant in her blue dress, her wavy hair cascading over her shoulders, her eyes twinkling, and her smile disarming. My shoulders relaxed at the sight of her.

"Hey, you look beautiful," I said kissing her cheek.

Her eyes roamed over me in a torturous, slow motion. "You don't look so bad yourself."

Carter Hills appeared in my peripheral vision. He was much taller than I'd pictured him to be. For a second, I prayed Derek could see this moment from that cloud…or wherever he was. I still couldn't believe this was my life at the moment. The musician towered over me by a few inches, and my back tensed again at the way he stared at me as if he could burn me alive only with his gaze. Flickers of apprehension woke up inside me. I felt so out of my element. Seeing him next to Dahlia, it all seemed surreal. She told me about his protective side, but right now, he looked like he was about to blow a gasket.

Ignoring him, I focused my attention back on Dahlia's face. She was even more beautiful than I remembered. Her smile eased my nerves, and I reminded myself that she was the only one who mattered—no one else.

A little boy, no older than three, with a mop of dark hair, the one I saw her with on the day we met—and a tiny spitting image of Carter Hills—wrapped himself around one of her legs. His grin was as contagious as his mother's. He looked my way with the tiniest of smiles, and the simple curve of his lips sewed back another loose part of my heart. We watched each other for a moment as if we could communicate without words. The boy averted his gaze, and Dahlia kneeled down to talk to him. Carter's eyes never left me the entire time, sharp and focused, like laser beams. Not once did he blink or look away. He wasn't at all like I'd pictured him, and our first encounter wasn't anything like I'd imagined. After a moment, he unfroze and padded toward the child and picked him up, his somber face holding no trace of friendliness. Anger undulated from him. Or was it annoyance? I couldn't tell for sure.

Once close to me, he held out his hand. "Hi. I'm Carter. Nice to meet you." He squeezed my hand hard, and I offered him a steel grip. I was from Chicago, not Chicken Town. His broody attitude had no effect on me. If he thought his fame or lousy attitude would rattle me, he clearly didn't know me.

"Nice to meet you. I've heard a lot about you," I said, standing tall.

"Please treat Dahlia with the respect she deserves."

"I wouldn't do anything less. I'll be a perfect gentle-man," I assured, holding his gaze.

Dahlia spun around to face him and backhanded him on the shoulder. "Really, Cart?"

They exchanged a silent look. Something passed between them. Carter's eyes turned to slits. Dahlia cocked her head as if to say, "Are you kidding?"

He then offered her a wide smile, and she batted her eyelashes at him.

Whatever they told each other silently, Dahlia won, because Carter relaxed his stance, nodded at me, then stepped back. "Okay. Fine." He managed a tiny smile. "You two have fun. Better?"

"Yep. Much better." She pressed a kiss to her son's head before following me outside.

"Good night," I heard Carter say before the door clicked behind us.

Once away from her best friend's inquisitive stare, I handed Dahlia the flowers I had gotten for her earlier. She brought the daisies to her nose and took a big whiff.

"There's something about flowers that makes me happy," she said. "Thank you."

Every time Dahlia and I texted in the last week, the words had come easily between us, and I hoped tonight wouldn't be any different.

"Jack is the cutest."

She laughed. "He has more of the Hills genes in him than any of mine. He's a replica of Carter and Jeff when they were his age."

"He has your face. It's just hidden under that tuft of dark hair."

"My Mama says the same thing, and she also says he's as easygoing as I was at that age." She shrugged. "He's my entire world and brightens up my days. He's the most caring boy I know."

We drove for the next few minutes in silence then pulled into the restaurant parking lot. Once I killed the engine, I rounded the car to open Dahlia's door.

Inside, the hostess led us to a black leather, half-circle booth, just as I requested, thanks to Greta's advice. "Can we order wine on a friend-date?" I asked in a teasing tone as the server handed me the wine list and left after promising to be back in a couple of minutes.

Dahlia snickered behind her menu. "I think it's allowed. Except with Carter—when he's in town—and Addison, my girlfriend, I rarely ever go out. My nights are usually low-key, spent at home with my son. I'm not really aware of the rules of a friend-date to be honest, but wine sounds really good right now."

Her enticing smile widened, and it vibrated through me as it exuded glee.

I winked, and Dahlia let out a heartfelt laugh. "I think we could make our own. Rules, I mean." She paused. "See? I've decided, and wine it is."

Radiance lit up her face.

"I like that. Dressing up and having a meal with wine is allowed. Dressing down and fixing a house too. I'm putting it out here since that day will come soon."

Her cheeks turned a flaming shade of red, and she rested her joined hands on the table, zest animating her features. "What about kissing? Is it allowed between friends? I love when the boundaries are set and clear."

I blinked. Did she really go there when every minute spent in her company made it harder for me to picture her as just another friend like Tucker and Jace?

"Yep," I said, taking a piece of bread to swallow the words that longed to be spoken out right now, but I knew shouldn't. "Kissing is okay. If we both agree."

She nodded, her stare fixated on me. "Will we know when kissing goes beyond the limits of the friend zone?"

I breathed through my mouth and thought about it for a moment before my words escaped with a mind of their own. Tension grew inside me. I exhaled to calm the discomfort rising in my lower half. With a hand, I adjusted my jeans under the table as much as I could. "Bah. I think when it happens, we'll just recognize it."

"Okay. I guess we'll find out," she added with a lopsided smirk.

The air between us got charged with the tension of unsaid promises and repressed sexual desire. Fuck, I had to get a grip on my body, and fast. It had been so long since

I'd last gotten laid that it misread every signal as a green light. Right now, if Dahlia kept eye-fucking me like this, I would require an extraction mission to get me out of the restaurant because my body would turn into an explosive device about to detonate.

I bit on that piece of bread, only to choke on it.

The server came back. "You okay, sir?" he asked.

"Yes." I swallowed. Hard. "Fine. Thanks. I'm all right."

No. I'm not. Not fine. Dying here. Unable to process anything because my blood is lava and moving south at a vertiginous speed.

Beside me, Dahlia sipped her water, staring at me, merriment dancing in her irises. I really loved being on the receiving end.

The server noted our orders, and Dahlia's gaze darted away from me. I shivered and felt the withdrawal deep in my bone marrow.

"How's it going with the house so far?" she asked, the mischief in her eyes now gone.

The molecules of attraction swirled around us, but not as dense. In my head, I thanked her for the change of topic.

"Good. So far, I've worked mostly on the front porch and deck. At least now, it's safe to enter the house. How's the shop going?"

A large smile spread across her lips. "Incredible. Ready for opening day. The two women I've hired are amazing. They'll look after the shop when I'm not there. Jack is too little and needs his Mama. He's my priority."

"He's lucky to have you."

Her cheeks turned a satin shade of pink. Was my presence or our chemistry to blame for the light coloring? Dahlia searched my eyes. We said nothing for a long minute, studying each other from across the table. The fascination broke when the server brought us our appetizers.

"How's the new job? Mike isn't being too harsh on you?"

"Nope. Things are kinda great. Running my own crew."

"Whoa, he must really trust you. He can be a bit picky with his employees."

I shrugged. "I have experience and ran bigger projects in the past. Our visions mesh together. We're a great fit."

"Would you like to have your own business someday?" Dahlia asked, sipping her wine, seemingly interested in what I had to say.

"In Chicago, it never occurred to me, but in a town like Green Mountain, I can see the appeal. I guess we'll see how it goes. Mike said something about it the other day." I took a bite, studying her.

She grinned at me, and my heart waltzed in my chest at the sight. "It would suit you. Yeah, I can picture you in charge of your own business. You have the look."

I frowned. "The look? What does that even mean?"

Dahlia sat there, watching me, not saying anything for a long beat.

My heart rate spiked.

Her cheeks flushed darker—something she did so well—the smile still anchored to her face. Her lips, deep cherry red, acted like magnets, requesting my complete attention and devotion.

"You know," she said. "The look. Handsome. Serious. Confident. No nonsense. Determination. Success. And a will only a few people possess." She shrugged and leaned forward, as if to tell me a secret. "*That* look."

Could all the patrons here notice the sparks flying between us?

"You think you got me all figured out?" I teased.

"No. Not yet. But I will."

She leaned back in her chair and winked, and I swore a little part of me melted right there, somewhere near my heart—or inside my heart—on the spot.

Dahlia Ellis was like no other woman I'd ever met. The more time I spent with her, the more I wanted to know everything about her.

Dereck, bro, where did you send me? Did you suspect all along I'd fall under this woman's charm? For a brief moment, I could daresay both he and Tucker conspired to manipulate me into coming here, and I wondered whether Green Mountain could really be where I was meant to be, where I belonged. As if my friends had known all along that Dahlia Ellis would steal my heart with just a glance my way.

———

Hours later, I pulled into Dahlia's driveway and stopped the engine. She angled her upper body toward me. For a long minute, we eyed each other, neither of us breaking the lust-filled silence. My gaze floated somewhere between her irises and her mouth. Her lower lip trembled, and right now, I would have given everything I owned just to taste it. To erase the distance between us and steal a kiss. In slow motion, my eyes wandered over her face, the moonlight showcasing her singular beauty, from the arch of her brow to the length of her neck.

Dahlia's chest rose and fell. The freckles leading down her dress, showing me the way to her cleavage, were begging to be traced over with my fingertip—or with my tongue.

I lifted my eyes.

Heat burned in hers. I cleared my throat, breaking the

spell we were both under. The fire between us blazed hotter than before.

"Stay here. I'll open your door," I told her as I climbed out of my truck and made my way around it.

"Thank you," she said, avoiding my eyes after I helped her out.

I walked her to her house, my fingers itching to brush against her lower back.

My breath hitched. I wasn't ready for the night to end. I still craved her and her presence, her joy, and her energy, even after spending an entire evening by her side.

On the front porch, standing close, we drank each other in.

I leaned forward, my breath grazing her cheek. My words turned into a whisper. "Can we test that third rule? As friends?" I asked.

Why was my voice so husky?

Heat traveled up Dahlia's face, the pink color on her cheeks making her even more beautiful under the porch light. My earlier thoughts swam back to my mind. Was I responsible for making her flush all the time?

"Yes," she murmured. "I thought you'd never ask. And since the rulebook agrees…"

Her breathing became shallow. She parted her lips, and I leaned in until mine connected with hers. Dahlia splayed her hand across my chest as if she required the support, her touch light as a feather, and I shivered down to my toes.

We both stood there as if we'd been transported to another dimension when our mouths connected. As if the world had dissolved all around us and we were raw from lust.

Fiery desire coursed through my bloodstream.

If Dahlia's lips carried that much power, I could

already imagine how the rest of her would feel pressed against me.

I anchored my hands on her hips, craving to fit her body against mine, to memorize every curve, every freckle, and every inch of her delectable skin.

Dahlia's lips danced against mine, and I melted into her.

We kissed a little longer, and I barely held back the groan threatening to escape. When she pulled away, I ached to taste her mouth a bit longer.

"Thanks for tonight," she whispered, breathless, as she raised her gaze to lock it on mine, her breasts still pressed against my torso. Was she as reluctant as I was to let go?

Right about now, the pounding of my heart could shatter the entire town. Every cell in me sparked to life as she pressed closer, her warmth coursing through me. My body erupted in a thousand flames.

"Dahlia, is it okay if I wish to do this again?" I asked, drowning in the green pools of her eyes.

A smile drew on her lips. "Mm-hmm, because I'd love to. Very much." She paused. The way her gaze bore into mine intensified the scorching ache consuming all my senses, a longing to touch her and know her better—every part of her. "Tomorrow, I'm having a pre-opening celebration for the shop. Would you come"—she stared at me, her lips pursed—"as my date?"

My heart drummed, its beat an addictive thrum. "Oh, you sure?" Whoa, I hadn't expected this invitation. Fireworks burst inside me. Would I look childish if I pumped my fist?

Dahlia nodded, nibbling her lower lip, never averting her eyes. "I am. It's a big night for me, and I'd like you there."

Her words struck me straight in the heart. The attraction I felt, it was mutual. She felt it too. Now, I had confirmation.

"I wouldn't miss it for the world. What time should I pick you up?"

"I'll be at the shop all day, but it starts at six. Meet me there at five-thirty. We'll have a drink beforehand. Some of my friends will come early too. It could be fun."

I could already picture Carter Hills giving me attitude. That should be interesting. "Perfect. Count me in."

She kept her hand over my heart, her touch steadying its rhythm, and her face glowing in the dark night.

I tilted my head and traced a line with my lips to the corner of her mouth.

"I already love our friendship," Dahlia whispered.

"Me too."

Her floral scent filled my nose—the same one that had knocked me off balance the day we met, and had been doing so all night. With my eyes closed, I inhaled deeply, wishing I could bottle it up.

"Night," I said with a step back as I forced the word out because there was no other place I'd rather be than here in that instant.

My eyes trained on her over my shoulder as I made it back to my truck. Earlier, I promised Carter Hills I'd be a gentleman tonight, but right now, the thoughts swimming in my head were a far cry from it. I wanted to kiss Dahlia Ellis. Not only to kiss her, but to be kissed by her. I wanted to hold her in my arms. Not only to hold her, but hold on to her, protect her. I wanted to touch her. Not only to touch her, but to connect to her so deeply that she and I became one.

Once in the safety of my pickup truck, I emptied all the air lodged in my lungs. There. Now I could breathe. I watched the house until all the lights went out, then drove away—not sure what I'd experienced, but longing for a do-over. Soon.

My body sizzled with need. In the comfort of my own home, I discarded my clothes, throwing them on the floor as I made my way upstairs, ready to relieve the tension combusting inside me and making my cock hard as a flag-pole. In the shower, it was so stiff that it hurt as I wrapped my fist around it and pumped myself under the curtain of water.

The images dancing before my eyes were all Dahlia's. Her hair the color of fire. Her alluring smile. The way her eyes reflected her inner beauty. Yeah, she was everything I loved in a woman and so much more. Here and now, she took center stage in my mind, my body aching for her. For some reason, she had wiped out from my memory the image of any other woman I'd ever laid my eyes on. Fuck, I wished the night could have lasted longer. I closed my eyes, reliving that kiss.

My neck tensed. A zing traveled down my spine. My balls tightened. I clenched my jaw, pumping myself faster, my teeth gritted together. "Fuck," I said as I shot my load all over the wall. I was doomed. Dahlia Ellis had made her way to the back corners of my brain—and my heart—and now I wanted more. A lot more of her.

Derek's Bucket List – ~~3. Kiss a girl until my heart beats fast~~

16

DAHLIA

"Who's watching Jack tonight?" my girlfriend Addison asked as we sat on the deck, having breakfast while my little boy played with his wooden blocks beside us.

"Paula's niece." Paula was the nanny. A woman in her early sixties who was head over heels in love with my baby boy. "Carter will pick him up later and drive him to his place, and she'll meet him there. I'm lucky he's still in town. It all kinda fits, the dates and everything. Jack and he are spending a couple of days together before Cart has to leave."

"You guys are doing a great job with Jack."

God, I loved my family. It wasn't typical, but it was us. Carter and Dahlia, grown-up and messy, raising a child together.

"Mama often says she isn't surprised we make it work and that it somehow suits us."

"I agree. You guys are my idols. Always have been. Jack is lucky to have you two."

I sighed. Yep. Everything about the way Carter and I raised Jack together made sense. At least it did to us.

"Are you nervous?"

I shrugged. "About tonight? Not really. I'm more excited than anything. Introducing Nick to everyone is much more stressful. They will assume we're dating. Not that I care, though, but I don't want him to feel pressured or left out. We're a pretty close-knit circle."

Addison lifted her eyebrows. "Oh yeah, the mysterious man you've been seeing. I can't wait to meet him."

With a sigh, I rolled my eyes in an overly dramatic fashion."Already told you. We're not seeing each other. It's more like a new exploratory friendship."

"Exploratory? What does that even mean? Is it a secret code word for oral? Dah, are you finally getting amazing sex? Is that guy tipping your world off its axis with his incredibly skillful tongue?" She closed her eyes and poked her tongue out, kissing the air.

I facepalmed, watching her antics, and we both burst into a fit of laughter.

"Addi. No. I'm not. Too soon. Stop doing that. You look ridiculous. And it's disturbing. Are you sure you've grown up in the last decade? Gosh." I shook my head. "Exploratory means exactly what it sounds like. Let's say we're getting to know each other. Minus the sex…for now. Anyway, we only went on two dates—if you count the lunch on the day we met. Don't get ahead of yourself. He's new in town, and I'm just being his friend."

"Yeah, yeah, friends."

I lifted both my hands between us. "I swear. You'll be the first to know if I dive into a serious relationship. It's been so long…and, huh, I feel rusty. I don't know how to date as an adult. It has never happened before. Jeff passed away when I was twenty. It will take some time to get used to the idea."

Addison's gaze stayed fixed on me as she brought her cup of tea to her lips. "Okay, I hear you. Why are you nervous then? It's no big deal if you're just being his good *good* friend. Unless"—she lowered the mug onto the table—"unless you like *like* him." She made weird kissing sounds with her mouth.

I tossed a balled napkin at her. "Stop being annoying, Addi. I'm not ready to date. Let's say we're just enjoying each other's company…for now."

She threw her head back as another fit of laughter bubbled out. "Yeah. Tell yourself that. After three years, you're more than ready for a man to rock your world, and your bed, Dah. I feel the change in you. Anyway, I can tell you like *like* this Nick guy."

With my hands covering my face, I laughed too. "Okay, fine. He's nice. And hot. Funny and smart. The truth is, I wanna be able to open my heart to love again. I've missed the rosy blush of a new relationship—the butterflies, the anticipation. I love the tingles that surface when we're together and the way my body ignites when he looks at me. We could talk for days, and I don't think we'd ever run out of things to say. Somehow, it's like I've known him forever. It sounds silly." I paused. "Is it a crime if I wanna see him again? Should I feel bad about it?"

Addison's amusement died, and she leaned forward to grab my hands in hers. "No, Dah. You've mourned Jeff for a long time. It's okay to start living again. To want something new. Something exciting."

"It's scary."

"Yes. But also, beautiful. It's okay to let your heart feel things for another man. You've just met Nick. See where this could go, but don't put pressure on yourself, okay? Take it slow."

"Tell that to my hormones. They've been in overdrive since the day he stepped into the shop. You should've seen him…shy, lost, ridiculously irresistible. It's like he stirred something in me I thought had been asleep that day. Big time."

"See? You may be readier than you think." Her lips grew into an oversized smirk, and I shook my head, standing up to clean the table.

Addison followed me inside. "Since I'm the official party planner for tonight, I should start making those last-minute phone calls. I'll meet you at the shop at noon and bring lunch. We'll spend the afternoon together."

I pulled my girlfriend into a hug. She and Carter had both been my rocks over the years, and lately, I'd been missing her more than usual. "Thanks for driving here. Tomorrow, we're spending the day at the spa, and I'm treating you to dinner afterward. Our last night out has been last fall. We're overdue."

"Oh yes, we are." She dropped a kiss on my cheek. "I'll shower and meet you later. Are your parents coming? I haven't seen them in forever."

I shook my head. "No. They're spending a few months in Africa. They won't be back for a while. We video chatted yesterday, and they wished me luck, so it's all good."

———

Hours later, Addison and I were helping the crew set up tables and the makeshift bar at the store. Shivers of excitement ran through me. Goose bumps blossomed on my skin at the thought I'd made this dream come true.

"Hey, Da-*aaah*," Addison called from the front, her voice dripping like honey, while I was changing in one of the dressing rooms. "There's a gentleman here for you." She relished doing that. I could hear the teasing in her voice.

A quick glance at my phone told me it was already five-thirty. Nick was here. That explained Addison's sultry tone. If it were any of my other friends, she wouldn't have used that voice—the one she used every time a male specimen she found attractive entered her peripheral vision. It was a daily, almost hourly, occurrence in her case.

"Coming," I called, zipping the strapless, silvery dress and fixing my hair one last time. Everything had to be perfect tonight. Me included. I only had a few grown-up nights throughout the year, and I intended to enjoy this one.

My breath caught, and I nearly tripped over my heels when I came face to face with Nick, dressed in a crisp white shirt with the top two buttons undone and the sleeves rolled up to his elbows. He had black trousers on, and his blond hair was artfully disheveled—a bedhead style that looked effortlessly sexy. His eyes drew me in, the moment they settled on me. He stepped closer and took my hand, heat rushing through me as he leaned in to kiss my cheek, his lips lingering for a long second.

My whole body tingled under his touch. The symphony in my chest heightened every sense. All I could hear was the steady thump of my heart. All I could smell was Nick's irresistible manly-woody scent.

"Hey, you look beautiful," he said, his tone faint and husky. The rumble of his whiskey voice rippled all over my skin as if he were under the same magnetic enchantment as I was.

"You don't look so bad yourself," I said, both of us

replaying the words we used the previous night. Nick grinned, and I beamed back. I forced my heart to calm down when all I craved was a do-over kiss. "Go get yourself something from the bar. My people should be here soon. I'll introduce you."

Nick nodded, let go of my hand, and sauntered over to the right side, where the bartenders were standing.

Addison neared me and elbowed my ribs. "Girlfriend, now I understand. Wow, this man is a hot piece of ass. No wonder he woke you from your dormant state. That gravelly voice…damn. It might even affect me. Is he for real?" I gave her a stern look as she fanned herself, flashing me a not-so-subtle wink. "Dah, the way he undressed you with his eyes… Whoa. He was about to eat you whole. Ohmygod, I deserve a man who looks at me like that. You're always snatching the best ones."

I tapped her hand. "It is too soon…right? To feel this much attraction?" Nerves hit me like a wave, fear, anxiety, and happiness colliding in my chest.

"Dahlia, I already told you. You've mourned Jeff for years. I'm sure he'd want you to move on and to be happy and live fully again. To be the fierce woman he fell in love with. He'd never wish for you to be alone. You know I speak the truth. Jeff Hills adored you too much—you were his entire world for most of his life—to ever forbid you from falling in love again."

"But I'll break Cart's heart once more."

"Dahlia, Carter can't be mad at you for following your heart. I know it's hard on him, and believe me, I get it, but the guy *has* to move on. It's been years, and your stance on the subject hasn't changed. You can't forfeit your own happiness just because he can't get over you."

My pulse raced, and I cupped my chest to calm the

palpitations I feared I wouldn't be able to contain for long. I blinked, keeping the tears threatening to fall at bay.

"Breathe, Dah. It's gonna be okay. I have your back."

I nodded.

Addison snaked her arm through mine. "Trust me, you've got this."

"I hope."

Riley and June, Carter's management team—Riley being my ex-manager and my friend—walked in. I smiled, grateful for the interruption, keeping me safe from the ache I got whenever I walked down memory lane. Stud, my ex-bandmate, and his wife Belinda followed close behind.

We exchanged a few words, and I directed them to the bar.

Addison, in full party-organizer mode, was busy talking to the caterer.

It suited her. This job. She had always loved throwing parties and having people over. She worked as a graphic designer in Atlanta, a few hours' drive from here. She was great at her job but excelled at being a people person. Whenever we saw each other, it was like no time had passed. I missed having her in my everyday life.

Carter arrived next, and all my worries faded away. Almost all my favorite people in the world were here, in *my* bridal shop, celebrating the realization of my new venture with me.

Nick came back the moment Carter joined me.

"Hey, Carter. Nice to see you again," my new friend said, extending a palm toward him.

Carter's face turned to stone as he shook Nick's hand. "Likewise. Dahlia forgot to tell me you were coming."

Nick's smile didn't falter. "A last-minute invite."

I fought the urge to wrap an arm around Nick's

midsection, staking my claim. Carter was acting like a child.

"Carter is not always that broody," I said with a shrug, trying to ease the tension between the two men now eyeing each other as if they were reenacting an old Western movie, ready for a duel.

Carter brought his glass of water to his lips. "Yeah, it only started a few days ago."

I backhanded his chest. "Enough, already. Come on, Nick, let me introduce you to some of the most important people in my life."

He nodded and followed me, exchanging words and joking around with Riley and Stud and complimenting June on her dress.

My ex-manager took him under his wings, and Belinda neared me, pulling me aside. "Dahlia, what you did with the store is pretty amazing. It's very much like you." I followed her gaze as she nodded in approval at the wall of heels—each higher or shinier than the last—against the powder-blue walls, the dark recycled-wood ceilings echoing the floors. She leaned closer. "Who's the guy?" she asked, pointing her chin toward her husband, who was talking to Nick.

"A friend. We met last week. Somehow, we hit it off."

"Are you guys dating?"

I hurriedly took a big gulp of my champagne and shook my head. "Gosh, why is everyone assuming we are?"

"Come on, Dahlia, it's me. I know you. We've been on the road for months together. I can perceive your feelings. Right now, I'd have to be blind not to see the sexual tension floating between you two. Both of you can't keep your eyes off each other. I would've bet you've known him for a long time and were keeping him a secret from us. I'm surprised you've never mentioned him before."

I lifted my hands before me. "We just met. I swear."

Belinda sipped her drink and waggled her eyebrows. "If you say so."

"I swear. He's hot, right?" I let out a warm laugh.

"Oh yes. Girl, you know how to pick them."

We both chuckled as we glanced at the guys, all friendly, Stud clapping Nick's shoulder as they laughed about something.

My friend leaned closer. "Don't worry about Carter, okay? I'll ask Stud to talk to him. I might even drill some sense into him myself. He usually confides in me when you're not around."

I bowed my head. Carter's feelings for me were out in the open. They weren't some dirty secrets only I was aware of. "Thanks, Belle." I sighed. "I hate breaking his heart, and for some reason, I keep doing it without meaning to."

We drank our champagne side by side, keeping an eye on the guys.

"Don't worry. It will all turn out fine. For everyone."

After showing a famous designer around, one I hoped would agree to feature one of her exclusive lines here, Carter cornered me by the dressing rooms.

"Dah, why did you bring him here? Don't you think it's too early to introduce him to everyone? Next thing I know, he'll be having breakfast with Jack."

I pulled at Carter's hand, his face a mixture of anguish and calm—just as I'd guessed—and led him farther away from everyone else. "Cart, you don't get to decide who I can and cannot hang out with. It doesn't work like that. Nobody said anything about Jack entering the equation yet, okay?"

Staring at his feet, Carter nodded. When he lifted his eyes to meet mine, I saw the spectrum of his pain waltzing across them, his melted-steel irises darkening."Dah, it's too soon."

"It's been three years, Cart. I'm not a nun. The last thing I want is to spend the rest of my life alone and sad. I want to thrive. To love. To do all the things I've dreamed of."

"I want them for you too…but not with *him*."

"Gosh, I can't believe we're having this conversation right now. Right here. You knew it was bound to happen someday. Carter, I am not replacing you in my heart. My love for you isn't something that can be pushed away or swapped. It's yours. Forever. You should be aware of it by now, but there's a place for someone else in it too…one day. I'm not your person in the way you want me to be, but I'm your person in every other way. For now, I'm just being Nick's friend. I can't predict what will happen in the future, but I owe myself the right to see where this thing will take me…if he wishes it too."

With a long inhale, I blinked my tears away—now wasn't the time to have a meltdown—and sighed, not in the mood to fight with my best friend over another guy.

Carter hugged me, and our hearts meshed together, beating to the same rhythm. The way they'd been doing all our lives. My friend was right. If I were in love with him, everything would be so much simpler. His steady heartbeat rocked mine until it calmed down.

"Cart, let me prove to myself that I can still do this. Date. Have fun. Trust someone else with my heart who's not you—"

"Dah, I—"

Addison walked over to us, and I thanked her in my head for the disruption. "Sorry, guys. My timing sucks, but, Dah, it's time for your speech. The servers have started passing *amuse-bouches* around." She pivoted to face Carter, her long blonde ponytail sweeping my face as she turned around. "Hey, Cart. Nice to see you. It's been too long." They hugged and kissed each other's cheeks. "Now come on, you two, and stop hiding in here."

Carter's eyes said what his mouth didn't. *This conversation isn't over.*

Mine answered. *Yes, it is. You're wrong about Nick. Trust me on this.*

He's not right for you.

In your eyes, nobody will ever be. Carter blinked, and I added. *It doesn't have to be this way.*

He cocked his head to the side, telling me he was done talking. For now.

Addison motioned me to the front of everyone gathered in my little shop, and I forced a smile while my stomach still reeled from the conversation with Carter. I swallowed and exhaled. I could do this. With my fingertips, I wiped the corners of my eyes, checking for any mascara smudges. Then I relaxed my shoulders and followed my friend.

"Hi everybody. Thank you for coming and celebrating this special moment with me. It means a lot. I hope you're having a great night." I paused to catch my breath. "I have moments of stage fright." People laughed. "Yeah, I know how it sounds, but it was usually Cart who did all the talking back in the day. Most of the time, I stood there with my heart racing until we started playing… True story. Not sure if I've ever admitted it to anyone but those guys," I said, pointing to my ex-bandmates and manager. "Anyway, I'm sure Carter will take over if I freeze."

My gaze landed on my best friend, our previous disagreement mostly forgotten. Carter grinned at me and mouthed, *Don't look at them, Dah. Look at me. I'm right here.*

Those words. They were the same words he'd spoken

to me before each performance over the years. Whether as kids performing on a makeshift stage in my backyard or the last time I played before retiring after our second world tour. The ones that always soothed the frantic beatings of my heart.

With my eyes trained on him, I continued, "Let's see if I can do this by myself."

He bobbed his head, showing me just how much he believed in me. It acted as a calming blanket around my hyperactive heart.

I inhaled a cleansing breath, straightened my back, and kept going. "It took me years to get to this place in my life where everything finally made sense again, and I couldn't have done it without many of you. Cart, you're my family. Forever." He offered me a lopsided smile, raising his glass of water in my direction. "None of this would have ever been possible without you. I love you. We've been through so much already, but one thing I wouldn't change is our everlasting friendship. It's one of the most important and precious treasures of my life. Addi, thanks for being by my side in all my ventures. You're the one person who knows how to cheer me up on the days I'm a mess. Your help today is priceless." I smiled at her. "You actually have no idea. And by the way, you're good at this. Riley, June, Belle, and Stud, all of you being here means the world to me. We don't see each other as often as I'd like, but I'm grateful I can still call you my friends—and my family—after all these years." I thanked all the people important to me. Those without whom I wouldn't stand here today. "And finally, thanks to my new friend, Nick. Consider this your official welcome to town. I'm glad you walked in here by mistake that day. All y'all, cheers," I said, raising my champagne glass.

"See? I knew you could do it," Carter said, as soon as I

joined him, still surfing the happiness cloud. He wrapped me in his embrace and kissed my temple. "I'm proud of you."

"Not too often, though. At one point, I thought I'd faint. Public speaking is your thing," I said, clinking my glass against his.

Carter's phone went off, and he excused himself.

I slithered through the small crowd to reach Nick, deep in a conversation with Riley about a commercial development in Chicago he had shares in. My heart did a happy dance. Yeah, Nick, fit right in with my friends.

Later, we were gathered around my ex-manager. "Okay, we were in France. And these guys had one show left to the European leg of their first world tour. We were in that restaurant, all of us exhausted and drinking a little too much when a man came to us, asking if we could pretend to be that band of country losers from the US to surprise his wife, who was a huge fan. We all looked at him without saying anything. I remember that day as if it were yesterday," Riley said, as I wiped the tears of laughter welling in my eyes, the memory still fresh in my mind.

"That was epic," Carter said.

"I can't believe I missed that," June added.

"What did you guys do?" Nick asked, engrossed in the story.

"We went to the hotel bar, took over the stage, and sang one of our songs," Stud chimed in. "Afterwards Carter said to the wife, 'Hi, we're those country singer losers you love so much. Care to take a picture with us?' Riley made one VIP ticket appear for the next day's show and gifted it to the wife, adding she was invited backstage after the concert. When the man argued she couldn't go alone, Riley added, 'We wouldn't want to force you to watch a bunch of US turkeys onstage for two hours. You'll be better off not going,' then clapped the man's shoulder and walked away as the wife yelled at her husband for insulting us."

"Shit. I wouldn't have wanted to be in his shoes," Nick said.

"Yeah. We have so many stories like this one. All worse than the others," Stud said. "A trip down band-days lane is always fun."

Riley lifted his glass. "Whenever you're ready, losers."

I hadn't laughed this much in a long time.

These people. My band family. No wonder they were still a part of my life. I loved each of them so much. They were my ride or die, and no matter how much time had passed since the last time we saw each other, our bond never faded.

We grew up together. And reached the top together.

Cried hard. And fought harder.

And saw each other at our worst. But still, we stuck with one another.

No matter what. Nothing would break us apart.

We loved one another. Unconditionally. Our friendship had only grown over the years.

We were family. All of us in it for the long run.

Around eleven, after the guests left, Riley made a crate of liquor appear. We drank, all of us sitting on pillows in the area in front of the dressing rooms.

Addison brought a tray, filled with leftovers, as we settled down. Eating and passing the booze around, we listened to Riley as he regaled us with more stories from our band days.

Carter scooted closer and draped an arm around my shoulder. From habit and years of doing so, I sank my body into his. His fingers played with the loose strands of my hair. We were just being Dahlia and Carter again. The kids unable to spend a day apart growing up. The teens sleeping in the same bed, doing nothing else but holding on to each other's hands for hours. The co-parents learning how to change diapers together and how to survive when their entire world crumbled.

Nick appeared in my line of sight, and my insides clenched.

Carter and I were nothing else but friends, but somehow, having Nick here, witnessing us being so close physically, felt wrong. Our friends didn't care, they were used to our antics, but Nick had no idea. Sure, I'd told him Carter and I were family and that we were everything to each other, but being *us*, like this right now, felt like a mistake.

Nick sat on our right, his legs folded before him, his crossed arms resting on his bent knees. I sensed his gaze on us, questioning.

I got to my feet and headed toward the restroom.

Addison caught up with me halfway there. "Hey, girlfriend. What's wrong? You have that look on your face."

"Wh-what look?" I asked, avoiding her eyes.

"*That* look. You know, when you're overloaded with emotions and I can't decide if you're sad, upset, happy, or about to throw a fit."

I poked my tongue out at her. "I don't have *thaaat* look."

"You do. What happened? Did Cart say something?"

I shook my head. "It's…it's Nick. It feels wrong being all over Carter when he sits next to *meee*. He's not…he's not used to our relationship. It looks… *I'mmm* sure it looks weird from an outsider's point of view, no? Nobody but *youuu* guys get it."

"Oh, so you do like *like* him," she said, her lips stretched wide.

I placed a hand over her mouth. "Shhh. Lower your

voice. He'll hear *youuu*." I lost my footing, drunker than I thought. "I'm desperate to kiss him again."

"*Again?*"

I gave her what I thought was my most innocent look.

My friend clamped my upper arms and shook me as if I were a palm tree and she craved a coconut. "Naughty girl. I knew it. You secretive little flirt. Way to go, woman. I've got to talk to him a little tonight, and he's perfect for you. Also, those golden eyes. They look like pools of whiskey. You've earned the right to get lost in them. He could do damage with those. Or set your panties on fire. Girlfriend, be wild for a change. Be like me. You'll thank me tomorrow."

"Addi, I...I've never done anything like this before. What if it destroys what we're building? What if it blows *uppp* in our faces?"

"Dah, do you want to kiss him?"

I bobbed my head multiple times, the same way my son always did.

"You have your answer. You don't need my advice. Or permission."

———

"Come on, girls, I'll drive you home," Carter said as Addison and I walked back toward the party, our arms interlinked, basking in our happy, booze-fueled bliss.

"Nah. I'll drive them home," Nick chimed in. "Carter, you should drive your friends to their cabins instead."

My best friend jumped in Nick's face, his scorching gaze strong enough to reduce him to ashes. "You're not driving anyone anywhere, pretty boy. Nobody here is in any shape to get behind a wheel. Call yourself a cab or something. News flash, in this town, it might be quicker to just walk home. Don't waste time. You should get going. We'll be all right."

Nick steeled his back, not breaking his stance at Carter's harsh words. "My last drink was more than two hours ago. I've been sipping water since. Don't worry about me, man. Don't picture me as a threat—or a villain —because you're wrong on both accounts. No need to give me shit either. I'll drive Dahlia and Addison home while you take care of them," he said with a firm voice, not open for discussion, gesturing in the direction of Riley, June, Stud, and Belinda, still laughing and drinking, not a care in the world about the heated exchange.

I swallowed hard. Nick had just reached a new level of respect in my mind as he stood up to my best friend. Every word escaping his full lips captivated me and took me hostage. They showed me the strength in him, and some-how, turned me on.

The idea of a do-over kiss prickled my lips. I blinked to escape his magnetic force. If my friends weren't here, I wouldn't wait another second to claim his lips. Because I'd been thinking about them a lot in the last twenty-four hours, obsessed about their taste and their feel.

Blinking away my fantasies, I neared Carter in one stride. "Stop. Nick's right. They are *alll* staying next to your house. *Youuu* have enough room in your truck for them. Addi and I will ride with Nick."

Carter sighed.

"We'll *beee* okay, Cart. Stop worrying about *meee* all the time. I-I can take care of myself, okay? Now let's get them out of here. I have to clean *uppp* and engage the alarm."

Carter's serious stare weighed on me. "Go. Don't worry. I'll take care of it and set the alarm."

"*Youuu* sure? I can help *youuu*," I slurred my words a little.

"Yeah. Go home. Get some sleep. We'll be out of here in no time."

Our gazes fixated on each other for a beat.

Carter moved forward to drop a kiss on my forehead. "Go, Dah. I'll call you tomorrow."

"*Thankkks*." I squeezed his forearm and nodded without another word.

"Be careful," he murmured to my back.

I closed in on Nick, who stood further away with Addison.

"Ready?" he whispered, his warm breath tickling the shell of my ear as I reached him and he leaned in.

"*Yesss*," I replied, my voice low, loving the bubble we always fell into when we were together.

We exchanged a smile, and my chest expanded at the way he glanced at me.

"Does Carter need help? We can stay to clean up."

I shook my head. "*Nopppe*. Let him. It will erase some of his annoyance. Believe *meee*, it's better if he does it by himself. On. His. Own. Anyway, the rest of the store has already been cleaned, *sooo* it's just this one room."

With his hand glued to the small of my back, Nick led me to his truck, Addison stumbling in front of us, singing, and contagiously happy.

Ten minutes later, we parked in my driveway, and my girlfriend got out on the pretext of a full bladder.

"Don't wait for *meee*. I'll be right in," I told her.

Damn. No way did Nick miss her not-so-subtle wink.

She closed the truck door behind her, and I let out a nervous laugh.

Nick shook his head. "She's crazy, but I like her. She reminds me of my best friend. Don't ever let me introduce them. They would be dynamite together. Hot but dangerous."

"She's the best." My eyes trailed her silhouette as she entered the house.

Heat coursed through me, my body smoldering with desire now that Nick and I were finally alone.

We stared at each other, and it killed the lightness we shared. The air in the truck cab crackled, and my skin prickled with growing awareness.

Nick's musky scent filled my nose, firing electric jolts through my heart.

His throat worked, and I zoomed in on the movement.

My eyes moved up and focused on those lips. The ones whose contours I wanted to draw with my fingertip and feel against my skin. Hear all their secrets and whispers as they tasted mine.

"I'll walk you to your door," he said, breaking the tensed silence and my slow exploration of his face.

Neither of us made a move to exit the vehicle for a minute.

My pulse quickened.

Restraint flashed in his eyes, mixed with something I assumed was desire.

Gosh, I was desperate to kiss him so bad but feared I would be swept away if I did.

Under the porch light, we faced each other, just like the night before.

"Thanks for inviting me tonight, Dahlia. I had a great time, and your friends are the real deal. You're lucky to have them. They all love you very much. That much was obvious."

I moved closer, eating the space between us. I craved Nick's touch. Perhaps it was the champagne I'd drunk, or the excitement in the air, but once again, I had a hard time focusing anywhere else but his mouth.

For the hundredth time tonight, I wondered if his lips

would be as soft on my flesh as they looked. If they would taste as great as they did last night.

Nick laced his fingers through mine and brought our joined hands to his chest. Heat shot through me and messed with my composure. His touch alone broke barriers I had set around my heart a long time ago. His heartbeat, strong and wild, mirrored mine. Before I chickened out, I rose onto my tiptoes and pressed my lips to his. Our connection stilled the whirlwind inside me.

As if we'd rehearsed it a million times before, our mouths fused together, like two magnets.

I entangled my fingers in his hair, deepening the bond we shared.

Nick drew in a sharp breath and closed his eyes before pulling away.

"I-I…" I winced. "I'm sorry. I thought…I, huh, I believed…"

Nick tugged at my hands when I tried to yank them away.

"Dahlia, don't. I'm very into you too. It's just—" He tucked a strand of my hair behind my ear, cradling the side of my face with his palm.

Shivers moved up and down my spine at the closeness of our bodies.

"We're friends. I think you made it clear tonight when you gave your speech. Thanks, by the way. I'm glad I walked into your shop that day too, for what it's worth. I knew we said kissing is allowed, according to our rulebook, but I'm scared if we do it a lot, I'll never be able to stop. I'm not into one-nighters, and you don't deserve to be just a fuck to me." Nick tipped my head up, his hand still glued to my face, as more heat shot through me. "Don't feel bad about this. I can't keep count of how many times I've wished to do this tonight, but our new relationship is precious to me. I refuse to mess it up by skipping steps."

My lips quivered. "Do you…do you feel it too?" I asked, my eyes brimming with tears. A sting of rejection hit me, but the feeling of being cherished washed over it, which was a weird mix. I had to know if I was making up scenarios in my mind.

My head and heart and everything inside me battled together. The alcohol I'd drunk didn't help to order my thoughts. As a woman, I craved Nick's touch, but my head knew what he said rang true. That we owed it to ourselves to see where this thing simmering between us could take us.

"I do. Which is why I think we better take it slow."

His lips connected with my forehead, and I swooned in his embrace. Every time Nick touched me, I burned a little hotter and melted a little more and fell a little harder in this exciting vortex. The symphony playing inside me had turned into an orchestra. Nick steadied me, one hand anchored to my hip.

With his gaze burrowing into mine, talking straight to my soul, he added, "Give us some time, okay?" I rested my hand over the one still pressing my cheek and held him there as he asked, "Can I call you in the morning?" His golden irises drank me in. The conflict in them must have mirrored mine.

I shook my head.

Nick's face fell, and a frown crossed his forehead.

I pinched my lips together as I watched him, looking defeated.

17

NICHOLAS

In the darkness of the night, Dahlia's mouth found mine. Fireworks shot in every direction, making me feel drunk too. Drunk on her. On her scent. On her touch. Our shared connection ran deeper than a physical need or an urge to tame. It was a whirlwind I never wanted to escape. Her mouth moved against mine, playing with the strings of my restraint, breaking through the walls I set around me, and saving my heart for the one I could see myself building something with.

Love. A future.

Some common sense snapped me out of the trance that had settled between us. Cursing at myself and fishing in the pit of my will, in the corners of my soul—something so deep and intense I couldn't explain—I leaned back.

Hurt and incomprehension flashed in her eyes. A blazing flush crept upon her cheeks, and when she started to step back, not ready to have her out of my energy field, away from my body, I tightened my grip on her hands.

Could she understand my silent words? My need to

treat her right. To not rush what we could be and kindle it to ashes.

Her lips trembled as I tucked her hair behind her ear and framed her face. My eyes lingered on her for a long beat.

"Do *youuu* feel it too?" she asked.

I did. So much, it floored me that I could feel things for someone I barely knew.

The words escaped my mouth of their own volition.

"Can I call you tomorrow?" I asked.

An avalanche of emotions crashed into me when she shook her head.

It broke something inside me. Something I didn't even know existed. I schooled my expression, doing my best to hide my confusion. I blinked. Dahlia was tipsy, and I'd wanted to be respectful, not kiss her when I knew the effect she had on me. In the heat of the moment we shared, I'd been afraid I'd be too bewitched by her to stop before things went too far. The sparks between us could easily ignite into an inferno if we weren't careful.

I'd wanted to be nice, not to be an opportunistic jerk, and I'd ended up being rejected—big time—by a woman I was falling for a little too hard and a little too fast.

My stomach turned to rock as Dahlia stood there, inches away from me, my hand still cupping her cheek. I'd never spoil what we shared because I couldn't be patient. She had to know, or I hoped she could feel it, that I spoke the truth.

Earlier, in her shop, she'd nestled against Carter and let him play with her hair. The sight of them, friendly and intimate, had shaken me to my core. For the first time in almost forever, I felt possessive of something—or rather, someone—who wasn't mine. Someone I had no right to lust over this way. The truth was that I couldn't help it. I hated his hands on her, the familiarity between them, and the unspoken history woven into their embrace. As if they were alone in a room full of people and couldn't care less.

I hadn't missed the way Carter Hills longed for her and watched her or only smiled when she stood by his side.

Dahlia pressed her hands to my chest, bringing my focus back to her, her touch powerful enough to get every part of my body twitching and begging for her attention.

Dahlia Ellis possessed a rare power over me. "Tomorrow, I'm spending the day with Addison. Jack is with Carter for a few nights, so we're enjoying ourselves."

"Oh." I exhaled and chastised myself for imagining the worst.

"She's leaving after dinner. If you're free, we could go out afterward? Hang out or something?"

"Yeah. Okay. Huh, I'd like that."

My eyes captured hers and before I changed my mind and claimed her lips, I leaned forward and pressed a kiss to her cheek, my heart banging, beating a chaotic rhythm in my chest.

"Night, Dahlia."

"Good night, Nick."

My thoughts eddied as I drove away.

Dahlia Ellis had kissed me twice now. The teenager part of me, mostly alive around Tucker, high-fived itself. Sure, it lasted only seconds, but it was a well-worth micro-moment of bliss. Her full lips had felt like velvet against mine. As I replayed the memory, I ran my tongue over my bottom lip. Vanilla. It still tasted like her. For some reason, I wished it would linger until the morning.

Dahlia had no idea what she had done.

With the kiss she had initiated, she'd opened the door

to my heart, the one I reserved for someone special, *my person.*

Judging by the intensity of the fire searing between us, I hoped that one day she would be. It sounded silly, but there was something about her I couldn't explain, something that appealed to all of me, even to my soul.

Earlier, the touch of her lips had electrified every cell in my body, yet it also stirred the doubts creeping into my mind and the sadness enveloping my heart.

"Hey, bro. Are you listening? Your intake on this would be much appreciated. And yes, I know you're just a child, but if I call Tuck, he'll give me all the wrong advice. You know I'm right." I sighed. "Dahlia and I just met. Why do I feel so protective and possessive of her? It makes zero sense. None. Yet there's something between us—I can feel it. And now I know she feels it too." I ran a hand through my hair, messing it up. "Like an idiot, I pushed her away earlier. Goddamnit. What's wrong with me? I'm so confused right now. Please tell me I did the right thing."

My heart jackhammered, and my body pulsed, vibrating at the mere thought of her.

To silence my racing thoughts and frenetic hormones, I turned the radio on.

"Bro, really? Are you kidding me right now?" I said through the windshield, my eyes fixated on the inky sky.

Carter Hills Band's "Monkey Business" song started playing on the radio. Again.

I smiled and shook my head.

"C'mon, is it your answer to everything?"

This time, the lyrics hit me differently.

I could only hear Dahlia's clear voice, and when she attacked the chorus, her voice unraveled my mind and sparked a slow, burning need low in my body.

The one that had only been a voice for as long as I could remember now belonged to the person I couldn't wait to see again. The chorus played once more. I was floating. Like an out-of-the-body experience as I hung to every word coming out of her mouth. The mouth I'd kissed and cherished. The one I could listen to days and nights.

I parked in the driveway just as the song ended.

"Bro, what are you doing to me? Are you telling me I was a fool for walking away, or are you just messing with me like Tuck would do and having a blast about it? Yep, I bet you're laughing from your cloud. I can see it clearly in my head." My cheerfulness died a little. "Derek, I just wanna thank you for always listening to me. I feel you. With me…always. Also, thank you for the song. If it's your way of telling me you approve, and I hope it is, I'm thankful. I haven't figured out that master plan of yours yet, but I will." Tension left my shoulders, and for a moment, I relished the solitude of my truck and the quiet of the night.

Glued to the seat, I watched the stars through the windshield, somehow wishing for another sign or something.

My lids grew heavy, and I could barely keep my eyes open, so I exited the cab.

"By the way, I've met Carter Hills. All right, you probably already know, but anyway, I'm not sure he's a fan of mine—grown-up stuff, don't worry—but he would've been a fan of yours for sure. I witnessed him with Jack. Yeah, you would have liked him. Go play now. I love you." I kissed two fingers and raised them toward the sky on my way inside. "Night, bro." Without turning any light on, I went to my room, undressed, and fell face-first onto the mattress, tired of replaying how I had turned Dahlia down earlier and hating myself for being so reasonable. Or chickenshit, as Tucker would say.

Derek's Bucket List – 45. Nick. Do something that's right even if it doesn't feel like it at first

———

The next morning, I woke up around six with renewed energy, ready to start my day. Still, I had leftover angst coursing through me. Outside, the sun was bright and the sky blue, so I decided to put my pent-up energy to good use and focus on the yard. With the freshly mowed lawn, painted walls and borders, the house already looked better and less like an abandoned dwelling. Soon, the exterior would be ready to impress any potential buyers.

At the garden center, I picked up bags of soil and garden tools. I halted when I stepped into the flower aisle. It was a riot of colors and species I hadn't expected.

A young man in a green apron made his way toward me. "Can I help you?"

"I'm looking to buy some of these," I said, indicating the varieties of flowers before me, "to fill the flower beds at my house. Any suggestions?"

The man laughed. "You should ask your woman. Full sunlight or shade, I can help you with that. Anything else, nope. Girls usually love that part, you know. They tend to be better too. Not that you're not—"

I lifted a hand to shut him up. "Yeah, I get what you mean. Gimme time to think about it." I didn't care which flowers I picked as long as they were purple. Dahlia mentioned something about loving this color the other night, and for a reason that defied logic, I loved the idea she'd find them pretty if she ever visited my place.

Just the thought of that woman was enough to curl my lips into a ridiculous grin.

In the next aisle, I admired the swatches of paint on card stripes. The front door could use a splash of color. Something vibrant. I'd seen it on a job the other day. A farmhouse painted in white with a red door. Not sure about the red, I spread sample cards on the counter, studying the display.

I rubbed my nape, my eyes drifting from one card to the next.

First, the flowers, now the door. Maybe that kid was right, and I really required a woman's help after all.

Digging my phone out of my back pocket, I sent a picture to my best friend in town. After all, didn't she tell me home decor was her specialty?

ME

> Hey. Want to paint my front door. Something fierce and good-looking. Give the house some personality, you know? Which color? Unlike you, I'm bad at this. Desperate for an expert opinion. Help a guy out.

I pressed send, wondering if she would reply. After all, Dahlia Ellis was a busy woman.

A thought popped into my head as the chime announced the message had gone through.

ME

> Forget it. I'll deal with this later. It's your day with Addison. Don't answer me.

My phone went off, and Dahlia's name appeared on the screen. I froze, my fingers debating whether to accept the call or not.

You're being ridiculous. You're the one who messaged her.

Drilling some sense into my brain, I answered after the fourth ring.

Her cheery tone melted my hesitation. "So glad you've reached out. I knew you'd ask for my help at some point. What color is the house?"

"It's a two-story white farmhouse. The front porch is stained in a walnut shade. Everything else is white, except for the shutters, which are black. What do you think about painting the front door red or some other color? You know I'm not skilled with decor stuff. I've been standing here for fifteen minutes, unable to commit to a color."

"Ohmygod. I wish I could see the look on your face right now. Are you scratching your forehead? Are your armpits wet?"

The sound of her laughter soothed me. Again. Even when she was teasing me. Especially when she was teasing me.

"Make fun of me all you want. It's a very serious decision, and I was hoping you could help me make the best choice."

"Switch to video chat," she told me.

"Why? So, you can laugh at my face?"

"Absolutely. And it will also be easier if I see what you're seeing."

"No. It can wait." I cringed. "I remembered it was your day off with Addison after I pressed send."

"Oh Nick, don't be silly. If it weren't the right time, I would have said so. Now switch to video chat. I'm actually proud and happy you're asking me."

I breathed out my relief as my finger fumbled with the

screen. Last night's rejection didn't shadow her words. The disquiet that had gotten me agitated all morning dissipated. Perhaps I didn't really require her help, but more the reassurance that we were okay.

Dahlia's face appeared on my screen, and I almost choked on my own air. "Oh, you're busy. Why didn't you tell me?"

She must have seen my amusement because she added, "Don't let the face mask distract you, Nick. It's avocado and concrete."

"Concrete?" I asked.

A loud chuckle resonated from beside her, and Addison's face replaced Dahlia's. "Hi, handsome. Don't make her laugh or that thing will crack. I wouldn't be surprised if it was actually made of concrete, though. Bye, Nick."

"Bye, Addi," I said as Dahlia grabbed the phone back from her friend.

Her lips tilted up, and I smiled back. Again, I was falling under her magnetism, head—and heart—first, with no security net to catch me.

Even with a green paste spread on her face, she looked stunning. She had her hair tied in a knot at the top of her head and some sort of pale pink bathrobe on.

Her moss-green eyes sparkled.

God, she was gorgeous.

"I have to say, the frown across your forehead made my day. Now turn the camera around." Oh yeah, the paint samples. Distracted, I regained some control over myself and did as instructed. "Teal," Dahlia said without hesitating. "Red would look great, but teal will give it a fresh vibe. Yeah, teal it is."

I blinked, speechless. "Love how assured you can be. Do you have time for another mission? Unless you gotta get rid of that huh…that thing," I said, my finger drawing circles in the air over the screen.

"Bring it on. Please. Anything to forget my face is itchy and feeling like it's carved in stone."

I heard Addison complaining from where I couldn't see her. "It's torture. Spa day is supposed to be relaxing."

Dahlia shook her head, unable to smile fully, thanks to that mortar-avocado mix.

Ten minutes later, together, we had chosen an assortment of flowers.

"Whoa, you weren't kidding. From now on, you'll be my personal interior designer. Or the chief of the landscape department. The job is yours. And don't even think about passing up on it."

She snickered, the sound addictive, her gaze radiating happiness. "Still on for later tonight?"

"Yes. Unless you're too tired after your day."

Her laughter intensified. "Nick, it's spa day. It's to relax and stuff, but I won't be exhausted from getting pampered. Believe me, I'll need some action after that."

"Okay then. Text me when you're free."

"I will. Bye, Nick."

Why did every time my name passed Dahlia's lips, my heart banged louder in my chest, and my body hummed to the melody of her voice?

Not ready to assess the *what-ifs* of our blossoming relationship, I buried the thought deep down and finished my errands.

The whole time, my heart moved around in my chest, unable to stay still.

———

The ringtone of my phone resonated through the bathroom as I stepped out of the shower, ruffling my hair to get rid of the water beads. My pulse raced at the idea that it might be Dahlia. Toweling myself off quickly, I grabbed the device on the countertop. My glee vanished a tad at the sight of my best friend's name flashing on the screen.

"Hey man, what's up?" Tucker greeted me.

"Not much. Getting ready to go out. What about you?"

"Is that a southern drawl I hear in your voice? The lumberjack effect?"

I let out a heartfelt chuckle. "Sure. Why not?" Anything to please him.

"Have you found friends for poker night, or are you having a date with your neighbor's dog?"

"Neither. I have a real date. Like with an actual human being."

My friend whistled, and I hated myself for taking the bait. How could I get so rusty in just a few weeks? I knew Tucker Philips like no other, yet I'd fallen into his trap like an amateur.

"Finally," he hollered through the line, so much that I had to distance my phone from my ear. Not ready to be deaf, I put him on speaker as I got dressed. "Who is she? Have you got your dick sucked already? Is she hot? Tits. Real or fake? And her ass? You know I'm an ass-man."

I shook my head, slipping a long-sleeved T-shirt on. "She's perfect. I like her."

"Shit," Tucker claimed. "I never thought I'd see the day when Nick Peterson would say a woman is perfect. God, are you high? Fuck, what did she do to you? Voodoo magic shit?"

I let out a nervous snicker. "It's powerful, man.

Anytime we're together, it's electric. Hard to explain. Never saw this coming—" A chime distracted me.

DAHLIA

Addi is gone. Karaoke or bowling?

Karaoke with Dahlia Ellis, queen of country music, not sure I was ready for this just yet.

ME

Bowling.

DAHLIA

Great. I know the perfect place. Meet you there?

ME

No.

DAHLIA

Why?

ME

I'm picking you up. Twenty minutes okay with you?

DAHLIA

Yes.

I pictured her in my head with an ear-to-ear smile.

"Nick? Are you still there, or did you dump me for that woman?" Tucker whined.

I smiled, not indulging in his childish ways.

"Nick? Should I worry? I should've known something wasn't right. You're going on a date. That doesn't sound like you. Do you need me to come over and shake some sense into you? Remind you of who you are?"

I huffed. "God, Tuck. Relax. I'm fine. In case you forgot, you live more than nine hours away. Anyway, I have to go."

"Wait." His voice had lost its teasing tone. "You sure you're okay?"

"Yep. I'll call you later, man."

I jumped in my truck, ready to pick up the woman who'd been on my mind all day.

Dahlia slid herself into the passenger seat before I had time to ring her doorbell, and soon, the floral scent of her permeated the air.

A flush of electricity bloomed along my nape, and my body that had been tensed with restless energy settled the moment she appeared.

In unison, we leaned over the central console and met each other's gaze. Every molecule of air fizzed around us. Every inch of me sizzled with awareness, tuned to her proximity. Her lips parted. Just before I gave in and claimed her, I pressed a kiss to her cheek.

"I'm glad we're doing this," she said in a low voice once I pulled away.

I swallowed. Hard. "Me too." My body told a different story, pulsing with the heady, undeniable attraction I felt for her.

Once I parked behind Freddy's Bowling, I rounded the vehicle to open Dahlia's door. She laced her fingers through mine the instant her feet hit the ground before pulling me toward the entrance. The contact of our skin messed with all my restraints. Even my dick enjoyed the simple touch of her hand on mine.

We changed our shoes and got set.

Dahlia went first, and her ball landed in the gutter. She swirled to face me, a pink hue coloring her cheeks. "I should've told you I suck at bowling," she admitted.

I rose to my feet to join her as I grabbed a ball. "Why did you wanna play then?"

She shrugged. "Because it's fun."

I mirrored her smile. "Okay, you're the most fascinating woman I know. Hands down." No other woman I knew, or person, in fact, would have offered to play something they sucked at on a date.

Dahlia curtsied. "They say it's part of my charm."

My fingers brushed her elbow as I took her place on the alley. Fresh electrical sparks crackled where our skins touched. "I have to agree."

On her sixth turn, Dahlia sent the ball down the lane and knocked over eight pins. She pivoted on her feet, bouncing around, doing a little dance, glee pouring out from her, as if she'd just won the lottery.

Every inch of her seemed to glow with happiness, and I couldn't look away.

"Nick, this is no joke. I *must* bowl a spare. My bowling skills cred is on the line. I can't risk it." She joined her hands under her chin in some sort of prayer. "Will you help me?"

I pointed to my chest. "You want my help?" My eyes studied the scoreboard. "I'm not even that good, you sure?"

She bobbed her head several times in quick succession. "Yes. Please help me make this happen. I'll owe you."

Firming my shoulders, I grabbed her ball as the pinsetter rolled it back to us. "Okay, let's do this."

Behind Dahlia, time stopped as I helped her position herself. Her warmth radiated through me. "Keep your eyes on that little triangle over there. The one that points to the pins still standing."

She sidestepped to the right. "Like this?"

I nodded, my airways struggling to open correctly to let oxygen flow to my brain. "Yeah."

"Don't let go of me, okay?"

"Never," I said, my voice husky.

Dahlia sent her ball rolling but lost her footing. I circled my arms around her waist as she faced me, her hand splayed on my chest. As if everything froze around us, we stood like this for a long minute, breathing each other in, mesmerized.

I lost the fight in me and claimed her lips.

The softness of her mouth sent a shiver through my body.

Only, a kiss could never be enough to quench my thirst for this woman.

Her lips danced against mine in a well-rehearsed tango of lust. They injected me with a passion unwilling to be contained.

I was in no rush to let go of her, to step out of her world. Our heartbeats quickened, perfectly in sync.

This moment we shared cemented something deep inside me, and I knew I could surrender myself to Dahlia here and now, if I had to. But I wasn't ready to free-fall without a safety net, to surrender my heart to love utterly and without reserve, to dive in headfirst. *Heartfirst.*

Because even if I had healed in many ways over the last couple of months, I still had remaining layers of pain that had to be dealt with. And no way I'd ask Dahlia to tackle them along with me. They were my issues…my bruises…mine alone to fix and cope with.

Dahlia's mouth, glued to mine, made me believe I could do this, though. Give love a shot and overcome the last fragment of grief sprinkled on my journey.

A flashing sign on the mounted screen above the alley caught my eyes. I ignored it at first, but it flashed again, and my sight drifted in its direction.

"You did it," I whispered against her mouth.

"I…what?" She blinked, confusion swimming in her eyes. "Oh, the spare?"

I nodded.

"I did it?"

I nodded again.

The smile painting her face tugged at my heart. Still in my arms, she leaned back to check the scoreboard. "Nick, I did it," she exclaimed, her arms winding around my neck.

Without thinking, I lifted her off her feet and spun her around. When I lowered her, her front brushed down my chest, and we both sucked in a breath, the electricity from our kiss seconds ago waiting to ignite again.

"Thank you," Dahlia said, before stepping back and returning to her seat so I could play my turn.

My eyes drifted to her, and while she looked in the distance, her fingertip traced the length of her lips, as if to commit to memory the kiss that meant much more to—I was pretty sure—both of us.

Around a pitcher of beer, at the back of the bowling alley, we sat at a high table an hour later.

"To your spare," I said, raising my glass.

"To great teamwork," she replied. "How do you like Green Mountain so far?"

My eyes locked on hers, and I didn't blink when I said, "More than I thought I would. That's for sure."

Dahlia's adorable blush confirmed she was well aware of the meaning behind my words.

A train of yawns left her mouth as I pulled into her driveway a little later. "Thank you. For tonight," she said. "I would invite you to—" Another yawn escaped, cutting her words short.

I smoothed her lips with the pad of my thumb and rested it at the corner. "Go rest. I'll see you later."

She closed her eyes and nodded, covering another

yawn with her hand. "Who knew a day off could be so exhausting?"

"Catch up on sleep. We'll talk later."

She moved closer and kissed my cheek. "Thank you, Nick. For being so understanding."

My body trembled with an untamable ache.

I unbuckled my seat belt, but she stopped me by placing a palm on my forearm. "Don't. I can go in by myself." She opened her door. "I had fun tonight."

I nodded my agreement. "I had a great time too."

Just when she was about to shut the door, Dahlia turned around. "Hey, Nick. Tomorrow I'm working till four. Carter will drop Jack around that time. He's had a change of plans and is leaving town for one night. What if we come over to your place? I could help with the flowers."

"You don't have to," I said, hating the words as soon as they exited my mouth.

"I'm pretty good with garden stuff. Better than bowling. You and I already proved that we make a great team. And I also wanna see those beauties with my own eyes. For real this time."

"You sure?"

"Totally."

"Come over when you're ready. I'll text you the address."

"I'll bring dinner."

"I—"

Dahlia lifted a finger. "Shhh. I insist. We're friends, remember? And friends bring each other dinner all the time. It's no big deal."

"But you're already helping me—"

"Nick, you're helping me all the time."

She turned and walked to her front door, waving at me before closing it behind her.

For a long minute, I stayed in my truck, unable to move, my eyes transfixed on her house as lights blinked through the curtains on the first floor, then the second.

Feeling like a creep, I drove away.

"Bro, I hope none of this is a dream." I kissed my fingers and saluted the sky as I made my way inside my house, unable to chase the happy feeling wrapped tight around my heart.

Derek's Bucket List – ~~46. Nick. Feeling like my life is moving forward and I am floating~~

18

DAHLIA

At ten to four, Carter dropped Jack at the store just when I was about to lock. "I thought you were meeting me at my place," I said, rummaging through my purse for my keys.

Carter scratched his forehead with his thumb. "Yeah, but I thought surprising you would be better."

I lifted my son from his arms and nuzzled his neck. "I agree. Ohmygod, I've missed you, baby." I refocused on my friend. "I was closing early to get to you two faster."

Carter pulled me against him and kissed the top of my head. "I'm sorry about the change of plans, Dah. You know I always look forward to spending time with him."

I squeezed his hand. "Relax, Cart. It's only for a night. You're already doing much more for the both of us than anyone would in these circumstances."

"Thanks. It means a lot."

We exchanged more with our eyes than any word could.

"Have you two stayed out of trouble?" I asked.

Jack giggled in my arms. "*Cattter* plays ball."

"You guys played ball?"

My baby bobbed his head.

Carter offered a one-shoulder shrug. "I got a soccer ball. We moved the furniture around in the den, and I taught him how to kick."

"*Goooal*," Jack hollered, and we all laughed.

"Dah, you look happy," my friend said. "Spa day did you good?"

I swallowed before speaking, praying for Carter not to notice the warmth I felt rising in me. "It did." To avoid looking at him, I peppered kisses across Jack's chubby cheek. I wasn't in the mood for an open-hearted discussion with the man I loved in a million ways except for the one he longed for.

When I met his eyes, he watched me with interest, his hands stuffed in his pockets. "Dah, are you okay?"

"Yes. I'm great."

He frowned and shook his head. "If you say so."

"Come on, Cart. If I weren't, you'd be the first person I'd tell."

He sighed. "Fine." He stole the keys from my hand and locked the door after engaging the alarm. Then he held out his arms, and Jack jumped into them. "When I leave, I'll miss you guys. A lot. I hate going away for weeks." He ruffled my son's hair.

I snaked my arm through his. "Cart, we'll be all right. Don't worry about us. We'll be here when you come back."

His lips found my temple. "Promise you'll call if anything happens. I mean, anything."

I smiled because my best friend was the most generous and caring human being to ever walk the face of this Earth. "I will. I swear. You have one more day left with him, so we'll say our proper goodbyes later."

"I'll spend the night in Nashville and be back in the morning. How about I pick him up around nine?"

"Nine is perfect."

Carter walked us to my car, buckled Jack in his seat, and kissed my cheek.

"Be careful out on the road," I told him as I got behind the wheel.

"Always."

I drove away as he waved at me from the sidewalk.

A part of me disliked not telling him about our going to Nick's, but another part of me, the rational side, knew it wasn't a good idea. Not now, at least.

The short drive home didn't give me time to dwell on the *what-ifs* or spin scenarios in my mind, and I breathed a sigh of relief.

After I gathered the ingredients to cook dinner and packed a handful of Jack's necessities in my trunk, I left to meet with my new friend. The one I couldn't get off my mind.

My eyes found him before I even pulled into the drive-way. He had his back to me—his white T-shirt glued to his skin—water dripping from him. Even from a distance, I noticed his back muscles through the thin fabric. Nick was fighting with a hose, water spraying in every direction as he tried to turn it off, a broken valve in one hand. I couldn't move, my foot resting on the brake, as waves of heat rolled through my belly. My body hummed low with sensation, a throb gathering between my thighs, a longing I hadn't felt in ages.

Busy fighting a water snake, Nick was oblivious to me ogling him. I parked the car and lifted Jack in my arms. My heart hopped in my chest as I watched the man I was staring at remove his wet shirt. I gasped as he revealed his bare chest, and our eyes met. My free hand flew to my mouth, silencing the embarrassing sound tumbling out.

Nick offered me a mischievous smile as he used the drenched fabric to wipe his soaked face.

He flexed one arm, and I drank him in.

This was bad. Super, super bad.

I hadn't set eyes on another man in years, but now, I had no idea how not to. I had no idea how to look anywhere else.

In a hurry to look away from the orgasmic vision before me, I popped the trunk open and reached for the grocery bag. Nick sauntered in my direction, dripping wet, still shirtless. Apparently, he'd won the fight with the water hose.

Was my jaw hanging open? Just in case, I forced my mouth shut and gave him a tight-lipped smile.

"Here. Let me," he offered, lifting the bag from my arms.

I kept my lips pressed together, unsure what to say. I'd been caught staring at him like a kid entering a candy shop for the first time, and nothing I said could erase that. Sure, Nick looked delicious. *No, not delicious. Delectable. God, not delectable. Scrumptious. Mouth-watering. Good enough to eat. Ohmygod.* What was wrong with my brain? I must have been hungry. *Nick looked good. Yeah, good. Good shoulders. Good abs. Good…* My gaze screeched to a halt as I followed the hair down his… Was my face all hot and bothered now because my body was—in all the places that mattered?

Nick's raw, woodsy masculine smell hit me next.

Okay, this was beyond bad. I was a hormonal mess and a danger to any man lingering in my vicinity for too long.

Could he tell? I hoped not. Oh God, it would be so humiliating. I inhaled, forcing my uneasiness deep down.

Had I been so deprived of tasting a man… *No, not tast-*

ing, this had to stop. Come on, brain, work with me here. Had I been so deprived of being with a man—*yes, better*—for years that now I felt like giving myself to the first one I met? Damn it. The night would be unbearable if I didn't find a way to leash my attraction.

Nick offered me a reprieve as he turned to face Jack, still in my arms.

I blew out a quick breath, letting go of some of the tension coiled inside me.

"Hi, little guy. I'm Nick. It's good to finally meet you. What's your name?"

Jack, who had his face pressed into the crook of my neck since I took him out of his car seat, straightened his body and granted Nick his warmest smile. "Jack."

"Nice to meet you, Jack," Nick said, shaking my baby's hand.

How had he befriended my son in less than two minutes? Jack was usually shy around strangers and rarely responded to their questions.

Every time I noticed something new about this man, I always ended up pleasantly surprised.

"You two make yourself comfortable. I'll go change. Be right back. Don't move." He tapped the tip of my son's nose with a finger, and Jack giggled.

Even if I wanted to move, I couldn't. My feet had taken root in the ground, and the entire scene felt like a dream.

Say something, Dah. I parted my lips, but no words came out. Instead, I nodded, as if I'd lost the usage of my vocal cords in the last minute or so. And I used to sing for a living. *Real smooth, girl.* Jack squirmed in my arms, wriggling as he asked to be lowered.

Nick wrung out his shirt on the front porch, and my mouth watered as his defined arms bulged. Drops slid down the length of his spine, capturing my gaze. Trouble, trouble, trouble. Was gawking at a friend allowed? Probably not. I should revise the rulebook. And fast.

Bare-chested, Nick entered the house—finally—and I got a grip on myself.

"Mama, look," Jack said, commanding my full attention, pointing to the left side of the house.

In my mind, I thanked him for putting my hormonal mess to rest once and for all.

The sight of my boy dashing toward an old dog made me forget every shred of awe as I hurried after him. "Baby, wait. Don't go near the dog. It's—"

"The dog is old, supposedly half-deaf and half-blind. Don't worry," Nick stated as he exited the house, dressed in dry clothes, two beer bottles hanging from his fingers, his blond hair tousled. Even in casual clothes, he looked stunning.

He offered me a beer and I accepted it, thankful for the distraction and relishing the cold liquid as it slid down my dry throat.

Next, he joined my son and squatted to his level. "Jack, you wanna pet the dog?"

"Yes. Doggy. *Woof. Woof.*"

They exchanged a smile.

"Yes. *Woof. Woof,*" Nick echoed. "Now gimme your hand. We'll let him know you're here. His eyes are really old—"

"Old?" Jack asked with round eyes.

"Yes. They don't work very well, so he can't see you if you are too far back. We should get him glasses."

"No glasses. He's doggy."

"You think?"

Jack bobbed his head, and Nick grinned at him.

My heart exploded into a million molecules when the

man grabbed my baby's tiny hand in his and brought it in front of the dog for him to sniff. The old fellow licked it, and the sound of Jack's crystal-clear giggles filled me with so much love and happiness. And contentment.

"See? He loves you already. His name's Buddy."

"Buddy?" Jack repeated.

"Buddy. I think he'd like to be your friend."

"Buddy my friend."

"Yes." Nick nodded. "You two will get along great. I can feel it."

"Buddy my friend," my son recited with a happy grin on his face and a convinced nod.

Who was this man? Now even a toddler had fallen under his charm.

"Come with me," Nick continued. "We'll bring him fresh water."

As if they'd known each other for a long time, Jack and Nick ambled hand in hand toward the house in search of a bowl to take to Buddy, my son bouncing on his feet.

Frozen, I stood there, my eyes following them, my heart swelling in my chest with elation.

My son sat next to the dog, patting his head, and talking to him in a quiet voice when they returned. "You my friend, Buddy. You a dog. *Woof. Woof.* Wanna play?"

He wound his arms around the bloodhound's neck, and the old dog licked his cheek.

Nick joined me. "See? Best friends," he said, his arms crossed over his chest and a twinkle in his eyes.

"Is Buddy your dog?"

He shook his head and twitched his thumb toward the neighbor's house. The one we could barely see through the line of trees. "No. He lives next door, but for some reason, he adopted me the day I moved in and follows me around all the time." He ran a hand through his still-damp hair.

"Dahlia, listen. I've been meaning to be honest with you for a while. The thing is…huh…I lied to you on the day we met."

I angled my upper body to face him, keeping an eye on Jack.

My lungs seized. What was he talking about?

I held my breath when he spoke.

"I led you to believe you were my first friend in Green Mountain, but that title had already been claimed by Buddy. He came to me the moment I climbed out of my truck and sealed the deal."

A loud laugh exited my mouth. I wiped my eyes as tears built in them. "Oh, you serious? Whoa, I think I can forgive you for this little confusing information. Let's say I'm your first *human* friend then. I can probably live with that. Sure, I'm sad, but I'll get over it. In time." I held out my palm, and Nick shook it. A charged warmth traveled from him to me, heating my body and electrifying my core.

As if magnets controlled them, my eyes drifted to his lips, and flutters rose inside me.

Coming here tonight was a bad idea. I would never be able to act innocent because sooner rather than later, my body would betray me. I already could predict.

Just a handshake and I was about to dissolve into a puddle of lust at Nick's feet.

In a quick motion, I yanked my hand away, rubbing it against my thigh to remove the persistent tingling. "About those flowers…" I said, deflecting the attention away from our hands and the blazing connection we shared. There was no way Nick hadn't felt it too, but I said nothing because I wasn't ready to examine what it meant.

His gaze, appreciative and alive, twinkling and playful at the same time, scanned my face.

It stole some of the air destined for my brain.

I blinked, trying to ease the tension swirling inside me, faster and stronger than a tidal wave.

Nick's eyes darted away. "Huh… Sure. The flowers. I already prepped everything. All you have to do is work your magic, so it'll look fabulous. I've got more soil in the cargo bed of the truck just in case, and I've bought you garden tools and gloves. You know… So you don't get dirt under your nails, because it's a pain to clean out afterward. So…huh…I've got you a…well…a garden kit…to avoid those muddy fingernails."

He looked cute as he rambled about dirty fingernails. Why was I getting the feeling he was as nervous as I was? His cheeks reddened, and I enjoyed the effect I had on him in that moment.

"Thanks. That's really thoughtful of you." I squeezed his forearm and turned my head. "Jack, come with me, baby."

My son jumped to his feet and beckoned the dog to follow him.

Slowly, as if he had to gather his energy from a source deep inside him, the old bloodhound stood on all fours and walked toward me. They both sat down on the pebble-and-soil-covered ground, not a care in the world about getting dirty, the dog now resting his head in my child's lap.

With my phone, I snapped a picture. Without thinking further, I sent the adorable shot to Carter, who replied almost immediately.

CARTER

I'm framing this.

Wait. Who's the dog?

Is it safe to let Jack play with him?

Did you get a dog, Dah? You know he's old,
don't you? I only left an hour ago. When will
you have time to care for a pet? Are you
okay? Do you need me to call you?

I sighed and smiled to myself.

ME

Don't worry. The dog is harmless. Aren't
they cute together?

FYI, I didn't adopt a dog. I'm fine. It's just a
neighbor's old bloodhound. Stop worrying.
Love you and be safe. See you
tomorrow xx

CARTER

Good. Got scared for a minute.

Love you too. Kiss Jack for me.

Nick gave Jack a red pail and shovel he'd bought, and my son busied himself collecting soil under Buddy's watchful eye.

I put my phone away, and kneeling in front of the flower beds, I got to work, arranging them until they looked charming, as my nana would have said.

The next hour flew by. I forced my thoughts to stay on the task, refusing to let them wander.

With pride coursing through my veins, I stepped back to admire my work. Yeah, I hadn't lost my touch over the years. Not wanting to throw out the small crate of leftover flowers, I ventured near the garage, looking for a bright idea. Rummaging around, I found an old tire and rolled it to the side of the house. After I filled it with soil, I planted the remaining flowers, creating a DIY pot. With my hands on my hips, I smiled at the result.

Unable to resist any longer, my eyes found Nick, busy painting the door, and to Jack—Buddy by his side—piling pebbles. If only life could always be this simple. I hoped for nothing more. Peace, dreams, and love. And this. Quiet and family.

An air of sadness surrounded Nick, flashing in his eyes whenever he thought I wasn't looking. Though it lasted only a second, I was certain I hadn't imagined it. The other night, at the store opening, I had noticed it too but didn't make a big deal out of it. As if he sensed my gaze on him, he cocked his head in my direction and smiled, the stretch of his lips erasing all traces of his inner melancholy and doing weird things to my aching body as it shone on me.

I cleared my throat, trying to look unfazed. "Jack, baby, are you coming inside with me? I'm going to cook dinner." My son raised his eyes from his old friend to frown at me. "If it's okay with Nick to use his kitchen."

"No. No coming. Stay with Buddy, Mama. *Pleeeease.* Buddy my friend."

"I know, baby, but don't you think Buddy could use a nap? I'm sure he's very tired."

Again, he shook his head. "No. Buddy not tired. Buddy wanna play with me, Mama. Buddy not sleepy."

I huffed as I joined Nick on the front porch.

"Come on, Jack, we'll invite Buddy inside." He moved to face me. "No way I'm letting you cook dinner by yourself, Dahlia. You're the guest here."

"You sure?"

"About the dog or about you being a guest?" he asked in a teasing tone.

I slapped his arm, the same way I did with Carter, sucking in a breath at the familiarity of the gesture. Nick didn't seem to notice my uneasiness because he jumped from the porch to get Jack and Buddy.

"Come on, little guy. Let's go help your mommy out. Buddy will come with us, right, Bud?"

"Okay," my baby said, slipping his hand into Nick's as they walked together, the dog trailing behind them.

Settled in the living room, Jack and the dog lay on their fronts side by side. I brought the bag of toys I'd taken from home. "I'll be in the kitchen if you need me," I told my son as he picked up his figurines.

"Okay, Mama. Buddy snoring. Buddy funny."

"Everything all right?" Nick asked when I met him in the kitchen.

I nodded as he poured two glasses of wine, handing me one. "Everything's better than fine."

We clinked to our friendship, our eyes locked, each of us consumed by the other.

"Thanks for having us," I said.

"Thanks for being here," he replied, his whiskey irises swallowing me whole.

———

Nick and I worked side by side prepping dinner as if we'd been doing this every night.

"Look at them," Nick said, signaling to where Jack and the dog were playing in the living room. Jack used Buddy as a play mat, running toy cars over his back as he lay peacefully. "They clicked. Best friends at first sight. They remind me of two people who met recently…" He winked at me, and I melted a little more in his presence.

The words floated between us.

"Thanks," I said, breaking the silence.

Nick stopped chopping broccoli and studied me, his eyebrows knit together. "What for?"

"This," I said, gesturing to my son. "Jack's happy, so I'm happy." I rose to my tiptoes and planted a chaste kiss onto his cheek.

Our eyes found each other, and for a long minute, we said nothing. Jack came running toward us, and we snapped out of our spell.

Nick held out his hand. "Come with me, little guy. Let's go grab Buddy some food next door. I'm sure he's hungry, and he'd like to eat dinner with us."

With Jack's tiny hand wrapped around Nick's forefinger, they strolled outside. Nick had a soothing aura that Jack gravitated toward, and it mesmerized me. I cupped my chest with both hands as I watched them, blinking tears away. My heart expanded, so big it almost erupted from my chest. Yeah, I could get used to a life like this.

Once we finished dinner, Jack traipsed away, going back to the living room, with Buddy trailing behind.

"I'm screwed. Now he'll ask for a dog. You know that, right?"

Nick coughed a loud chuckle. "Which means I'll be seeing more of you two in the future, then." He sipped his wine, giving me a sorry-not-so-sorry shrug.

"In no time, you'll beg us to stay away. I doubt you're ready for a woman and a toddler to take over your bachelor life. Don't worry, we won't invade your space. I pretty much invited ourselves over tonight. That was rude. I'm really sorry—"

Nick's face fell. He shifted in his seat to stare at me. "You're always welcome here. Both of you. And you didn't invite yourself over. Nah, you came to my rescue after *I* asked you for *your* help. Also, you brought dinner. I'm the one in debt right now. I owe you. Whatever you ask, I'll be there."

His liquor-colored irises darkened, becoming a dark shade of brown. They descended and stopped on my mouth before moving back up to my eyes. My breathing halted. I saw stars, feeling lightheaded. What was going on with me? I tried to speak, but no coherent words came out.

My heart hiccupped in my chest, the wild rhythm making me excited. And scared.

Nick blinked and resumed talking as if nothing had happened.

But something had happened, right? Was I going crazy or hallucinating? I had no idea how to put into words—or even rational thought—what had passed between us. I shook my head to push the notions away, unable to define the waves of heat crashing through me.

"I'll go check on Jack," I said, standing up, trying to escape the heavy air surrounding us.

With his arms around Buddy, he had fallen asleep, spread on the old bloodhound, his head buried in his fur. A rush of emotion filled me at their sight.

"I'm officially in love with this dog. You should warn your neighbors I might have to kidnap him one of these days," I said as Nick joined me, nudging him in the ribs with my elbow.

"Please don't, or you won't have a reason to come over anymore."

His words stayed suspended in the air between us.

Something hot ignited deep in my core. Flames? Or was it a pure, raging fire, so powerful it could burn me alive?

I swallowed hard, glancing down to avoid Nick's piercing gaze and escape the moment. I failed. My eyes returned to him. We faced each other, neither of us saying a word. My heart inflated even bigger in my chest, and it did some dance I wasn't used to anymore. Nobody, except Carter, had looked at me with so much heat in years.

The back of my eyes burned at the intensity of our exchange. I tried to blink, but couldn't, fearing I'd miss something if I did.

Nick rubbed the back of his neck, his gaze steady on me, his attention unwavering. He erased part of the distance between us and reached for my hand, tracing circles over my palm with the tip of his finger. "Do you have to go?" he asked. "Maybe we could lie Jack on the couch or—"

"I'd like to stay. If it's okay with you." When did my voice become so throaty?

He grabbed a blanket, and we settled Jack on the sofa. I kissed his head and tucked him in. "Sleep tight, baby. I love you," I said, caressing his dark hair.

On wobbly legs, I followed Nick to the kitchen. We filled our wine glasses and moved to the den.

"I like this house," I said after taking the room in, once we sat on the cream loveseat. Large windows, a piano in a corner, and a second stone fireplace.

"You play?" Nick asked, pointing to the piano.

"Not really. I know a few songs, but it's not my instrument of choice."

I took a sip of wine to ease the dryness in my mouth.

"One day, I'd like to hear you play. Do you still sing?"

A soft chuckle left my mouth. "I do. Sometimes. Mostly to Jack."

"Don't you miss it? Playing in stadiums. The fans. The hype."

I folded my legs beneath me and shifted to face him, lost in thought for a second. "Yes and no… I miss parts of it. But mostly, I don't. Hard to explain. I love my life. What

I've built for Jack and me. I'm satisfied with what I have, and I don't need an extravagant lifestyle or loads of cash to be content."

"Jack looks like a happy kid. You did great," Nick said, sipping his drink.

"Thanks. It wasn't always easy, but we made it work… In our own way." I paused. "Do you think—?"

A loud thud resonated from the other room, cutting our discussion short.

"*Mammma?*" a trembling little voice, thick with tears, cried out from the living room, sending my heart racing.

19

NICHOLAS

A soft thud coming from the living room startled us. Dahlia and I exchanged a panicked gaze before leaping to our feet.

Buddy made a yapping sound.

"*Mammma?*" Jack cried. "*Mammammammaaaa.*"

We rushed to the other room.

Dahlia lifted her son, curled on the floor, and kissed his head. "What happened?"

"*Pouf.* Fell, Mama. Buddy caught me. Buddy my friend."

She hugged him to her chest, rocking him back and forth. "Yes, Buddy is your friend, baby. Let's go home and put you to bed, okay?"

Jack nodded, shiny tears filling his eyes. "Buddy come home?"

A small smile spread across Dahlia's lips. "No, baby. Buddy must go home too. He lives next door. And it's late."

Jack's lips trembled. "Buddy my friend. Buddy sleeps with me."

Dahlia rocked him some more, and the little boy's

eyelids fluttered until they closed."It's okay, baby. We'll come see Buddy another time."

She kneeled to put Jack's toys into the bag, but I grabbed her elbow and helped her up. "Let me. Please. Go buckle him into his car seat. I'll bring you your stuff."

Her eyes clouded, a myriad of green mesmerizing me. "I'm sorry, Nick."

I tipped her chin up with my finger. "Hey, it's okay. You're a mom. It should always be the top priority. Don't ever say you're sorry again for taking care of your baby, okay?"

She nodded, and I kissed her forehead.

Minutes later, we faced each other in the darkness, Jack now fast asleep in the car.

"Thank you for today. And tonight. And for dinner. And after dinner," I whispered.

Dahlia inched closer and looped her arms around my midriff, drawing a breath in. My arms locked around her, keeping her against my throbbing heart.

Her mouth slowly rose to mine, her lips tasting like wine and vanilla lip gloss. It didn't last long, but the gentle caress brought me down to my knees and was enough to rattle me to my core.

"Thanks for everything. And for entertaining my baby." She leaned back, a gleam in her eyes.

"Jack is awesome. You should be proud."

"I am," she said, her eyes on me. "Nick, I'm a mother. Sometimes, it makes things unpredictable." Her gaze drifted to her sleeping son through the car window, her irises overflowing with love. When she brought her attention back to me, tears pooled in them, and she blinked them away.

With both hands, I cradled her face until our gazes collided, for the umpteenth time tonight. "Hey, it doesn't have to be. We won't rush anything. I'll wait for you. Until you're ready. Let's just see where this is going first, okay?" She nodded as I kissed her tears away gently. "I'm here. Whenever you need me. I'm not going anywhere."

"Thanks, Nick."

I kissed her forehead one last time before she hauled herself into her car and drove away.

Minutes after Dahlia disappeared, I stood still, wondering if I was ready to put my heart out there, knowing it could be crushed in the process. Despite myself, tonight had changed things. Never would I have thought I'd get attached to people I hardly knew this fast. In ways that probably made no sense, Dahlia and Jack fit right into my life. Complicated or not, after today, no way could I let them walk out of my life without fighting for them. They had woken up a dormant part of my heart, one I thought had died after Derek passed away. A part that could still care deeply for someone, beyond what I thought possible.

Buddy trotted toward me and sat at my feet, butting my leg with his head.

I bent down and caressed his fur. "They are amazing, aren't they?" He pushed his head deeper into my palm. "Yep, I think so too. I'm happy you guys got along. Jack is a great kid. He reminds me of my friend I told you all about…a bundle of sunshine."

In silence, we watched the street where Dahlia had driven away, neither of us in a rush to get inside.

The night replayed in my head, and my lips curled at the memory.

Yes, Dahlia Ellis was special. And yes, something I couldn't quite define had simmered between us again tonight. Now I couldn't wait to see her again..

"Let's get you home, old pal," I said after a beat, strolling into the darkness.

. . .

Derek's Bucket List – ~~2. Make 1 new...no, 3 new best friends~~

———

Two nights later, I was hanging out at a bar with Dean and Willis, two guys from work. After we took seats side by side at the wooden counter, I ordered a pitcher of beer for us. Its dark oak finish, matching the floor and ceiling, gave the space a relaxed vibe. Off Main Street, it was the kind of place people flocked to on nights when there was a game on TV or to enjoy after-work happy hour.

A group of people played pool in the far corner, next to one of those vintage-looking jukeboxes. Country music wafted through the air, muffled by the chatter all around us. Two women, dressed in jeans and matching plaid shirts, practiced line dance moves, laughing as they gripped glasses filled to the brim with beer.

"Are the rumors true?" Dean asked, pouring the amber liquid into glasses after ordering a side of fried pickles.

I sipped my beer. "Which ones? Do you small-town people only feed on gossip? You know food is actually better for your health, right?"

Willis let out a loud chuckle. "Nah, it keeps things interesting."

I shook my head and sighed. "Bring it on. What's the new rumor this time? Last week, it was about my moving here to escape the Chicago mafia because people said it was the only viable reason I'd relocate to Green Mountain, Tennessee."

"Nah, you're good. Nothing to do with your affiliation

with the mafia or the Godfather this time. Rumor has it that you're hanging out with Miss Country."

I choked on my breath. "Miss Country?"

Willis offered me a pointed look. "Carter Hills's girl. Dahlia Ellis. Someone was at Freddy's Bowling a few nights ago and said you two looked cozy together. Also, my neighbor saw you hanging out with her at her store opening party. You should be careful, man. Carter Hills is known for his temper. I wouldn't dare to play with his toys. My cousin saw him punch a photographer once. Everyone in town knows Miss Country is Hills's property. Nobody in their right mind here would ever ask her out, except if they have a death wish. No wonder she's still single. So sad, the poor girl is quite a catch. Always smiling and being nice to everyone."

My glass hit the bar top with a loud thud. "Whoa, can you repeat that? I believe my hearing is messed up. C'mon, are you being serious right now?"

Both guys nodded.

"Only someone from out of town would risk dating her," Dean said. "If you value your life, keep it in your pants, Nick. Just sayin'. Take the advice…or don't."

I moved my hands up between us. "Geez. You guys are talking nonsense. This isn't the eighteenth century anymore. Women don't belong to men." Why did I feel like I had to defend Dahlia and Carter's relationship to these idiots who believed rumors instead of seeking the truth? I was sitting right here with them, so why didn't they just ask? "Dahlia and I are friends. True. That's all. Don't feel obligated to print it in the newspaper or tell the whole town. We enjoy each other's company. True. Last I checked, it wasn't a crime."

"Just saying, Nick. You should be careful. I—"

My phone chimed, and I welcomed the distraction.

DAHLIA

I was thinking… I'm home alone. Are you free?

No pressure. I just thought I should ask. In case you're alone too and are looking for something to do.

I blocked out Willis's and Dean's voices as they droned on about why I had to follow their advice while I typed back.

ME

I was having a drink with guys from work, but I'm done here.

What are you up to?

DAHLIA

Night in or night out?

After what the guys had just told me, the temptation to go out seemed like a perfect way to shut those gossip kings and queens up, but I decided against it. *Night in* it would be. I didn't feel like feeding the rumor mills. And like an egotistical jerk, I relished the idea of having Dahlia all to myself.

ME

Night in. Pick a movie. I'll take care of the rest. Be there in fifteen.

I fished a twenty out of my wallet and placed it in the middle of the counter. "Guys, gotta go." They waved at me, now busy watching a game on the TV mounted behind the bar. "Please stay away from the rumors." I winked and left, all that nonsense making me smile.

With a giant bag of popcorn in one hand and a six-pack of beer in the other, I rang Dahlia's doorbell.

Dressed in silver cotton pants and a long-sleeved white shirt, her face bare and her hair tied atop her head in that messy knot thingy women often wore, she looked mesmerizing when she let me in.

I leaned in to kiss her cheek after she took the snack from me, burning her scent into my memory and savoring the peaceful feeling it gave me.

"How was your day?" I asked, placing the crate of beer on the kitchen counter.

"Great."

I returned her enticing smile.

"How was your happy hour with the guys?"

I shrugged. "Okay, I guess."

My eyes traveled around the main floor of the house as I followed Dahlia across the family room, two bottles hanging from my fingers. White walls with Jack's art pieces framed on them, maple hardwood floors, a toy chest in a corner, and a play mat in the middle of the room. Every detail reminded me of Dahlia. Simple and elegant with a touch of warmth.

The house wasn't big, but it was decorated with care.

We entered the living room. It had high ceilings and a small fireplace with a screen mounted above it. The oversized L-shaped couch stretched across almost the entire opposite wall. A fluffy, colorful rug under the coffee table filled the space in between, its shades echoing those of the decorative pillows. A large window on the third wall offered a view of the side yard.

"I love what you've done with the place," I said.

"It was a model house when I bought it three years ago. I didn't have the energy or will to renovate an existing house or build a new one. It's home. I like it, but it misses the old farmhouse charm I have always pictured myself living in. There's not a lot of history between these walls. Only the ones we've created and it's okay, but I love old houses. Their walls can tell stories. Those that came before you lived in it and the others, long after you're gone." She shrugged. "This house is the first one I've bought on my own. It means something to me. It's our home for now, and I'm grateful for it, but I don't think it's my forever home. We'll see how it goes."

We sat side by side on the large couch, keeping a respectable distance between us.

"Why did you move here? You know, when it all went to shit. Why not stay close to your family?"

Dahlia grabbed the beer bottle I handed her after I twisted the cap off. "Carter and I used to play at Green Mountain Fest every fall when we were teenagers, and again, after we reached stardom. I've always felt at home here. There's something about this town that calls to me. It's bigger than me, and I can't explain it. When I left White Crest, it wasn't even an option not to come here. I love everything about Green Mountain. It's my place in this world. Somehow, I've always known it."

"Yeah. It's growing on me, and I've been here about three weeks. I spend way too much time looking at the mountains from my deck. The view is spectacular. And peaceful."

"You should see Carter's cabin. It's atop a mountain, about three miles from here. It's huge, and the view is magnificent. When he bought the lot, he offered me the chance to move up there, next to him. To build a cabin of my own. But I love it here, and I like my independence more than anything. He's a bit overprotective, so the distance is good."

I shifted my upper body to face her. "Can I ask you a personal question?"

Dahlia tucked her legs under her and turned to face me.

"Sure. As long as it's not *too* personal," she replied with a wink.

"Why aren't you two dating? I saw the way he looked at you the other night. You two have history…" *And people in town believe you belong together*, but that I wouldn't tell her. Not yet at least.

Dahlia's expression turned somber. She blinked, chasing away a memory or something. "It's hard to explain. Even Carter doesn't seem to get it most of the time."

She sighed, bringing her beer to her mouth and taking a big gulp, my eyes transfixed by the sight of her lips closing around the bottle's neck.

"I love Cart. With everything I have. And I know I always will… He's been my person for as long as I can remember…but not in a romantic kind of way. At fifteen, I thought for a moment I was in love with him. Until I fell for Jeff. Hard. Then I knew what I felt for Carter was a different kind of love, one that was more like brotherly." She shrugged. "He and I aren't meant to be together this way. Carter loves me—I know he does—but I'm not the one for him, and I hope one day he'll finally understand and see what I've been telling him for years. That life will prove to him that he has a special someone who isn't me."

I studied her as she said those words.

No, Dahlia wasn't in love with Carter Hills, but my gut wasn't wrong when I assumed he was madly in love with her. How could any guy in his right mind not fall under her charm? It wasn't even about the fame. She genuinely cared for the people she loved. I witnessed it at her store opening every time she interacted with her friends…and even with strangers. Dahlia Ellis possessed a pure soul that drew people in.

She pressed play on the TV remote, and halfway through the movie, she scooted closer, sinking her body into mine, as if she belonged there, by my side. As if she required my warmth and my closeness. It felt like the most natural thing in the world. She and I, spending time together, our bodies molded to each other.

The credits rolled across the screen, and she tilted her head to stare at me, my arm still draped over her shoulder. My heart flipped in my chest. I wasn't ready for us to break apart. Her lips enticed me. Again. I had no idea how to be indifferent to anything related to Dahlia Ellis.

"Wanna go for a walk?" she asked.

"Sure. But there's no streetlight. It might be a bit dark outside."

Her face lit up with mischief and a hint of adventure. "Nope. I have everything we need. Follow me." Seconds later, she fetched two headlamps from a drawer.

"You serious?"

She bobbed her head, like Jack did so many times the other night. "Come on, it'll be fun."

With drinks in hand and our flashlights on, we strolled down the street. Dahlia slid her free palm into mine, and with our fingers intertwined, she gave me a tour of her neighborhood.

"Do you miss Chicago?"

"Honest answer?"

"Always."

"No. I believed I would. I've never thought small towns were my thing, but you were right about the mountain air. It's addictive. I can see myself living here full time. Ask me again in six months, though. But I'm pretty certain my answer will be the same. People here take the time to just be. To live and be happy. It's refreshing."

She pressed her head to my shoulder. "Glad to hear it. If you didn't like Green Mountain, you'd break my heart. Big time."

"Don't worry. It's the last thing I wanna do."

She pulled me onto a rocky path between two lines of trees. It was pitch black there, moonlight not reaching us in this tunnel of branches.

"Where are we going?" I whispered. "If you're going to kill me, you can do it here. I think we're far enough from civilization."

"C'mon, it will be worth it. I forgot my ax, so your life is safe. For now."

I helped her over a low fence made of old birch trees, and we remained suspended in time as I held her in my arms, my hands clutching her hipbones. Her floral scent spiraled into me, both of us panting as if we'd just run a dozen miles.

When I released her, Dahlia smoothed her shirt with her fingers and glanced down until her breathing evened. "Let's go. We're almost there."

"Never in a million years did I think I'd end up trespassing on private property with the famous Dahlia Ellis. Not even in my wildest dreams."

She grimaced and punched my arm. "Shut up, we're not trespassing. I know the owners. Mr. and Mrs. McLoughlin. See, I know their names. Jack and I always come here."

"In the dark, with a toddler, sweet move."

Dahlia poked me in the ribcage. "Stop messing with me. You'll see it's worth getting caught." She lowered her voice. "Even if they chase us with a rifle."

"A rifle? People use them around here? I thought it was only in movies."

"Guess we'd better not find out."

We walked through high grass for two minutes before stopping in front of a dark barn. I couldn't make out the color of the siding in the darkness, even with my headlamp on.

Dahlia let go of my hand and slid the doors open, gesturing for me to follow her. Once inside, she flipped a switch, and a soft glow cast shadows on the walls. A strong odor from the stable hit my nose, wiping away every trace of her perfume. I scrunched up my nose, adjusting to the scent, a mix of sweet hay, sun-warmed wood, and the unmistakable musk of horses and earth.

Once my eyes got used to the low light, I perused all around me, taking in every detail of this place: open rafters soaring thirty feet above, wood-paneled walls, and a haystack tucked in one corner. Three horses—one white and two brown—in separate stalls. Dahlia neared the biggest one, brown with a black stripe going from its muzzle to its crest.

"Nick, this is George Maloney," she said, petting the horse between his eyes.

"Like the actor?"

She nodded. "Come closer. Let him sniff you."

"Hey, buddy," I said, the horse butting my hand. "You like that?"

"Jack and I visit these fellows at least once a week. It's so calm in here. Brownies," she said, pointing to the smaller brown horse, "is Lady Baba's pony. She had him four years ago after Mr. and Mrs. McLoughlin rescued her from a pony farm. George isn't his dad, but he adopted Brownies as his own. They are one big happy family now." Dahlia grabbed my hand in hers. "Come."

She climbed a wooden ladder that led to a mezzanine on one side of the barn. I followed close behind, not wanting to risk her falling if she lost her footing. We sat on stacks of hay covered with a tarp when Dahlia produced a guitar from somewhere behind us.

"You keep it here?"

She smiled, the sight warming my heart like wildfire. "Something Stud used to do when he was a kid. He had it rough and kept a guitar in an old barn, music giving him the courage to keep dreaming. I loved the idea. One night, not long after I moved to town, we wandered together and stumbled upon this place. He told me that whenever I felt sad, I should come here and play. Sing my sadness and heartbreak away." She lifted one shoulder into a shrug. "When Jack is with Cart and I feel alone, this is my go-to spot. My special place where I follow my friend's advice. Somehow it works. Also, the horses downstairs are a great crowd."

I scooted over on the makeshift bench, clearing my throat. "Dahlia, would you sing for me?" I asked as she settled between my legs, her fingers strumming the chords while she adjusted the tuning keys.

"What do you want me to sing?"

With my eyes closed, I inhaled a cleansing breath, my body thrumming at her proximity. My voice sounded huskier as I spoke the words out. "The song that speaks to you the most."

**Oh, oh, oooh, you walked into
the room
And suddenly I couldn't
breathe
You looked at me with
those eyes**

And suddenly nothing existed
but you
You took my hand in yours
And suddenly my entire world
became you

Dahlia had the most beautiful voice, raw and clear, soft and strong. All my hair stood on end as she sang one of Carter Hills Band ballads, one that was barely ever heard on the radio. One I didn't know the lyrics to.

I leaned back on my straight arms, every word from her mouth powerful enough to shake my very soul.

You and me, that's how the
story should be
You and me, forever it will be
Oh baby, you and me, forever
it will be

Dahlia strummed the last chord, my heart vibrating in the same rhythm.

"Wow. I'm speechless. Wow. That was beautiful. You have an amazing voice." I pushed her hair over her shoulder, in a movement way too personal for two friends, my lips shuddering to connect with the skin of her nape. Shivers crept along Dahlia's spine as my hands landed on her hips. I felt the tremors as they traveled through me too.

All my senses were attuned to this woman.

Dahlia leaned back into my arms, her back pressed against my chest, and I fought the overwhelming urge to pull her tighter against me.

"I haven't sung to anyone but Jack in three years," she said, breaking the silence, the words floating between us. "You're the first one."

"Thanks. I'm flattered."

A heartfelt laugh bubbled out. "You should be. I gave you a private concert. It counts for something…a seal on our friendship."

"Thanks for giving me a sneak peek into your world. It means a lot to me."

Dahlia began to say something but stopped. She turned in my arms, folding her legs before her, pressing them against my chest. "I've never brought Carter here. He doesn't know about this place…"

I quirked a brow. "He doesn't?"

She shook her head.

"Why?"

"I…I don't know. It just never came up. All my life, I've shared everything with him. Except this. Only you and Stud know."

I felt like puffing my chest out as pride traveled through my bloodstream.

Dahlia grinned. "I told you it would be worth it."

My throat tightened with emotion. The setting was perfect. I would've spent the night here, in this barn, with her nestled against me—far from everyone and everything —if she'd only asked. Just the two of us, savoring the moment until dawn, uninterrupted.

My lips descended to hers, stealing a kiss. My body agreed, every fiber of me responding to her closeness. I brushed her hair back with my fingers and mirrored her grin when we pulled away. "I'm glad you opened up to me. Your secret spot is safe with me. For the record, I'd never try to upstage you because I can't sing for shit."

Dahlia's clear laughter filled the space around us. "It can't be that bad."

She spun until her back pressed against my chest again, and this time I locked my arms around her, holding her tight as her head rested in the bend of my neck.

"Can I ask you a favor? Something personal to me?"

She nodded.

"Can you sing 'Monkey Business' for me?"

She angled her head and watched me with furrowed brows. "You like that song?"

"It means something to me."

From the corner of her eye, Dahlia studied me for a beat, as if she could read the thoughts I didn't speak out loud. As if she was communicating with my soul, leaving me out of the exchange.

Once she seemed satisfied with whatever she saw, she settled back against me, her back pressed to my chest. Picking up her guitar, she strummed a few strings and began to sing.

> **...I thought there was a hippo**
> **in your closet**
> **A monkey hidden under**
> **your bed**
> **I thought I saw a lion in your**
> **kitchen**
> **And a snake hanging from the**
> **chandelier**
> **Because that's what your love**
> **does to me, baby**
> **You turn my world**
> **upside down**
> **My imagination runs wild**
> **I can become a pirate, a ghost**
> **hunter, or even an**
> **astronaut**
> **There's nothing I can't do**

**No, nothing I can't do
As long as you're beside me...**

As Dahlia plucked her guitar and crooned the funny lyrics that made Derek laugh so many times in the past, I mouthed them from behind her, wishing once again this night would never end, my heart so big in my chest, it could barely be contained.

Derek's Bucket List – ~~*47. Nick. Being speechless (in a good way)*~~

20

DAHLIA

Nick's hands stayed anchored to my waist as I sang the lyrics of a song I hadn't performed in a while. The whole time, I had to force myself to focus on the music, feeling dizzy from just being close to him. Everything that made him who he was seemed to hang in the air between us. I could tell there was a deep sadness inside him. I recognized the signs. I felt his pain. The shadow in his eyes, the way his arms tightened around me. After the song ended, I relaxed into him, and his arms stayed around my waist like he was afraid I'd disappear. I could feel his steady heartbeat against my back. Something had happened to him. Had he been through something life-changing, like I had when I lost Jeff while pregnant with Jack?

I had a hunch life put him on my path for a reason bigger than just us.

Something in me felt right in his presence as if I was meant to be a part of his life and he, of mine. This moment together, this air we breathed, it felt right too.

My heart had loved before and had splintered with

agonizing pain. From then on, I'd lived only for Jack—and Carter. Because while I cared for those I loved the most, I forgot about my own suffering and the fissures scarring my heart. It took me years to start living for me again and to give room in my life to the happiness I deserved too. To enjoy each breath of fresh air filling my lungs. In a way, I could see the same struggle in Nick. The tug of war between dwelling in grief or living life to the fullest.

We stayed in the moment for a long time, his thumb grazing my abdomen with distracted caresses. Against his firm chest, my body relaxed and my mind calmed.

Our silence connected us, enveloping us in an oyster of peace. Whatever tomorrow brought, today was meant to be. I turned my head to look at him, his smile reaching the innermost end of my heart.

Something I'd been wanting to talk to him for a while but wanted the moment to present itself. Butterflies woke up in my chest. With a deep inhale, I looked straight ahead and whispered, "Remember the day we met? You told me about your friend who died…" I paused.

Nick's hold on me stiffened.

"I just wanted to say… I-I understand. Some aches in this world seem like they have the power to break us in two, yet we must stay strong. I've been there. So, if you ever wanna talk about it, you don't ever have to, but if you did want to, then I'm here. One call and I would leave everything to be with you. Even if you didn't want to speak, but just wanted me to be there to share your silence. I am here, okay? I know how it feels…and how destructive grief can be…"

The strokes of his fingers stilled at my words.

I placed my hands gently over his, waiting out his grief, his arms locked around me as the emotion poured through the space between us. I stayed silent. The air tautened with tension, then captured its prisoners. Nick sighed and allowed me in his sacred orb, listening to his unsaid words as my mind swam in the memories of the trauma of my husband's sudden death that shook me to the core.

In a hushed tone, I explained, "When Jeff died, I withdrew into myself for months, unwilling to accept anybody else's support. Once I did, though, it helped with the grief. With the emotional overload. I'm extending the offer. Paying it forward."

For a beat, I let the words sink in.

Moving closer, Nick rested his forehead in the crook of my neck.

I pinched my lips together, willing my own emotions to slacken their grip around my heart. I hadn't revisited the struggle of Jeff's death in a long time.

Nick splayed his hands across my stomach, his warm palms shooting their heat through me, as he held me closer. With me in his arms and these shared emotions binding us stronger, we stayed silent, grieving our past experiences together.

For the longest time—I didn't know how long—we stayed like this. Time had no meaning. It just moved around us, helping us heal.

Nick pressed a gentle kiss to the nape of my neck, and the fear prickling my insides, the idea I had overstepped, died. He understood and had accepted everything I was without question.

With a deep breath in, I pulled away from him and whirled around.

With my fingertips, I pushed tendrils of his hair away from his forehead, taking in the sliver of pain in his eyes and acceptance tinting his features.

I held his face in my hands, tracing his scruffy jaw with my thumbs. "Don't lock it all inside when it gets to be too much. Promise me you'll find someone to share it, okay? Even if it's with your silence."

His eyes slowly met mine, and I saw the relief my words brought. His chest expanded with a deep intake of air, and he nodded.

Little by little, I watched his pain melt away, his expression softening under my touch.

When our gazes joined again, something shone in his whiskey-dark irises. "Thanks, Dahlia…for, huh…for everything."

He closed his eyes, pressing his lips to my forehead, lingering for a long minute as if our touch alone could soothe his bruised heart.

21

NICHOLAS

That song. Every word Dahlia sang pressed hot tears behind my eyes, threatening to spill. And somehow, every lyric also stitched up pieces of my heart I hadn't realized were still bleeding.

One moment, I could barely breathe. The next, my lips curled faintly, warmth spilling through my chest and settling deep in my core.

The song Derek had loved so much now felt like it was meant for me. Every chord, every line, carried something sacred. Like a message meant for my ears alone. Like her voice, low and steady, held the power to reach inside and fix what had long been broken. My heart. My soul. And every bit of me.

She set the guitar down, then tucked herself against me like she belonged there. In that instant, I knew that I didn't want to let go. Didn't want to take another breath without her in my arms.

Something I couldn't name, stronger than anything I'd ever known, wrapped around us. Pulled us closer. It wove our past and present together—the ache of old wounds, the quiet knowing in our souls—all blending into a single moment that felt a lot like healing.

Dahlia Ellis and I shared more than our eyes could see and than our hearts could define. We'd both lost ourselves to grief. In different ways, but similar at the same time. Neither of us had woken up on the other end unchanged.

The smile she offered me, from over her shoulder, filled me with a mix of joy and hope. Hope that whatever remnants of sorrow lingered in my heart, everything would eventually make sense again. That I would outgrow my feelings of helplessness, which still haunted me every now and then.

My journey since leaving home had brought me a new sense of peace. Even if none of it erased the memory of the night I pressed that button, I now believed it had set Derek free—that he was grateful, watching over me, guiding me toward the life I deserved. A life that would truly fulfill me.

Dahlia brought her attention to our joined hands and whispered, "Remember the day we met? You told me about your friend who died…"

The atmosphere surrounding us strained, and I struggled with my breathing.

Her words went straight to my heart. Every one of them.

She trusted me enough to open up completely, telling me her story without holding anything back. She talked about her grief. I wanted to say something in return, to show her I understood, that everything she said hit home for me, but the words wouldn't come. They stayed stuck, buried deep in a place I couldn't reach.

A rush of emotion blindsided me, squeezing my chest and dragging up every painful memory I had of Derek and what I did—and what it had cost me, not in money, but mentally. I was the one left living with the memory of unplugging his ventilator that night. In a way, I would be haunted by that instant forever, even if it lasted only a microsecond.

Dahlia rested her hands on mine, and the simple gesture eased the throbbing inside me. Strength shot through me, filling me with the certainty that I would be okay. My hands stayed on her stomach, drawn to her, absorbing every particle of courage radiating from her. My forehead pressed into the curve of her neck, where I felt safe. And accepted. Our souls fused in the quiet, sitting together, comforting each other, healing together.

Still, my words refused to pass my lips.

Sensing my reluctance, the woman—whom I was now certain could change my life and whom I hadn't met by chance—twisted in my embrace. She combed strands of my hair with her fingertips, her eyes confirming what her words promised: a safe haven. Understanding and compassion. The sincerity in her gaze eased my angst, and the upward tilt of her lips in the low light of the barn became my sole focus.

All I craved in that moment was to kiss her. To tell her she was right, that everything she said hadn't been in vain. Her words had done more for me than any therapy ever could. Without even knowing it, just being with her was enough to seal the remaining cracks in my heart.

"Thanks," I murmured. Just one word.

I pulled her closer, first pressing my lips to her forehead before slowly descending them to hers, taking everything she offered and promising to give everything back.

Serenity found me. And I wished it'd stay with me forever.

Derek's Bucket List — ~~48. Nick. Having a soul-connecting experience~~

22

NICHOLAS

I t had been four days since Dahlia and I had seen each other—not since that intimate night in the barn. Between being a mom to Jack, the store opening, and time with her friends—Stud and Belinda were still in town—she'd been too busy to see me. The memory of the night we shared kept me going. Days later, I still clung to her words.

Determined to show Mike how much of an asset I could be to the company, I threw myself into work, and I was pretty satisfied with how the construction was coming together so far.

My boss called me as I unclasped the tool belt around my hips and was about to call it a day.

"Nick, still on site?"

"Leaving now. Why?"

"You're aware you can leave when everyone else does, right?"

"I know, but I like to set the next day before going home."

"Speaking of home, on your way there, could you stop by Main Street? We've got a service call, and you're the only one still on the clock."

"Yep, no problem. It's on my way. What is it about?"

"A front door requiring some adjustment. It shouldn't take you long."

"No problem, boss. Text me the address."

"I'm very impressed by your work dedication, son. Tucker was right. I'm glad you're here. Keep up the good work. You and I will do great things together."

Mike's words reached my heart. I blew a silent breath, doing a little victory dance in my head.

Yes, I fit right in.

I parked my truck in the spot facing Dahlia's Bridal Shop, waiting for Mike's instructions. In the meantime, I hoped to catch a glimpse of her. Four days without seeing her had felt like an eternity after that amazing night we'd shared. I was about to call Mike when Dahlia appeared on the sidewalk, her curled hair draped over one shoulder, catching the low sunlight.

She spotted me, and a wide smile spread across her lips. She gestured for me to join her, and I waved back, hopping out of my truck, light on my feet.

"You're here," she said as if she'd been waiting for me.

"Yeah. Doing a service call and waiting for instructions from Mike."

Dahlia's lips stretched wider. "I know. *I am* your service call."

"You are?" I asked with a tipped brow.

"Yes. I can't lock the store because the front door is giving me trouble. A delivery guy bumped into it earlier with a buggy, and now it won't close properly."

"You know you didn't have to place an official request

for me to check the door, right? I would've done it on my own time if you'd asked."

She grinned. "I know, but it's more thrilling this way. With you coming to my rescue without knowing it. I asked Mike to send you but didn't want him to tell you it was me who made the call. I figured I needed to see your hands-on skills before helping you renovate the interiors of your house."

I neared her, erasing the gap between us until we breathed the same air.

Tension rose between us. Electric.

Dahlia's eyes sharpened with interest.

My voice sounded rough. "You're right. You haven't experienced any of my manual talents so far, Dahlia."

Her face turned crimson.

"Red looks good on you, by the way. I've wanted to tell you since the day we met."

She brought both hands to her face. "Nick Peterson, you're doing this to me on purpose. That whiskey voice of yours isn't helping."

"Whiskey voice?"

"Yeah. It ripples. Like when you have too much liquor to drink. It's husky and gives me goose bumps every time you speak. Like whiskey, it's pretty strong."

"Oh, my voice has an effect on you? Now that I'm aware of it, I'll have to tease you all the time."

"Stop or I won't tell you the proposition I have for you after we're done here."

"Dahlia Ellis, you want to proposition me? I like the sound of it." She pushed against my chest with both hands, her grin disarming as I continued, "Let's look at that door while you tell me all about your devious plans for tonight."

I got to work, and she watched me, looking as beautiful as ever, her purple top making her green eyes pop. My body vibrated at her frequencies. Standing so close to that woman was driving me crazy. In the best ways possible. But also in the most frustrating ways, since I'd told her we'd take our time.

"Here's the proposition. Would you like to have dinner with Belle and Stud tonight? It's their last night in town. They're leaving tomorrow."

I caught her gaze. "Oh. So, you want me to entertain your friends?"

She let out a warm laugh. "Oh God, you're not going to make this easy on me." She grimaced, and I laughed too. "We're meeting at six at a pub in town." She paused and drew in a breath. "Nick, would you be my date tonight?"

She glanced at me with a mix of heat and nervousness, chewing her bottom lip.

My tone lost its playfulness. "Dahlia, I'd like nothing more than to be your date for tonight. Any night, in fact." *Just ask and I'll come running.* Yeah, I had become that guy.

She jumped into my arms and threw her arms around my neck. "Great. Stud has been texting me all day, begging me to invite you."

"Oh, so I'll be more like *his* date then? Because *he's* the one who wants me there."

She shook her head, her lips still tilted up. "No. You're coming with *me*. Stud is just annoying me because he likes to. And…huh…he likes you too. You'll be *my* date, no one else's. For your information, I wanted to invite you face to face, which is why I didn't say anything sooner."

We stared into each other's eyes, neither of us daring to break the moment. Our faces were inches apart, and I held my breath.

Dahlia's chest rose and fell against mine. Her words were so soft-spoken I almost didn't hear them. "It will be fun."

My ribcage felt like it was about to burst, my wild heart threatening to explode in a cascade of fireworks.

The idea of a double date hit me like a cold shower. A one-on-one date would have been a better fit, because Dahlia's presence heightened every sense I had, and I could barely contain it. Somehow, I feared the dam would rupture at any moment, exposing my desire.

Every spot where our bodies touched burned, as if she were the gasoline my body needed to ignite.

In the privacy of her bridal shop, I yearned to kiss her, and so much more. To take her, and make her mine. To throw caution to my stupid, reasonable principles and lose control for once. To let go and enjoy the ride. See where it would take me…take us. A voice in my head kept telling me to be patient, to wait for the right time. When it would make perfect sense to break every rule I forced myself to follow and finally release the suffocating need to contain my passion.

I parted my lips, fighting with myself to stay in control. "Yes," was all I said.

"You okay?" Dahlia asked, her voice low, careful. "You look like you're in pain."

"I…am…" I swallowed the uneasiness clawing at my throat, trying—and failing—to hide how my body reacted to her.

Her brows drew together, concern softening her expression as she stepped closer.

I didn't move. I just couldn't.

I was too afraid she'd pull away.

And even more afraid she wouldn't.

Derek's Bucket List – ~~49. Nick. Share something with someone I cared about that can't be described with words~~

23

DAHLIA

The four of us sat at a round table in the middle of the pub. The booth's blood-red leather back curved up high enough to block us from the rest of the patrons, giving us a bit of privacy.

Stud had ordered a bottle of champagne and after the server poured each of us a glass, my ex-bandmate lifted his. "To Dahlia and her great new venture, and to Nick, who I'm happy to call a friend. Man, we have a lot more in common than just our shared love of woodworking. Cheers."

Nick bowed his head, and Stud exchanged a quick glance with his wife, sharing a smile.

"Thanks for being here," I said to my friends. "We don't see each other often enough. Next time, you gotta bring Tristan along." Belinda—or Belle as we all called her—and Stud had a boy a little younger than Jack, who'd stayed back in Oregon with his grandparents.

We all drank to that.

The whole time, my eyes stayed fixed on the man sitting next to me. The firm line of his jaw. His tousled blond hair. When he laughed, the amber of his eyes glinted. My heart skipped a beat each time his fingers skimmed mine over the table. He slipped his arm over the backrest behind me, and as if it were the most natural thing in the world, he pressed a gentle kiss to my lips. Not earth-shattering, but enough to make my breath catch and send jolts of desire and happiness coursing through me. I let myself sink into the familiarity of his touch—and the woodsy scent of him.

In that instant, I felt at home. Exactly where I should be. Exactly where I belonged.

Tonight, like so many times before, it felt as if Nick had always been there—woven into the fabric of my life without me ever realizing it—but waiting for the right moment to walk in and wake that part of me I believed had been quelled years ago. That spark in me I thought had vanished when my heart had gone missing. The one that now begged to express itself, to shine, and conquer the world. Nick's world.

"Okay, one of these days, you'll have to come visit us," Stud said.

Lost in the contemplation of my date, I had missed most of their conversation.

"Our property has a few acres, and we'd like to add a B&B. Right now, I'm building a new barn because my little woodworking business is really taking off, and soon I'll be running out of space."

"Man, we were destined to meet," Nick said, bumping his fist with his.

"If you ever go into business, you and I are gonna have a talk. Right now, my brain is running at full speed," Stud continued. "I see a future here."

"The day I decide what I'm going to do, you'll be the first to get the memo," Nick added.

They clinked their glasses.

Belinda watched me, amusement dancing in her irises, and shrugged.

I knew the meaning of every twitch of her lips and every twinkle in her eyes. In the time we'd traveled the world together, she had become a sister to me, but also a confidante and a friend.

Don't let him go, she mouthed my way.

I knew it. Since the shop's pre-opening celebration, she had become a Nick fan too.

I'm serious, Dahlia. Hold on to him. He's good for you, she continued.

I sipped my drink, etching the moment into my memory, hiding my flaming cheeks behind the rim of my glass. *I will*, I mouthed back.

The blood rushing to my face burned even hotter now, as I made the commitment in front of my friend.

Five hours later, Nick drove me home. I didn't want the night to end. We sat for a few minutes in comfortable silence, engine idling, my head resting on his shoulder, his arm stretched across the center console to pull me close.

"Thanks for inviting me tonight. I had a blast. Stud and Belle are great. If Tucker were here, he and Stud would be a terrible match. It would be a very tiring night."

"Yeah, Stud is pretty intense. He has energy for days. He just never stops. No pause button. But he's a true artist. Everything he touches turns to gold. And on top of that, he's the sweetest guy. Now I can't wait to meet *your* friends and learn interesting things about you too. I'm sure they have great Nick Peterson life stories to share."

Whoever that Tucker guy was, I bet he'd have a lot to say about Nick's antics over the years. Was I moving too fast? I'd kind of blurted out a not-so-subtle request to meet his friends…without really meaning to say it out loud. The last thing I wanted was to freak him out or make him think I was rushing things instead of letting us take our time.

For a short moment, I looked away, breathless, my pulse beating at the realization. First Belinda. Now, this. I swallowed. Nick had made it clear we needed to take things slow and get to know each other first, and I had agreed. I just couldn't seem to remember that with him sitting beside me, so close it short-circuited my common sense.

"How's the house renovation project going?" I asked, steering the conversation toward safer ground. Less personal. Much better.

"Good. So far, I've focused most of my energy on the exterior. The haunted-house vibe is fading, one wall at a time. Soon it'll look sharp. The interior doesn't need nearly as much work."

"Sorry I haven't had much time to help you out…been pretty busy. Tonight was nice, though. A well-earned rest after the whirlwind of the past few days."

He let his fingers glide up my arm, stopping at my shoulder where a tight, stiff spot made me wince. "Tensed?"

I rotated my head and rolled my shoulders to loosen up. "Yeah, I guess I am."

"Turn around."

Nick shifted closer and placed his hands on my upper back. My body responded instinctively, relaxing under his touch. With skilled hands, he worked out the tension, using his thumbs to knead the knots from my back.

"Oh, Nick… Wow. It's even better than what that woman at the spa did the other day. Yes, right there." I moaned, unable to hold the sound in. My whole body seemed to sing beneath his palms. "Keep going." I purred and dissolved under his soothing touch. Nick kneaded my flesh, moving his fingers down the length of my arms and along my back. "Where did you learn this?" I asked. "No way you're this good by accident."

He snickered from behind me, and I savored the intimate closeness between us in the truck's cab. "My mom is a massage therapist...or used to be. She trained my sister and me at a young age. It's been years since I offered someone a massage, though."

I turned my head and grinned at him. "I feel like a VIP. Thank you. Do you also offer foot massage? I'm a sucker for those."

Nick laughed with me, the baritone sound clear and contagious."Yeah, my magic touch also goes to feet." He paused. "And other places..."

My cells tingled at his words. I could've tilted my head and locked lips with him, but refrained, lost in the pleasure he brought me, and in our promise not to rush things. Because right now, if I gave in, nothing would hold me back—not until we reached the edge and free-fell, together, into whatever came next.

Nick's hands continued their wonder, grounding me to the present.

I gasped every time he loosened a knot.

He trailed his hands down my arms, stopping on my thighs. This could be it—the moment we'd combust together. I could throw caution to the wind and give in to whatever was brewing between us.

Air barely reached my brain as a flood of sensations surged through me. It had been years since a man had touched me this way.

My head spun in a rush of dizzy heat. The flutters his touch had sparked the other day now surged, pulsing in a steady rhythm low in my belly. A single spark could blow the entire truck to pieces.

Nick moved his palms to my hips, kneading the tender flesh there with his thumbs.

Could I climax just from a massage?

I heard his breath hitch behind me, sharp and shuddering.

We were playing a game neither of us seemed able to step away from.

"Dahlia."

Ohmygod. My name rolled off his tongue, slow and deliberate, sending shivers down my spine. His mouth traced the curve of my nape, and I saw stars.

I hadn't been touched, or loved, by a man in so long. It felt like I was seeing the sun after a few years of hibernation, and I savored the feeling. I wanted more. No, scratch that. I needed more.

I twisted in my seat, ready to set aside all our pseudo-friendship rules and give in to what my body, mind, and soul craved most when a ringtone broke the lust-filled silence.

Nick groaned, and the throaty sound only heightened the desire coursing through my bloodstream. I wished to hear it again, but with our bodies entangled, and blissfully satisfied. God, keeping those thoughts—the images I'd painted in my mind—at bay grew harder with every passing second. I felt bereft when his hands left my body to grab the phone and decline the call. Why were we always interrupted? Panting, I watched his face over my shoulder as he scowled at the device.

The phone rang again.

"Tuck," he muttered, his eyes shooting daggers at the flashing screen.

The interruption—unwelcome, but maybe necessary—diffused the storm raging inside me. Within minutes, the air in the cab felt normal again, and I sank back against the seat.

My voice dropped to a whisper. "I have to get inside. I told the babysitter I wouldn't come home too late."

The man who could so easily steal my heart nodded as I traced the shape of his mouth with the pad of my thumb. My breath sizzled as his tongue darted out to lick the tip. "Yes. We'll talk later, okay?"

We intertwined our fingers, and I had to summon superhuman effort to let go as longing rose inside me, swelling and refusing to be tamed. Now that Nick Peterson was a part of my life and held an important place in it, I found myself savoring the way we existed together. Every hour with him strengthened our bond, yet I had no way to explain the effortless chemistry between us.

I ran my fingers through my hair after I closed the front door behind me and pressed my back against the panel, begging my heart to quiet its violent thrum.

What had just happened?

24

DAHLIA

The next few days went by quickly. I was so busy with everything that I barely had any time to myself. I hadn't seen Nick since that night we went out with Stud and Belinda almost a week ago.

We texted a few times, exchanging *hellos* and *good nights*, but with both of us so busy, it lacked its usual warmth. Ever since that night at the barn and our double date, things between us had shifted from good to something truly amazing. Our bond felt stronger and deeper. Nick had become a huge part of my life in a short period of time, and if I was being honest with myself, after days without seeing him, I kind of missed him.

Each time we talked, a smile lingered on my lips for hours afterward. The man had a way of teasing me, challenging me, and caring for me all at the same time, and I relished the feeling.

"Dah, you've been talking about Nick for the last ten minutes. You should call him or pay him a visit. Are the sparks between you still there?" Addison asked as we video chatted once I'd put Jack to bed.

I grinned like an idiot. "Yes. And they've only intensified with each time we spend together."

"Then don't let him walk away."

"The other night when we had dinner with Stud and Belle, it was…huh…it was… I'm not sure I possess the right words to explain it."

"Try anyway."

"When we're together, it feels as if we've always been like this. Dahlia and Nick going out with friends. Easy. Simple. Matter-of-factly. During dinner, he kissed me like it was the normal thing to do… It's like we've known each other a long time."

Addison's voice turned high-pitched, and she clapped her hands in joyous enthusiasm—just like a kid. "Okay, I hear you. It's perfect. You didn't scare him away by bringing up his grief the other night or by suggesting he talk about it. And I'm pretty sure your near-orgasm during that massage only turned him on. Either he needs time to deal with everything going on in his life, or with whatever he left behind, or he's just busy with work. Don't wait. What you two could have is precious. Priceless. Fight for what you deserve, girlfriend. What are you waiting for? Call him already."

"I know we're both fairly occupied and stuff, but what if he's changed his mind?"

"What do you mean?" my friend asked. "You told me yourself that you almost came the last time you were together, when his hands traveled all over you."

"I did." Oh God, if I shut my eyes, I could relive that instant with great details. "But he's the one who insisted we take our time. Maybe he could tell I was on the verge of giving in, and he's not ready for that yet."

"Don't be silly. If it's not his work, the only logical explanation is that he got spooked because you brought up his late friend the other night. Guys aren't exactly known for talking about their emotions. Not all of them are Carter Hills. He's one of a kind."

The words lingered between us. Addison once had a serious crush on Carter, but since he didn't reciprocate her feelings, it never went anywhere. Sometimes she still wondered what might have been. She admitted it one night after a bad breakup, when she came over to vent and talk shit about her ex.

"Back to Nick.Give him time. Maybe he needs to work through some emotional stuff…on his own. Anyway, grow some balls, girlfriend. If your words opened his wound, use them to help heal it. Be brave. Be fearless. Be the friend you promised to be—the one he can share his sorrow with, even without words. You're Dahlia Ellis. You've been through much more than this. Woman up. Take the lead. Take action."

"Ever thought about leading group therapy sessions?" We both chuckled until I spoke again. "Addi, I know you're right. I'm just not sure what I should do. Or rather, how to do this."

"Dah, I'm just thinking out loud here. Do you think the whole "star thing" could have scared him? Like, you used to be super famous, and maybe that intimidates him. You said he and Carter didn't click… Perhaps he finally decided it's a bigger deal than he realized."

I sighed. "Nah. If it were the case, it would have happened sooner, no? Why now?" I nibbled my thumbnail. "No, it can't be that. We were good, I swear. After the night I brought up his late friend, we went on that double date, and the sexual tension between us was undeniable. But now, he's sending short texts and is suddenly too busy to spend time with me…" I sighed again. "Nothing makes sense."

"Ask him. Plain and simple. Or take a page out of my Wilde's playbook and do something crazy. Go to his place, kiss him—you're both being too reasonable by sticking to that friendship rule, by the way—and show him what he's missing. Use that sexual energy you've both been basking in to rock his world. He'll thank you. I know I would."

I snickered. "Yeah. This is the perfect recipe for disaster. I'm not sure I remember how to flirt…or be upfront. The night at the shop pre-opening, I kissed him first, and…he…he recoiled."

"Forget it. He explained why. You two have spent a lot of time together since, and you kissed many times. Go to him. Set the record straight."

"Why are you always my voice of reason? You're right. I should. I will. Tomorrow."

"See? Easy peasy. Keep me updated. I'm rooting for you."

I giggled. "You better."

I moved to my bedroom and unclasped the chain around my neck. The one that held my wedding ring.

"What are you doing?" Addison asked as I stored the ring into a box after pressing it to my lips.

"Moving on. It's about time. Jeff lives in here," I said, pointing to my heart.

"You sure?"

I nodded. "Yes." I blew out a long breath. "It feels right. It's time…to let go. If I wanna move forward, I have to put the past to rest."

"Dah, I'm proud of you. You're amazing. Nick is a lucky man. Don't worry, okay? Things will work out between you guys. I can feel it."

"I love you. Night, Addi."

"Love you too. Night, girlfriend."

In the upstairs bathroom, I undressed and slipped into

a hot bath with a glass of red wine in hand. Country music played on a small speaker set on the countertop as I sealed my lids, my thoughts drifting to Nick—for the thousandth time today. He'd been center stage in most of my dreams since the day we met, taking up way too many of my brainwaves during the day.

Addison was right. Our friendship was too precious to let it go to waste and not explore it further.

As I sank into my thoughts, the sound of the doorbell startled me. In one swift movement, I dried off and wrapped a towel around myself. Who could it be at this late hour? The only person who ever stepped onto my front porch, day or night, was Carter, but he wasn't in town, so I really had no clue who it could be.

Hurrying down the stairs, I rushed to the front door. The man on the other side looked nothing like Carter Hills. Blond hair, broad shoulders, tanned skin.

Nick stood there, his head hanging low, kicking the deck with the sole of his shoe, still in his work clothes—a white T-shirt, a dark plaid vest, dirty jeans, and tan boots —looking hot and messy, his stubble longer than usual.

"Hey," I said, folding my arms over my chest, remembering I wore nothing but a towel. A smile tugged at my lips at the sight of him.

"Dahlia, I'm sorry for coming here so late." He paused. "I-I just wanted to apologize, and…huh…it couldn't wait."

"You are? Why?"

He shook his head. "I ghosted you, but I didn't mean to. It has nothing to do with you, and everything to do with me. The last week has been crazy, but now I was afraid you'd think you did something wrong, which is far from the truth. I shouldn't have come here at this late hour, but I wanted to explain."

"Did you just leave work?" Or had direct access to my

naughty thoughts? Because seeing Nicholas Peterson dressed in construction attire was something my eyes would never get enough of. He looked effortlessly masculine, hot, and focused, like he'd just stepped straight out of a fantasy.

A black smudge grazed his upper brow, and several more marked the front of his white T-shirt, which clung to his toned abdomen.

His tousled hair gave him that boyish-manly look I loved so much.

I ogled him with no shame as his irises, two golden gems, scanned the length of me.

I blinked, breaking our silent flirtation.

Nick gave a single nod. "I pulled a lot of overtime this week. An unplanned project landed in my hands, and I wanted to get ahead. I was used to working much longer shifts in Chicago, so adjusting to the shorter schedule here has been tough. Anyway, someone asked for my help—"

"Wanna come in? I can warm something up for you… or huh…make you a sandwich. If you haven't eaten yet. In a past life, I was crowned the Sandwich Queen. That's how good they are, I'm telling you. You won't want to miss one."

His lips curled at the corners, and the sight sent bursts of longing through me. "It's tempting, but I'm not staying. It's late, and you must be tired. I just wanted to clear the air. Friendship is sacred to me, and I'm never letting my friends down. Oh, and I brought you something."

He handed me a small, square cardboard pastry box.

"What is it?" I asked. "I love surprises."

"Every night this past week, I've been working at that cookie shop that's opening next weekend. The owner gave me this as a thank you. I thought you and Jack would like it. There are frog and rabbit-shaped cookies in there. Oh, and they're organizing a kid's cookie decorating workshop in a couple of weeks. Maybe Jack would like to go. Just in case, I booked him a spot—"

My eyes rounded. "You did?"

"Yeah. It lasts about twenty minutes, and he'll get to decorate a bunch of cookies with frosting and eat them afterward. I thought it could be fun. The lady told me even a toddler would love it."

I blinked. "You brought us cookies and booked my son a workshop?"

"Oh shit. Is he allowed to eat sugary treats? I didn't think about asking first."

I grabbed his hand between mine. "Yes, he is. Just not every day. Anyway, that's very sweet of you. Now come in, you must be starving. I'll feed you." I winked, and he snickered with a shake of his head. "For the record, I'm not taking no for an answer. Also, I could use the company because I've missed my friend this week."

After I changed into a pair of lounge pants and a seafoam-green cotton long-sleeved T-shirt, Nick and I sat on the opposite sides of the table, and I watched him engulfing his sandwich. No. Attacking his food would be a better word.

"This is amazing," he said with a mouthful.

"For how long have you been underfed?" I teased.

"Nah. I'm not. Just haven't eaten all day. Too busy."

A smear of mustard clung to the corner of his lips, catching my attention.

"You have—" I pointed to his face.

A soft blush colored his cheeks. "I what?"

On my feet, I neared him, and using the pad of my finger, I wiped away the yellow blot, then brought the coated finger to my lips.

Time stood still.

The air froze between us, around us, enveloping us.

A warm tide rose from somewhere deep inside me.

I swayed, leaning on the table to stay upright.

I couldn't find the right words to explain the swarm of butterflies in my stomach, each bigger and more beautiful than the other. They multiplied at a vertiginous speed, and I had to blink to break the trance I'd fallen into.

Nick swallowed, and it soon cast another spell on me. One I wished to never escape.

The heat radiating from his muscular frame stirred something deep within me. With a deep inhale, my eyes fluttered closed as one of his hands molded around my nape while the other rested on my hipbone. My body drank in his masculine scent, and my soul basked in his glow.

Every touch of him branded my skin through our clothes.

My thundering heart pounded in my skull, its rhythm dizzying.

I closed my hand around his elbows, my anchors to stay grounded in this world.

Nick skimmed my forehead with his warm lips, and a new tide, now flooded with raw lust, surged within me.

A small gasp left my mouth when his lips trailed to the side of my cheek and lingered there for a long moment.

My head spun as Nick's grip on me tightened, and I reminded myself to breathe.

Caressing the shell of my ear, his rough voice sent shivers through my heart. "Thanks for dinner. Again, I'm sorry I've been distant. Never again. I've missed you too much."

If only I could hold on to him like this forever. Through the storms and the fun times. Through darkness and complete illumination.

A long exhale escaped his mouth, and his shoulders

slouched slightly as he stepped back, breaking the moment. He gathered the empty glass and plate and loaded the dishwasher while I stood there, still entranced by everything he was.

After a while, he came back and pressed his forehead to mine. "Are you gonna be okay?" he asked, the whiskey-deep tone of his voice, diffusing shivers through me.

I nodded.

"Good." Why did the word sound so painful coming from his mouth? As if he hoped I'd plead for his help, his presence, his care, so he wouldn't have to leave.

He lowered his head and pressed a kiss to my cheek—so soft, that tremors shook me. And so intoxicating, I believed for a moment I was drunk.

Nick stepped back, my hand nestled in his. "Night, Dahlia."

He flashed me a hint of a smile, and my heart kindled.

I blinked again, and he was gone. The door clicked behind him, taking a piece of my heart in its wake.

Air returned to my lungs, oxygen made its way to my brain, and I regained control of my body. I blew out a long breath, wondering if I'd dreamed the entire scene. My hand flew to my cheek. The whisper of his kiss was all he left behind, the sole reminder of him.

———

The next day, I surveyed the business I'd created from scratch. Gowns made by local and foreign designers, prom dresses, bridal attires, accessories like shoes, purses, tiaras. Dahlia's Bridal Shop had something for everyone. Including a kid's section with smaller versions of high-fashion labels. It even carried an exclusive line of bridal wear by a coveted designer from Milan, along with a more affordable collection bearing my name that I co-designed.

As the owner, I spent a lot of time dealing with orders and numbers. Even though I enjoyed the business side of things, I also loved meeting with women and helping them choose the most beautiful gown for their perfect day—making their princess dreams feel within reach.

The shop was busier than I'd ever expected, which forced me to hire another employee. I couldn't keep working ten-hour shifts seven days a week. Jack spent most weekdays with Paula, but his nights and most weekends were mine. No matter what, that wouldn't change.

Truthfully, I could have chosen never to work another day in my life. My future was already secure. But I still had dreams—I still wanted to reach for them—and this bridal shop sat at the very top of the list.

Right after finding love again.

And maybe having another child.

Someday…one day.

Anyway, being a retiree in my early twenties didn't suit me. Not at all.

Today, I came home early, wanting to spend some quality time with my baby.

"Jack's still asleep, Ms. Ellis," Paula said as I dropped my purse on the kitchen island.

"Thank you, Paula, and please call me Dahlia."She nodded, but I knew she wouldn't—just like the fifty times before I'd asked her. "You can go home. I'll take it from here."

She left, and after I changed into a pair of cotton shorts and a hoodie, I climbed into Jack's bed, molded my body to his, closed my eyes, and let exhaustion lull me to sleep by his side.

We woke up from our nap two hours later, rested.

"Nick came over last night and brought you something. Hungry for a cookie?" I asked my baby boy as we sat on the back deck, watching squirrels jumping from trees, basking in the final hour of daylight.

"Yay," he screamed, hopping all around me. "Cookies. Cookies. Love cookies. Mama, gimme."

After fishing the pastry box out of the kitchen, I joined him back outside and lifted the lid.

"Oh," Jack said. "Frogs. *Boing. Boing.*" He paused to imitate the animal. "*Boing. Boing.*"

I watched my son, his adorable grin in full bloom, clapping his hands as he reached for a green-frosted sugar treat.

He licked his lips, and I couldn't hide my smile.

"Good?" I asked.

He nodded, gulping down the last bite, his fingertips green with frosting.

Unable to resist, I tasted one too. "Ohmygod, you're right. Wow, these are delicious."

"*Deciliticious*," he repeated, scooting over to settle on my lap.

With my palm, I ruffled his thick hair and kissed the top of his head.

Soon he squirmed out of my embrace and dashed toward the slide, sending the squirrels scattering as he ran after them.

Left alone, my thoughts drifted back to Nick and how much I missed him. Last night had been nothing but a tease, making me yearn for him even more.

Jack called my name, and I joined him, scooping him up in my arms and tickling him while he laughed his heart out.

On the swing, with my arms wrapped around him, I

rocked my son back and forth as an idea popped into my head.

25

NICHOLAS

I got home early, ready to paint another wall of the house. The sun sparkled in the azure sky, not a cloud in sight. I stood atop a ladder with a paintbrush in hand, letting the warm mountain breeze brush my face. Country music—something I'd come to really like, thanks to a certain redhead I couldn't get out of my head—played from a portable speaker I'd set on the banister below. I hummed softly, lost in my task when Chaz joined me, Buddy trailing behind him.

"Hey, guys," I greeted. "Bud, I thought you weren't coming today," I added with a smile.

The bloodhound made a noise that sounded like a sigh and huddled in a quiet corner beneath his favorite tree.

Both Chaz and I exchanged a laugh and a shrug.

I leaned back to admire my work. The top of the wall looked fierce with a fresh coat of white paint.

"From down here, it looks pretty great. Need a hand?" the teen asked, approaching the base of the ladder where I was still perched.

"Are you skilled with a paintbrush?"

"Huh…not sure, but I'm afraid of heights. Please don't ask me to come up there with you."

I let out a warm chuckle. "Not a chance. You can paint the windowsills if you wanna give it a try. It's pretty straightforward. I already sanded them the other day. Grab a can of paint and a brush from the back of my truck, and you'll be all set."

In no time, Chaz got to work. After an hour of painting in silence, he asked, "Do you miss Chicago?"

"Everybody in this town has been asking me that question." I smiled with a shake of my head. "The truth is, I don't. Which, to be honest, surprised me at first. I love how simple life is around here. The absence of traffic is a huge plus. People here are happy, and friendly. I'm still not used to the rumor mills, but other than that, I get why people would want to move to Green Mountain and raise a family." I climbed down the ladder, shifted it to the right, and climbed back up. "Have you been to Columbus yet?"

"No," the teen said. "My parents and I are going soon, so I can get to know the city and everything before the big day. We'll go to—"

My phone rang.

I reached for my back pocket, only to realize I'd left it on the banister."Chaz, can you get that?"

"Sure." A pause. "Hi, this is Nick's phone." Pause. "No, I'm his neighbor." Pause. "Yes." A longer pause. "No."

I snickered. By the sound of the interrogation going on, I'd bet Tucker was on the other end of the line.

"Nick," Chaz said, "this guy named Tucker says it's an emergency." He held my phone above his head.

With a huff, I climbed down and snatched it from his grasp. "Hey, Tuck, what's up?"

"Man," he said, "where have you been? I've been

texting and calling you nonstop like a clingy girlfriend, and you never reply or call back."

"Sorry," I said, wiping my stained hands on my jeans. "Been busy. Working overtime and all that stuff."

"Yeah, yeah. We almost never talk anymore since you moved. I'm beginning to think you prefer the company of a dog to mine." He sighed, and I was pretty sure he rolled his eyes too. Tucker was always aiming for the drama.

"Seriously, you should leave the finance world and go straight to Hollywood. You'd be a much better actor. And knowing you're the best at your job, it's saying something. What's the emergency?"

"None. Just a marketing strategy to make sure you wouldn't avoid my call this time."

"Huh…okay, but I'm in the middle of something, and you're being paranoid."

"No, there is actually something. How is it going with that girl you told me about? Still in the friend-zone or did you score a goal like pussy-whipped Jace would say?"

Why did I open my mouth about Dahlia to him of all people? "Yep, we're friends. For now."

From the cooler on the ground, I fetched a bottle of water, uncapped it, and took a long swig.

"What does that even mean? You get sucked on the side, or you tap that pussy only on the weekends? Unless you jerk yourself off to oblivion every night. Do you fix roof leaks in Green Mountain too? I bet your services are in high demand. Uncle Mike could start a new department."

Water spilled from my mouth as I burst out laughing. "Fuck, Tuck. No roof leaks. And don't drag Mike into your kink. No need to brand these images into my head. C'mon, man." I shook my head and wiped my dripping chin with the back of my hand. "For what it's worth, and I can't believe I'm actually laying out the facts for you, our relationship is not like that. Why am I even trying to explain myself?"

Beside me, Chaz faked to be fascinated by his phone screen, but he was clearly listening to our conversation, judging by the grin on his face.

Tucker continued as if I hadn't said a word. "Nick, you're confusing me. Why no sex? This is fucked-up. Are you sure you're okay?"

"Tuck, I'm great. Never been better."

Chaz mouthed, *I gotta get going*, when my eyes landed on him.

I moved the phone away from my face. "Thanks for your help. See you around."

The teen waved and disappeared behind the line of trees.

Buddy raised his head to watch him leave, but didn't make the slightest move to follow him home.

I exhaled a chuckle. This dog.

"Neighbor?" my friend asked once I brought my attention back to him.

"Yep. Was helping me paint the house." I sat on one of the front porch steps, elbows resting on my bent knees. "To answer your question, that woman and I are friends, but I'd like us to be more. Eventually. When we're both ready to give it a real shot. I don't want us to be a fling. She's long-term commitment material, man, not a woman you fuck and forget all about. She's special."

"Shit. So, she's out of my league then."

I spit a laugh. "Forget it. She's too good for you. They all are. I have to go, not done with the wall yet."

"Call me later."

"Sure thing. Please stay out of trouble."

Tucker's deep laughter filled the line before we hung up.

Soon my thoughts drifted to Dahlia. As if she'd read my mind, she sent me a text message followed by a picture of her and Jack eating cookies.

> **DAHLIA**
>
> You should have at least kept one. These are amazing. Can I join the kid's workshop? I'd do anything for cookies.

My stare locked on their happy grins as my thumbs typed.

> **ME**
>
> You like cookies? My bad, I pictured you more as a joystick kinda woman.

> **DAHLIA**
>
> Dear God. You're the worst.

> **ME**
>
> You make it too easy for me. Anyway, you've got green frosting at the corner of your mouth. If you were here, I'd take care of it.

I pressed *send*, savoring the flirting we always indulged in. Since the night at the barn and the double date happened, I wasn't convinced we could stay just friends for much longer.

> **DAHLIA**
>
> Wish you were here with us.
>
> Can we talk tonight?

> **ME**
>
> Wine and midnight talk? Sounds good.

I pictured her laughing with her head tilted back.

———

At eight fifty-seven, my phone went off. Not that I had been checking the time. Okay, fine, I had. My pulse raced when Dahlia's name flashed on the screen. A warm flush hit me. Great, now I felt like a teenager on a first date.

I scratched the column of my throat before answering and smoothed my T-shirt as if Dahlia could see me. "Hey you," I said the moment I accepted the call.

"Hey, Nick. Free for our chat and wine?" she asked, her voice low, with a hint of a smile.

"I wouldn't miss it for the world. Since I don't have the honor of picking you up for our date, I have a few questions for you first."

"Go ahead. Hit me."

My lips curled. "It's just one, in fact. What are you wearing?" I asked, slouching on the couch with my feet resting on the square ottoman.

Dahlia's sharp intake of breath resonated through the phone, followed by a low chuckle. "It's not really sexy, but it's comfy. Cartoon PJ pants and a T-shirt Jack painted for Mother's Day. It's a modern-style piece of art with blue as the dominant color. Very fancy and unique. Every designer's dream."

"You should frame it. Could be worth a fortune someday." My phone pinged, and a photo of Dahlia, gorgeous with her hair loose and rosy cheeks, her wineglass in hand, and wearing that piece of clothing, filled the screen. "Yeah, I agree, definitely museum material. Jack is awesome."

"He is. Being pregnant at twenty was a surprise, but in the end, it was for the best. He's the greatest thing that has ever happened to me. As if life knew I'd need him to keep living. Now your turn to send me a picture. You've seen my outfit. Let me see yours."

I pointed the camera of my phone at me and smiled. Okay, I looked stupid. I ran a hand over my face and tried again. It took me about five poses to get a good enough result.

"You know, I've never done this before," I said.

"What? Being charming over the phone?"

I sipped my wine, shaking my head. "No. Sending a selfie to someone… Well, not exactly… I mean sending a selfie to a woman."

"So, I'm your first?"

"You are."

"Oh, I like the sound of that," Dahlia teased.

And, for some stupid reason, it made me proud. At that moment, I missed being able to touch her. To kiss her. To hold her.

"Please don't judge me if I didn't nail it. I might need a couple more tries." I lowered my voice. "Or a private lesson."

"Nick, stop. You're perfect." Her gravelly voice turned my insides to mush. "Nice shirt, by the way. You're a solid nine out of ten. Don't let it go to your head."

"God, you're a tough one to please. Dully noted. You subtracted a point. Why?"

"The lighting. There's a shadow on your left side.

Other than that, it would have been a perfect shot. I'll still keep it, though."

Dahlia's laughter lit up a thousand fires inside me.

"I had no idea you were also a photography critic. Is there something you can't do?" I asked, taking another sip.

"A million things. But you'll have to stick around to find out."

My playfulness faded, my tone turning serious, every cell in my body vibrating. "I can't wait to learn about them. I'm sure you're being too hard on yourself."

"We'll see. And just to be clear, you'll be allowed to grade me too." Silence stretched between us. "Nick, I just wanted say…thank you."

"For what?"

"For being you."

My heart swelled and pushed against my ribs as her words streamed through me.

"Thank you for being you too. Walking into your shop by mistake that day is the best thing that's happened to me since I got here." I breathed in some air and a hefty dose of courage. "Can I tell you something?"

Her voice became a throaty whisper. "Yes."

"I wish I could see you right now."

Was she panting? "Open your video chat. I wanna see you too."

"Hey," I said when her face filled my screen.

Dahlia was sitting on her bed, holding her phone in one hand and her wine glass in the other. How much would I give right now to be able to kiss her? Just another kiss to relive the ones we'd shared and feel her warmth against my chest. And get lost in her green irises. Trace the curls of her hair between my fingers. Touch her. Hold her. Fuck her.

Uncomfortable on the couch, I moved to my bed, my

phone resting against my folded legs, my glass in one hand and the other cupping my junk, the tightness in my crotch becoming unbearable.

"Do you believe in soul mates?" Dahlia asked, breaking the painful threads of my thoughts.

"Sure. I believe we're all destined to be with someone for a reason nobody can explain. A force greater than us placing people on our road for a purpose. Why?"

"Because I've been asking myself this question a lot lately. Can someone have more than one soul mate in life? Don't answer…it's silly."

I searched her gaze through the small rectangular screen. "Dahlia, it's not silly. If I were in your shoes, I'm sure I'd be asking myself the same question. I love when you're offering me a window to your thoughts…and to your soul."

I'd trade everything just to hug her right now and chase away the doubts shining in her eyes.

Silence fell between us, both of us lost in our own minds for a moment.

"What's your favorite travel destination?" I asked, trying to get rid of the heaviness enveloping us.

"Why?" Dahlia furrowed her brows, and I traced them on the screen with a fingertip, as if I could smooth them out from here.

"Because. I think people's tiniest preferences tell a lot about them."

"New Zealand. Favorite food?"

"Chicken wings."

"Sweet or spicy?"

"Spiciest, the best," I said. "Favorite season?"

"Spring. I love how everything wakes up. Favorite sport?"

"If I'm playing, baseball. If I'm watching, hockey. Your middle name?"

"Elisabeth. I love this game. Yours?"

"Jake."

Dahlia's eyes flared. "Nah, you don't look like a Jake. I much prefer Nicholas."

The sound of my name—my full name—leaving her lips sent shivers up my spine to the very tip. Nobody except my mother—and strangers—called me this, and it had never sounded as sexy as coming from Dahlia's mouth.

"Nick, thanks for doing this with me. Talking, sharing, laughing. Being a mother, sometimes it…it scares people away."

I set my empty glass on the nightstand and turned to my side, my phone propped up against a pillow and one arm folded under my head. "It would take a lot more than that to chase me away, Dahlia. I think it's amazing that you're a mom. I'd never see this as something negative. It's part of who you are. Part of what makes you, *you*. What makes you amazing."

A faint blush colored her cheeks. "I have no idea where you come from, Nick Peterson—"

"Chicago," I whispered while she grinned.

"Now that I know you, if you didn't exist, I would have to invent you. I'm kind of a fan."

The way the last word left her mouth with that southern drawl broke me in the most delicious way. All I craved now was to drive up to her place and kiss her senseless until neither of us could breathe on our own anymore. And to do nasty things to her. I remembered the taste of her lips, and every night, I prayed to taste them again and devour all of her right after.

"So, you're telling me I have my own fan club now?"

"And I'm the president. I'm not crazy, I swear," she said, using the words we exchanged the day we met.

"First, don't get ahead of yourself. I'm sure there are things about me that would drive you nuts."

Dahlia chuckled. "I doubt it. I've learned a long time ago that people are complex individuals with many layers, but the truth lies within their hearts. That's where you gotta aim. In your case, your heart is pure gold. I'm a good judge of character. Don't try to sell yourself short." She stared at me, her tongue tracing her lower lip. "Tell me something annoying about you. I'll tell you if it's *that* bad." She arched a brow, challenging me with her eyes.

Damn, I loved how her power over me made me confess all my sins to her.

"I hate lies. My temper usually flares up when people tell me half-truths or lie right to my face. I also hate when things get chaotic. It drives me insane, and I withdraw into myself until I straighten them up."

"If those are your flaws, then we're good." Dahlia yawned, and I followed suit.

"You tired?" I looked at the time. "Whoa, it's already past midnight. Where did the time go?"

"A little, but I don't wanna hang up. I like our late-night talk. It feels like I know you better…or in a more intimate kind of way." With my finger, I traced her lips on the screen. "I enjoy being your friend tonight."

"Anytime."

Dahlia's voice grew warm and steady. "After Jeff passed away, I've made it my mission to end each day by telling the people I care about how important they are to me." Her eyes turned glossy in the dim light. "It's something I have to do… I-I never got a chance to tell him those words or to hear them from him one last time…"

My throat worked. A truckload of emotions knotted

around my stomach and rattled my heart. "I know what you mean. Been there too." I pinched my lips together, holding back my emotional overload before it could spill over. The last time I went to see Derek, he slept the entire few hours I was there, and I never got a chance to tell him one last time how important he had been to me. "I'm glad we found each other." Through the screen, we gazed at each other for a long moment before I spoke the words lingering on the tip of my tongue. "Dahlia Ellis, you're passionate and strong. And fearless in your convictions. Your energy is soothing. I'm sure everyone around you feels loved."

She locked her eyes on mine. "Nick, there's something about you… A vulnerability. I'm not sure what it is, but it's there. I sense it." She paused. "Not a lot of people reflect the wisdom you possess. It's a great quality. You left everything you'd ever known behind to start afresh. That's very brave of you. You should be proud of yourself for being strong when you could have been weak."

"Guess we both ran away when things got too tough."

She shrugged. "You and I, we both had two choices. Stay and be miserable and haunted by our past, or leave, rise from the ashes, and wish for something new. Something better. We're very much alike."

"I wouldn't say my level of courage equals yours, though."

"Having a broken heart isn't a competition. When facing it, we each handled the pain as best we could. For what it's worth, I'm glad you left Chicago."

Something twisted in my stomach.

I didn't want to let her go. I wanted to hold on to her for a little longer. "Me too."

We contemplated each other. Something passed

between us. Fascination. Understanding. Interest. And flakes of lust too.

I was right when I said that from the moment we met, it felt like I'd known her forever.

Right here, right now, our souls were living a journey of their own as if they had to connect because they could understand each other, learn from each other, and heal together.

I cleared my throat. "Now, go to sleep. I'm here, and I'll watch over you."

"Why?"

"Because. You're important to me."

"Good night, Nick," Dahlia said between yawns.

"Night." Our gaze bored into each other for a few more seconds until she looked away, moving to turn off her bedside lamp.

Watching her drift into sleep, the steady rhythm of her breaths stirred feelings in my heart I'd never experienced before.

This was the most surprising date I'd ever had. Dahlia was her own person, and I loved how careful, yet willing to open up to me, she had been tonight.

I hadn't dated lots of women in my life—my dating records didn't compare to Tucker's—but Dahlia had an almost virgin record. She'd told me once Jeff had been her one and only. Deep down, I loved how sweet and innocent she was about everything, a contrast to the self-assured woman she usually projected. This new side of her grew on me. From an outsider's point of view, she appeared to have everything figured out, but this version of her tonight showed me just how fragile she could also be.

And damn, everything about her enticed me.

With my thumb, once I made sure she was deep asleep,

I ended the video call. A pinch squeezed my heart when her face faded on the screen. "Good night, Dahlia."

For the first time in a long time, my last thoughts before dozing off didn't travel to my memories of Derek and the day I pressed that awful button.

Sleep claimed me, and my dreams swarmed with the woman I was beginning to crave more and more every single day.

Derek's Bucket List – ~~20. Nick. Go on a different kind of date~~

26

DAHLIA

"How are you doing?" Carter asked from across the ocean a few days later. I squeezed the phone between my cheek and shoulder as I hung up the new bridal lingerie I'd just received. A teal lace babydoll set with matching panties caught my eye, and I held it up in front of the wall-length mirror, imagining myself wearing it.

I had no idea when was the last time I'd dreamed of wearing something sexy and beautiful underneath my clothes. The realization filled me with a heady rush of secret thrill.

"Dah, you there?"

Carter's voice brought me back to the present.

"Huh, yep. Sorry. Distracted. I'm great." I put the lingerie aside, ready to take it home. "How was the concert last night?" I asked, giving him my complete attention. Carter's new tour had kicked off in Europe yesterday.

"Uneventful. Is Jack through the night these days? He was having more nightmares than usual the last time he stayed over."

"He hasn't had any in a few days. He woke up once last night, and that's been the only time so far."

"And the fever?"

Yesterday, my little boy had woken up with a fever, but it had subsided during the day. "Gone. He was still asleep when I left him with Paula this morning, but he was in top shape before bed last night."

"Call me if it returns. I hate knowing I won't be there to help you out if he's sick or something. If you need me, I can hop on the jet and be there within a few hours, though."

"Stop worrying. Nightmares aren't life-threatening. And the fever only lasted a couple of hours. Nothing serious. We'll be fine. Do your thing. Anyway, Nick is around if I need a hand."

"Dah—"

"Stop it, Cart. Nick and I are friends. Like you and I."

"Fuck. It's not the same, and you know it. All that guy wants is to get into your pants."

"And that's not what you want?" Carter remained silent as I apologized. "Sorry. That was a low blow. You care about me and want what's best for me. Listen, I'm just enjoying the idea of having someone around to spend time with. Nick is good for me. We get along great, and he makes me smile. Our relationship is new…and exciting. No matter what, the best friend title will always be yours, Cart."

"Dah, just say the word, and I'll drop everything and stay with you forever—" His voice cracked a little on the last word.

My heart too.

"I know, and I love you even more for saying this, but it wouldn't be fair. You shouldn't have to choose one or the other. Anyway, we'll never be together *that* way. For what it's worth, you're incredible onstage, and I'd never ask you to throw your gift away. Even if you begged me to. The stardom has always been yours, and I can't wait to see you the next time you play around here."

"In the fall, I'm playing in Nashville. You guys are staying with me at the penthouse for an entire week. We'll find someone to manage the shop, but I need both of you with me. I fucking miss you when you're that far away, and I'm stuck in some impersonal hotel room, on the other side of the world."

"Gosh, we always miss you too. How's Spain?"

"Just landed my ass in the suite. You are my one-call." I chuckled at the pun. "Can you believe I haven't done a show here since the Band days? It will be weird to be up there on my own tomorrow night."

"Carter, I'm always onstage with you…even if I'm not physically present."

"I know… Do you remember that guy we met who showed us around town the last time we came here? He's still working at the hotel. I saw him minutes ago, and he remembered us. Called you the fiery angel."

"Ohmygod. He did?"

"Yep."

We talked some more, then hung up.

At fifteen past four, I left the shop and hurried home to relieve Paula of her duty.

"Baby, wanna go see Buddy?" I squatted to hug Jack as he squealed in delight.

My son pulled away from me, and a heartwarming smile tugged at his lips. "Buddy," he singsonged. "Buddy. Buddy my *bestest* friend."

His contagious optimism warmed my heart.

Something clicked inside me as I watched my baby, sending tingles of excitement through me. Not because of the dog, but because of the man the dog had befriended. I couldn't help it—my heart ran wild for him.

"Let's go then," I said, gathering what we might need after I changed into denim cut-offs and a loose shirt, ready to leave. "We're having dinner there. My friend Nick invited us over. We wouldn't want to keep him and Buddy waiting for too long, right?"

A permanent grin was now etched on my face. No matter how ridiculous I looked with a smile too big to hide, nothing could wipe it away. Honestly, the idea of seeing Nick again sent sparks shooting through me.

With Jack's tiny fingers wrapped around mine, I knocked on the door. My pulse had started its berserk dance the moment I parked the car, and with every passing second, the rhythm grew even more berserk.

"Here you are," a masculine voice greeted me from behind. I nearly dropped the bag slung over my shoulder at the sound.

Nick.

He looked scrumptious.

My insides clenched.

There was no denying it. Nick Peterson possessed a hold on me and my hormones—and every inch of my womanly parts.

Jack's here. Act cool, I repeated in my mind because there was nothing calm about me or my demeanor right now. I was an explosive device on the edge of detonation. My insides twisted with need. My body amplified every signal Nick sent, tugging at every string of my composure.

Somehow, that phone date the other night had proven to me that we were meant to be. That what Nick and I shared was bigger than we could comprehend, that our connection was beyond words.

Jack let go of my finger and rushed toward the man

who was looking at me with a barely concealed desire—
something unfamiliar I hadn't noticed until today.

Nick picked him up and ruffled his hair. "Hey, little guy. I thought I heard you arrive. I was in the garage. Wanna gimme a hand? I made a bird feeder and was waiting for you to choose the perfect place to hang it."

"Yes," Jack said, squirming to be set down.

"Buddy's waiting for you under his favorite tree. Let's go see him first."

Jack ran toward the backyard as I climbed down the stairs to meet with Nick.

His arms pulled me closer the second I neared him, my heart now a throbbing mess inside my chest.

"You know you're wonderful with Jack, right?" I asked, breathless.

"Just with Jack?" he asked with an arched eyebrow, his smile hitting me straight in the heart.

I rose onto my tiptoes. "Not just Jack," I murmured against his lips before kissing him. Because that was all I'd been thinking about since that phone date.

"I've missed you too," he said, voicing the very thought in my head. He intertwined his fingers with mine, and hand in hand—as if we'd done this a hundred times—we walked toward my little boy.

Our smiles grew as we watched Jack tell Buddy all about his day. The dog twitched his ears in response, as if the stories were the highlights of his canine day.

"Little guy, ready to feed those birds?" Nick asked after their conversation was over.

My son moved to his feet and nodded.

"Great." Nick swiveled to face me. He traced his lips down my cheek, leaving a trail of goose bumps in his wake. "There's a glass of wine waiting for you on the back deck.

Make yourself at home. We'll be right back." I closed my eyes, my heart hiccupping in my chest, as Nick kissed the side of my face. "I won't be long, and I'll make it up to you later."

Air sizzled, and I almost lost my footing, drunk on his promises.

He turned to grab Jack's hand, and my lungs deflated with a woosh. How long had I been holding my breath?

———

After dinner, we went for a walk with Jack and Buddy, then my son fell asleep on the living room floor again, next to his best friend. Nick and I spent countless minutes watching them, enjoying the picture-perfect moment: Jack lying on his side, his arms wrapped protectively around the dog's neck.

"I feel bad about moving him," I whispered.

"They look so peaceful," Nick said. "We could try slipping a blanket underneath him, then cover them both without disturbing either one."

"That could work. Let's try."

We repositioned Jack alongside Buddy and spread a quilt over them.

In the kitchen, we refilled our wine glasses as I settled on the cool surface of the island, and Nick sat on the countertop next to the sink, three feet away from me.

"Thinking about moving here full time?"

His lips stretched. "I am."

"Told you. The mountain air."

He raked a hand through his hair. "Not sure it's the air, Dahlia."

Why was he looking at me like that? As if he were starving.

In a swift move, he jumped to his feet and stalked toward me.

"Gotta tell you something."

I gasped, choking on my own breath.

The room temperature soared to searing levels.

His lips parted, and my grip around the wine glass tightened, my heart bracing for whatever Nick was about to say.

I inhaled through my mouth to put to rest the jitters awakening inside me.

Nick stopped a foot from me, and I was pretty sure I melted as his eyes rested on mine.

My throat was parched from the heat radiating off him. My lips parted, my tongue tracing their length, but no sound followed. I swallowed hard, the silence thick between us.

Tremors shook me.

Nick stepped forward, and my gaze drifted to his mouth, waiting for him to say something—anything—to soothe the tension rising at my core.

27

NICHOLAS

"**F**uck, Dahlia. I'm not sure I want to be your friend anymore."

Hurt flashed in her eyes. Replacing the intensity that had been burning there all night. "W-why not?"

"Because I wanna kiss you so bad."

Her voice became a throaty whisper, and it tormented my agonized cells. "We already kissed. Many times."

"Dahlia, friends aren't supposed to kiss each other. Not the way I'm itching to. Not how I intend to. It's not in the rulebook… I checked. Believe me, I'm sure. And your being here right now, all beautiful and sexy, is driving me crazy." I paused to breathe properly. "Big fucking time."

Her breathless murmur quivered in the air. "You do? You…you did? The thing is"—she inhaled—"maybe it's time to change the rules. Nick, we've played long enough. I'm a mess because I think about you kissing me *this way* all the time. I do."

Pure unleashed electricity traveled through my veins. A fire sparked through my body as I discovered the depth of her desire, every nerve ending alive and hungry for more.

My lower body twitched just at the thought of her lips on mine…and mine, well, all over her soft flesh.

The woman was like a drug. She got me addicted to her essence with just a glance my way, and now I was a junkie craving her.

Dahlia's sharp intake of breath commanded my undivided attention. "Kiss me, Nick. Like you mean it. Like you want to. Like I belong to you."

She nibbled her bottom lip and molded her upper body to mine. Each thump of her heart reverberated through my chest. She captured my eyes, and I lost the battle within me.

With deliberate slowness, I took the wine glass from her hand and set it on the counter behind me, desire making my fingers tremble. A rising tempest within me made it hard to be gentle. I wanted to take her hard, the way I pictured myself doing so every night—every day. And every aching minute in between.

I slammed my lips on hers, tilting her head back, claiming her as mine, wanting to inhale her completely.

My heart probably skipped a few beats.

Dahlia gasped, and I thought I'd lose it.

Nothing was delicate or slow in the way I captured her lips. All the restraints I'd held onto for the past few weeks flew away. The roughness of my jaw brushed against the softness of hers. Desperate whimpers whirled around us. My torso pressed against hers, caging her and keeping me upright as my body convulsed, her lips savage against mine, accepting everything I demanded.

This wasn't a kiss. It was a seismic wave of desire washing over both of us. A tsunami of burning want.

I closed my eyes as I imprinted this moment on my heart.

Dahlia anchored herself to me. She fisted my T-shirt,

urging me closer. Her other hand curled around my neck, a vice grip forbidding me to step back.

I stopped breathing. Only Dahlia existed for me in that instant.

She sucked on my tongue, and I swore I could have come right there.

Blood boiled in my veins as a sudden surge of need electrified me. I tangled my fingers in her hair, clutching her to me. My lips crushed hers. I bit them before soothing them with my tongue.

Her whimpers were my undoing.

I tugged her bottom lip between my teeth, barely able to contain myself. My eyes fluttered open, just enough to notice how beautiful she looked, lost in the moment between us.

Shivers of pleasure shot down my spine as she half-moaned and half-growled and pulled my lips back to hers. My tongue darted into her mouth, hungry and intense, eager to play with hers. I clamped my fingers around her hips while sensations spiraled with a searing need inside me. She shuddered in my arms, and my heart swelled as if it would burst out of my chest. My dick was about to drill a hole through my pants. Heat flared between us as we lost control, Dahlia's sounds awakening something wild within me.

Feral.

Animalistic.

Wild gasps and yelps.

Her body undulated against mine, hot and untamed. Mine dissolved under her touch as she caressed my chest and pinched my nipples between her fingers. I felt more alive than I ever had before. Thrilling. Only desire existed between us. We were lost in each other, in this connection, breathless and dazed.

This time, I looked at her. A thunderbolt called Dahlia had cleaved my body, igniting my core, scorching my spine.

She owned me. Every single bit.

We were about to crash and burn, and it scared me as much as it excited me.

Soon, we would explode together, consuming each other. I tried—I really tried—to talk myself out of it so our friendship could blossom for a little longer, but my body had a mind of its own. My soul too. And I gave in to both.

I curled a hand around her nape, my fingers digging into her skin, hating even the slightest space between us. Our mouths collided again. She tasted like a forbidden fruit, sweet and addictive. The taste of her wasn't enough —it would never be. If we crossed that line, there'd be no going back. Dahlia Ellis had become my *raison d'être*. My sin. My obsession.

Our lips moved in perfect sync, like a rehearsed choreography. No teasing. No hesitation. Just raw need and the urgency of wanting each other. Dahlia was offering herself to me, and like a greedy man, I intended to take all of her and give back ten times stronger. I wanted to blow her mind until she couldn't think, her body completely satiated.

Fire traveled through my bloodstream. My lower body pulsed, desperate for an immediate release.

Dahlia quivered in my arms, wild moans echoing from the back of her throat.

My brain went blank.

My senses sharpened.

My heart pounded in my chest.

One look into her eyes, and every nerve in me ignited.

Without another word, I cupped her cheeks as her gaze, demanding and scorching, found mine. So heavy, I almost forgot my own name.

I angled my mouth and sucked at the seam of her lips, dueling with her tongue in a delicious tango. Dahlia pulled me closer, her hands charting the searing ridges of my abdomen, goose bumps rising in their wake. I slid her forward until her hips reached the edge of the counter. She pressed herself into me, her body chasing the ache of something deeper. Tension wrapped around us until we were coiled tight with an urgency we could no longer ignore.

Every breath she took sent aftershocks through me, turning my flesh into a blazing inferno.

My hands roamed all over her still-clothed body. Too many layers of fabric separated us, preventing me from touching her, like really touching her in the way I'd been dreaming of since the day we met.

"Where have you been all my life?" I whispered against her mouth, ravenous for the woman rocking my world.

She moaned, her need for me woven through her words, the sound waking the beast inside me. "Here. Waiting for you to show up."

My hand ventured between her thighs, and she shivered when I traced the seam of her cut-offs, sensing her heat through the denim.

I drew circles over her clit through the fabric with my thumb, and she gasped. Taking advantage, I pushed my tongue deeper into her mouth, meeting hers in long, enticing strokes.

"Nick." Dahlia cried as she pushed her breasts forward while I traced her jawline, the column of her throat, and the contours of her collarbones with my mouth. "More," she demanded. "So much more."

With one arm, I lifted her into my arms and locked her ankles behind my back. I slid my hands beneath her shirt, my fingertips enjoying the feel of the warm skin of her back, before moving to her front. Squeezing her plump breast, I rolled a nipple between my fingers, the lace of her bra adding to the fiction. A low growl rumbled from her throat as she fisted my hair and consumed my lips.

I ground against her center, my dick seeking her warmth. Dahlia rolled her hips in an age-old dance, a symphony of purrs escaping her luscious lips.

"Shirt off," I ordered as I unclasped her bra, my hands greedy, not wanting to let go of her breasts, even for a second.

She lifted my shirt over my head, her eyes singeing my torso.

My body pulsed, and my heart rattled inside my chest.

This woman was killing me.

Taking her sweet time, she removed her top, her unclasped white bra revealing the most perfect mounds I'd ever seen. Creamy, round, big enough to fill my hands. My dick, now rock-hard, twitched in my pants.

I grazed the skin of her arms with my fingertips, from her shoulders down, freeing her from the dangling piece of lace. We both watched it fall as it landed on the planked floor. Our palms came together, and our fingers wove around each other.

"You're beautiful," I breathed out, still wrestling with myself not to give in and take her right here on the kitchen island.

Tilting her head back, Dahlia bit her lower lip, eyes alight with sparks.

My mouth grazed her earlobe, slowly tracing its way downward, licking and tasting. I nipped the flesh of her neck with my teeth, trailing over to the fullness of her chest, famished for the stiff buds pressing against my torso, pleading for attention.

"More," Dahlia begged, her voice husky, the sound orgasmic.

My dick pushed against the zipper of my pants, wanting to be let loose in this game.

I close my lips around one stiff nipple, and I sucked on the tip, flicking it with my tongue.

Dahlia moaned, a dark flush rising from her neck up.

"You taste like summer."

A low gasp escaped her lips.

"What does summer taste like, Nick?" Her voice shuddered, pleasure building inside her as I attacked her other nipple with my tongue, so hungry for her I could never stop.

Fuck, Dahlia's sex voice was like pure ecstasy shooting through my veins. And the way she said my name, with her southern inflection, destroyed me in the most delicious way.

"Sweet. Smart. Sexy. Sassy. Irresistible. Delicious. You. I have to taste all of you now."

She cupped my face in her hands and drew me up, her mouth claiming mine, plundering it with her ravenous tongue. "I can't wait…to know…what you taste like too," she said in between kisses, panting.

Those words. They shattered me. My brain, my resolve, my willpower, they all left me. Only my mouth, my dick, and my hands existed.

Dahlia unbuttoned my pants, her fingers set on their own mission. Her tongue darted out, tracing the curve of her lips.

I groaned, and another chain of my restraint clattered to the floor.

Before I could feel her touch on the burning piece of me aching for her, I stopped her with a hand.

She raised her gaze, question marks floating in her moss-green eyes.

"You first. Let me make you come. If you touch me, I won't last, and it will be over before we even get started. I'm about to explode just from the way your lips taste."

"But I—"

I silenced her with a bruising kiss, the kind that would sear itself into my lips forever. "You'll have plenty of time."

With steady fingers, I unbuttoned her cut-offs and pushed a finger inside her panties, relishing the wet warmth of her coating my digit. Dahlia screamed in delight, and I swallowed it as our lips sought more, never satisfied, never still.

"Fuck. Even your pussy is addictive."

I slid a second finger in, and Dahlia gripped my biceps, digging her fingernails into my skin, and arched her back, mewing like a kitten.

"Oh, God, Nick... Yes. It-it's been so long since someone touched me like this. Please, don't ever stop."

I cupped my junk, making sure my dick hadn't drilled a hole through my pants. Everything was fine. Except that I was so hard, I wondered if all the blood in my body had pooled to the tip.

"Oh, yes. There... More—"

Giggles reached us from the living room.

My brain didn't really register them.

More giggles.

This time, there was no mistaking the sound for anything else.

Dahlia and I froze, my digits concealed deep inside her, her wetness and heat wrapped around them.

Bubbly laughter spilled from the other room this time.

I fished my phone out of my back pocket.

Ten thirty-seven.

Dahlia and I exchanged a quizzical stare.

I extracted my hand just in time as Dahlia jumped to her feet and buttoned her shorts. She offered me an apologetic smile and a shrug.

I grabbed both our shirts from the floor and handed Dahlia hers.

Dressed and decent, we made it to the other room.

The scene playing in front of us made me smile, but it also put to rest my horny self.

On the floor, Buddy was licking a sleepy Jack's face, the boy laughing his heart out.

Dahlia and I shared another look. She winced, and our eyes traveled back to Jack and Buddy cuddling on the floor, and we both burst out laughing.

Dahlia angled herself to face me, her arms circling my waist. "Nick, I'm so sorry."

My lips found hers. "Don't be. Look at them." We turned our faces in their direction. "This is priceless."

Half an hour later, I walked the woman of my dreams and her son, now fully awake, to their car, Buddy in tow, listening to Jack singing to him, energized from his power nap.

Once she buckled Jack in his car seat, Dahlia joined me. "Again, sorry," she said as my lips found her in the darkness of the night. "I'm already counting the days when we can continue where we left off."

I lowered my palm to her ass and gave it a squeeze as she kissed me one last time.

"Night, Nick. Sweet dreams," she said with a wink.

My body overheated. "After what we did, I'll never be able to sleep. I'll have a hard-on for days to come."

She ran her hand along my erection. "How rude of me to leave you like this." She offered me a lopsided smile, palming my hard flesh.

My knees buckled. "Geez, this is as much incredible as it is torture."

Humor left her features. "I don't know when we'll be able to resume this." A long huff broke the silence. "I'll miss you."

With one finger, I lifted her chin up, staring into her eyes. "As I already said, I'll wait for you. We'll be fine. Each time we get interrupted, I'm just burning hotter for you afterward." As if to corroborate my words, a rush of heat spread through me. "I'll see you soon. Go now, or I'll kidnap your pretty ass and lock it in my cave and never let you go."

A smile returned to Dahlia's face, and I silently congratulated myself for putting it there."Thank you, Nick. One day, I'll let you capture me and do nasty things to me."

If only she knew. *You've already captured my heart, Dahlia Ellis.*

"I can't wait. Go. Now," I ordered, teasing, as I kissed her forehead and opened her car door. "I'll miss you too."

She waved at me, and as soon as she rounded the corner, I escorted Buddy home in a rush to return, the tension still clawing at me, knowing it wouldn't relent until I took care of it—myself.

28

NICHOLAS

The next morning, I woke up at dawn, too restless to stay in bed. I had tossed and turned for hours, my mind drifting to the woman who had taken a chunk of my heart hostage last night.

The taste of her lingered on my lips for a long time after she left, and I hoped it could stay there forever.

My thoughts churned in my head. I dragged a hand over my face, trying to ease the new wave of desire pulsing through me.

"Fuck," I screamed to relieve my frustration, as my fist connected with the kitchen counter. This thing between us had me all bothered, and now I was in my kitchen, wishing she'd appear at my front door and we'd pick up where we left off last night. With my tongue in her mouth and my fingers playing her body.

With a mug of coffee in my hand, I watched the sunrise from the back deck. The sight helped me pull myself together. For a moment, I simply appreciated the view, pushing away the images in my head. This brief moment of peace and quiet—taking in the beauty nature had to offer—had become my ritual on most mornings.

My mind stopped spinning, and my racing thoughts slowly fell into order.

I breathed easier.

Maybe it was the lack of sleep that had sent me into a state of mental agitation this morning, but now that the trepidation and angst had eased, I could see more clearly.

"Hey, bro," I said, slouching in my chair, glancing at the sky.

Derek and I were due for a meaningful talk.

"How are you doing? Touching base with you. Things move fast around here. Just so you know, you were right. I can see it now. I have no clue how you could, but hey, I'm not questioning the process. Back home, I was missing out on so many things. Home… Why does my chest tighten whenever I think about Chicago as my home? Is it weird? Now I can only picture myself living here, in Green Mountain."

I paused to regroup my thoughts.

"Anyway, I'm glad you sent me on this journey. And guess what? I checked another item off your list. I made three best friends so far. Our lives entangled in a way I can't explain, but there is something there. It's real. And powerful."

I let the silence hang in the air after I spoke.

"By the way, I never thought I'd befriend a dog, but here he is, proving me wrong. It's like Dahlia, Jack, and Buddy were destined to enter my life. Some way… Some day… When I was truly ready to welcome them. It feels so damn right to share pieces of my life with them. If you're the mastermind behind all this—and I truly hope you are —thank you. I can't wait to see how far our relationships will go, but I know in my heart I'll forever be grateful they've become part of my journey."

I closed my eyes to chase the emotional turmoil shaking me.

"I miss you, Derek. Every day. I wish you were here. I wish you could meet them. I wish you could have come on this adventure with me. Go, have fun, okay? Love you, bro." With my fingers, I saluted the sky.

A scratching noise echoed through the ajar patio door. Buddy yapped from the front porch, and I hurried inside and crossed the kitchen to let him in. He sniffed around, and after pacing the main floor of the house twice, he curled into a ball on the floor with a loud sigh.

"You miss them too?" I asked, wishing he could talk back for once. "Yeah." I sighed. "I know the feeling."

I refilled my mug and was about to start my day when Chaz, my young neighbor, came knocking. "Hey, Nick. Can I talk to you?" he asked through the screen door.

"Yeah. Sure. Come on in. What's up?"

He sat on a stool and buried his head in the bent of his elbow.

"Coffee?"

"Sure," he muttered.

"Everything all right? Huh, you looked…confused?" I asked, lacking a better word.

Chaz nodded, not meeting my eyes. "You know the girl—"

"The one who dated your best friend?"

"Yeah. Jolie. She asked me to this dance in town next month."

"That's great, man."

The teen groaned, his face still hidden in the crook of his arm. "No, it's not. She was *his* girl first. He'll kill me if I go with her. He told me many times she was off-limits. I'm screwed. I really like her. And I…I think she likes me too."

"Your coffee, black?"

"One milk and too much sugar," he muttered.

"Tell me the truth, Chaz. What do *you* want?" I asked, making my way to the refrigerator to get the milk.

He lifted his head, his face flustered. "Her. I've been in love with Jolie since third grade. And she'll be in Columbus too next fall."

"Did—what's his name?—your friend know about your crush when he asked her out?" I placed the cup of coffee before him and leaned back against the counter next to the sink, sipping mine.

Chaz was about six or seven years younger than me, but right now, I felt like decades separated us. He looked so clueless and inexperienced that it made me smile and I felt for him.

"Yeah."

I shrugged. "So. He broke the bro code first."

"You think?"

"I'm sure. Come on, man. He made a move on the girl you loved. That's really shitty of him. Best friends don't do that."

Chaz's face lit up as if I'd shot him with pure caffeine through an IV line.

He cast a glance down, and a single deep wrinkle carved a line across his forehead.

I followed his gaze and cursed all the saints in my head. Nested underneath the kitchen cupboards, a foot away from me, was a piece of fabric.

White lace.

I blinked, urging my brain to think—fast.

With my index finger, I directed Chaz's attention to my right. "Look who came to visit me this morning?"

The teen turned his head, and I kicked my leg out to hook Dahlia's bra lying abandoned on the floor. In a ninja-style movement, I picked it up and shoved it into a drawer.

Chaz huffed a loud breath. "He's getting weaker by the day. At this pace, I'm not sure he'll be here by the end of summer. I got him when he was a puppy, you know. He's been my best friend forever. I'm glad he has you now that I'll be going away to college."

Tears glistened in Chaz's eyes.

I stepped around the kitchen island and clapped his back. "I'm sorry. I know it's hard, but I'm sure he's had a great life."

He shrugged. "I guess."

"I lost a best friend too. A couple of months ago. I know the pain, believe me." I forced a tight-lipped smile, though it felt anything but natural, hoping Chaz wouldn't ask questions I wasn't ready to answer.

"I'm sorry. That sucks."

He turned his attention back to the kitchen floor, scanning for the white piece of lingerie. He arched a brow, stared at me, then shook his head. "What should I do about Jolie?"

"Life is short, man. Seize the chance or you'll always wonder what could have been. Face your friend. Tell him the truth. If he's upset and throws a fit, then he's not worth your time and friendship, and you don't need him around."

Chaz listened to me, nodding, as if all of this occurred to him for the first time.

"What do you have to lose? You'll be gone in a few months, anyway. Will—"

"Hank."

"Will Hank be in Ohio too?"

"No. He's staying here."

"Go for it then. Don't let him ruin what you and Jolie could have."

Images of Jace and Pam flashed through my mind. Since I moved here, I'd barely had a chance to talk to him. Now my friend had no reason to drop by unannounced, and we had no more excuses—like poker nights—to see each other. Even Tucker mentioned the other day that he'd only seen him a handful of times since I left the city. But hey, if it meant Jace was happy in his marriage, what could I say? It wasn't my decision, but I missed him.

Chaz firmed his back, resolve now flashing in his eyes. "You're right. Hank has no right to pull the bro code card on me. Thanks, Nick."

Without another word, the kid left, his cup half-drunk, confidence radiating from him.

I took the bra out of the cutlery drawer and twisted it between my fingers.

Last night's memories swirled back in my mind, suffocating me as they replayed in my head.

My lower body hardened, and my mouth watered.

Was last night just a one-time thing? A flood of lust we had to tame? Or was Dahlia truly serious about moving forward in our relationship—just as much as I was? *Wait and see, man. You promised her friendship. Stick to it. Unless she makes a move,* the naughty voice in my head added. I breathed out. Could I do that? Wait and see? I had to. For both our sakes. Dahlia already had a complicated past, and she didn't deserve a fling. She deserved the real thing. Flowers. Date nights. Love. Commitment. And forever.

I was busying myself in one of the bedrooms upstairs, taking measurements to replace the broken window, when an idea hit me.

It planted a little seed of hope in me that shot jitters to my stomach.

After I changed, I hurried downstairs, ready to run some errands.

With my phone, I snapped a picture of Buddy, sleeping in the same exact spot he'd shared with Jack just the night before, and sent it to Dahlia.

ME

Look who's missing his new best friend?

She replied minutes later. For my plan to unfold, I had to know if she was at the store right now.

DAHLIA

I'm telling you. This dog is a keeper.

ME

I'll put a lock on his leash to make sure a redhead who's been seen lurking around him won't be able to steal him away from me.

DAHLIA

I wouldn't.

ME

Oh yes, you would. I heard you all right last night. And the other times before.

I can tell you have a plan.

Picturing you wearing a ski mask, dropping cookie crumbs to create an evasion path, waiting in a white van while your toddler sidekick eats those chunks, messing with your mission.

What would your thief name be? Firecracker? Red Devil?

DAHLIA

Firefly.

ME

Firefly? It doesn't sound badass enough. You sure?

DAHLIA

Why not? I like those bugs.

ME

Girl, you'll never cease to amaze me. Let's call you Fireworks.

DAHLIA

Why?

ME

Because. It fits you. You're no insect, Dahlia. You're a spectacular, colorful display, setting me on fire each time you rest your eyes on me.

Imagine the headline: "Fireworks Thief and her Spark sidekick have stolen a dog. Wanna catch them? Offer them cookies."

DAHLIA

Stop. I'm laughing so hard right now, my ribs hurt.

Be honest, though. Jack would look cute in a ski mask, eating pieces of cookies.

ME

Absolutely. But not sure he's the man for the job. If it were for any other mission, I'd drive the getaway car.

DAHLIA

You would?

ME

Without hesitation.

Big day at work?

DAHLIA

It was earlier. Prom dress fittings. I'm all
alone now.

I jumped into my truck, and minutes later, I parked in
front of Dahlia's Bridal Shop. In Green Mountain, I could
be about anywhere in only a couple of minutes, while in
Chicago it took usually over half an hour to get from one
place to another. I loved it. The small-town charm and
simplicity.

ME

Got something else you might miss.

DAHLIA

?

ME

*sending her the picture of her bra I took
before leaving my place*

DAHLIA

OMG I'm so relieved you can't see my face
right now. It must be neon pink. I'm sure it's
bright enough that it can be seen from
space.

ME

Don't be ashamed, it's a pretty piece of
lingerie. I'm just not sure it's my size. I may
have to return it to its rightful owner.

By the way, pink is a good look on you.

Through the store's big, square window, I watched
Dahlia as she perused around, searching for me. I waved at
her when our gazes met. She shook her head and ran a
hand over her reddened face.

I shrugged as I opened the door.

"You're the worst, Nick," she said, backhanding my chest. "I almost died of embarrassment."

"You're lucky I didn't bring it here." Her eyes widened. "Anyway, if you wanna get it back, you'll have to come over and have dinner with me," I said, raising my hands between us.

Dahlia looked thoughtful as she said, "I supposed it wouldn't be fair to Jack to deprive him of spending time with his best buddy."

And my body from the withdrawal last night caused me.

"It would be like another double date with friends."

A chuckle left her mouth. "Okay, fine. You won. You got me at double date."

I grinned like a fool because that was how spending time with this woman made me feel.

Long gone were those spells when I went through life mechanically, back in Chicago, where every day was almost a duplicate of the previous one. I used to love my job, but looking back at my life before I moved here, it missed the excitement. I wasn't unhappy. No, I didn't think it was that. But it was predictable—an awful lot. If I had agreed to the contract Cody urged me to sign, the next five years would have looked exactly the same. Thanks to Derek, I'd escaped the routine I thought I'd miss, but didn't. All the plans. The expectations. It would have soon become too much, weighing me down. I hadn't thrived like this in a long time, and I could easily become addicted to this slower, more content lifestyle.

"See you at five." I whirled around to leave when I remembered the paper bag in my hand. "Here." I handed it to her.

Dahlia gave me one of her quizzical stares. "What is it? I hope it's not a new bra." A pink blush returned to her cheeks. Her lips curled when she eyed what was inside, discovering the treat I got her.

"Saw it next door. It reminded me of you."

She halted, her hand midway between the bag and her mouth. "You saw a glazed donut in the bakery window, and it reminded you of me. How?"

I shrugged. "It's sweet and sparkly. Like you, Fireworks."

She tilted her head back, laughing. "Okay, it's actually nice of you." She bit into the pastry as if she hadn't eaten in days. "Want some?" she asked with a mouthful.

"Nah. You look like you can use it. When was the last time you ate?"

She flicked her wrist as if it was no big deal. "I had tea at six this morning."

"Glad to learn I'm not the only one starving himself. Still, you shouldn't run on an empty stomach."

"Sometimes I'm so focused that I forget."

"Gimme a sec," I said, hurrying outside, not giving her time to argue.

I crossed the street, reached Ivy's Café in a dozen strides, and ordered Dahlia a sandwich. After I came to an agreement with Ivy, I returned to the bridal shop and handed Dahlia the takeout container.

"Eat. I'll watch the store while you do. Take your time."

"You sure?"

I nodded.

"Thanks," she said, her hand finding mine and giving it a quick squeeze before moving to the back of the store.

Fifteen minutes later, I left, ready for the next step in my plan.

Back home, I carried the packages I'd bought to the bedroom upstairs, and after I fixed the broken window, changing the glass and sealing the edges, I sat on the floor and unwrapped everything, ready for phase three of my plan.

Derek's Bucket List – ~~*24. Nick. Make someone smile*~~ ~~*my newfound mission*~~

29

DAHLIA

Jack ran toward Buddy, a plastic firefighter truck in his hand, the moment his feet landed on Nick's doorstep.

"Thank you," I said after Nick lifted the bag from my arms.

He rubbed his jaw and turned to face me. "I've been thinking about remodeling the upstairs bathroom because there's a leak in the shower, and getting rid of the wallpaper in the master bedroom. I was wondering if your offer to gimme a hand still stands. I might need your help picking out tiles, faucets, and paint…those sorts of things."

"Yes. Absolutely. I'd like that. Already told you I used to be a master fixer-upper… Back in the day." My throat closed as images of Jeff and me fixing the old house he bought for us when I was seventeen resurfaced.

"You okay?" Nick asked.

I blinked and nodded. "Yeah. Got lost in old memories for a second." I forced a smile and chased those flashbacks away. "Can I get a tour? To see what we're dealing with?"

He leaned in, and his lips grazed mine. "Sure, follow

me. I can't believe I never took the time to give you a proper tour. Guess we've been busy."

I grinned at the teasing while Nick lifted my son in his arms, and climbed the stairs after them.

The farmhouse was old, but it had a lot of charm. Since the first day I came over, I could picture all its potential in my mind. The tour cemented my vision. One wall down here, an opening there, new windows, an updated banister, some black wrought-iron light fixtures, and a terrace off the master bedroom.

"Looks like your brain is in high gear," Nick remarked after we exited the bathroom, and he explained his vision for the room.

"I can see it clearly in my head. It's a shame we can't do it all. I love the bones of this house, though with the right budget, the right plans, and enough time, it could be so much more."

"My mission here is only to fix it up for future buyers, but I agree. With a bigger budget and a few additions, we could easily turn it into an incredible home."

"What's this room for?" I asked as we passed a closed door.

Nick breathed out and straightened his back. He looked around for a few seconds as if debating with himself whether to tell me or not. "If I show you, promise me you'll listen to what I have to say before freaking out, okay?"

I knitted my brows together. "Tell me you're not a serial killer and this isn't your trophy room."

He relaxed at my words before offering me a devilish smirk. "Only the heads."

"Then it's fine. I would've run away if you'd said only the feet. Not a fan of toes. Heads are safe."

He wiped imaginary sweat from his forehead with the

back of his hand, pretending to be relieved. "Since I was hoping you'd embark on this remodeling journey with me, I did something. It's no big deal. You hate it, and we don't talk about it anymore. You love it, then great. Don't feel obligated to anything… I feel stupid right now. I should've asked you first. I'm sure you'll think I'm a weirdo—"

Before he could finish his sentence, I turned the knob, opening the door slowly as if it could detonate somehow.

My hand flew to my mouth, and my heart did a three-sixty-degree rotation in my chest.

Jack squealed and wriggled in Nick's arms, silently begging to be lowered to his feet. My child entered the room, a huge smile brightening his face.

"Is it what I think it is?" I asked, standing motionless, as though gravity had doubled beneath my feet.

Nick cleared his throat, keeping his eyes from mine, his head bowed as he rubbed the nape of his neck with one hand. "Yeah. Well… It's a…it's a playroom. It's not much, but I thought Jack could use a safe place when we're tearing apart the old bathroom. Assuming we do it together… Somewhere he could play or"—he pointed to a tiny plush sofa-bed in the corner—"nap if we work late. It's silly. Huh, I get it. In my head, it sounded smart, but now I feel ridiculous for not asking your permission first."

A street-patterned rug, a few plastic vehicles, and other toys were lined up against the wall. A shelf with half a dozen picture books was set up next to the royal-blue sofa-bed, decorated with two stuffed animals.

"You made this?" I asked in a voice so thick with emotion, it barely sounded like mine. "For my son?"

Nick nodded, his fleeting gaze meeting mine.

Without thinking further, I jumped into his arms, brushing my lips against his. "It's beautiful. And thoughtful. You didn't have to, but I like it. A lot. You're amazing."

"Look, Mama. *Vroommm. Vroommm*," Jack said, opening his fist to reveal an orange toy car.

"You like that, baby?"

He bobbed his head and grinned.

"Say thank you to Nick."

"*Thankliounick.*"

We both laughed as my son wrapped his arms around this incredible man's leg.

Nick kneeled before him. "You're welcome, little guy. I'm happy you like it. How about you and I go get Buddy? I'm sure he misses you very much. He was looking for you earlier today."

Jack bobbed his head and stepped back, holding out his hand to grab Nick's finger. "Cookie, *pleaseiounick.*"

Nick rolled his jaw back and forth, as if he were thinking it over. "Are you sure your Mama is okay with that?"

Jack bobbed his head once more as I watched their exchange.

"Then let's ask her." Nick, still on his knees, raised his eyes toward me. "Dahlia, can Jack and I get cookies? *Pleeeease.*" He glanced at Jack next and whispered, "You think she'll let me have one too?"

Jack nodded, giggling.

I rested one fist on my hip and tapped the side of my chin with a finger. "Will you two eat your dinner later?"

They both said "Yes" at the same time.

"Will you brush your teeth before going to bed?"

They said "Yes" again.

"Cookies it is then." I scrunched up my face. "Can I get one too?"

Nick jumped to his feet and winked. "Oh yes, I forgot how your Mama loves cookies."

My face heated up, no doubt, as I remembered our innuendos from the other day.

Jack lifted a finger. "Wait, Mama. *Nickandme* get cookies, okay? Wait."

Five minutes later, the three of us sat on the playroom floor eating our snack. Once we finished, the boys left to get Buddy, Jack tugging at Nick's hand, while I attacked dinner.

We sat around the table as if we'd been doing it for years, and Jack perched himself on Nick's lap. They laughed together at something Nick said, and in that instant, I wished I could stop time and savor this moment of bliss a little longer.

I had no idea how we had slipped into this comfortable routine, but I was thankful for every second of it. Most nights, when I closed my eyes, I still believed it was all a dream.

———

After dinner, Nick and I were seated on the kitchen island, wine glasses in hand, going over the pictures on his laptop, finding inspiration for the upstairs bathroom. At some point, Nick sauntered off—only to return seconds later with my bra folded neatly in his hand.

"I have this piece of equipment I gotta return to its rightful owner. I must ask, and I have a right to know. Did you leave it here on purpose? Was it to tempt me, or were you trying to find a not-so-subtle way to snatch an invite again?" He wiggled his eyebrows, and I buried my face in my hands, feeling warmth pooling in my cheeks.

"I figured it might add some personality to your trophy room… Or give it a little edge, you know?" I pinched my lips together, not quite sure how I felt brave enough to speak these words out loud.

"Considering it's now your kid's playroom, I'll have to hang it on my bedroom wall instead."

My body tingled. I clenched my thighs as heat billowed between them. "Maybe it was the plan all along," I said, the blush on my face now hot enough to melt my skin.

"I'm sure we could find a way to make it part of the new decor."

The heated exchange between us was turning me on, my body melting into a molten pool of sizzling need.

We stared at each other, the chemistry between us so palpable, I could almost taste it.

"I have to get going," I muttered.

Nick framed my face with his hands. "I know. Our time together always flies by too fast."

In the living room, I scooped up a sleeping Jack from the little sofa-bed we'd brought down there two hours ago and made my way to the car.

"Thanks for the room," I said when what I really wished to say was: *you're awesome. All I hunger for is for us to pick up right where we left off last night. I'm a mess since you've entered my life. I think about you all the time. Every night I touch myself, imagining these are your hands on me, your heartbeat that's vibrating through my chest, your lips that are between my thighs.*

"You're welcome. Thanks for your help. Now I owe you twice."

I know exactly how you could pay off your debts.

I mirrored Nick's smile. "No, we're square. You fed me today, remember?"

I'm desperate for you to feed me every day, but I want more than sandwiches and dinners. I want the entire buffet. Every last bite.

What were all these thoughts popping into my head?

Nick leaned forward, and my heart skipped a beat. If

he got any closer, we'd get burned. There was no way I could resist him. To try would only fan the blaze. We'd start a wildfire, and everything in our path would combust.

"Night, Dahlia," he said, his lips tasting the corner of mine.

His scent rushed through me, heightening all my senses. Man, soap, and wood. It imprinted itself on my nose.

"Goodnight." I climbed into my car, not looking back, desperate to be as far as possible from this man who could shatter my existence with a single flick of his tongue and a brush of his fingers.

———

The next five days flew by in a haze. I stayed busy at the store, training my newest employee. I'd talked to Nick a few times on the phone since Jack and I went over there the other night, but we hadn't seen each other—not even once.

Every day, around noon, I received a special delivery from Ivy's Café—wraps, sandwiches, soups, salads—with a note.

> *Friends take care of each other.*
> *Don't go a day without eating.*
> *Take a few minutes for yourself, you deserve it.*
> *Life is brighter when you're around.*

After three days, I begged Ivy to tell me the truth. Nick had asked her to bring me lunch every day since he told her I had a tendency to forget to eat. Ivy loved the idea, and together, they had planned the entire thing. I'd asked Nick about it on day four, but he told me he had no idea what I was referring to. This was one of the sweetest things someone had ever done for me, and now I couldn't wait to thank him the proper way.

In person.

My phone rang, and I answered it without checking the screen. "Hey, Nick. Still on for tonight?" We were supposed to go shopping for the new bathroom an hour's drive from here.

"Dah, it's me." The sound of Carter's voice startled me, but it also grounded me. My best friend had a way to calm my nerves just by talking to me.

"Hey, Cart. Still in Germany?"

"Yeah, leaving in the morning. Heading to Scotland next." His words were clipped. Carter was upset. I could read his moods even from thousands of miles away.

"Cart, it doesn't have to be like this," I said, trying to soothe him.

"Do you like him?" he asked.

I said nothing.

"Dah, be honest. Do you like Nick?"

I sighed. "We're friends. We get along and have fun together. He's nice."

"He's not right for you."

"Stop already. You don't even know him," I argued, strangling the phone in my hand.

"My gut tells me he'll break your heart."

"Well, your gut is wrong. He won't."

"Fuck, you like him. A lot. I can tell. Why am I always the one you push away?"

I closed my eyes, knots tightening my insides.

I inhaled—and exhaled—trying to calm my jumbling thoughts. "Because. You and I, we're best friends, Cart.

We're not lovers. We got too close once, and it complicated everything… We're still surfing the aftershocks."

"Dah, you never gave me a real chance. You gave one to Jeff. No, you granted him many. Even when he was acting like a shitty piece of shit. I loved my brother, but he was wrong. Still, you stayed with him through it all. And… and you forgave him. Now Nick. Why not me? You never even gave us the chance to prove how perfect we could be together. How incredible our relationship would be. That night we shared…it…it meant something. I know you. Better than you know yourself. It was out of this world. Don't try to deny it. Fuck, Dah…I'm the one who's been by your side all these years…through everything. No matter what… Never asking anything in return, but a chance at love. This is freaking hard. To see you fall for other guys while you refuse to just acknowledge what we are or what we could be. I'm so sick of being parked in the friend zone. No man relishes that spot. It's like being benched during the last game of the championship. It sucks. Bad. Life is much better when we're together, Dah. I only feel alive when I'm by your side. Gimme a shot too… to prove to you we belong together."

"Cart, I love you. With all my heart. You're one of the two most important people in my life, but I'm not in love with you the way you want me to be. I'm sorry… We've been over this a million times already. You have to move on and chase your own happiness… To find *your* person. Maybe Nick is mine or maybe he's not, but I won't know unless I try. It's not about giving you a chance or not. It's about what my heart desires. Believe me, I have no control over this. Things would be so much simpler if you and I were together, I agree. It would be so much easier with Jack too. I'm aware. But for a reason I can't explain, I can't go down that road with you. We'll always be more than friends, but we'll never be lovers. Friendship is all I can offer you… My heart breaks every time I think about how I'm hurting you."

I paused.

Carter said nothing, so I continued. "Every time I push you away, I fear you'll have one of your episodes. That you'll withdraw into yourself and lose touch with every-thing and everyone around you. I hate knowing I won't be there to care of you…to calm you down. To bring you peace. When you find the one—"

"I already have," he rushed out.

"No, Cart. You haven't. I swear on Jeff's grave. Your soul mate, your other half, she's out there, searching for you too. She wishes for you as much as you wish for her."

Carter remained silent on the other end of the line.

"Be open to give her a piece of your heart. Be open to love. Elsewhere."

I imagined him scratching his forehead. Or clenching his fists.

"Dah, I'm in love. With. You. Always have been. For over twenty years. It's a fucking long time, so I can tell you it's not just something that will go away. I want everything with you. Love. Family. It's us, Dah. Carter and Dahlia against the world. And Jack. We're a family, the three of us. My feelings won't go away just because you don't recipro-cate them. In my heart, I'll keep hoping you realize I'm the one for you too. Be assured I heard everything you said, but it doesn't mean I have to believe it…or agree." His voice cracked on the last word.

Tears pooled in my eyes.

My best friend continued, "You are my destiny. The day you stop fighting it, you'll realize the truth. In the meantime, I'll put on a happy smile the next time I meet

Nick. If he hurts you, though, I'm killing him with my own hands, Dah."

I chuckled through my tears. Carter was the least violent person I knew.

"I'm not kidding."

"Cart, I wish things were different. I do. No matter how it turns out, I'll always be there for you. In every way I can. What would I do without you in my life?" I breathed out, drying my tears with my fingertips. "For what it's worth, you don't even kill spiders, but whatever. If you wanna act all rough and tough around Nick, suit yourself." I sucked in a jagged breath.

Carter sniffled.

My heart vibrated. "I miss you. All the time."

"Me too. I love you," he said after a moment.

I kept my eyes shut, fighting back my emotions. "I-I know. I love you too. Be safe out there."

"Talk to you tomorrow, okay? I'll video chat with Jack."

"We'll be here. Whenever you're ready. Bye."

We hung up, and tears streamed down my cheeks as I locked the store.

For a couple of minutes, I sat in my car, my heart breaking into many pieces as I thought about how much I kept hurting my best friend. Why did it have to be this complicated? Why couldn't Carter love someone else? I heard everything he said and it all made sense, but right now, I craved Nick's touch. My heart longed for him too.

"I'm sorry, Cart," I said out loud before starting the engine once I dried all my tears.

Nick was already parked in the driveway when I made it home.

The sight of him chased my emotional breakdown away. It brought a smile to my face, hope to my heart, and heat to my core. Yeah, Nick happened to be the one my entire body burned for.

"Finished early today. Thought you might like a hand with Jack while you get ready. If we feed him before we get going, we could grab takeout somewhere, both of us later," he offered, opening my car door.

That fuzzy feeling returned to my chest—and my lower belly.

I climbed out and moved closer to him. "Ohmygod, you're a savior. I thought I wouldn't have time to shower."

I hugged him, my pulse spiking when his arms curled around me in return. The way our bodies connected quieted every doubt swirling inside me. I tightened my grip on him, needing him more than ever.

We breathed each other in before finally breaking apart.

I smoothed the fabric of my powder-blue maxi dress with my fingers, trying to busy my hands.

Paula left, and after I snuggled with my son for a little beat, I put Nick in charge of feeding him some leftover macaroni while I got ready.

Dressed in a denim skirt, a teal tank top, and cowboy boots, I braided my hair and added a little makeup to my eyes and lips.

Satisfied, I went downstairs, only to find both guys sprawled on their stomachs on the floor, building a tower with wooden blocks.

Jack pushed it until it toppled over, his laughter warming up my heart.

Nick faked being sad, and together, they built it up again.

I could've stood there in the doorway, watching them for hours.

"Mama," Jack said, jumping to his feet when he noticed me and running into my arms as I crouched down.

"Hey, baby. Ready to leave?"

He bobbed his head. "See Buddy?"

I said no with my head. "Not today, baby. Some other time, okay?"

"Okay. Buddy my friend. My best *bestest* friend."

"Yes, he is."

Five hours later, Nick pulled into the driveway, the bed of his truck loaded with boxes of bathroom tiles and other supplies needed to start the farmhouse's interior renovation.

Jack snored in his car seat behind us, deep asleep.

"I had fun tonight," I said, not ready for the night to end.

"I did too." Nick leaned closer, tracing the rim of my lips with his thumb. "Listen, I can't stay away from you, Dahlia. There's something powerful that exists between us, and no matter how much I tell myself I should back off and be content being your friend, I can't. The line we crossed the other night can't be uncrossed. I don't wanna go back to being just friends."

I remained silent, searching for the right words.

Shivers tickled my spine.

My heart danced behind my ribs.

I blew out a long breath, doing my best to keep my fears at bay.

"I have no idea what I'm doing. I might be a mother, but my love life has been dead for years. It's scary to trust someone else with my heart."

"I—"

I spoke before he could finish his thought. "But I'm willing to try with you. My heart tells me you're worth the risk. That you'll be gentle and careful with it. It hasn't healed completely. It might still break again from time to time, but I'm okay. I just need the reassurance you'll be patient with me."

"Dahlia, I'll never hurt you. I'll be gentle, and we'll figure it out. Together."

"I'd like that."

"Can I kiss you?"

I nodded. "It seems like forever since you did the last time."

Shifting in my seat, I leaned over the central console, meeting Nick halfway.

Our mouths explored each other, careful at first, as if it were the first time, but soon we kissed with unchained zeal. And passion. And something else I couldn't name. Our tongues entangled together.

Nick feasted on my neck as much as he could with the console between us. "God, you taste even better than I remember."

My skin ignited. All rational thoughts left me. This. This feeling. The desire. I'd missed it more than I thought. A pool of scorching heat filled my lower belly.

"You wanna come inside?" I asked, breathless, barely holding it together.

"You sure?" he asked, his eyes full of sparks, his pupils dilated, sending my heart in high gear just by the way he stared at me.

"Yes. Don't leave already."

He cradled my cheek with his warm palm, and he said "Yes" against my lips as I melted into his embrace.

We broke apart, and eager to return to kissing the man who had turned my world upside down since he'd first wandered into my store by mistake, I released my baby from his car seat and lifted him into my arms.

Nick moved closer and extended his hands. "Let me. Show me the way to his room."

I placed my son in his arms, seized with emotion at the sight of them, when Nick's lips connected with the top of his head.

Once in Jack's bedroom, I tucked him in his bed as Nick stood beside me, watching my baby for a long time with cloudy eyes, his head dipped forward, and his shoulders low.

"Wanna go downstairs?" I asked, caressing his biceps with my fingertips.

He nodded and swallowed. "Sorry," he said, dragging a hand over his face. "I killed the mood."

"It's okay," I said. "Remember, I'm here if you ever wanna talk about it."

He averted his eyes for a few seconds before bringing them back to me. Caring. And hurting. All at the same time. "Not now. One day I will."

I fetched two beers from the fridge and offered him one as we made it to the living room.

"Whenever you're ready."

A sigh left my lips. I knew Nick had lost someone he loved. I didn't know what he'd been through, but I knew despair and heartbreak when I saw them—because I felt them too. I recognized the signs.

I scooted closer, and Nick draped an arm over my shoulders. With my head pressed against his ribcage, I drew figures over the plane of his abs with my finger, drunk on his heartbeat, strong and steady.

"It's nice," I said.

Nick cocked his head, waiting for me to continue.

"This. It feels right. And good."

With a twist of his upper body, he moved to face me. "I

was serious earlier. I want this. With you. Whatever *this* is." I closed my eyes as he smoothed my lips with the pad of his thumb, sending shivers to my core. "Can I kiss you again?"

"Do you really have to ask?"

When his lips, sure and warm, locked on mine, I dissolved in his arms.

He groaned. I whimpered. He swallowed every sound coming out of my mouth. My back arched as Nick trailed kisses down my throat.

How did I survive all these years without this man's touch?

"You wanna keep going or stop?" he asked, his voice rough and rippling with lust.

"Stop."

He jerked away from me fast, and I felt the cool air rush between us.

With my bottom lip between my teeth, I moved to my knees, and without a word, I straddled him.

"Dah… What..? I-I thought—"

I placed a finger over his lips. "I don't wanna stop. I just want to do it this way," I said, barely recognizing my own voice, strained and husky.

Nick hooked his hands around my hips, and I shifted over him, feeling the hard part of him taking residence between my legs. He stared at me, waiting for me to make the first move.

With a tilt of my head, I grazed his lips, savoring the way they felt against mine. How they reacted to my teasing.

"Now kiss me and don't stop," I said, almost pleading, my entire body combusting with restrained need and aching desire. And a whole lot of different sensations I couldn't define.

His muscular hands ventured under my top, pushing the cups of my bra down, his palms hot on my bare flesh.

I threaded my fingers through his blond locks, tugging his head back to lock eyes with him. My heart raced in my chest. His tongue dived into my mouth, and the fire burning inside me turned into an inferno, fed by his oxygen as it mixed with mine.

With my hands splayed across his chest, we devoured each other with our eyes, his whiskey irises bright and dark at once.

I rolled my hips over his, relishing the sensations of his thickness as it rubbed against my most sensitive spot, sending bolts of electricity to the deepest part of me and igniting all my cells.

Nick clutched my hips and increased the friction between our bodies. I moaned so loud I feared I'd wake Jack upstairs, but I was unable to keep it bottled up inside.

"Come for me, Dahlia. Let go. Now." As if he possessed a special key to controlling my orgasms, his words acted like a magic formula. I hadn't reached a climax with a man in years. We were still dressed, and I became a pile of sizzling flesh in his arms as I dropped forward, pressing my forehead to his chest.

"Are you okay?" he asked, brushing the tendrils of my hair away from my face.

I grinned as euphoria flooded my veins. "Better than fine. I'm fabulous. I'm flying. You've unlocked something deep inside me…and now, I'll be craving more. So much more."

Nick mirrored my smile. "I'll give it all to you. This satisfied smile is a good look on you. I can't wait to see your *I just got fucked* expression. If it's half good as this one, I'll be addicted to it. I can already tell."

His hands found my breasts, and he kneaded them, making me hot for him all over again.

I sat on my ankles, and moving back, I unbuckled his belt and freed his erection. It pulsed in my fist, hard and warm, and ready for me. With my hand around the base, I worked him slowly, getting used to the feel of him.

I ran my tongue over my lips as wild and dirty fantasies whirled inside my head.

I pushed his shirt up, revealing his tantalizing abs, the ones I'd dreamed about since the day I saw him shirtless, water rolling down his chest. The vision had kept me warm most nights—and every time my vibrator showed up for a little private party of our own.

"I wanna taste you," I said, my voice sounding more like a sex kitten's than my own.

Nick nodded. Then shook his head. He nodded again, his head thrown back and eyes closed, as if torn between liking the idea or not. "I'm clean. Got tested a few months back. I haven't slept with anyone since," he said, panting. "Oh God, Dahlia, just your touch is enough to shatter me."

I smirked, relishing the power I had over him in that instant.

With my eyes trained on his face, I moved down and swept my tongue around the tip, enjoying the taste of him for the first time.

His hips buckled off the sofa as an animalistic growl escaped him.

I lapped at it again, eating him up as if he were made of ice cream. His pre-cum coated my tongue as I engulfed him deeper into my mouth.

"Fuck, you're good. Oh yes…God."

I sucked him harder. Pumped him faster. Pushed him deeper inside my mouth.

Every roar leaving his lips made me hornier for him.

Every pulse of his cock got me hungrier for him.

Nick grabbed a handful of my hair and set the pace. I had no time to catch a breath as he fucked my mouth. Our eyes found each other. His had never looked so dark before, the pupils dilated to the brim. Glints danced in his irises. The look on his face was a combination of pleasure, pain, and control. I had every intention of robbing him of the latter. I stroked him faster, drunk at the way he stared at me as if he was receiving head for the very first time and had no idea how to abandon himself to the pleasure, half-conscious and half-lost in it. A train of growls left his mouth, and he let go of me. A few bobs of my head later, his body stiffened.

"Dahlia, I'll—" He pushed my head back, fisting himself until his cum covered his stomach in jolts.

With a swipe of my tongue, I licked the swollen tip of his erection. Nick blinked, staring at me as if I'd blown his mind.

I shrugged. "Told you I wanted a taste of you. You stole that moment from me. I had to sample the product."

"Fuck, you're hot."

Pulling me to him, he crashed his mouth on mine, devouring my lips, our tongues dancing a tango. He wove his fingers through my hair and deepened the kiss, sucking my tongue in his mouth and sending a flood to my panties. His thick semen transferred to my tank top, hot against my skin.

"You are amazing, Dahlia Ellis. Now I wanna eat your pussy until you beg me to stop, until I drain every orgasm out of you. Fuck, you're gorgeous."

"I can't wait," I replied, leaning back to catch some air. "Not tonight, though. We both have to get up early tomorrow."

His gaze lowered after we broke our embrace. "Damn, I ruined your top."

"No, you just branded it. It might actually become my favorite one." I winked, and he groaned against my mouth.

Nick cleaned his abdomen using the warm washcloth I brought him as I removed my sticky top. We kissed goodnight in the doorway, our mouths still hungry for each other. After a long shower, I slid under the covers, sleep claiming me as I dreamed of all the things I couldn't wait for Nick to do to me, my lips stretching into a ridiculous grin, and my heart playing a cheerful melody in my chest.

Only then I realized something. Music had finally made its way back into my heart.

Into my life.

30

NICHOLAS

"Can we talk?" I asked Dahlia a few days later while Jack was keeping himself busy with Buddy, rolling on the lawn after dinner as we sat on the deck. The sound of the boy's laughter healed parts of my heart, a little more each time, and I had to force my eyes off him.

Dahlia leaned over the table and grabbed my hand in hers and quirked an eyebrow.

My pulse quickened at her sight. We hadn't had a chance to be alone since the night we made out on her couch like horny teenagers. I couldn't wait for round two, but her responsibilities as a mother and business owner were her priorities—and only added to her charm—so I had to be patient.

I mirrored her stance and kissed her lips.

Something inside me grew quiet, a voice…a calm settling deep within.

For a long minute, we stared at each other until I could finally name the new sensation unfolding inside me. My pulse didn't even hasten at the thought of it. No, because it felt right. About damn time.

I exhaled. "There's a reason I left Chicago. You already know about my friend who passed away."

She nodded, a tiny wrinkle marring her forehead.

"His death hit me hard…huh…for many reasons. Anyway, one night, I received a delivery. Something Derek had put together for me. A letter… Stuff he loved… And somehow, as I was searching for the meaning of life, surfing through my grief, his words spoke to me. In a strange way, it was as if he wanted me to go on a self-discovery journey or something. As if he had planned the entire thing and knew I belonged elsewhere…"

I swallowed and tightened my grip on Dahlia's hand.

"I went to see the ocean first. There, I met a nice woman and her little girl. Their hospitality touched me. I patched their roof while they helped me patch my broken heart…or some parts of it, at least. A week later, I left and ended up meeting an old couple by the side of the road, arguing about a flat tire. After I helped them out, I spent three weeks working alongside them at their ranch. None of it was planned. It just happened… As if Derek was pushing me toward an ultimate goal…an endgame I couldn't really see at the time."

I shook my head, smiling at the memory of it all.

"Mike told my friend Tucker about the job here, and the next thing I knew, I was agreeing to move to Green Mountain. For a longer period of time than I imagined I would at first…but something in me whispered it was the right decision. That I had to do this. And now that I'm here with you, it feels like my instincts were right…"

Dahlia brushed my hair back with her fingers, letting her soft touch linger on my temple as she watched me.

"There's this list… Huh…how can I explain it?"

A curve graced her lips, and the tension in me eased.

"Well, Derek made it before he died. Some sort of bucket list. Or more like a 'Things he wished he had experienced in his life' list, as he called it. Somehow, it became our common bucket list. It was…it was in the package I received." I closed my lids for a split second and cleared my throat. "Derek was twelve when he died… Cancer."

Dahlia's sharp intake of breath vibrated through me. She squeezed my hand, offering me support. And a listening ear. "Nick, I'm sorry. It's devastating." Her gaze shifted to her son, and she watched him for a minute, her eyes soft and loving, brimming with unshed tears. "I can't imagine…"

I started speaking to avoid falling into the chasm of my grief and memories. "Anyway, when I set out on my big journey, I challenged myself to tick off everything on the list—and add a few personal goals along the way. That's why I drove to the coast. Since I left my hometown, many things I can't explain have happened—often matching the list, for some reason. Go figure. Anyway, there's one thing I haven't done yet, and I think we could do it together. The three of us… If you're up to it…"

Dahlia's eyes lit up. "What is it?"

"Okay. I don't know if you like the outdoors, but I've been thinking about it. A lot. And I'm sure Greta wouldn't object to Buddy having a sleepover."

"Nick, tell me what it is."

"Derek wanted to go camping…to sleep under the stars. Jack is little, and I'd never ask you to bring him into the woods with bears and all sorts of wild animals. And honestly, there's no way the dog would make it through the trek." My gaze shifted to the old bloodhound, panting next to Jack, as the boy hugged him and whispered into his ear. "What if I build us a platform? Nothing fancy, but some sort of stage, and we could add inflatable mattresses and sleeping bags, and camp here. Under the stars," I said, surveying the backyard. "We could light a campfire and roast marshmallows or have s'mores and even cook dinner or whatever. What do you think?"

Dahlia's irises glinted with thousands of stars. "Ohmygod, this would be so much fun. I haven't gone camping in forever. I'm not even sure I remember when the last time was." Her gaze darkened, and something passed in it. She closed her eyes and swallowed. When she glanced back at me, whatever memory had resurfaced had already faded.

I flipped my hand under hers, and she interlaced her fingers with mine. Leaning forward, I lifted her chin with a finger until our eyes met. "Whatever it is, you can talk to me. I know you had it all before me, and I'm okay with it. It's part of who you are. I'm just happy that we've found each other now."

A lone tear rolled down her cheek, and I caught it with my thumb. We got lost in each other's gaze for a moment before I stood and rounded the table.

"Come here," I said, sitting on a vacant chair and pulling her onto my lap. With Dahlia nestled in my arms, we watched Jack running around, Buddy puffing, too tired to follow him.

I really could get used to this life—more than I ever thought possible.

A simple life with the people dear to my heart. Love. And family.

I fastened my arms around Dahlia's waist, and she rested her head on my shoulder, soft and warm against me.

"Thank you for being you," she said, cocking her head until our mouths fused. "And I'd like to go camping with you. It sounds fun. As a teenager, I used to love stargazing and making out. Would it be allowed?"

"Absolutely. It's mandatory," I said, kissing the tip of her nose. "Next weekend. It's a date. Do you have sleeping bags and stuff like that?"

"Nah. But I'm on it. Build that stage and I'll take care of the gear."

"You sure?"

She nodded. "Yeah. Jack and I will go shopping sometime next week." She brought her attention to her son, now running in our direction, his friend snoozing in the shadow of a tree. "Baby, we gotta go soon. I have a long day tomorrow at the store."

"Not going. Stay with *NickandBuddy*," the boy said, folding his arms over his chest.

I let go of her, and Dahlia squatted before him. "I know, baby. You still have a little time before saying good-bye. Next week, we'll go camping together. The four of us."

"Buddy no camping. Silly."

"He will come. Nick will make sure he can sleep with you. But you must be a good boy. Do you think Buddy prefers marshmallows or hotdogs?" she asked, tickling her son's tummy.

"Buddy doggy, Mama. No people food. Doggy food, *Nicksaid*. You funny." He grimaced. "Buddy don't like *hontdogs*."

Dahlia nuzzled his neck and kissed him on the crown of his head. "You're right. What was I thinking? We'll find doggy treats for him then. Does it sound better?"

Jack bobbed his head with so much energy I feared it would fall off, and hurried toward the now snoring dog.

Dahlia and I busied ourselves cleaning up the table and filling the dishwasher inside.

"Before I go, kiss me," she ordered, her voice raw and overflowing with lust. She looped her arms around my neck, her soft breast pressing against my chest and sending so many signals to my lower body as our tongues danced together. "I've missed you."

With both hands, I pushed her hair away from her face, wanting to look at every inch of her.

"I'm sorry I've been so busy lately," she said.

"It's okay. Don't worry about it."

"It's not, but I'll make it up to you." She winked, and my entire body ignited at her promise. "Will you show me that list, or is it too personal? I don't want to intrude. I'm just curious. If I'm overstepping, please tell me. Your friend must have been wise to send you here…to me."

My stomach knotted.

I breathed in to calm my rumbling uneasiness away.

After all, Derek's list wasn't some secret. Tucker had seen it. Yeah, he'd even snapped a picture for good measure.

I tugged at Dahlia's hand. "Let's settle Jack, and I'll show you."

"It doesn't have to be today." She shrugged. "Next week is fine. Or some other time. You don't even have to if you're not ready."

At that moment, something unfurled inside me. I had no idea what it was, except for the certitude that this woman belonged in my life for as long as she would have me. Everything about her made me want to do better. Be better. Aim higher.

"Let's do it now. I hate secrets. Not that this is some world-shattering one, but I'm ready to share it with you. Because it's important to me. And you're important to me too."

Jack lay in his small sofa bed, dressed in the monster pajama set Dahlia brought over, with a blanket in one fist and a sippy cup in the other, Buddy curled up next to him.

As they watched bear cartoons with an annoying theme song, I led Dahlia upstairs.

Jitters surged inside me, my heart threatening to leap from my chest at any moment.

Now I would be sharing a past that only a few people knew about. It was scary opening up and showing my vulnerability. It felt like a big step in our relationship, but one that needed to be dealt with. Dahlia's sensitivity would heal the final rift in me. I had no more doubts.

We sat side by side on my bed after I fished the list out of a drawer.

Dahlia unfolded it with care, and I observed her expressions as I shared an important part of my life with her for the very first time.

She cleared her throat and read what Derek had written out loud. "Derek's *I wish I had experienced in my life* List + Nick's *Bucket* List. Ohmygod, this is so sweet." She sucked in a breath. "Okay, let's see. One. Go to a hockey game with Nick and the guys." Then she read the comment I added below. "*It was a great night, bro. Hope you saw the ribbon with your name on it after each goal. I'll forever remember that day.*" She turned to face me. "Wow." After blinking, she continued. "Two. Make one new…no, three new best friends. *I thought I already had all the friends I needed in Tuck and Jace, but I was wrong. Three new best friends came into my life unexpectedly, and they stole my heart the moment we met.*"

Her lips bent as she read my words.

"*Jack is a little boy. I'm sure you two would have hit it off in no time. He's sweet and adorable. And smart. Like his mother. He's always happy. Every time he's around, I can't help but smile. And it's amazing to be able to smile again. His innocence reminds me of yours. He has a way to appeal to my heart. Buddy is my neighbor's dog. You never specified if the friends had to be humans, so I take it upon myself to say it can apply to any living species. He came to me the moment I parked my truck in the driveway and has been by my side since. There's something between us. It's strong, and I can't really explain it, but I consider him my friend too. And there's Dahlia—"*

I recited the words out loud, knowing every line by heart. "I don't know where to start, bro. I feel like I've known her all my life, which is silly since I only met her not too long ago. There's a connection between us. Something powerful. She fits right into my life, her heart next to mine. Her smile makes my knees weak. You know like that song you enjoyed so much. I wish you could have met her because I'm sure you too would have fallen under her charm right away."

My gaze met Dahlia's, the blush covering her cheeks unmistakable. My heart rate kicked up at the way she stared at me.

"Nick," was all she said, her hand cupping her heart. She straightened her spine, and her lips found my cheek, filling me with new sensations, before continuing. "Three. Kiss a girl until my heart beats fast."

Once again, I interrupted her with words etched in my memory. "It happened. Go to point two. *She kissed me back. And I thought my heart would explode. It had never felt this way before. Never. She's special. I'm telling you. And she wanted to kiss me again, but like a fool, I stopped her. What's wrong with me? I yearn for more, bro. It's too soon to know, right?"*

Her voice was a breathless murmur, aimed for my heart, when she said, "You're not a fool. You're one of the best people I've ever met. You're smart, funny, caring, handsome… Definitely not a fool." She rested her head on my shoulder and kept reading. "Four. Go camping and sleep under the stars. Five. Watch the sunrise every morning. *I do that most mornings, talking to you as if you're listening to me. I hope you are, or if someone hears me, they'll think I'm going* nuts. *It's our moment, you and I. Buddy always comes to me right after. As if he senses I might need him in these moments. Yeah, Buddy is definitely one of my best friends now."*

Dahlia smiled, her eyes glossy.

"Nick, this is beautiful. Six. Dip my toes in the ocean, even if jellyfish are gross." A snicker left her mouth. And one left mine too. "Seven. Go to a Carter Hills concert because duh, he's the best. Ohmygod, Cart would be so proud. Derek was a true fan?"

I nodded. "Yep. He could listen to his music every day, all the time, on repeat."

"I love it." She frowned, her brow knitting as she read my next confession. *"Okay, this one is tricky. See, for a reason I still can't wrap my head around, I've met Carter Hills. No kidding. I have no idea how this journey brought me to the rock star, but it did. Even though our first encounter was a bit tense, he seems like a nice guy. And he is Dahlia and Jack's family. He cares about them so much. Their love knows no boundaries…no beginning and no end. It's beautiful. I'm the guy getting in the middle of it. I understand his reservation. I really do, but I hope one day we'll be okay—for Dahlia and Jack's sake—because they mean a lot to me too. Oh, and by the way, Tucker gifted me two tickets for his show in Nashville in the fall. You'll get to see him in concert, after all."*

Dahlia turned to face me. "Nick, about Carter—"

"It's okay. We only met twice, and I love that he cares enough about you that he's willing to scare anyone who's not good enough for you away. The thing is, I'm not scared easily, so he'll have to try harder if he wants me out of your life."

She moved onto my lap, straddling me, and grabbed my hands in hers. "Carter barks but doesn't bite. Believe me. And I'm big enough to choose who I bring into my life…and my heart. He doesn't have a say in it." Her lips widened into a smile, one that tipped my heart over. "But I'm really happy you're ready to fight for me. It's important to me. For what it's worth, I'd fight for you too. Any time of the day. Or night."

She kissed me, her lips light over mine, then continued reading the list.

"Eight. Do something deemed impossible. Oh, I like that. Nine. Build something with my own hands that I'll keep forever or gift someone. Ten. Nick, go on an adventure (now you must pick one). Wow, this kid was smart. I already love him." She read the words I added next. "*I did it. I packed my stuff and followed your advice. I don't know where this trip will take me, but it feels right. I'll keep you updated.*"

She paused, contentment painting her face.

"*Update. I'm in Green Mountain, bro. It was Tuck's idea. You know how he is. He even got me a job. And I'm fixing an old house. It's beautiful here. People are nice. They smile all the time. You would fit right in. I met someone this afternoon. Got lost and entered her shop by mistake. She stole my breath away the moment we locked eyes. We spent the entire afternoon together, chatting and laughing. She agreed to be my friend. We're having a date next week. Wish me luck.*"

Dahlia fastened her arms around my neck. "Nick, you didn't need luck. For the record, I was starstruck too."

I leaned in until our mouths were a hair's breadth apart. "You, Dahlia Ellis, the country music star, was starstruck by a guy like me?"

She nodded. "Nick Peterson, you're not just a guy. You're the guy I wanna spend all my time with. The one I never seem to get enough of. It means something."

Bringing her attention back to the list, she read the other points. "Make someone smile my newfound mission."

I jumped in, gazing into the eyes of the woman still sitting on my lap, as I read aloud the words that spilled from my heart. "*Dahlia smiles all the time. Big gestures, little ones, she finds beauty in everything. Today I gifted her a donut, and she bit into it as if I had given her the world. I'm telling you, this girl is different. She's the best thing that has happened to me since I left the city. As if all my life, I was destined to meet her. To fall for her. I wish for her smile all the time and want to be responsible for every curve of her lips. Because her smiles make me smile too.*"

My voice faded out as silence enveloped us, my heart beating fast inside my ribcage.

"What's the last point on Derek's list? You left it blank," Dahlia whispered, her hands trembling, and a river flowing down her face.

I shrugged, battling the emotions stirring inside me. "I have no idea. He didn't finish it. I added a few and still do as I go. The last one has to be something meaningful. I haven't found what it is just yet."

Dahlia folded the sheet and handed it back to me.

"This is beautiful…and sad, Nick." She sucked in a shaky breath. "I'm amazed by you. You have such a huge heart. Derek sounds like someone great."

"He was."

Her moss-green eyes bore into my soul. They soothed me and shot me with doses of something close to love. Something that made me long to never leave her sight— and her side.

Our mouths collided, speaking everything we didn't say out loud.

"Point twenty. You're the reason I smile so much. And about points two and three," she said, whispering against my lips, "I agree too. Now kiss me again because I love it when my heart beats fast."

And just like that, Dahlia added another point to the list. One that mattered. A lot.

Derek's Bucket List – ~~22. Nick. Share parts of my life with the person who means the most~~

31

DAHLIA

"Nick, it's charming. I can't believe you made this for one night. Did you even sleep at all last week?" I asked, covering my mouth in awe as I took in the raised platform he'd built and stained in the same walnut color as the porch. Located behind the old garage in the backyard, it resembled a giant bunk bed on stilts. Fairy lights hung from the tree branches—as if he knew I loved them—casting a glow that made the whole scene feel magical. It would be even more enchanting once the sun set.

On one side, there were wooden stairs to climb up along with a ramp for Buddy's old bones. Okay, this was the cutest thing I'd seen in a long time. Nick's thoughtfulness and caring ways made my heart tremble with eagerness and need, lust or something I couldn't exactly define. All I knew was that spinning in his orbit made me happy—and content.

Before he could say anything, I turned and slammed my lips against his, craving the taste of him. He jerked and stiffened in shock, then leaned into the kiss as heat flared between us. I bit his lower lip, then soothed it with gentle, brushing strokes of my tongue before inviting his tongue into my mouth, sucking it hard. His lower body stiffened in greeting, a fitting reply to my bold move. Maybe I wasn't so rusty after all. The idea alone sent a thrill through me, filling me with jitters and excitement.

Breaking off the kiss, I panted heavily against his mouth. A new sensation washed over me. One I could easily get addicted to. Never before had I been so rough, taking what I wanted without restraint. But right now, all I craved was to play dirty. Silence hung around us, broken only by the harsh cadence of our breaths.

"Let's check out the view from the top. You'll see, it's fantastic," he suggested, putting my horny hormones to rest—for now.

I nodded and gestured for him to climb up first. He gave me a weird look, and a silent giggle escaped me.

Nick started up the wooden stairs, and I followed, pressing close, deliberately brushing my body against his. I gave his butt a hard squeeze, and he stumbled on the steps.

"Hey. You're not playing fair."

My eyes widened with fake innocence as a lascivious grin spread across my face. "What? Just admiring the view. As you said. With my hands. I agree it is fantastic and mouth-watering."

He waggled his finger at me over his shoulder as a wry smile overtook his lips. His gaze flashed with mischief. Clearly, he hadn't met my brand of naughtiness yet. "Woman, behave."

He wrapped his muscular arms around me when we reached the top, and I sank into his embrace. The view was quite impressive from up here.

"I had no idea the property was sitting on such a big piece of land."

The trees lining the boundaries created a much-appreciated intimacy, offering us no view of the neighbors. I bet the owners had some great parties in this yard. If it had been me, I would've pitched a big white tent and hosted all my get-togethers here. Birthdays, anniversaries, weddings. A place to bring families and friends together. To create memories.

The pillows and sleeping bags we brought over were laid on the mattresses, and my eyes lingered on the cozy display.

"Perhaps this could be our thing. Sleeping under the stars once a week," Nick put forth with a shrug.

I agreed with a nod. "It's magical. Coming here once will never be enough." His hardness pushed against my back, and I whirled around in his arms. His grip on me slackened, and I watched him, amusement returning to my face, my cheeks heating up. "Oh, I'm not the only one feeling naughty."

His lips tilted in an innocent smile, the opposite of the heat flashing in his gaze. "W-what?"

I gave him a pointed stare, then deliberately dropped my eyes to his erection. The bulge in his jeans slowly swelled beneath the denim. "Dahlia, don't play with fire. You will get burned."

"Yeah, but what a way to go. I tried safe, now I want the inferno. The hotter the better."

My breath hitched as he combed my hair away from my face gently, then curled it around his fist and pulled until my lips opened. The flutters in my belly turned to raging fireworks. Hot air whirled between us. Mine or his, I couldn't tell. Nick's lips rubbed against mine as he cupped his junk with his other hand before pushing his hard-on against my softness. My insides melted as his length hit my sensitive nub. More. I wanted more. I needed more.

Hungry for release as steam vaporized my sanity, I thrust against him. Demanding. Unapologetic. Anyone could walk on us, but I couldn't care less. I was finally taking everything I had been craving for weeks now. I bit his lips after he sucked on mine until they felt sore. I wanted to be marked by him and brand myself on him. Nick Peterson was mine. No one else's. It was about time we made it official, and I staked my claim.

We kissed for a few intense minutes, rough and hard. Playful and steamy. Bit by bit, sanity returned, and we separated, gasping for air. The desire that arose within seconds of our bodies touching each other couldn't be contained. I didn't want our first time to happen out here on the platform. I wanted it to be intimate, comfortable, and secluded. I wouldn't be opposed to it next time—but not today. Today, I had plans. For him.

Nick framed my face with his large palms, holding me in place. I grabbed his shirt to stop myself from tumbling onto the mattresses and dragging him down with me.

"Dahlia—" He was flustered, his gaze smoldering.

I tried to speak but couldn't find the words. The only thing that I could think about was our imminent release. Mine. His. Entangled together in bed sheets. And breathless. The only words echoing in my mind were "Fuck me." The tidal wave of pure need rising inside my core was demanding to be satiated.

Nick cleared his throat and broke the tension—the one wrapped tight around us. "Tonight, I prepped some food for grilling over the campfire and treats for dessert. Hope you're hungry."

Yes. *Hungry.* Not for food, though. For him. I salivated at the mere thought.

My body refused to temper down. To settle.

His hands all over me, his hard body pressed against

mine—inside mine—his mouth mapping every inch of my bare flesh were what I craved. They were all I'd dreamed about since the day I saw him in my shop for the very first time.

With my arms wrapped around his midsection, I stared into his eyes. "Starving." Huskier than normal, rougher than before, the single word rose from the well of my desire.

Nick's eyes burned with a fiery heat. Tracing my cheekbone, down to my neck, right down to my cleavage, his finger hovered over the valley between my breasts.

Against his lips, I whispered, "Jack is still napping in the playroom. How about you and I have a little playtime of our own?"

Coils of heat snapped into my body as his pupils dilated.

"You serious?"

I gave a sharp nod.

"You sure?"

"Never been more sure."

"Gosh Dahlia, I want you so bad."

"I want you too. I don't wanna wait anymore."

Without another word, he jumped from the platform and raised his arms to give me a hand, allowing my body to rub against his slowly as he helped me down. A blaze snaked around us, between us. He swept me off my feet, scooping me over his shoulder and carrying me straight to his room. With my hands caressing every part of him I could graze, I stoked the fire, letting it burn hotter and brighter.

This moment would be mine—ours—and I would savor every second. Over the past few years, I had always put myself last. Not this time. This was my time.

Nick kicked the bedroom door shut and lowered me to

my feet, my toes barely brushing the floor as I melted into a body of lust, conscious only of the thrumming pulse deep between my thighs, desperate for a release.

All the naughty dreams I'd had about our first time, about us, could now turn to reality, and none of them involved clothes or being rational.

The mere thought of us tangled together, enveloped by the scent and taste of him, sent a zing through me. The image in my head of his weight pinning me down, the feel of his rough stubble rubbing against my cheek, and the desire pouring out of him made me weak in the knees. Bits of me I'd long thought dead were slowly coming back to life, and now I wanted to take charge, to rock his world, to show him just how far gone I was for him.

His greedy palms molded to my ass, taking a handful. His mouth, as if under some magnetism, lowered over mine.

"Wait," I said, leaning back.

A frown creased his forehead as he looked confused.

I moved a step away from him, never breaking eye contact. With a twist, I unbuttoned my shirt, letting it fall open. The shadow between my breasts teased him with tantalizing glimpses.

His eyes widened as realization hit him. "No bra? Did you ditch it to mess with me on purpose? Had I known this, I would have lost my mind long before."

"None whatsoever. Lost it the other day, remember? Didn't wanna risk losing it again. So sad, I have nothing to hang on your bedroom wall this time. Maybe this shirt. Do you want it?" Nick's gaze could set the world on fire. With a seductively slow movement, I slid my hand lower, just under the waistband of my shorts. I tugged the dark pink lace up and winked. "Or maybe these."

"Yeah." Nick cleared his throat, his voice rough. "Yes. Gimme."

A victory smirk spread across my lips.

Sucking on my finger for a second, I glided it to the dip of my collarbone and down to my navel, swaying my hips, taking a few sideswipes over my half-hidden breasts, squeezing them, pinching my nipples until they poked out from under the fabric of the shirt.

Nick's eyes were at risk of bulging out, following every movement.

Feeling brave and beautiful under his ardent stare, I wetted my finger and dipped it into the waistband of my shorts, a low grunt escaping. I could see his restraint wearing thin, and I relished the power I held over him in that instant.

Keeping my shirt on, my way to titillate him, I used my other hand and unbuttoned my cutoffs, pulling the zipper down.

Nick's sharp intake of breath rippled through me.

Like a predator hunting his prey, he prowled toward me in one stride.

I shook my head. Slowly, I shimmied out of my denim shorts. I pushed the lace to the side, slipped a finger inside me, allowing the wetness to coat my finger. I added another digit and dived them in and out of me, chasing a release that would tip me over the edge. Removing my fingers from inside me, I showed him the evidence of my desire. "Look what you do to me. Want me to share?"

His tongue darted out to wet his dry lips, ravenous hunger etched across his face as he bobbed his head like a little kid.

Good. I loved that he was as hungry for me as I was for him.

I winked. "What about a striptease?"

"What?"

"Strip for me. Then you can fuck me as many times as you want, however you want."

Heat flared as determination rose in response to my challenge. He pulled out his phone, his thumb swiping across the screen for a few seconds. A low, soulful song—hot and heavy with beats—filled the room. His body began moving to the rhythm. I backed up until my calves brushed the bedframe, then slowly crawled backward across the mattress, all the while keeping my eyes locked on him as his body swayed to the rhythm.

In the most jaw-dropping move, he lifted his shirt, one inch at a time, enticing me with glimpses of his chiseled body—his sculpted abs, strong pectorals, and broad shoulders. As if he'd rehearsed it multiple times, he took a handful of the fabric behind his neck and peeled it off, the piece of clothing falling from his fingertips. His entire bare chest was now exposed to my gaze. So hot. He turned around, his back presenting me with another delectable treat. I would love to sink my teeth into those muscles and lick the golden skin that was tempting me.

Nick's firm butt twerked as he jerked to the music, then swayed, my mouth salivating at the sight. The sound of the zipper coming down became the biggest aphrodisiac. I wanted him. Every hard inch of him. He spun around and, in one sweeping motion, removed his jeans, his hardness pulsed, pointing straight at me.

"No boxer briefs?" I asked with an arched brow. "Did you ditch them to mess with me on purpose?"

"Didn't wanna hide the effect you had on me all night." He fixed his gaze on me.

I swallowed, my voice trembling, laced with unchained lust. "Nick. I want you. Right now. On me, against me, inside me." I slid out of my shirt, letting it drop to the floor, ready to lose every piece of clothing standing between me and him.

He inched closer. "I believe those are mine." He pinched the thin fabric of my panties between his fingers. "I earned them, no?"

The way he watched me, eyebrows dancing, had my throat dry and pulse racing.

"Yeah." My voice sounded as if it was coming from far away.

He crawled over me, his lips a hair's breadth away from my aching flesh, his harsh breaths caressing my bare skin. He curled his fingers into the waistband of my panties, and a shiver traveled the length of my spine. Tremors rattled me.

Nick's palms brushed against my ass cheeks as he pulled the flimsy fabric down.

I arched my back, aching, my head spinning, about to combust right here on his bed. "No more playing." My voice was shaking, barely sounding like my own.

"You started this," Nick argued, my underwear locked in his fist like a prize he refused to surrender.

With my legs spread wide, I beckoned him to taste me with a flick of my finger. My insides melted as his gaze became an erupting volcano.

With measured movements, Nick slithered in between my thighs, and his lips grazed my sensitive bundle of nerves as he inhaled the scent of me. His skillful tongue took a sweep of my lower lips, rubbing my clit, nibbling it gently. A rhythm overtook me as his finger joined in and entered me, hitting the spot that could send me over the edge in no time. He played me like an instrument. His hands, strong and calloused, took what they wanted. I twined my legs around his shoulders, opening my thighs wider to take more of his tongue.

How did I survive so long without this man devouring me in the most intimate way? My hips bucked to match his every move. I closed my eyes while he squeezed my breasts and pinched my nipples, then cupped my thighs almost painfully. Deliciously.

He firmed his tongue and dipped it deeper into me, reaching a spot that triggered spasms from my core. With the pad of his finger, he rubbed my clit to the same rhythm. I moaned as heat spiraled inside me. His hand moved away from my sensitive flesh to lift my hips further, leaving me bereft. I slid my fingers downward between my thighs and rubbed my bundle of nerves until I was filled with raw, explosive need.

Nick, his lower face shiny with my imminent release, watched me.

I arched my back further to meet with his expert tongue as he went back to his mission, hoping to take more of him, not ready to let go just yet. Desire lashed shivers through me. I gulped in air, savoring the sensation as it washed over me. Heat coiled within me, spiraling toward a point of no return—toward madness. My body shook, unable to postpone the climax any longer.

"Nick, oh God… More. Now."

He curved his fingers as they replaced his tongue, rubbing that aching spot inside me. His tongue joined my digits in massaging my clit, faster and faster as my head thrashed on the pillow, my breaths escaping in shallow pants. I reached a pinnacle where time stopped, and I convulsed against his mouth, gripping and releasing him, as waves of unleashed pleasure rippled through me in surges of exultation.

The pounding of my heart deafened me.

I surfed the climax, touched the high, breathing hard, dots dancing before my eyes as all my muscles tensed, then relaxed. I rode the surge of my release with soothing strokes of Nick's tongue as he licked every drop of wetness and stayed still until I returned to Earth, bliss flooding every inch of me.

On his knees, my lover watched me with a satisfied—part amused—glance.

A mischievous grin took over his face as he leaned forward. His greedy, and oh-so fantastic, tongue returned to my pulsing flesh.

I writhed my hips, trying to escape the hotness of his mouth. "Stop. Too sensitive," I pleaded. "I-I can't."

He snickered and pushed one, two, three—I had no idea—fingers back inside and I gasped, knowing the stars were still reachable if he moved them just the right way. Oh yes, this felt so good. So perfect. So intense. "Better?" he asked, positioning himself over me.

Could he feel how fast my heart was racing? How completely I had fallen under his spell? And how much more of him I still craved?

Gliding his fingers lazily in and out, his mouth found mine, hungry.

I tasted myself on his lips, the mix of us, sweet and musky, lingering on his tongue. My appetite for him had multiplied, feeding the yearning that had taken permanent root inside me, settling deep in every cell. Propping myself on my elbows to deepen the kiss, I wrapped one hand around his throbbing erection, unable to go slow anymore.

It vibrated in my fist, all thick and ready for me.

A hissing sound exited his lips as I worked him, loving how even his hard-on fit in my fist like it'd been carved just for me.

Nick pushed his head back, breathing heavy. "Dahlia, if you keep going at it like this, I will humiliate myself… Oh, fucking fuck."

Unable to hide my smile, I moved my hand up and down his steeled shaft, relishing the effect I had on his body and the control he could barely keep as I toyed with the hard part of him.

I bit my lower lips when our gazes collided, and I beckoned him closer with a finger.

Nick crawled over my body, and my hand curled around his nape, pulling him in.

One of his palms grazed my cheek, his eyes boring into mine, aiming straight for my soul.

"I'm ready," I said.

His finger tipped my chin up. "You sure?"

I nodded.

"I'll be gentle."

I shook my head.

"What?" A frown creased his forehead.

"Don't be gentle. I need this. I need you. I want it all… with you. I've been patient long enough. *We've been patient long enough.* Just rock my world, okay?"

He nodded and shifted to the side, grabbing a condom from the nightstand.

With deliberate precision, he guided me onto my back. His tip teased my entrance and I purred, the sensation only about to push me to the point of no return.

With his eyes glued to mine, he slid inside me, inch by inch. Frozen, we both looked at each other as my body adjusted to his for the very first time.

Neither of us breathed, too enthralled in the moment.

I smiled. Nick smiled back.

He reached for my face with one hand, and I sucked on his thumb, desperate to keep my mouth busy to muffle the cries I knew would soon tumble out.

Nick thrust slowly, gauging my reactions.

I locked my ankles around his back, changing the

angle, pulling him deeper inside me, relishing how his body grazed my clit with each roll of his hips.

His eyes darkened under heavy lids as if he was trying to prolong the pleasure, to stitch himself to me, to live in this moment forever.

Snapping out of my daze, I threaded my fingers through the hair at the nape of his neck and pulled him down to me, desperate for his mouth on mine—and every part of him against me. I kissed him with fieriness.

With a moan, I detached our mouths and pushed my chest forward and his head down, silently begging Nick to cherish my breasts. He tugged at the sensitive tips with his teeth, drawing a loud gasp from me, his hands busy kneading my achy flesh.

Blazing fire set up there while he toyed with the hard tips with his tongue, as if to tame the flames.

Once satisfied, I propped myself up on my elbows and devoured his mouth, unable to go slow. I slid further up, and with open palms, I pushed Nick onto his back and impaled myself on his erection. A series of curses left his luscious lips as a whimper left mine once I rolled my hips over his in an erotic tango.

"Dahlia, fuck—"

Nick fused one hand around my waist, the other tracing every curve of my face, his gaze traveling from my lips to my eyes.

This, this moment with this man, was one I would cherish forever.

I felt more alive than I had in years—and more womanly than I'd known in just as long. I felt beautiful in the way he looked at me, in the heat burning behind his gaze. I lost myself in the amber of his eyes, in every sensation his body stirred within me.

With my hands splayed across his toned chest, I started

moving up and down. Short gasps left my mouth while I rode him like I'd pictured doing so many times since we kissed for the first time.

Spasmodic groans escaped him as he clenched his teeth.

Increasing the friction, he lifted his pelvis, and with quick jerks of his hips, I welcomed him further inside me.

I closed my eyes as pleasure built in every fiber of my being, and my spine buzzed.

We both lost ourselves in the bliss we brought to each other.

"Dahlia, I won't… I-I can't…" He breathed fast. "You're beautiful. Look at me."

I opened my eyes, and without breaking contact, I lay back, pulling him down with me in the tumble. Positioned between my legs with my knees spread on each side, Nick pounded faster. His lips firmed in a thin line, his features taut, and his eyes focused on my face the entire time.

"Like this… Don't stop. I…I… *Yesss*." The orgasm tore through me as I surrendered myself to him completely.

He slowed his movements, clamping my hips, keeping me still as he emptied his load in jolts.

He grunted as we both convulsed in each other's embrace, our hearts beating to the same rhythm, our breaths fighting for the same air.

His hands anchored me at the waist, keeping me flush against him, while his lips rained gentle kisses over my eyelids. "You're beautiful. All of you. It was…you are…" —he sucked in a puff of air, trying to even his breathing— "amazing."

My emotions fought to spill out all at once. What we'd just shared was out of this world, making everything between us feel more real than ever. "Don't go, okay? Don't leave. Don't die. Stay with me." The words, mixed with tears, left my mouth before I could hold them back. Or think them over. "I've been alone for so long…and…and now that you're here, I never wanna be alone again. What we share is special. It's ours…us. It's everything. What we just did only cemented that feeling."

A sob wheezed out. Nick had a way of making me feel vulnerable, a sensation that had felt foreign ever since I'd had to steel myself to keep going three years ago.

He dried my tears with his thumbs. "Hey, I'm here. With you. I'm not going anywhere. As long as you'll have me in your life. This. What we just did…you're right. It welded something between us. A force neither of us can deny."

His words felt as if he could read my deepest thoughts and the language of my soul.

It stole the last particle of air from my lungs.

Words I hadn't spoken in years resurfaced in my head —and my heart. I pushed them down, not ready to assess what we were to each other or what we could be, but knowing it wasn't a dream. A mirage. Or a figment of my imagination.

No, these words had now planted seeds in my heart.

And they wouldn't go away.

32

DAHLIA

Nick handed me a sausage he'd just grilled over the campfire. Jack and Buddy rested on a blanket behind us, the dog being used as a play mat and a car track once more.

"Naughtiest thing you did as a kid?" I asked.

Nick's eyes flicked up toward me, and he hiccupped a laugh. "Easy. One night, I found my Christmas presents and unwrapped them all," he whispered.

"Oh no," I exclaimed, slapping a hand over my mouth. "Did you get caught?"

"I was very careful to wrap them back up afterward. But somehow, I mixed the name tags. My parents had a long talk with my sister and me about Santa. And nosiness."

"Is your sister in Chicago?"

"No. She was in Europe for a while. Came back, somewhere on the East Coast. Met a guy… A surfer. One who escaped the expectations his family had put on him and moved to Australia. Last I knew, they lived in a van on the beach and were happy."

"Oh, this sounds fun. I wish I could live like that." I paused. "Santa, huh? I can't imagine you being naughty."

Nick shrugged. "I had my moments growing up. Tucker got himself into lots of fights—mostly about girls—and I had to jump in to save his ass more often than I can remember. This scar on my eyebrow, I got it after Tuck was assaulted by the entire football team in junior year because he made out with the quarterback's girlfriend under the bleachers and everyone saw it. I couldn't let him get his ass kicked—again. Not that he couldn't defend himself, but he's my friend, so we always had each other's back. We still do." He snickered. "He loved that. No, I take my words back. He still loves that. Trouble. And girls."

"Oh, this is terrible. I can't wait to meet him. He sounds like an…huh…interesting guy."

"Believe me, he is. But he's also the most loyal person I know. And there's nothing he wouldn't do for the people he loves. He's the best, and you're right. You can't be bored with a friend like that."

"Addison is the same. She was the popular girl in high school. Always having a boyfriend. Attending parties. Experimenting with everything before anyone else our age even dared. She got me my first beer at fifteen. Whenever we're together, it's like no time has passed since high school. She pushes me to try new things…to be more adventurous. To follow my instincts." I shook my head as some of Addison's and my best memories flashed in my mind. "What are your parents like? Are you close?"

"No, they live in Italy. I don't see them very often. They rarely come to visit me. Maybe once a year at the most. I try to fly there when I have some free time. Tuck feels more like family to me. But you should see my parents together. They're the real deal. Love at first sight. They were made for each other. Even after all this time, they're still madly in love. They're the definition of couple goals. Sometimes I think they love each other more than the idea of having a family. It's okay, though. As long as they are happy. Are your folks around?"

"Still living in White Crest. In my childhood home. My dad's a lawyer. He used to manage Carter's and my career when we first started. Got us our big break contract when we signed up with Riley. They come here from time to time, but usually, I'm the one driving there to see them. After Jeff died, I pulled away from everybody I loved because it hurt too much. All those memories... Carter refused to gimme my space. In a way, I'm happy he didn't. He prevented me from drowning."

I averted my eyes, memories of my past hitting me at full force.

Nick scooted his chair closer to mine and held my hand in his. "It's okay to be sad. I already told you. How was he?"

I met his eyes. "Who? Jeff?"

"Yeah."

A warm laugh came out. "Where do I even begin? I'd known him all my life. He was almost three years older than Carter and me. The three of us grew up together, but never did it occur to me that we could be more someday. Jeff always volunteered to help Carter and me whenever we needed anything... Always gravitating around us. He used to brag he was our biggest fan. And honestly, he was. From day one. Thumbs-ups, smiles, driving us around. He never missed a show unless he had to. He's the one who got us on Riley's radar. He would have done pretty much anything to see us succeed."

"Did he sing too?"

I shook my head, grinning at the memory. "Nah. And he couldn't figure out a guitar either. If he had, we would have been unstoppable the three of us. Our chemistry was through the roof. He only sang while doing hands-on work around the house, and believed me, it was bad. Really bad." I paused. "From the outside, he looked fearless and always in control. He knew what he wanted, and no one could change his mind if it were set on something. But with me—and Cart—he showed that softer side of him… his vulnerability. And huge heart. He was smart, caring, hardworking. He struggled to find his place in this world. Somehow, even when we tried to include him as much as we could in the band, he felt like a third wheel. So, he decided to follow a path he thought to be his calling. War changed him, though. Jeff wasn't cut for the army, and deep down I'm sure he knew it too, but he hoped to make a difference and leave his mark on the world. To make it a better place…in his own way."

I breathed out with a tight smile.

"That's pretty noble of him. How did you two happen?"

"One day, I was at his home, and he paraded in front of me, half-naked, still wet from his shower, only a towel wrapped low around his hips. He told me years later he had had a crush on me for years but had no idea how to tell me, so he came up with this idea to catch my attention. I was fifteen."

"Did it work?"

"Oh yes. After that, I couldn't stop thinking about him. He woke up my dormant hormones, and I became obsessed with him. He asked me to prom, and things evolved between us after that. Our relationship changed the dynamic of our trio, and we never went back to what we used to be. For a long time, Carter resented us. He acted as if it was all fine, but deep down, he was hurting. A lot."

"But he stayed by your side, no matter what, no?"

I nodded. "Yeah." I lost myself in my thoughts. "Jeff was my first everything. We grew up together. We'd been through so much. Just when we finally figured out how to be with each other for the long run, his heart stopped. I never got a chance to tell him goodbye. Never got the opportunity to tell him all that he meant to me. How sorry I was for the years we missed being happy, too busy fighting." A lump filled the back of my throat. "We had it all—*I* had it all—and it crashed and burned without any notice."

I used the shoulder of Nick's hoodie I'd borrowed to wipe the tears welling up in my eyes and sniffled. My heart shattered in my chest. It turned to dust.

Nick squeezed my hand a little harder, letting me know he was there, then smiled at me. He didn't have to say anything. Everything I needed to mend the remaining fractures of my broken heart swept through his eyes. It warmed me up. With him, I felt more alive than I had in years. The particles of my heart flying around in my chest found their way back together. They built my heart back up, piece by piece, until it felt whole again. I flipped my hand into his and returned his squeeze.

"Any ex-girlfriend who broke your heart? A lost love? Anyone who got away?"

Nick's shoulders dropped as he sighed. "There was this girl. Zoey. Like you and Jeff, we started dating in high school. Back in the day, I thought what we had was true love…that she was the one for me. Until one day, after college, she packed her stuff and moved to California to be with a guy she'd met online. I wanted us to move in together. We had dreams…or so I thought. Turned out she had dreams of her own, and they didn't include me. I took it hard. Met all kinds of girls afterward, thanks to Tucker being on the prowl almost every night, but it always felt wrong. Then I started seeing Pamela on a regular basis. We weren't dating, just being exclusive. After a year she hinted for more. I couldn't see myself going the distance with her. Just to piss me off, she hooked up with one of my two best friends—who apparently had a huge crush on her I knew nothing about—and they eloped months later. She's kinda controlling and crazy at times, but Jace loves her. If he's happy, what else could I want for them?"

I pivoted to face him. "Your ex-girlfriend—or whatever you were—married one of your best friends and you're okay with that?"

"I aim for what my parents have, and I won't settle for any less. If they're happy together, that's fine by me. I would've never married her, anyway."

"Okay, I knew you were amazing, but that, right now, blows my mind. Can I send Pamela a *thank-you* card?" My smile washed off, and I brought my attention back to Nick. "Does this mean you can see yourself going the distance with me?"

His eyes found mine, gleaming with so much heat and power, I had a hard time swallowing. "Yes. I do."

We stared at each other, and flutters danced around in my belly. My pulse kicked up.

Nick's lips parted, but Jack joined us before he could add anything else, and broke the moment.

He tugged at Nick's sleeve. "Play with me? Buddy sleepy. Go swing."

Nick squatted to align his face with my son's. "Oh, you want me to push you on the swing?"

My baby's eyes filled with delight, and he bobbed his head fast.

"You sure you're brave enough to go high?"

He nodded again.

"Okay. Come on then, little guy. Let's see if your toes can touch the sky."

With both hands over my heart to prevent it from running away or combusting, I watched my men sauntering away, hand in hand, toward the swing set Nick had built for Jack last weekend.

My men.

When did I start referring to Nick as mine?

I had no clue, but the thought didn't scare me. No. Instead, it soothed another chunk of my bruised heart.

The realization struck me hard, knocking the air out of my lungs.

33

NICHOLAS

"Scoot closer," I said to Dahlia as we positioned ourselves on our stargazing deck, Jack sleeping beside her, tucked in a red sleeping bag, Buddy snoring on his right. With my phone, I snapped a picture of the four of us. "I'll get it framed."

Dahlia pressed a kiss to my chin as I took another shot of us. "Thanks for letting Jack and I be a part of Derek's list. I had fun today. I'm glad Joan could take over the shop all afternoon. She's been amazing so far and knows everyone in town. I found someone I could count on, and she's exactly the right person."

"It's all you. You make people want to be the best versions of themselves. It's a gift you possess, Dahlia Ellis. I know because it's rubbing off on me too."

"Thanks, but look who's talking. You're pretty *extra* extraordinary yourself, Nicholas Peterson. We make a great pair, you and I."

I kissed the nape of her neck, pushing the copper tresses over her shoulder and relishing the floral scent of her. With her back to my front, I hooked an arm around the curve of her waist and pulled her against me, my body hardening at the mere thought of spending the night together.

"You're lucky we have company, or I would've made you scream my name right here. All night long."

Dahlia writhed her ass against my erection, testing the limits of my willpower.

"Thanks for the double sleeping bag you got us, by the way. This makes camping so much more worth it." I rolled onto my other side and flicked off the fairy lights with the switch I'd installed beside my head on the platform. Darkness settled around us.

Nestled in my arms, the woman I never knew could steal my heart turned to face me. Entangled, we stared at the dark sky, the stars shining like someone had sprinkled diamonds from space.

"This is perfect," she said.

I ventured a hand under her shirt, sliding my fingertips along the length of her ribcage, then back up to trace the line of her spine, repeating the motion like a slow, deliberate dance.

A low quivering gasp left her mouth and her body tense.

I kept going, savoring the shivers that blossomed beneath the pads of my fingers. Dahlia squirmed against me, pressing herself deeper into my arms.

"Now this is perfect," I said, my palm molded to her backside, holding her close.

In the pitch-black darkness, we couldn't see each other clearly, but by instinct, my mouth found hers, and I swallowed the soft whimpers that escaped her lips.

We pulled apart before things escalated, and she anchored herself to me, clutching my shirt. In the safety of each other's arms, we sank into the quiet.

My eyelids fluttered as I tried to stay awake, but I lost the battle, lulled to sleep by the gentle rhythm of her breaths.

"Nick?"

I blinked, unsure if it was part of a dream or not. "Hmm."

"I really like us together. Thanks for everything you do for us. It means a lot, and I'm thankful for all of it. I'll never take anything for granted ever again. This is me telling you I'm grateful to have you in my life…in our lives."

"It all comes naturally with you and Jack…as if you've always been a part of my life. I'm the lucky one. Now sleep. I'm watching over you," I said, as she sank her body into mine, fastening my grip around her. "I'm glad I found you too. I'll never wish to be anywhere else. And I'll always make sure you're happy and safe."

"You expecting someone?" Dahlia asked as I got up to answer the door the next afternoon.

I shrugged.

The pounding intensified on the other side.

"No. None of the guys from work said anything about coming over, and the neighbors are gone for the day. Everyone else I know is here."

My eyes traveled to Jack drawing in the living room, Buddy napping next to him, and Dahlia sitting at the kitchen table, looking over the paint samples I'd picked up for the bedroom.

Another knock on the door.

My grin stretched from ear to ear as I yanked it open. My best friend stood on the front porch, a duffle bag slung over his shoulder, looking like his preppy self, dressed in dark trousers and a purple button-up shirt with the sleeves rolled up to the elbows.

"Hey, man. What are you doing here?" I asked, pulling Tucker into a hug. I failed at holding back the smile curling my lips. "Are you lost? Those clothes have no place around here."

He took a step back and tsk-tsked. "You're just jealous that I'm better looking than you, man. I thought coming to town for a surprise visit would be a good idea. You know, just to throw away any plan you might have."

I stepped aside to let him in.

As if his eyes were magnets only attracted to the opposite sex, Tucker's gaze landed on Dahlia. "Oh, you have company." He elbowed me in the arm, probably thinking he was being subtle.

Jack, curious, came to me, and I picked him up and kissed his cheek.

"Man, how long have you been here? Did time fly by and I didn't get the memo? Whoa, you've got yourself a family." Tucker bunched his dark eyebrows, giving me a what-the-hell stare. "Did I miss an entire episode of Nick Peterson's life?"

Tucker slapped his chest, his dramatic side on full display, and I rolled my eyes as Dahlia rose to her feet to meet him.

"This little guy here is Jack. Jack, this is my friend, Tuck. Don't listen to anything he says. He's a troublemaker."

They both studied each other with frowns, but Jack held out his fist for Tucker to bump, just like we practiced all the time. My friend and I burst out laughing. And like a dad, pride overflowed in me.

"Nice to meet you, Jack. I see you already know the

secret code to our friendship." He ruffled the boy's hair. "You can call me Uncle Tuck."

I flipped a palm over, glancing at my friend. "Uncle Tuck?"

He shrugged. "Yeah, thought it sounds good."

I shook my head but ended up laughing along with him.

My woman neared us, interrupting our chuckles.

Tucker gave her a slow once-over, panty-melting smirk in place, his playboy ways untamed. "Hey there. I'm Tuck, Nick's best friend. And the most handsome between the two of us."

Dahlia furrowed her brows, looking at him, unimpressed.

I silenced my snicker with a closed fist.

With round eyes, Jack watched the interaction as closely as I did.

"Dahlia," my girl finally said, shaking his hand. With a loud sigh, she shook her head. "You see, I thought I was Nick's best friend. This isn't working. We've already agreed that in this town, I get to hold the best friend title. Sorry, man. You're now second best."

"Did you just *man* me?" Tucker asked with a stunned expression.

Dahlia failed to reel in the grin spreading across her lips. "Yep. I think I did. *Man.*"

Tucker pivoted to face me, his eyes wide. "Nick, I like her. She's a keeper. Are you single?" he asked in his most flirty tone—the one he used every time he tried to hook up with someone.

I clapped his shoulders. "Off-limits, man. Sorry. She's too good for you."

Dahlia's gaze traveled between us, her smirk getting

bigger by the second. "And I'm already taken," she said, locking lips with me.

Those words pinned me to the floor. The way she said she was taken—as if it were the most natural thing to announce—sent my heart into overdrive. Dahlia had staked her claim on me in front of my best friend. This meant a lot. At least, to me, it did. Her words replayed in my head, and my body sizzled. The thought of sending Tucker away and kissing her until her lips caught fire popped into my head, but I pushed it away. For now. *Later*, I promised myself. Instead, I pulled Dahlia against my chest and pressed a kiss to the top of her head.

"Welcome to Green Mountain, Nick's friend," she said to Tucker.

"Thanks. Staying for the weekend. Hope you guys have room. I thought I should make sure Nick here was thriving far from the city. He kept ignoring my calls, and it didn't sit well with me."

"Drink?" I asked.

"Beer, please." He brought his attention back to Dahlia. "Tell me all about you," he said, a hand on her lower back, leading her to the table and taking a seat next to her.

Thirty minutes later, we were alone on the deck, enjoying a drink under the warm, late spring sunshine.

"Man, no wonder you didn't tell me anything about your relationship," my friend said. "Fuck, you've got yourself a rock star. Is this a prank? Am I hallucinating?"

I huffed a laugh through my nose. "She's the best thing that has happened to me in a long time. We clicked. From the moment we met. Hard to explain. It's more than just… simple attraction." I let the words simmer between us. "It's everything."

"You're aware she has a kid, right?"

"Thanks for the heads-up." I shook my head. "Didn't notice."

"Are you ready for this? Being a dad and everything. Because that boy will look up to you. Like Derek did."

I took a sip, searching for the right thing to say. "It doesn't have anything to do with my being ready or not, man. All this," I said, waving my free hand around me, "fits. It's where I'm supposed to be. Where I belong. It came naturally with Derek. And it is with Jack too."

"Whoa. You, the city boy, turned into a country man. Damn, you have it hard for that girl. I never saw this one coming. I thought you'd be ready to leave town before the six-month mark. Tell me. Are you pussy-whipped like Jace?"

"You met her, man. Dahlia is nothing like Pam. She's her own woman. If you haven't noticed, she does pretty good for herself—and I do too. But together, we're great. We're thriving. This thing between us, I can't describe it. It's rare. Addictive. Something I lack the words to explain. Something bigger than us."

"Okay, why do I feel like I'll hear the L-O-V-E word soon coming out of your mouth?"

I took a sip. "You're just jealous."

Tucker tilted his head back, laughter spilling out. "Keep trying to convince yourself, man. Hey, speaking of her, where did your woman go?"

"On a walk to get Jack to sleep. Should be back soon. Do you wanna go out for dinner or stay in? We could order in too."

"In. I want to get to know the woman who's about to own your heart—and your balls—and that little boy you can't stop gushing about."

"Fine by me. Let's hit the grocery store then." I jumped to my feet. "Come on, follow me."

Tucker halted before we made it down the deck. "Did you tell her about Derek?"

I scratched the side of my face. "I did. Even showed her the list." I inhaled through my mouth to calm the jitters waking up inside me at the mention of my deceased friend. "I didn't give her all the details, though. I will… When the time is right. It's still hard to talk about him. Baby steps, okay? Right now, I'm happy—we're happy—and it's all that matters. I've decided to focus on that."

Tucker downed the rest of his beer and got in step with me as we sauntered down the driveway toward my truck.

———

I attacked the dishes while Dahlia put the leftovers away, and Tucker hung out in the living room with Jack. My friend had never been a baby person, but Jack had won him over pretty quickly.

Perhaps it helped that Tucker was about five in his head most of the time.

"Got an idea. I should be awarded the *best friend of the year* title. Hope you'll vote for me when the time comes," he called out from where he sat, his tone serious. "You two should go out for a few hours. Enjoy each other."

I stopped breathing. At least, I'm pretty sure I did. I should get my ears checked. Perhaps I heard him wrong.

"Me and my friend, Jack, we'll play with his car toys or watch some TV shows meant for us guys. Aka cartoons meant for kids under five because they're my favorites too," he added with a wink.

"Good one, man. Even I believed you for a second. Don't repeat it or I'll take your words for granted."

Tucker sighed in the most dramatic way. Yeah, he should get a degree in theater, he was that good. "You want to spend some time with Uncle Tuck?" he asked the boy.

Jack, now perched on his lap, nodded.

"See? Even he can't resist me. Go out, make out, do whatever you want. We'll be fine. There are no bottles or diapers involved, so I'm capable of babysitting this little guy." As if to prove his point, Jack leaned back against my friend's chest, completely at ease. "Say bye Mama, bye Nick," Tucker said.

Jack echoed his words, waving his tiny hand at us, watching my best friend as if he'd painted the moon—and the stars.

"Are you sick? You're not trying to bribe me to go out with you like you usually do? Something is wrong."

"Bah, me and Jack-Man are bonding. I'll go out some other time. I'll still be here tomorrow night. Anyway, the nightlife in this town looks a bit boring. No offense. I also don't feel like hanging out with Uncle Mike in his semi-retired community." He brought his beer bottle to his lips and offered me the smuggest smirk.

I leaned in and brought my mouth close to Dahlia's ear. "Babe, if we wanna go out, now is the time. I under-stand you don't know Tuck, but I vouch for him. And Jack will be asleep by the time we leave. It's your call."

"Won't he feel left out?" Her heart, big and selfless, made another appearance. My chest brimmed with pride.

"Nah, I'm sure he already has a woman on speed dial, whom he can't wait to call later."

Dahlia rolled her lips and chewed on them, looking hesitant for a second. "Okay, let's do this, but tomorrow you'll spend time with him. He's your best friend. He came all the way here to check up on you."

"You've got yourself a deal. Now let's go before he changes his mind."

"Where are we going?" Dahlia asked once we tucked a sleepy Jack in and kissed him goodnight.

With our fingers knitted together, I brought our joined hands to my lips and kissed her knuckles. "I was thinking we could head to your place and have dirty sex because my mind has been entertaining the idea all day."

Her face flushed with excitement as if powered by a thousand volts. "Oh, I like how you think, Nick Peterson. Drive us home then."

Home. I liked the sound of it.

Derek's Bucket List – ~~23. Nick. Feeling like the cracks in my world are healing~~

34

DAHLIA

Warm lips teased my nipple through the fabric of my shirt. A yelp came out, and I arched my back, pleasure traveling through me in addictive waves.

"I'll never get tired of this," Nick said.

His deep voice stirred something wild inside me. His grin set every nerve in me alight. The heat between us blazed hotter than ever, and my skin tingled wherever his eyes lingered.

I squirmed on the bed, my resolve hanging by a thread.

Clutching the hem, I tugged my shirt over my head.

Nick traced a path with his lips from my breasts to my belly. He hooked his thumbs into the waistband of my jeans, and in the most painfully slow movement I'd ever witnessed, he lowered them to my ankles. I shimmied out of them and kicked them off, unable to wait any longer. We only had a few hours to ourselves, and I intended to make the most of them.

Nick eye-fucked me as he stood by the bed, undressing as if he had all the time in the world, his irises gleaming.

"God, you're so hot when you stare at me like you wanna eat me up." The moan escaping me sounded foreign. "Don't leave me like this, all worked up. It's cruel."

Now naked as the day he was born, he hovered over me and used the back of his hand to skim the skin between my breasts, moving down to my stomach and grazing the junction between my thighs.

Shivers ran through me. My hips bucked off the mattress.

His hand ventured south, tracing the length of one leg, then the other.

My nipples were so stiff they tingled. My clit pulsed from all the prickling sensations shooting inside me and all the dirty promises I could read on his face.

I gasped. "Fuck me or kill me, choice is yours, but stop messing with me, Peterson. Give it to me already."

Nick snickered and bit one nipple. I grunted…or purred. I wasn't sure. Pain and pleasure blurred together.

"Did you just *Peterson* me?"

I nodded.

"Oh, I see you mean business."

I extended my arm to caress the wooden piece of him begging for my attention, but he jerked away from my reach. "Hey. Not fair." My breathing turned shallow, and scorching hot desire flew through my bloodstream.

"Listen, I have a plan, and you'll love it. So much that you'll ask for more. Want to hear all about it?" Nick's smirk widened. "You know that friend of yours?" He tipped one eyebrow, looking devilishly handsome in the moonlight spilling through the window.

"Which one?" I blew the words out, tremors of unfulfilled need rippling through my body.

"The one you told me all about. You know, the one

who has been warming up my place for the last three years. That vibrating thing you like…"

"*Yesss*," I murmured, clenching my thighs together, barely able to stay put. "What about it?"

"Tonight, he'll join the party. Funny fact, I've never had a threesome before. Have you?"

Did I dissolve on my bed? Yeah, I probably did.

Nick's gaze fixated on me, waiting for me to say something.

"I've never had one before either." I breathed in slowly, focusing on his lips that I couldn't wait to feel all over me. "Being naughty with you, you think I'd like that?" I asked, my voice out of tune.

He cupped my cheeks and pulled my bottom lip between his teeth."Oh, believe me. I know you will, baby. Until you're so satisfied, you'll beg me to end you."

My breath hitched on its way in. Nick hadn't even started feasting on me, and I was already insatiable, every inch of me combusting with need. "Peterson, stop wasting my time and touch me already."

Relishing the idea of messing with him too, I dipped one finger between my thighs, and Nick's face turned a dark shade of purple. I flicked a nipple between my moist digits and thought he'd explode before my eyes.

"God, you're the hottest thing I've ever seen right now. Dahlia, no cheating, though. Don't start your fun without me."

With his body positioned over mine, he kissed me senseless, leaving me light-headed. At some point, we had to break apart to catch some fresh air, my lips sensitive and numb.

"Where's that friend? I can't wait to meet him."

With his hands locked around my waist, as if he feared I'd vanish, I slid to my side and opened the drawer of my nightstand. With one hand, I rummaged inside until I presented a very-expectant Nick with a neon-pink silicone dildo.

His eyes flared, and his tongue darted out.

He studied the toy, and with his hands still clinging to my body, he glided me further back on the mattress. "Ready to play?" he asked, every word and glance dripping with naughty promises.

I blinked, drunk on the hunger pulsing in his eyes. That was the moment all hell broke loose—the moment I lost touch with reality, and gravity abandoned me.

Without waiting for an answer, my man dived forward and spread my legs with his muscular hands. He lapped my soaked center with his greedy tongue, and I shivered underneath him.

He increased the pace, fucking me with his tongue.

A train of unintelligible words, mixed with cries, left my mouth, turning him into a starving man. Without letting me catch a single breath or savor the heat building inside and along my skin, Nick grabbed the pink toy from my hand and pushed a button. It played a vibrating rhythm in his fist, and he stared at it with awe. When he recovered from his daze, he coated the toy with my damp heat, sliding it inside me with ease, my vagina convulsing around the shaft.

Holding the vibrating toy in one hand, gliding it in and out of me at a dizzying pace, he plunged back between my legs and sucked my clit harder, my bundle of nerves feeling raw between his lips.

The few brain cells I still owned left my body.

My breathless whimpers echoed in the room as my entire body stiffened for a moment, then melted, satiated and spent. I fisted the sheet at my sides, trying to anchor myself to this world and stay grounded in the moment.

Nick moved over me, thirsty for my mouth. "You like this dirty, don't you?"

While he kissed me, he kept maneuvering the toy in and out of my tight channel at a steady pace.

Throaty moans spilled out of me, wild and unrestrained, creating a chaotic symphony. My cheeks flared, a rush of heat radiating through me.

Our eyes met.

The affection pouring from him healed every remaining scar on my heart—even the deepest ones.

"Dahlia, you've seen nothing yet." His voice cracked on the last word.

How had I been lucky enough to find a man like him? What could I have done to deserve him? Why was life granting me this second chance at happiness?

I looped a hand around his neck and pulled him down to me. My mouth ravened his, pouring into him all the particles of love dancing inside me. Yeah, love. What we shared looked a lot like it—and felt a lot like it too. In every possible way.

"Gimme a sec," he said, lifting himself off me and reaching for his discarded pants on the floor.

"Listen…I-I was thinking," I said as he froze, a condom in hand, waiting for me to continue. "You're clean. I'm clean. Except with you, I haven't had sex in years, and I'm on the pill. What do you think about ditching this?" My gaze zeroed in on the foil package. "Only if you feel comfortable."

I heard his sharp intake of breath as he studied me, furrowing his brows.

"Or we can use it. I just thought… I don't know…"

Without a word, Nick tossed the condom over his shoulder, looking hotter than ever, determination tightening his features, a lopsided smirk tugging at his lips.

I swallowed, my head spinning from all the unspoken promises etched across his face.

The sexual energy radiating off him was so intense, I swore I could've gone up in flames

He crawled over me, and I held my breath.

Discarding the vibrator, he dived inside me, where he belonged, in a long slick thrust. Where our bodies and souls merged, and we became one. Goose bumps bloomed all over my skin at the feel of him, bare and swollen, making me his.

I shivered as he pounded into me and circled my puck-ered nipples with his tongue, alternating between them both, until I shuddered underneath him. His name, a whis-pered breath, trickled from my lips, pleading for him to stop, my flesh too tender, and imploring him to never stop, my yearning for him untamable. Insatiable.

Longing for ecstasy, I ground my hips against his.

Nick cursed when I dug my fingernails into his biceps.

I locked my legs around his waist, keeping him close to me.

His body rubbed against my clit and wiped out every bit of fight I had left, making me feel alive—and about to explode in euphoria.

Unable to process anything anymore, I begged him. "Never stop… Deeper… Faster… Fuck me harder. Yes… like that. More… Oh, *yesss*…"

"Keep talking dirty. That's sexy."

I shook my head. "No talking. More kissing."

His irises turned almost black as he plunged forward, allowing me no time to catch my breath, his tongue showing me just how turned on he was. Our hips moved together, a perfectly rehearsed choreography, drawing me toward my climax with each thrust.

Nick grabbed a fistful of my hair as I braced myself on my forearms, keeping our mouths fused together.

He moved to sit on his ankles, bringing me up with him. I straddled him and circled his waist with my legs as he rammed inside me from beneath me, never missing a beat. I kept him close, my arms locked around his neck while he gripped my ass, anchoring me to him.

We surrendered to the pleasure coursing through us, until the world beyond the bedroom vanished.

Nick's fingers traveled all over my back as if he couldn't get enough and had to touch me everywhere.

Breathless, he kept the pace steady, my body bouncing over his, all the sensations he brought to me clashing together until I cried his name and came undone against him. He fastened his arms around me, holding me upright as I tried to come back from the rush.

When our eyes met, the air between us crackled, every flicker reflected in his gaze. My heart sizzled at the realization.

Before I drowned in the golden depths of his eyes, I reluctantly drew my body back, fighting the pull of him. The hollow ache between my thighs throbbed, a raw reminder of the void.

Nick's lips pursed, but I silenced him with a finger. Under the weight of his watchful and confused gaze, I bent forward, taking him all in my mouth. His dick twitched at the contact of my tongue.

"Fuck… Dahlia… Wow… Jesus…"

Pride filled me as I stole his ability to form a complete sentence.

A taut expression painted his face, and it almost looked painful. He fucked my mouth for a few minutes, then halted the rocking of his hips. With a string of curses, he ran a hand over his face and tilted his neck back, granting me all the power.

With one hand curled around the base, I pumped him, enjoying the tremor of his erection every time my tongue laved the tip. I took him all in, sucking him with vigor until his cock lengthened to reach the back of my throat.

Nick breathed in—and out. His control stretched thin, until it shattered. With one swift movement, he flipped me around, and I had to release him. He positioned himself underneath me until my soaked center rested against his mouth.

He lapped at me with his tongue, and shivers skated the length of my back. My mouth returned to his dick, sucking it so hard, he stiffened under me. His mouth continued his teasing of my flesh, and I purred in bliss. Nick patted the bed, grabbing his newfound friend. With the hammering vibration on, he brought it back between my thighs until I shook, unable to stay still as surges of pleasure washed through me. And then he let go, a loud animalistic grunt escaping his mouth, as we came undone together. I gulped every drop of milk flowing from him in jolts, my tongue licking and teasing the now oversensitive tip. Until he couldn't take it anymore and had to writhe from underneath me.

Two could play this little game he was indulging in, and it turned out the bedroom sins were my ultimate weakness.

Moving back, I wiped my mouth with the back of my hand. We locked eyes, both panting. My chest rose and fell in a quick tempo as I tried to get a full breath in.

On his knees, Nick inched closer and kissed me with everything he possessed, no doubt tasting himself on my lips. "Dahlia, you have something that belongs to me right here," he said, licking the corner of my lips clean of any trace of him.

And I died right about there.

35

NICHOLAS

"Okay, here's the thing," I said when I stopped by Dahlia's shop before the opening hours. "I've learned from a very reliable source that today is Buddy's birthday. How about we throw him a party tonight? I'm sure Jack would love that."

Dahlia moved to my right, removing wrinkles from yet another gown with a portable vapor machine.

"It looks good," I said, taking a step back and admiring the wooden shelf I'd just fixed on the wall next to the shoe display, making sure it was level.

"I love it," she said, a smile in her voice. "What do you have in mind?"

I gave her a grin laced with mischief. "Lots of things."

She poked my arm with a finger. "Buddy's birthday, Nick. Focus." My gaze traveled down her body. "My eyes are up here," she said, pointing to her face with two fingers. "You seem to love planning stuff, so I'm all ears."

"How about we bake him some dog cookies? I found a recipe online, and it's super easy. We could get party hats and balloons and all the silly things kids love. My neighbors are away for the weekend, so Buddy is staying over with me."

"Would it be just us three?"

My hands found her hips, and I drew her to me. "Only Jack, you, and me. And Buddy, of course. I'm sure Jack would love the party setup."

Dahlia skimmed her lips over mine. "He will. And thank you for always thinking about him and making him feel special."

"You two deserve the best. I'm the lucky one. Would tonight work? If you guys can make it."

When did I get excited at the idea of throwing an old dog a birthday party?

"Yep," Dahlia said. "Very important question, though. Will we be able to kiss after the party?" She quirked a brow, offering me a cock-awakening smile, her eyes glistening.

I removed the vapor thingy from her hand and placed it back on the rack, looping my arms around her. "You're right. I love plans. Always have. Right now, I can tell you I did a lot of strategizing this week, and most of them involved a very naked me and a very naked you and a lot of kissing. Last weekend seems like ages ago."

I leaned in to claim her mouth, her pink lips tasting like cherry. My balls tightened as she rubbed my junk over the fabric of my shorts.

"Birthday party for the kids, then naked after-party for us. That's the plan."

She purred into my ear, the sound almost bringing me to my knees."Keep planning, Nicholas Peterson. I can already tell you're mastering the art quite perfectly. Do you need me to bring anything?"

I motioned *no* with my head. "Everything's covered.

Recipe printed. Shopping list is on my phone. And the girl has agreed to be my date."

Dahlia laughed in my arms, and I got harder for her.

"Anything else you want me to take care of before I get going?"

"Oh yes. I almost forgot. There's a light bulb to change at the back, and I got some black and white framed pictures I'd like you to hang on the wall between the dressing rooms."

"I'm on it. Show me the way."

"And if you have a little more time to spare, there are some heavy boxes to move around. They're piled up in front of the emergency exit. If the fire department stops by, I'll get fined."

I flexed my biceps, and we kissed some more before Dahlia led me to the back of the store after calling me a show-off.

"What time do you open today?"

"In about forty minutes. We still have time."

Once in the backroom, before I could catch up with what was happening, Dahlia jumped into my arms and wrapped her legs around my waist.

I clutched her ass, and she kissed me until I had to lean back to breathe on my own. "I love it when you're not wasting any time. Want to do this here?" I asked, lost in her starving eyes.

She nodded and pushed the straps of her dress down, exposing her bare chest. Her nipples, puckered and pink, pointed at me, begging me to feast on them. "One week is far too long," she whispered against my mouth.

I freed my cock with one hand, and I sat Dahlia on a pile of boxes. I lifted her maxi dress until the fabric bunched around her waist, kissed her with purpose until my lips hurt, and rammed into her, my pants low around my ankles. I kneaded her breasts with my hands the entire time while she tipped her head back and cried my name over and over. We moved together in flawless rhythm until we both came in a tangle of pleasure and contentment.

"Wow," I said between kisses as we both free-fell back to Earth.

I zipped myself up after I lowered Dahlia down onto her feet. She swayed, and I offered a hand to steady her.

"I'm drunk," she said with a smirk, a dark blush coloring her cheeks, and her eyes glossy. "Drunk on you."

"Don't say stuff like that because I'll never get out of here."

"I'm glad we got it out of our systems. Now I'll be able to focus. It wasn't fair having you around, looking all sexy with your tool belt, and doing nothing about it."

I turned my head to kiss her again. This woman.

Together, we moved the boxes with a shared awareness, our gazes speaking the unspoken language of our hearts.

———

Hours later, Dahlia, Jack, and I stood around the kitchen island, Jack perched on a stool, molding dog cookie dough into bone shapes.

The boy's arm fell to his side, and Buddy got to his feet to lick the sticky dough from his fingers. He giggled, the sound pure and heartwarming, and we joined in. "Buddy likes cake. His tongue wet."

After we put our creations in the oven, I sat the toddler on my shoulders, and together we hung red balloons and a *Happy birthday* banner over the door leading to the back deck.

"If this house were mine, I'd move the kitchen to the north side and the living room here, where we can look over the mountains through those giant windows. I'd paint the walls white to light up the space like you did at your place but keep the old hardwood floors and planked ceilings, though. They give this place its charm. I'd also build a barn where the garage stands. It's old and must be replaced soon, anyway. All white, like the house, with black shutters and teal doors. Maybe get a horse…or two. Or use it as a wood workshop or a place to have people over," I said. "I haven't really thought about that part. It's just an idea… The way I see it in my head. The land is big and flat. It has so much potential."

"Ohmygod, I can see it all too. It would look amazing. Your vision is very similar to mine. Except for the barn, which, to be honest, I hadn't thought about, but it would be the perfect addition. One day, when you start your own construction business, you'll be able to build houses the way you see them in your head. You could even use a barn as an office."

I gave Dahlia a pointed look. "How are you so sure I'll own a business one day?"

She shrugged. "Call it instinct, but I just know it."

"Let's make a pact. If I do, I'll name you president of the interior design department. Mike wants to retire in about a year. He talked to me about taking over. We'll see."

Dahlia wound her arms around me. "It's sexy when you're making plans to stay in Green Mountain. By the way, I would love to join your business. You're kinda hard to resist when you're in construction mode. That tool belt… Think you could wear it more often?"

I snickered, tucking her hair behind her ear.

The air tensed.

I looked between her lips and her eyes, torn between holding her gaze and kissing her. "Dahlia, you're making it hard for a man to walk away. The mountain air is great, but you're greater. My home is here now. I can't imagine living anywhere else."

That was the truth. I didn't miss Chicago. I loved the new life I was building for myself here, and as long as Dahlia and Jack were in it, I'd never be able to be anywhere else. No matter how I missed my friends back in Illinois.

Dahlia batted her lashes, her big moss-green eyes locked on mine. "I'm very glad you feel this way. Now that I've found you, I'm not ready to let go of you. I kinda like having you around." She buried her face into my chest and took a big whiff before lifting her gaze back in my direction.

"You do?"

"Yeah. You're kind of nice. And good-looking. And skilled with your hands. And you smell great too."

I mirrored her lopsided smile before claiming her lips, our mouths fusing in a slow, intoxicating tango.

Time stood still as we lost ourselves in each other's embrace.

"About that tool belt, I'm pretty sure we can put it to good use," I said.

Dahlia's eyes became stars.

We kissed until Jack bounced our way, Buddy in tow. "Buddy wants cake now. Cake, cake, cake," he singsonged.

"Let's see," I said, lifting Jack into my arms and turning to check the timer on the oven. "Five more minutes." I opened my palm, holding up all five fingers. "But it'll be too hot. Tell Buddy he has to wait twenty minutes, okay?"

I lowered Jack back onto his feet, and he raised one finger. "Buddy, wait twenty minutes. *Nicksaid.*"

The dog hung his head and let out a huff.

I squatted before the bloodhound, rubbing him behind the ears, just the way he liked it. "Come on,

Buddy. Don't be sad. It's still your birthday. Just get some fresh air, and I'll come get you in a few minutes."

He sat, his gaze set on me.

"Okay, time to get real, my friend. To have a discussion man to man. Or rather, man to dog. Or whatever. We're throwing you a surprise party here. If you could spend the next twenty minutes outside, it would help us put the finishing touches on things."

Jack perched himself on my bent knee, looping one arm around my neck. He bobbed his head. "Surprise, Buddy. No peeking."

I pinched my lips together to hold back the snicker threatening to escape. My eyes drifted to Dahlia, who shrugged. I found it adorable whenever Jack repeated her words.

With his head hanging low, the dog tottered outside when Jack moved to his feet to hold the door open. "Surprise Buddy. And cake. No peeking, okay? Go play."

About ten minutes later, the rains started, and Jack called Buddy in. Greta said he was half-deaf, but I wasn't so sure. Every time Jack called his name, he came running. Well, not running, but he came. In his old and slow dog version of a jog.

"Buddy, Buddy. Buddy," the boy yelled through the ajar door. "Birthday cake ready. Come eat, Buddy. Peek now. Buddy. *Buddddddy. Nicksayitsokay.*"

The downpour intensified, and I grabbed a rain jacket. "I'll go get him. I'm sure he can't hear us through the rain. He must be hiding somewhere. Old fellows like him don't like getting wet and stinky."

Jack giggled.

"Buddy doesn't deserve to catch a cold on his birthday, does he?"

The boy shook his head. I ruffled his hair before making it to the front porch.

Outside, I rounded the house, looking for the birthday boy. No trace of him anywhere. I searched under the back deck. No sign of him there either.

Rain streamed down my face.

The property was big, but most of the grown trees outlined the perimeter so I could see far ahead. Anyway, Buddy never ventured away from the house. No doubt he hated the walk back whenever he ventured too far, his body quickly wearing out.

After I looked behind the garage and the firewood shed, I went to his house next door. Greta and Brett were still away, and there was no trace of Buddy there either.

"Where are you, old pal?" I asked, mostly to myself. "C'mon, Bud, time for your party. Stop hiding."

I circled the perimeter. Still nothing.

Jack's voice resonated through the rain as he kept calling Buddy's name from the back door. "Buddy. *Buddddy.* Cake ready."

My heart drowned in my chest.

Sweat lined up my spine.

A nagging feeling twisted my stomach.

This wasn't good. This was fucking not good.

It couldn't be happening. Not tonight. Not on his birthday. I wasn't ready to say goodbye to another friend.

I would never be able to face Jack again if I came back inside without Buddy.

I rounded the house to the left and locked eyes with Dahlia from the kitchen window. She pursed her lips. I shook my head, and her face fell. Even through the pouring rain, I caught the panic taking hold in her eyes.

"Buddy, where are you? Come back home now. It's cake time. I'm sorry I asked you to wait." My voice cracked on the last word. Why wouldn't this sick feeling go away? Why was my stomach tied so tight it hurt?

I turned around just in time to witness Jack running in the rain to meet me, Dahlia after him.

"Guys, go back inside. You'll get soaked."

"Buddy, your cake ready," Jack yelled.

I caught him and picked him up, using my body to shield him from the downpour.

Dahlia neared us and lifted him into her arms.

"Mama, want Buddy," he said, a tremolo in his voice. "Buddy my friend. Where's Buddy? *Buddddy*."

"I don't know, baby," she said, pulling him close, unable to protect him from the rain.

"We'll find him." I removed my jacket and placed it over their heads. Better. With the sleeve of my T-shirt, I wiped my drenched face. The rain picked up, each drop feeling like a tiny needle as it prickled my skin.

With one arm around Dahlia's shoulders, I urged her to go back inside. "Don't worry, I'll keep looking." A clap of thunder startled us, and she didn't argue, hurrying into the house, her footsteps splashing around as she retreated. I was about to give up too when I heard a muffled yap. "Come on, Buddy, talk to me."

That sound again.

My heart hit the ground. I swallowed the giant lump down my throat. Tears burned the back of my eyes. On my knees, I looked under my truck, and there he was, huddled down, his eyelids half-shut, his breathing fastidious.

"Oh God, Buddy. What happened? Come here, big guy, let's get you inside." On my front, I stretched my body until I could pull him into my arms.

In the entryway, Dahlia waited for me with a pile of

towels in her hands. We glanced at each other, no words required to understand how bad the situation was.

Jack put a blanket over Buddy as I laid him on the living room floor next to him, now dressed in his PJs, in the same exact spot they always had their playdates.

"I sing you a song, Buddy. *Cattter* sings to me when I sick."

Buddy butted Jack's tiny hand as if to say, "Okay."

My eyes brimmed with more tears. Right about now, I would've done anything to ease all their pain.

Dahlia's arms rounded my waist from behind. I cocked my head to watch her, tears flowing down her face at the sight of her son and his dog friend together. Both of them saying goodbye to each other, even if Jack couldn't truly understand the magnitude of the situation.

Holding on to each other, Dahlia and I stood there, watching them, neither of us able to speak. The emotions soared in my throat, choking me. Dahlia's shoulders heaved.

Jack finished his song and kissed Buddy on the head. "I love you, Buddy. You my most *bestest* best friend."

I dried my tears with the hem of my still drenched shirt.

"You should go home," I said, spinning around to face Dahlia, rubbing her upper arms with my hands. The sight of her broke me. "Don't cry. It'll be okay." I pulled her into my arms, hugged her like my life depended on it, and kissed her forehead. I was a liar. It wouldn't be okay. None of this was. And honestly, I wanted her by my side. But I didn't tell her that. "I'll take him to the vet. I don't want him to suffer. You don't have to go through this. It's unfair to you. Buddy is my responsibility. I'm the one who offered to babysit him for a few days."

"Nick, I'll stay. We're doing this together. I'm not going

anywhere. When you get back, I'll be here. I'll wait for you." Dahlia choked on her words. "I know how much he means to you. We'll…we'll wait for you."

I bowed my head. "Let's get Jack to bed first, then I'll take Buddy to my truck."

Dahlia nodded and lifted her son, now fast asleep beside the dying dog. "Say goodbye to Buddy, Jack," she said, waking him up. Sobs shook her body, but she kept them in, for her baby's sake.

Through my broken heart, all I hoped for was to soothe her pain. To add permanent sunlight to her life… and to her heart. Jack and Dahlia had already been through so much together. My instincts kicked in every time they were around, asking to protect them to make sure they'd be safe and sound.

When did I get so attached to this family?

How did it happen?

Jack's eyelids fluttered open, and he petted Buddy's head for what would be the last time. "Good night, Buddy. Sweet dreams. Be a good boy," he said, echoing the words his Mama told him every night.

A piece of my heart unglued itself and bled onto the floor, leaving a trace of me behind.

I bit my inner cheek to avoid crying.

With deep breaths in and out, I kept some sort of control over my own broken heart.

In the playroom that had become Jack's bedroom whenever he stayed over, Dahlia laid him on the sofa-bed and tucked a blanket around him. With her fingers laced through mine, we made it to my bedroom. I put a pile of clean clothes on the bed. "Take a shower and change. You can sleep in here. Or downstairs. I have no idea how long it'll take."

"Nick, I wish I could go with you…"

"I know. But I gotta do this on my own. As long as I know you and Jack are safe here, things will be fine."

She nestled her body in my embrace, and we stood there, our heartbeats fusing through our chests.

In a foggy state of mind, I changed and kissed Dahlia one last time before lifting the dog into my arms and settling him in the backseat of my truck. I found a veterinary clinic still open at this hour, a forty-minute drive from here, and followed the instructions once I entered the address into the GPS on my phone.

Time stopped. Had I been sitting here at the clinic for two hours—or six? I had no idea, no sense of how the moments had passed.

"I'm sorry. Buddy won't make it through the night. His body is too old and tired," the vet explained. "There's nothing we can do except make him comfortable."

In the privacy of an exam room, I fished my phone out to make a call, and the idea of being the one breaking the heart-crushing news shook every cell of my body. I inhaled. Air barely made it to my lungs before it wheezed out.

Greta picked up on the fourth ring. "Hey, Nick. Is everything all right?"

I swallowed, trying to speak the words tying my organs in knots.

I exhaled, pinching the bridge of my nose, my head bowed forward. "Sorry to…huh…bother you at this late hour. It's just…"

I heard the hitch in her breath. "It's Buddy, isn't it? It's okay, Nick. We knew this day was coming. You can tell me."

Keeping my eyelids sealed to force my racing heart to calm down, I muttered a breathy, "Yes." I could do this. I had to. My neighbors deserved the right to say goodbye to a dear member of their family, and my friend deserved the right to hear their voice one last time.

"Is he gone?" Greta asked.

I swallowed. "Not yet. We're at the vet. Nothing… nothing they can do. I'm so sorry."

"Can we see him?"

I nodded as if they were standing right beside me. "Sure."

"Gimme a sec. I'll get the guys in the other room."

I rubbed the heels of my hands over my burning eyes before switching to a video call, angling my phone so all they could see was their dog. In an attempt to offer them some privacy, I pushed the chair I'd been sitting on into a corner by the door, leaned forward, elbows on my knees, and buried my face in my palms.

"Hey, Buddy," Greta's voice resonated from the other end. It sounded more emotional than before. "I hope you can hear us."

The dog's head twitched a little, his eyelids fluttering as to reply he could.

"I'm sorry we're away. You're…" Her voice drowned away, the pounding in my skull blocking most sounds out.

With both hands, I scratched the back of my head, my fingers unable to erase the tingling sensation spreading to my scalp.

The buzzing in my ears lessened, and Chaz's voice made it through. "Life will never be the same without you, Bud. I'll always remember you. I-I love you so much."

The sound of his sobs hijacked my heart.

Greta's voice, now strained and wobbly, spoke next. "Nick?" I cleared my throat and took my place next to Buddy and picked up the phone. "Thank you. Thank you for giving us the opportunity to say goodbye." Sobs strangled her words. "Buddy was lucky to have you too. I know you two had a strong connection, and you'll miss him. Also, I'm sad for that little boy. I could tell Buddy loved him very much."

The lump in my throat had turned into a rock.

I said nothing. Because I lacked soothing words.

"Thank you, Nick," Chaz echoed. "At least he's not alone."

We exchanged a few more words and hung up.

For a moment, I watched Buddy, trying to comprehend everything that was happening. To make sense of the idea of losing another friend.

With his soft paw resting in my palm, I stayed by his side as the minutes quietly slipped away. I'd never leave him when he needed me the most. His eyes gleamed in the golden light as we held each other's gaze. Then they closed, and his breathing slowed, turning shallow. I rested my hand over his ribcage, making sure he was still alive.

I bit the inside of my cheek and finally let the words out—the words coming from my heart. "Hey, Bud. I don't know if you can still hear me, but I wanted to say thank you. For being my friend… And…and for watching over Jack. You welcomed me the moment I came to town and never left my side, even though I wasn't family… You accepted me, and you accepted Jack and Dahlia as if they were family too. Every morning after the sun rose, you joined me…as if—God, this is hard—as if you knew I needed someone to lean on after talking to Derek and telling him about my life here. You said nothing, but you were there, listening to me. And that…that was priceless. True friendship."

I closed my eyes and evened my breathing.

"I'm sorry… I'm sorry you have to go. Our time together has been too short, but it has been great. You'll finally meet Derek, okay? He's a nice kid. I'm sure he's already waiting for you up there. Yeah, I'm sure. Please watch over him. He needs a friend too…a best friend. The kind he's been wishing for, for a very long time. Please say *hi* to him for me, would you?"

I wiped my eyes with the heels of my hands.

"I can't believe I'm doing this again… Losing a friend is hard. Losing a second one in a matter of months is fucking impossible. I know I'm not alone. I-I have Dahlia. And Jack. If I'm allowed to ask you one last thing, can you watch over them too? I know Jeff is doing just that. How… how could he not? He had the most amazing family a guy could dream of. But maybe, just maybe, you could help him too… Or be his friend. Everyone needs a friend, and I'm sure he'd like the company. He must feel alone up there all by himself."

I cleared my throat.

"I don't know him, and never did, but he must have been quite a man. Tell him I'll take care of those he loved the most. Because I love them too. With all my heart. I-I'm sorry for rambling. I have no idea how all of this works."

With my forehead pressed against the fur of his neck, I squeezed his paw harder.

Buddy took his last breath, blinking as if to thank me—as if telling me he would be all right, not to worry, that he heard me.

My throat clenched.

I pressed a final kiss to the top of his head.

"You can go now, old pal. You've earned your rest. Thanks for being my friend. I'll forever miss you…" I tried to swallow, but couldn't. My throat was raw, tight, almost sealed shut. Breathing felt like work.

Tears burned behind my eyes before spilling freely down my face.

My very first friend here in Green Mountain had left me.

Somehow, it felt like he took a piece of me with him. The first piece of my heart that made all this move-across-the-country journey thing worth it. Somehow, in the short time we'd spent together, Buddy gave me my hope back. He made me believe I could do this. Start afresh. Start over. Be happy.

A little over an hour later, with Buddy's collar hanging from my fingers, I made it home. Rain was still pouring outside, and I was drenched and cold by the time I made it inside.

Dahlia was waiting for me in the kitchen, a cup of tea cradled in her hands.

Her lips looked thinner than usual, and sadness lingered in her green eyes.

She lifted her head as I entered, and I gave a small shake of my head.

Without a word, she padded toward me and wrapped me in her arms. I pressed my forehead to hers, savoring the warmth and closeness of her body against mine.

After a moment, she leaned back. "You're all wet. Let's get those clothes off you. Follow me." Holding my hand, Dahlia led me to the upstairs bathroom. I had gotten rid of the tiled floor, but the shower was still usable.

In the middle of the room, I stood frozen, as if I couldn't remember what I was meant to do.

Dahlia turned on the water, then peeled my shirt off, her fingers scorching against my cold skin.

She unbuttoned my jeans next and helped me shimmy out of them.

After she pushed me under the hot stream, she removed her own clothes and snaked her arms around me from behind, the hot steam of the shower cascading over us.

"It's okay to be sad…just don't be sad alone."

"How's Jack?" I asked after a long moment.

"Asleep. He'll be fine."

"I'm so sorry. That's not how I planned the night—"

"Plans don't always work out, Nick. And it's okay. It's life. You gotta learn to let go and ride the tide once in a while."

I shuffled on my feet, and with my woman in my arms, we stayed like this, bringing each other comfort.

The water turned cold, and after we stepped out of the glass box, we dried ourselves in comforting silence.

"Do you have to go home?"

Dahlia shook her head.

"Good. I want you here. With me." I pressed a gentle kiss to the tip of her nose, my knuckles skimming the soft skin of her bare arms. "I think we have to mourn Buddy together. The three of us."

I put on cotton shorts and a clean shirt and watched Dahlia tug at the T-shirt I had loaned her, along with the panties she had washed earlier, heat rising in me imagining her bare legs wrapped around me.

"I can't believe I didn't notice earlier how sexy you look dressed in these. You should raid my closet more often. I might actually like my clothes better on you."

We exchanged a smile, and I led the way downstairs. In the kitchen, I cut a large piece of the birthday cake I'd bought, and side by side, we attacked the chocolate dessert with our forks, sitting at the island.

"Why do you think he chose to die here? With me? With us?"

Dahlia shrugged. "Buddy felt safe with you. We all do.

It kinda makes sense." Tears glistened in her eyes. "You made him feel special."

I put my fork down, too many knots strangling my stomach to eat another bite. "I'll miss him… This place will never be the same without that dog around."

Dahlia scooted closer and rested her head on my upper arm. "You're a good man, Nicholas Peterson. You're strong. Fearless. And wise." She pressed a kiss to my shoulder. "And you're incredibly sexy."

"You think I'm sexy?" I pushed back, studying her expression.

She bobbed her head the same way Jack always did. "Yeah. And it's distracting. Let me show you the effect your sexiness has on me." Her eyes undressed me as they roamed over me in tantalizing slow motion. She bit her bottom lip, looking utterly irresistible.

I blinked, still amazed by the connection and chemistry we shared—and by the intensity spiraling between us.

In the most enticing way, and without breaking eye contact, she lifted the T-shirt over her head and dropped it on the floor.

My gaze lowered to her plump rose-tipped breasts and her center barely covered by her panties.

My throat worked.

"God, you're beautiful."

"Touch me, Nick. I can't stand not being in your arms any longer. We both need this. To feel better."

Fuck. This woman. She had a way of burning down the last thread of my willpower. Every single time.

I tipped her chin up with my finger.

Dahlia smiled. The kind of smile that could make me do nasty things to her.

Sadness lingered in her gaze, but now desire was taking over. Pure and raw.

My heart was bruised, but my body came to life. Scorching heat coursed through my blood, igniting each one of my cells.

My lips found Dahlia's, and a gasp left her mouth when our tongues touched. Desire shot through me, shaking my foundation and playing with my restraints.

My girl tasted as good as she looked. Exceptional. Sweet. Brave. One of a kind.

We explored each other's mouths with our tongues, taking our time to memorize every corner as if it was the first time.

All the pain that had been clinging to me since I ran away from Chicago died.

I wasn't scared anymore.

Everything in my life clicked into place.

I was where I was supposed to be.

Dahlia Ellis *was* where I was supposed to be.

All the puzzle pieces now made sense together. They had a purpose. I could finally see the big picture. Nothing that had happened was in vain.

I lowered my head and licked the swell of her breasts as I pushed them up toward my greedy lips with my hands. She shivered underneath my touch. My lips couldn't get enough of her as I feasted on her body.

With the pad of my thumb, I rubbed one pebbled nipple, and the moan that escaped her mouth got me even harder for her.

We moved to our feet, and with a step forward, I pushed Dahlia against the wall and lifted one of her legs, wrapping it around my waist. I ground my hips against hers, and nested my erection between her thighs. I cursed under my breath as she anchored herself to me.

"You're all I want, Nick. All the time. It's like you're

born from my fantasies. My wildest dreams. And I can't get enough of you," she whispered. "Ever."

I kissed my way down her throat, sucking and nibbling her skin, leaving my mark."You'll be the end of me."

Her fingers moved down.

I let out a loud growl as she freed my erection and curled her hand around it.

Every inch of me trembled.

She moved her hand up and down—in the most torturing, yet excruciatingly good way.

In that moment, it hit me. Every curve, every inch of me had been made to fit hers.

My thoughts bounced around in my head. All the things I'd wished we could be together now seemed possible.

"Bed?" I asked as we devoured each other with our mouths, voracious and burning with lust.

It was as if all the emotions we had been bottling up had erupted into a storm of passion neither of us could contain. Yearning. Desire. Need. And something bigger—more potent, almost hellish, yet beautiful. Something we had to face together.

Dahlia raised her eyes to mine. They had turned into molten emeralds. "No. Right here. Right now. I can't wait." The words trembled as they slipped from her reddened lips.

Her touch, soft and delicate, as she stroked my throbbing hard-on, sent ripples down to my toes. With her fingers, she shifted her panties to the side, exposing herself, and I groaned at the sight.

I replaced her hand with mine and pushed one finger inside her wet heat, testing how ready she was for me. Her warm arousal coating my digit was all the encouragement I needed. With one hand still holding her leg locked around my waist, I used the other to guide my way in, and entered her in one hard thrust.

Dahlia gasped.

I growled.

I dug my fingers into her ass cheek as we adjusted to each other.

Longing and lust overflowed from her eyes as I searched them to make sure she was all right.

She nodded, killing me and bringing me back to life all at the same time.

Without breaking eye contact, Dahlia pinched one of her stiff nipples.

The vision shattered me, and I could have shot my load right there without even having to move inside her.

She flicked the hard pebble between her thumb and forefinger, the sight propelling my hormones into overdrive.

Every nerve in my body sparked, my muscles tensing to the point of no return.

Shivering, electrified and taut, my body teetered on the edge of explosion.

My hand found her other breast, and I played with the tip the same way she did.

She let out a string of unintelligible words as she arched against me, clenching around my shaft, making me her prisoner.

Lifting both her legs around my waist, I slid in and out of her, unable to go slow any longer. "You're mine," I said, breathless, all the oxygen now busy fueling my dick.

"I'm all yours. God, I won't last long. Nick, don't stop." She breathed hard, her tone brooking no arguments, shattering the last of my restraints.

Without another word and with my mouth glued to hers, swallowing all her whimpers, I rammed into her.

Her back hit the wall behind. Again and again.

My balls were rock tight, ready to explode, stealing every shred of my common sense. Yeah, my brain had left the building, and only my body was in charge.

I lowered my head and ravaged her mouth. My entire being vibrated as her body swallowed me deeper. Until I could almost touch the deep end of her. Until I was about to be fused to her forever.

"There. Don't stop," Dahlia cried, her pupils dilated, and her lips swollen.

I ventured one hand down, and when my fingers connected with her clit, she detonated against me.

The walls of her vagina strangled my dick as they tightened around it.

She froze for a moment, her eyes closed, bliss painting her face.

When she opened her eyes, something had taken over her gaze. Something wild. An urgency.

"Fuck me harder, Nick. I'm not made of glass." Her voice, husky and low, unleashed something wild within me. I ripped her panties off, not wanting them in the way anymore. With my hands attached to her ass, I pounded into her harder.

The wall behind her quaked every time I speared into her.

Another orgasm hit her. Stronger. Her skin glowed in the low-lit kitchen. I lost myself in her eyes.

It took Dahlia almost a minute this time to come back from the rush as I licked a trail from her breasts to her jaw, relishing the tremors shaking her body.

She whimpered as I pushed into her with everything I had. Until my legs weakened when I came, and she collapsed into my arms, on the verge of fainting.

We both caught our breath before talking again.

"Evidence submitted. Case closed. Proved you are sexy." She claimed my mouth, stealing my breath away, and I forgot even my own name. "The sexiest. I hope you recharge fast because we're not done. I still need you," she said, with a twinkle in her eyes. "And you need me too."

"Don't worry about me. I have plenty to give. We'll see who calls it quits first." We untangled from each other's arms, and I guided her upstairs, toward the shower. "This time, I won't be gentle with you. I'll imprint myself on every square inch of your flesh, and you'll feel me in all your cells."

"I can't wait," she said, running away, her hearty laughter enveloping me.

"Don't hide. There are a million things I still wanna do to you."

Dahlia circled back toward me, splaying her hands across my chest, her naked body all shiny from sweat. "Then you better start now 'cause I won't be the one stopping you."

In the most natural way, Dahlia healed more pieces of my broken heart as if she were born to. As if she could soothe me just by being here.

With me.

And she had a magical way of keeping the darkness of the night at bay.

Derek's Bucket List – 24. Nick. Being brave even when it scares me

36

DAHLIA

I lay in bed, my mind replaying the last few hours on a loop. My body ached in the most delicious way. The man curled around me slept, his soft snores brushing my skin.

When Nick had returned home earlier, I had no idea how to comfort a man so completely shattered, standing in the doorway with his wet clothes clinging to him like a second skin. Shoulders slumped, chin lowered, he looked soul-weary. Saying goodbye to his dog-friend hadn't been easy for him. Buddy's collar was dangling from his fingers, and something inside me had twisted at the sight. Buddy was gone. Forever. The realization had hit me hard, a crushing weight squeezing the air from my lungs.

One glance at him was enough. I saw the hurt, deep and unspoken, churning within him and knew how help-less he must have felt.

My words were useless. Nothing I could have said at the time could have erased or eased the turmoil inside him. On my feet, I'd hugged him instead. In all the years I'd fought with my late husband, after he came back a changed man from the war, I'd learned that our bodies were much better at communicating pain and sadness than our words.

In that instant, I hadn't planned to shower with Nick, but with the anguish that had flashed in his eyes when I'd undressed him, his body rigid and unresponsive, I'd figured he might need this. Affection. And warmth.

Both naked, our bodies had been pressed together in the most intimate way, and yet there had been nothing sexual about it. I'd let my hand rest over his heart as mine had beaten steadily against his back.

I had the certainty in that moment that this man had infiltrated every corner of my mind, my heart, and my soul.

His sorrow had become mine.

Nothing could have broken us apart, not when grief had held us prisoner.

I watched Nick's sleeping form beside me, my stomach twisting at the thought of telling Jack about Buddy's passing the next morning. I didn't know how to explain death to a toddler. He still didn't understand the part where his own daddy had died. My heart shrank in my chest at the thought of breaking his, my pulse faltering.

In the kitchen earlier, I'd studied Nick as he ate a slice of the cake meant to celebrate Buddy's birthday. Only one thing could fix us. Love. No matter the form or how it was expressed.

Under his watch, I'd removed the shirt he'd given me and let it fall to the floor. Nick's smoldering gaze had drunk me in, his irises darkening, his lips pulling into a thin line.

He had scanned me from head to toe, and an ache had built low in my belly. Heat—hot, rousing—had rolled off him, the sexual tension between us rising to a peak.

"God, you're beautiful." The tone of Nick's raucous whiskey voice had warmed each inch of me.

"Touch me, Nick. I can't stand not being in your arms any longer. We both need this. To feel better."

At my words, something in his expression had turned feral, and I'd wondered if I could dissolve with only one sweep of his tongue?

Or from the intensity with which he was eye-fucking me?

He had stood still, my body quaking from the lack of attention.

Days when my vibrator was my best friend had become insignificant. Not when I'd experienced the real thing— warm flesh, whispered promises, lingering kisses. I would never go back.

I had brought one finger between my legs, and fire had burned in Nick's gaze. The animalistic side of him had taken over, and his own finger, thicker and longer than mine, had replaced my digit. Waves of unleashed ecstasy had surged through me. Why was Nick's touch always better? As if his fingers had a sixth sense when they fucked me. As if he could get me high just by embedding them inside my body.

A loud gasp had escaped my lips, mixing with his groan.

I had come, chasing the last waves of nirvana, my back hitting the wall as I drifted in the aftershock of bliss.

I'd yelped when he'd ripped my panties off, and that was the sexiest thing I'd seen in a long time. This man. One request, and Nick had turned into an unapologetic, dominating alpha. Gone was the sensitive, careful man I usually encountered. He'd gripped a handful of my ass and rammed into me until my vision blurred, and I believed I would never get down from this high.

Afterward, we had showered together for the second time in less than an hour, but this time around, the sexual tension between us had reached a new height. Nick's mouth was all over my skin, biting, teasing, licking, and kissing. My head had spun, desire and pleasure rushing through me in delicious waves. I'd spread my arms to either side, bracing myself against the shower walls to stay upright. My legs had felt like jelly, my pulse racing, my heart banging against my ribs.

"Stay with me, Dahlia. I'm not done yet. You woke up the beast in me. Now you'll have to tame it, or I'll eat you up all night. I'm ravenous and can go on for hours. Nothing will make me stop. Except you begging me to. You taste too fucking good, and only you can sate this thirst I have for you that's urging me to continue."

I'd swallowed hard as Nick had whispered dirty promises in my ear, making me even hotter for him.

All my wishes were being granted, here and now.

I'd swayed at the touch of his lips over the seam between my thighs, and Nick had caught my hips to steady me, his warm breath teasing my bare flesh.

"Hold on to me. You've seen nothing yet."

Another surge of heat washed through me as the memory faded, and I watched him for a few seconds, looking peaceful in his sleep.

When I finally followed him into his dreams, the grin curling my lips hadn't left, and the feeling rooted deep inside my heart had only increased.

It had only amplified my will to come clean. To be honest. And to take a leap of faith.

———

The next morning, I woke up early, and Nick was still asleep. The man who normally got up at the crack of dawn had been undone by the events of the previous night. I watched him for a long minute, making sure the worried lines that had marred the skin around his eyes last night had truly disappeared. Once satisfied, I snuck out of bed. Careful not to disturb him, I tiptoed outside the room and went to check on Jack. Through the ajar door, I peeked into the small bedroom that had become his. He was still deep in sleep, his fist clutching his fluffy blanket. The sight of him made my heart quiver and my eyes well up with tears. When I'd learned I was pregnant at twenty, it had been such a shock, but now I couldn't imagine a life without my baby in it. He was my whole world.

Strong arms locked around my waist, and warm lips trailed kisses down my neck. I shivered. If only I could wake up like this every day. With the man I loved next to me. I swallowed the words, spun around, and wrapped my arms around Nick's neck.

"Good morning," I said, kissing him back. My pulse sprinted. Yeah, I loved him. More than I ever could have imagined. My stupid heart was messing with me. In many ways, it didn't make any sense. Our relationship was still brand new. Yet, it felt right in every way. The other day, I wondered if my heart had mistaken the bond we shared for affection—because it had been starved of love for so long and couldn't process the rush of flutters invading me every time my mind drifted to Nick...or whenever we spent time together. No. I knew all about love. I had it. I had lost it. And now I could feel it again, burgeoning inside me, its branches spreading, their sap coursing through my veins.

"Good morning. Sleep well?"

I smiled against his lips. "I did. What about you?"

"As if in a dream. I can't believe we slept for less than four hours, and you look this good in the morning. It's unfair," he said.

"You should get in front of a mirror. You'll see you look way much better than I do," I said, combing his hair back with my fingers. "Are we ready to do this?"

"What?"

I straightened my back, trying to infuse myself with the courage I feared I lacked. "Tell Jack about Buddy…"

Nick bowed his head. His body stiffened. I kissed him, trying to show him he wasn't alone. That I was right there, by his side. And we could do this together. That we were stronger together. His arms held me closer, and I relaxed in his embrace.

"Yeah. I think I am. Are you?"

"I will be. I'm not sure he'll really get it, though. Death. It's kind of an intangible concept for a child…"

"How about we do something special? To commemorate Buddy's life. When my friend Jace's dog died years ago, we had a little ceremony in the backyard. We made cards and buried them in a hole, saying nice things about him. Perhaps we could do something like this. It's just an idea…"

I fastened my grip around him. "I like it. I'm sure Jack will, and Buddy would too."

We hugged without a word for a beat, losing ourselves in the comfort we brought each other.

The heaviness of the moment evaporated, and I became conscious of every inch of my man's hard body pressed against mine. I swooned in his arms as his lips locked on mine, taking their sweet time cherishing my mouth.

As if he sensed we wouldn't break apart if this dance between us didn't end soon, his hand met with my ass cheek. "Go, shower. I'll make breakfast. There's a special pancake recipe I want you to taste. I'd join you, but I don't want Jack to wake up and be afraid and alone," he said.

"You're too good to us, you know that, right?"

"Nah, Dahlia. I'm the lucky one."

Thirty minutes later, we sat around a plate of pancakes —Kelly's recipe as Nick called it—and fresh fruits, Jack sitting on my lap, not yet reaching the table by himself. I should get him a booster seat like the one he had at home. Yeah, that would make sense, since we spent so much time here these days. I forced my mind into the present and twisted strands of his hair around my finger as I spoke the words I dreaded most.

"Baby, we gotta talk about Buddy." I firmed my back and inhaled through my mouth. "He was really, really old, and last night he left… To become a star." I gestured to the ceiling to emphasize what I was saying.

"Like Daddy," my baby said. Not a question but an affirmation.

"Yeah, like Daddy. I'm sure they're already best friends."

"Me go on star? With Daddy and Buddy?"

I shook my head, a steel clamp strangling my heart. "No, baby. You can't."

Jack's lower lip shuddered. "Buddy my *bestest* friend. I want Buddy. *Buddddy*." Tears shone in his gray eyes, the same color as Carter's.

Unable to speak, I hugged him to my heart as tears made their way down my cheeks. "I know, baby. I know," I whispered, my voice cracking.

My eyes found Nick, and his expression mirrored mine.

Holding out my hand, I grabbed his, unable to let go, all of us needing one another to get through this. He offered a small nod. We were in this together. No matter what.

After breakfast, we made cards and wrote nice messages to Buddy. Nick found an old metal coffee bin in the garage, and we placed our treasures inside.

"I'll begin," Nick said as the three of us stood around the little hole he had dug under the bloodhound's favorite tree. "Buddy was my friend. He came to me the moment I arrived in Green Mountain, welcoming me to my new life. He followed me everywhere and made sure I always had a friend around. Just in case. As if he sensed I was alone, heartbroken, and lost. As if he could tell I had no idea why I'd come here and required his guidance. Buddy, you showed me love had no limits and that it was possible to love someone you've just met, even if it made no sense in your mind. When I left Chicago, I did not know what to expect. I embarked on this journey because I had something to gain. Something to accomplish. Something to prove to myself. Now that I'm here," he stretched his hand to intertwine his fingers through mine, "I've never been so sure of where I belong. Thanks for being my friend, Buddy. I'll always remember you."

Nick sniffled and rubbed at his teary eyes with the heel of his hand.

"Jack, do you want to say something?" I asked my son as I squatted to look at him, barely containing my own tears.

He nodded.

"Go ahead, baby."

"I love you, Buddy. You my best, best, *bestest* friend." He kneeled in the dirt and dropped a handful of pebbles, leaves, flowers, and bits he'd gathered minutes ago into the hole. He moved to his feet but bent over to pick up a stone he'd dropped. "Bye," he said, a satisfied expression on his face as he waved at the coffee bin.

The sweet gesture brought a fresh batch of tears to my eyes and permeated my heart with pride and love.

"You did great, little guy," Nick said, fist-bumping him as emotion clogged my throat.

No matter how big or small, grief was something I really struggled to deal with.

With a finger, Jack beckoned my man to lean forward. Nick opened his palm, and my son placed a pebble in it. They stared at each other for a long second. Nick's throat bobbed. Without a word, Jack slipped into his arms. They embraced for a long minute, neither of them speaking.

When they finally pulled apart, Nick's face was a map of tears and tenderness. He lifted my son into his arms, kissed the crown of his head, then threaded his fingers through mine, bringing me comfort.

We exchanged a glance. I'd met only a few people in my life who could read my heart—and my mind—easily. And over the weeks we'd known each other, Nick had become one of them. A look my way and my soul let him in. No questions asked.

With my eyes closed, I inhaled a cleansing breath. "Okay, let's do this," I said, lowering my shoulders as I breathed out. I cleared my throat before speaking. "Buddy, you and I didn't know each other very well, but you brought so much joy to the men I love that I'll be forever grateful to you. I wish I could have known you better, but even if your journey amongst us was brief, you made a great impact on all our lives. Rest in peace, Buddy. And thank you for loving us. Go find Jeff now. And tell him we're doing great. And I'm sure Derek is waiting for you too."

I dried my tears with my fingertips, my shoulders heaving.

Nick released his grip on my hand, and my fingers trembled.

The softness in his eyes when he pressed a kiss to my cheek sealed the tiny fractures of my heart.

"Gimme a minute," he whispered, tucking tendrils of my hair behind my ear.

I nodded, watching as he lowered Jack to his feet, and they both used toy shovels to bury the coffee bin.

When Nick rose back to his feet, he pulled me to his heart and kissed my temple. "I'm here, Dahlia. It's okay. We'll be fine."

I buried my head in his chest, taking comfort in the beating of his heart and the sound of his breathing. He was alive. We were alive.

Jack roamed around, picking more treasures to place on the fresh mound of soil.

Our eyes followed him, matching grins stretching our lips.

My heart was all over the place.

Whirling around, Nick placed himself in front of me and cradled my face with both hands. An anxious laugh bubbled out. "Dahlia, can I ask you something?"

I frowned, trying to decipher the look he gave me. "Sure."

"Did you just tell Buddy you love me?"

I leaned back and covered my face with my hands for a split second, feeling his heavy gaze on me. Oh, he didn't miss that. Through a timid chuckle, I drew in a bit of courage and met his eyes.

"Okay, hear me out. I kinda did. Because I do. I know it's too soon, and I'm sorry if it scared you because that's the last thing I wanted to do. Gosh, I wasn't supposed to say anything yet. It…it just slipped out…in the heat of the moment." I closed my eyes, Nick's stare about to drill holes into my skull. When I opened them again, his irises **sparked**, the glow so bright I had to avert my eyes. "I hope what I said won't change anything between us. Please don't run away. If you wanna panic, it's okay. I'll understand. To be honest, I probably would if I were in your shoes." I winced. "But let's talk first if I freaked you out. I can't take my words back, but we can…I don't know. If you prefer for us to go home so you can deal with everything, just say the word. I won't be upset. Oh gosh, I'm talking nonsense…"

Nick grabbed my upper arms, forcing me to look at him.

His eyes had darkened. The bent in his lips had receded.

I swallowed my uneasiness down as the man I knew I loved bored his heady gaze into mine.

"Dahlia, stop." The tilt of his lips returned. The ones I was dying to kiss to make him forget the last five minutes. "I asked you because I had to make sure I didn't dream it. At the vet last night, I told Buddy how much I love you. And that I hoped it was reciprocated. I don't know how it happened—or when—but my heart is all yours. Every fragment of it. I love you, Dahlia Ellis. Never had I imagined I'd find love here. Certainly not this fast. Yet I can't stop thinking about you… You've become the center of my universe. Knowing I was coming home to you yesterday after Buddy left eased the pain. You were the only one I wanted by my side through it all. Somehow, somewhere along the way, you stole my heart, Dahlia, and I'm thankful. And for what it's worth, I don't want it back. I want you to have it. To keep it. And for you to trust me enough with yours so I can care for it the way it should be."

My voice trembled. "You love me?"

"I do." Nick kissed me, and a kaleidoscope of butter-flies took flight deep inside me, turning everything that was gray and dull into a spectrum of bright colors.

Jack came running between us and pushed us apart, snaking an arm around each of our thighs. My fingers met Nick's as we both caressed his hair. As we both stepped back, my son reached for our hands, his little fists curling around our fingers, and the three of us headed back inside.

"Mama kissing Nick." He giggled. "Mama loves Nick."

We all burst into a fit of laughter.

"And Nick loves your Mama," my very hot and perfect boyfriend said. *I love you*, he mouthed my way, and I'm pretty sure I flustered because a wave of heat crawled up my cheeks. "And Nick loves Jack too," he added, picking up my son and nuzzling his neck.

"Nick loves Mama." My little boy hiccupped between giggles.

Nick loves Mama.

I would never get tired of hearing those words.

———

"How about the three of us do something fun today?" I asked as we played with Jack's toy cars in the den, the warm late-morning sun spilling in through the panoramic window. "I need to get home first for a change of clothes, then we can go hiking. See the waterfall. After-ward, we could float down the lazy river in those big inner tubes."

"Is it safe for kids?" Nick asked.

"You know you're cute when you worry about us, right? But yes, it's safe. I walk faster backward in heels than those tubes. He'll wear a lifejacket, and we'll sit him on either one of us. You'll see, it's really fun. Not much adrenaline involved, but it's romantic."

"Do you have one of those hiking backpacks to carry children for the hike?" he asked.

"Cart has one. We'll stop by his place to pick it up."

"Great. Gimme ten minutes to put a picnic together and then we'll get going."

I tugged at Nick's T-shirt and pulled him to me. "I love you." I sighed. "I'm happy it's finally off my chest. Now I can tell you every morning. And every night. And every minute in between."

Nick brushed his lips against mine."I love you. Go relax and let me get to work."

"But I wanna help," I pouted.

He shook his head. "Not this time. If you stay next to me, I won't get any work done. Dahlia, you're way too distracting for my sanity." His hand connected with my ass cheek, and I yelped. Stretching my neck, I kissed him, my lips molding to his. Yeah, I loved him. Way more than I ever thought I could love anybody else.

Nick carried Jack up to the waterfall in the backpack, my son whooping as we spotted a fawn and its mother. My man held my hand the entire time, as if afraid I'd get lost in the woods—or maybe just to make sure we stayed connected. The trail was marked and five feet wide—there was no way I could drift away—but I didn't mind, loving the way he watched over me. Loving how special and important he made me feel.

As if Jack sensed Nick and I were in it for real, he sat on his lap during our picnic, then fell asleep in his arms once we were done.

The sight of them filled my chest to the brim.

"You two look adorable together," I said, snapping a picture of my men. "How did you happen to walk into my life that day? How could you have mistaken my shop for Hilton and Sons?"

Shifting Jack to his right arm, Nick pulled me to his chest and kissed my forehead. "It was you, Dahlia. You blinded me with your smile and your beauty that day. And I just followed you in. Without thinking straight. Because even back then, I could tell you were special. That you held some power over me."

A seed that had been planted in my head—and my heart—weeks ago finally made sense.

I rested my head against his torso, Nick's strong hand pressing against my back. The rhythm of his heart, blending with Jack's soft breathing, soothed the jitters stirring inside me. Fiddling with the lint on the picnic blanket, I tried to muster the courage to speak. My heart thundered in my chest at the idea of giving voice to the thoughts running around in my head.

"Nick, I gotta tell you something," I said.

Leaning back, he searched my eyes until they locked with his, questions swimming in his gaze.

"It's big. I haven't told a lot of people… Huh…in fact, only Addison and Carter know. And…well…Jeff did too." I drew a deep breath through my mouth, attempting to settle the nerves twisting in my stomach. "See? I can't start this relationship without being honest with you first. You said you hate half-truths so… Ohmygod, it's harder than I thought it would be."

A weight pressed against my chest.

With my eyes closed, I inhaled and exhaled.

Nick grazed my cheek with his knuckles, and he forced my glistening eyes toward his. "Dahlia, it's okay. Nothing you say will make me walk away from you…from us. I'm here to stay. For the long run. If that's what you wish too."

I nodded, drying my teary eyes with my fingertips. "It's big. And kinda scary to admit out loud."

He scooted closer until I could sink my body into his. "It's me, Dahlia. You can tell me anything. I promise I won't react if that's what you're scared of."

"You might see me differently. Or think…gosh, please let me explain before jumping to conclusions, okay? It's complicated."

He raised a hand. "Trust me."

I nodded and scooted back, desperate for some fresh air, before telling him the secret that had been haunting my nights for years now. "Here we go. Promise me you won't get mad."

"I promise," he said. I saw the truth flashing in his eyes. The commitment. The love. The trust.

"There's a chance Carter is Jack's biological father." My throat worked as I swallowed the lump clogging it. I slid my now-moist hands under my thighs and hung my head low, avoiding looking at Nick for a few seconds. Until the storm in me dissipated—a little at least.

A strong hand curled around my nape. "Dahlia, look at me," Nick said. I tried to fight it but lost the battle, so I did. My eyes, as if he controlled them, lifted in his direction. "I knew."

"You did?"

He nodded.

"How?"

"To be honest, I didn't know but suspected it. The way Carter acts around you two is much more than just love. When you guys say you are family, it's way more than that. You are *a* family."

We both said nothing for a long moment. Until Nick broke the heavy silence.

"Everything makes so much more sense right now. I'm

glad to know I wasn't being paranoid. Carter behaves like he *is* Jack's father, not just his uncle. And as if you're his girl, not just his childhood best friend."

The words lingered between us, floating in the air as fragile drops that could either make us stronger or break us altogether.

"You said you two never dated…"

I drew in a jagged breath. "We didn't. It was one night. But somehow, that night changed a lot of things between us." I averted my eyes, staring in the distance. "Are you mad? I'd understand if you were." I sealed my eyelids as more tears streamed down my face.

"Jeff knew?"

I bowed my head. "I told him. Before we got married. But, since the day I learned I was pregnant, I've always been sure Jeff was the father. Even now… I don't know how to explain it. It's a gut feeling. After the shock subsided, Jeff and I had a long talk. We cried, we hugged, we cried again. And he finally decided to stay with me. And trust life."

I broke into sobs.

How could this day have turned sour? First Buddy, now this. There were just too many emotions swirling around. With just a spark, I was sure I could set the air on fire.

With my legs folded under me, I buried my face in my hands and let go of all the guilt I'd been keeping in for so long.

"How did Carter react? I don't know him much, but I'm sure the news didn't sit well with him."

I snorted. "We lost him for a moment. Darkness took over his life. He drowned his sorrows, pushed us away, acted recklessly. It was bad… I-I didn't recognize him. Us, as I said, was a one-night thing. A mistake… Something I think had to be settled between us because we would've always wondered if we were meant to be…" I paused. "But then Jeff died. And Carter came back to me." A long silence stretched between us. "There's this paternity test. He has it… I gave it to him after Jack's birth. I would never prevent him from knowing the truth. He deserves the right to. I'm just… I'm just not sure that *I* want to. Or that I can handle the truth if it's different from the story in my heart. The three of us had a complicated but beautiful relationship. Jack is the product of it…of unconditional love. It's precious." I swallowed. "Carter has never looked at the results. Not that I'm aware of…"

I blinked back some of my tears before continuing.

"After Jeff passed away, Carter and I decided we'd raise Jack together. We'd be like co-parenting him. I know Carter has been hoping for more, but I can't give it to him. Even if Jeff is stated as Jack's official father on his birth certificate, Carter is also his. In all the ways that count." With a cock of my head, I stared at Nick. "And now there's you… If we do this, you and I, Jack will consider you his daddy too. You must be willing to play that role. Eventually. He'll become yours too… In all the ways that matter. It's the only way this thing," I said, gesturing to the three of us with my hand, "can work. If we all commit to this child. He might have lost his daddy. He might have never known him—and never will—but Carter, you, and I, together, we can offer him something great. I know it's a lot to ask, but it's my reality."

"I—"

"Don't say anything if it means you'll change your mind afterward. You don't have to decide today. I'm just putting it out there. That's something you'll have to accept if you're with me. And as much as I love you, I'll never force you to a life you're not ready for. We'd both be miserable."

Nick laid Jack on the blanket beside him, extra careful not to wake him up, and on his knees, stalked toward me.

His eyes, amber in the sunlight and full of sparks, bore into mine—into my soul—and I braced myself for whatever words would leave his lips.

———

"Are you staying with us tonight?" I asked Nick as we drove back to my place. "Unless you desire some time on your own. I know the last twenty-four hours have been emotional. And then I dumped that piece of info on you. It wasn't considerate. I should have waited."

He brought our connected hands to his lips and kissed the back of mine. "Don't ever apologize for speaking what's in your heart. I already told you I'm not going anywhere. And no way am I letting you walk away either. We'll make it work, okay? You two are stuck with me."

We exchanged a heartwarming smile before I turned to stare out the window, emotions still filling my eyes. "I love you," I whispered.

"I love you too," he said, leaning in my direction to tug me against his side.

Feeling safe in his embrace, I rested my head on his shoulder and breathed him in. His masculine scent tingled my senses, and I lost myself in the newfound familiarity of him—of us.

"So, are you staying?" I asked again after a beat.

"Wouldn't it be weird…me sleeping over? Waking up together, the three of us?"

"We do it all the time at your place…"

Nick breathed out a soft laugh. "I know. But this is your home, your family nest. I won't feel good barging in."

"But I want you here. With us."

He parked the truck in the driveway and framed my face with both hands. "I know you do, and I love you even more because of it. Because you wanna share all those things with me…as if I'm already part of your family. And I told you, I'm all in. For the long ride…for the entire journey…but there's more than just you and I involved here. Let's not rush things. I'll stay for dinner but go after, okay?"

With my eyes closed, I nodded at his words. A lone tear traced down my cheek.

"It's been an emotional day. Let's order in," Nick offered.

My shoulders felt heavy and tense. With a breath out, I nodded again.

"Go inside, take a bath or anything you do when you wanna relax, and take a nap. Jack and I will take care of everything. We'll take care of *you*. You're always the one thinking about everyone else. Let me be there for you this time."

I hugged him tight against my heart over the center console of the truck before moving to get out. "Thanks, Nick."

With more tears sliding down my cheeks, I walked toward the house.

My heart jammed in my chest, its beats irregular, when I heard Jack and Nick's conversation.

"Mama sad?" Jack asked.

"Mama's tired, little guy. Let's have some fun together while she rests, okay?"

I made my way inside, and from the window, I watched them, laughing together, knowing in my core everything would be all right.

They raced toward the front door, Jack screaming his happiness the entire time. Nick ran after him, lifted him over his head, turning him into an airplane.

Their contagious giggles multiplied and reached my heart as I climbed the stairs to my bedroom.

Later, after we put Jack to bed, Nick and I snuggled on the couch. The day had been an emotional roller coaster and right now, we required each other to calm the storm.

After he made sure Jack was safe and he tucked me into bed, he left. I missed him the moment the front door clicked behind him and the engine of his truck filled the silence of the night.

37

NICHOLAS

Standing in the doorway a month later, I rubbed my hands together, admiring the newly renovated bathroom. Yeah, it looked sharp. Gone were the old tiles and leaking faucets. Mrs. Rutherford had allowed me a decent budget to remodel the room, and thanks to Dahlia's interior design skills, it surpassed anything I'd envisioned.

I hadn't seen my girl in almost a week, and somehow, it felt like forever. With the store thriving and drawing clients from everywhere, she'd been busier than she'd ever hoped for. It didn't make things any easier that her employee Joan was home caring for her sick grandchild. At night, after work, Dahlia spent some time with Jack and went to bed early, exhausted. I didn't mind, though my body was aching in withdrawal, making the most of the time apart to work on the house. At least now I had one less room to worry about. Every day, we talked on the phone in the morning and at night. The last time we saw each other, I brought over pizza, and Dahlia had fallen asleep just minutes into the movie. Even when we hung out at her house, I still didn't spend the night. After I put her to bed and made sure Jack slept tight, I always drove back here—alone in this house too big for one person.

Hungry, I went downstairs and surveyed the place, still struggling with Buddy's absence. Whenever I was home alone, I missed my old pal. Even if he were as active as a piece of furniture, he still brightened up my days.

I dropped my ass on a stool in the kitchen when a knock on the door startled me. I wasn't expecting anyone at this early hour on a Saturday morning. Rising to my feet, I straightened my stained work clothes and ran a hand through my hair, hoping to look somewhat respectable.

My frown transformed into a grin—one I was sure made me look stupid—at the sight of Dahlia cradling a sleeping Jack in her arms, standing on my front porch, her hair falling loosely around her face. My smile vanished the moment I noticed the worry lines around her eyes.

"What's wrong?" I lifted Jack from her arms, inviting her in. "Are you okay?"

Her chest caved, and her voice wavered, devoid of the usual confidence. "Paula is home with a bad case of flu, and I got called at the store because one employee didn't show up because her car broke down. The girl who's there right now can't hold the fort by herself. I hired her a week ago. She's not trained to do everything yet."

I leaned forward and brushed my lips against hers. "Tell me what you need. I'm all yours for the day."

"In fact, I was wondering if you could watch Jack for a few hours." She gave me a once-over. "Oh, you were working. This is so embarrassing. I should've called. Don't worry about it. I'll take him with me and find another solution. I'm sorry I bothered you. Please go back to what you were doing. I'll go now."

I clutched her elbow. "Dahlia, stop. I'm here. Don't

ever feel bad asking for my help. I love you and will always be here for you two. You're what matters most to me. Both of you. And no, I wasn't actually working… I was just appreciating the work I'd done last night."

She drew in a nervous breath, fingers fidgeting with the necklace around her neck. "Nick Peterson, you're my hero in more ways than you can imagine." She sagged into a chair at the table. "Gosh, I'm drained. You're a lifesaver. I should only be gone for a few hours. Jack's stuff is in his bag. You can put him down for a nap after lunch. I'll be here as soon as I can."

She rubbed her temples, and the sight of her, overwhelmed and visibly exhausted, with dark circles under her eyes, pained me.

I laid the boy on the couch and took a seat beside her, grabbing her hand in mine. "Don't worry. I've got everything under control. We'll be fine. Do your thing and come back later. I'll cook dinner, and you'll spend the night here. You have to rest. I'll watch over Jack. You can trust me."

Dahlia tilted her head back and met my eyes. "I trust you, Nick. I always do. Thanks for being here. I'm usually better organized than this."

I pressed my forehead to hers, breathing her in as I basked in her energy. Our souls fused for a second, and mine comforted hers.

"You're a great mom. These things happen. As you said, sometimes you've just got to ride the tide. And just so you know, the upstairs bathroom is now fully functional, and the new shower is much bigger." I wiggled my eyebrows, and Dahlia burst out laughing.

There. The wrinkle across her forehead vanished.

Her lips, soft and warm, claimed mine, and I melted into her embrace. Torn between what I had to do and what I craved, I gently pushed her away.

"Go. We'll be here when you get back."

I kissed her one last time, committing every second of her lips on mine to memory before she slipped away.

"You're amazing," she yelled over her shoulder, waving at me. "I love you."

In the living room, Jack was still deep asleep. I observed him for a moment, peaceful, his fist closed around his favorite fluffy blanket.

Minutes later, I placed him in his portable bed, fearing he might fall from the couch like he did the first time he came over.

On the kitchen table, I spread the blueprints for a new development project starting next winter.

Mike said he'd put me in charge of it, and according to him, a project of this size, here in Green Mountain, wasn't a common occurrence. I intended to be ready to impress him, more than ever, with my planning skills, leadership, and dedication. Excitement ran through me. I'd missed those—the big projects with hefty budgets and tight deadlines.

A few weeks back, over the drinks we'd agreed to have when I first moved to town, Mike confided that Tucker had told him about the condo mishap in Chicago—and that he was more interested than ever in selling me parts of the business. Or even the whole thing, whenever I'd be ready. His proposition sounded good, and I promised I'd look into it seriously.

Bent over the table, I studied the plans for over half an hour before Jack woke up. He came to me as soon as his eyes sprang open, his tiny feet padding on the hardwood floor.

"Hey, little guy. How was sleep?"

Jack yawned as he lifted his arms, asking me to pick him up.

I sat him on my lap. "Those are construction blueprints for retirement homes I'll be building. Right now, I'm building cabins. We could ask your mama to bring you to the site one day to see the big trucks," I said, stretching my arms as if to prove my point, "and the excavators. Would you like that?"

He nodded, his face still flushed and innocent from his slumber. "Mama?"

"Your Mama had to go to her store for a few hours. She thought you and I could spend some time together. Do you think it's a good idea?"

He nodded again.

"Great. I might ask for your help later. I'm removing the old disgusting wallpaper in the bedroom upstairs and I could use those big muscles of yours." I scrunched up my nose, and a smile glowed on his face. "Gimme a fist-bump," I said as we connected our balled hands. "Hungry? I could make you something. I'm not sure you had breakfast earlier."

"Hungry," he echoed.

"Let's see what we've got." I sat Jack on the kitchen countertop, a hand around his waist to prevent him from falling, as I rummaged through the refrigerator.

Jack poked my arm, and when I turned around, he held a banana in his hand.

"You want that." He nodded. "With toast?" He smiled. "I'll bring your toys down here, and you can play while I make you a five-star restaurant worth breakfast."

Ten minutes later, with Jack perched on my lap, we ate breakfast together. I studied the blueprints still spread before me, making calculations so Mike could produce an estimate.

The sippy cup tumbled onto the floor, and when I

leaned forward to grab it, my eyes took Jack in, and my breath hitched.

My heart plummeted to my stomach, and my body froze. Everything came to a standstill. Time stopped yet moved at supersonic speed.

Jack's face was turning blueish. His body stiffened as he tried to take a breath. He brought one hand to his mouth, and his body slumped.

"Breathe, little guy. Breathe."

All my movements seemed too sluggish.

Jack's eyelids fluttered.

No air came in and out of his lungs—nor mine.

As if he'd forfeited the fight, his tiny body turned limp in my arms.

"Stay with me, Jack. Oh God, stay with me. Please, hold on. Come on, little guy."

Life had a twisted sense of humor. Derek, Buddy. And now Jack. No way. Not under my watch. I'd give my life for this boy. Any day. Any time.

My last CPR class had been back when I'd started working for Cody years ago, and it only covered what to do on a construction site—not in a kitchen with a child.

Even though I knew the basics, I had no idea what technique to use on a toddler.

My body woke up. Adrenaline stirred in my blood.

The numbing of my mind washed away, and I jumped to my feet and laid Jack on the floor.

Taking the phone in my hand, I called nine-one-one.

"…must be choking. Have you checked his mouth? How old is he? Do you know CPR?"

I put the device on speaker. My bent finger swept Jack's mouth cavity, searching for a piece of food lodged there. Images flashed before my eyes. Yes, I had cut the banana into small bites. And the toast too. That I was certain. Still, was it enough for him to choke on it? Or could he have swallowed something else?

"Sir, please confirm your address. We'll send an ambulance." I did, and the lady kept talking to me, assisting me as I hunted for a piece of food clogging Jack's airways.

Nothing.

I flipped him over my forearm as instructed, his head low, and hit his back at an angle with the side of my other hand.

"Breathe, little guy. Breathe. Come on. Do it. One breath. That's all I'm asking for."

My eyes were trained on his lifeless body. I could do this. We could do this.

My chest hurt, my aching heart about to rip it open, twisting on itself. Now wasn't the time. I kept my focus on the child.

I hit his back again. And again.

"Breathe, Jack."

I hit his back once more.

"Don't even think about not breathing. That's not an option. Not while I'm here. Spit whatever is in there. And breathe. Do it. Now." I refocused on my technique. "Derek, help me here. Please. I can't go through this again," I muttered through clenched teeth. Because right now, I needed to believe in every saint.

Holding my breath, I hit his back one last time.

A tiny half-chewed piece of banana flew out of his mouth. Jack squirmed in my arms, color returning to his cheeks.

My heart untangled itself. I coughed, whizzing air.

Oh God, he's breathing. He's alive.

"I'm sorry. I'm so sorry, little guy," I said, pulling him close to my chest, tears scorching the back of my eyes, raw from not blinking, my adrenaline running high in my bloodstream, as a mix of relief, fear, and helplessness stirred inside me. "I'm so, so sorry. I don't know what happened."

All my thoughts went chaotic inside my head.

How could Jack choke on such a tiny piece of food?

I exhaled my relief, my heart thrumming in my chest.

With my fingers, I combed his hair back.

"Sir, the ambulance is on its way. Wait for it. How's the boy? Please check for any signs of breathing distress."

I bobbed my head as if the dispatcher could see me. "Thank you. I'm fine… We're…we're fine."

She kept talking, reassuring me, making sure we really were okay.

I hung up as the sound of sirens got closer.

"Thanks, bro," I said, looking at the ceiling. I kissed two fingers and saluted over my head. "Thanks for watching over us."

A tightness grew in my chest, and a sensation of dread filled the cavity.

I could have lost Jack. *You didn't,* a voice in my head said. *Jack is okay. He's alive. Stop worrying. He's here. With you. Breathing.* But still, I had trouble believing it. The reassurance did nothing to calm my jittery nerves.

While Jack and I waited, I gasped to control my shallow breaths, my emotions swirling so fast inside me I couldn't get a grip on them.

With my eyes squeezed shut, I took a deep whiff of his hair, the baby-shampooed chamomile scent laying a balm over my thundering heart.

With both hands, Jack pushed back. Was I hugging him too tight?

We stared at each other for a moment.

Without looking away, he framed my face with his tiny hands as if I were the one who had to be comforted. The one who'd stopped breathing. "No cry, Nick. No cry. It's okay. No tears, okay?"

How could he be so calm? He was the one who had almost choked to death.

The ambulance arrived a few seconds later, and the paramedics checked Jack's vitals before laying him on a stretcher.

Rushing to the living room, I grabbed his blanket before joining them.

When we settled at the back of the emergency vehicle, I relaxed my stance. Soon enough, I dreaded the phone call I knew could change everything.

"Sir, you did good. The boy is fine. We're taking him in just for observation. He should be released quickly," the paramedic, a man in his late fifties, said, clapping my shoulder. "He's lucky to have you." His smile resuscitated me, and the giant clamp that was crushing my insides released its grasp a little.

Jack wrapped his fingers around mine.

My eyes drifted to our joined hands, and I blew out a long breath.

The boy was alive. Nothing else mattered.

"It will be okay. I'm here." I ruffled his hair, kissed the side of his head, and grabbed my phone, knowing I'd potentially just lied to him.

With a roll of my shoulders, I cleared my throat. "Hey, Dahlia, it's me. Listen…" I paused my breathing until I drew in enough courage to deliver the news.

She screamed. She cried.

And I died a little more inside.

38

DAHLIA

In the middle of my shop, I crumpled to my knees, my legs too weak to support my weight. Nick's words played on a loop in my head.

"Jack choked."

"Couldn't breathe."

"Turned blue."

"Called the paramedics."

"Ambulance."

"Hospital."

No one was around. The only employee was busy hanging gowns we'd just received in the back of the store.

My eyes burned from all the tears I shed.

My throat itched from all the cries I let out.

My heart was bruised from all the times it banged against my ribcage, beating too loud and too fast.

My stomach hurt, tied too tight with bands of thorns coiled around it.

The little angel living in my head, the one I could trust, told me Jack was okay.

Jack was breathing.

Breathing.
Breathing.
Breathing.

My brain reset, and some of the fog around me dissipated. That was when I remembered Nick, still on the line.

On all fours, I reached for the phone I'd dropped seconds—or was it minutes?—ago and brought it to my ear.

"Nick?" My voice sounded so far away and weak. So not-me. "Are you still there?"

His voice—masculine and unmistakably his, yet missing its usual self-assurance—grounded me. "Yes. I'm here. Not going anywhere."

"Thank you."

"No. You can't thank me. I almost cost your baby his life."

"Nick. Stop. He's fine. He's alive. It wasn't your fault."

Sobs strangled his next few words. "If you decide I should go when you get here, just say it. I'll understand. I messed up. Big time."

"No," I said, my voice catching and distorted as it left me. "You're one of us. I need you. We both need you. Please don't go. Don't leave. I love you."

How could he blame himself?

How could he not see he'd saved Jack's precious life?

I wanted to be by his side, by both my men's sides, to hug them. Kiss them. Love them.

Nick exchanged a couple of words with a man—probably the paramedic—then I heard him tell my son, "The ambulance ride is pretty nice, huh, little guy? We'll have to go inside the hospital when we get there with the nice man here. You'll ride on this magic rolling bed, then a doctor will check on you with this thing he uses to listen to your heart. And your Mama will meet us there. How cool is that?"

Jack's voice, the reminder that his life was safe, reached my ears next. "Do the *wee-oww wee-oww*?"

Every crushed part of my heart healed at the sound of his request. Yeah, my baby was fine.

"You want the sirens?" Nick asked.

I pictured my son bobbing his head with too much energy, like he always did. The curl of my lips turned upside.

"I'm sure Johnny here can get you some *wee-oww*."

Seconds later, a high-pitched sound filled the phone for a short moment, followed by Jack's clear laughter.

This man. I had no idea why life had sent him to me, but I'd be grateful for the rest of my life. Someone I treasured. The way he looked at me. And loved me. And how he always made Jack his priority. As if he was his own. How could I not fall in love with him a little more each day?

From the moment Nick and I met, something strong had seared between us. As if we were destined to meet. To love each other and to be together.

"Sorry, Dahlia," Nick said, bringing my attention back to him. "Are you okay to drive?"

I nodded, then remembered he couldn't see me. "Yes. Mary is on her way. I'll be there as soon as she gets here. We have a fitting in thirty minutes." I sighed, feeling so far away from the ones I loved right now. "Thanks for being with Jack. Please kiss him for me a million times."

"Wanna talk to him?"

An invisible vice squeezed my heart. I did, very much, but I knew I shouldn't. "No. It will just make him miserable and cranky. Hold him. Kiss him. And tell him I'm on my way, okay? Don't leave his side." I shut my eyes and swallowed the mountain-big lump down my throat. "I love you guys so much." Tears spilled from my eyes and streamed in silence down my cheeks. "Thanks for being there for my baby." The sound of voices and doors opening resonated on the other end of the line. "Oh, you're already there. I'll be with you as soon as I can. Keep me updated, okay?"

"Of course. Drive safe, please."

"I will." We hung up, and after I found some of my composure back, I called Carter. I needed him and his strength, and he needed to know. Because no way I'd ever be able to hide anything from him. I knew from where he was he couldn't do anything, but I wanted to hear his voice to find my balance. And it was better he learned it from me than from anyone else—even Jack.

"Hey, Dah. I was about to call you."

The sound of his voice tamed the jitters jumping around inside me.

"Hey, Cart. I miss you." My voice broke. Carter knew me like no one else. No way I'd ever be able to fake being okay around him.

"Fuck, Dah. What's wrong? Is it that guy? He broke your heart, right? I knew he would. Damn it." The sound of his palm hitting a hard surface startled me.

"No. Carter. Don't say that about Nick ever again. He's been nothing but good and selfless around Jack and me."

"What is it then? You sound upset. And I can tell you've been crying."

"It's Jack—" The words died on the tip of my tongue. Even if Jack was okay, I knew Carter wouldn't be. And it broke my heart just thinking about worrying him.

His tone turned serious. "Dah? What about Jack? What happened?" Panic was lightly veining his words.

I had to tread carefully here. Carter had been having

panic attacks since Jeff passed away, and everything and anything could trigger them.

I breathed in a big gulp of air and some courage. "Listen to me. Carter, you gotta listen to everything I say. Jack is fine…but something happened… This morning. He choked while eating breakfast. He's okay now. The paramedics said Nick did all the right things—" I bit my tongue as I spoke the words. I cringed. Why did I include Nick in the conversation?

I swallowed the acid rising at the back of my throat.

"Nick?" Anger filled my best friend's voice. "What about Nick? Where were you? Why was Nick with him? Are you fucking with me, Dah?"

"Stop. It's not fair. You aren't here." Wrath sliced my words. "You know nothing."

Rolling my shoulders back, I explained everything. Because no way would I let things get strained between Carter and me. They had been, years ago, and it had almost killed me. Never again.

I could feel every layer of his tension, even from hundreds of miles apart.

"Carter, Nick and I are together. He's a part of Jack's and my life. You better get used to it. You're not allowed to insult him and his intelligence. Imagine how he felt at that moment. How he still feels… Nick loves us, Cart. And we do too. I called you because I thought you deserved to know. Because Jack is yours too. But if you gimme shit, I won't tell you a thing next time."

I blew out a long breath, filled with hurt and anger.

After a moment, Carter spoke again. "Fine. I'm sorry, Dah. You know how I hate not being there for you two. Most of the time, it kills me. You're the only family I have left. You can't be mad at me for caring about you and

Jack." Emotions laced my best friend's voice. "All I'm asking is for you two to thrive and be happy. And safe."

I softened my tone. "I know you do. And that's one of the many reasons why I love you." I paused. "Where are you now? In Canada already?"

Carter told someone to wait and brought his attention back to me. "Landed in Toronto fifteen minutes ago. On my way to Montreal. But change of plans. I'm boarding a flight to Tennessee. Should be there in two hours, okay?"

"Okay," I repeated. The thought of Carter flying to be with us calmed the throbbing of my heart. "Oh, Cart, I must go. Mary just walked in. I'll be able to leave the shop. I'll call you with the updates. Be safe. And don't worry, Jack is all right. They're just keeping him under observation because that's the protocol. Can't wait to see you later."

"Dah, I'll be right there…with you guys."

We hung up, and I gave my employee all the instructions before hurrying to be with the men I loved.

The ones my heart belonged to.

The ones waiting for me right now.

39

NICHOLAS

I padded down the hallway, my fingers interlaced at the nape of my neck, and a frown probably digging trenches across my forehead. Dahlia was inside the room, lying next to Jack on the hospital bed, brushing his hair with her fingers. The image brought painful memories back to the surface. Hospital room. Derek lying on the bed. Murielle by his side. Caressing his bald head.

Air couldn't get through. I was hyperventilating.

With my face turned toward the ceiling and my eyes closed, I drew in a calming breath, trying to steady myself —and my emotions. My stomach twisted. I'd spent too many hours in the hospital in the last few years. My throat tightened with unshed tears at the thought.

I knew I should go in there, but I required some alone time to calm the fuck down. The adrenaline rush I'd experienced earlier had dissipated. Hospital rooms, emergency, doctors. It was just too much for me to take. My insides quivered, spinning at lightning speed, building a tornado and shattering every particle of control and calmness I had left.

I huffed, dragging a hand over my face, rubbing my jaw. The back of my neck prickled, my hair standing on end. My eyes locked on Dahlia, and she smiled at me. A warm, tight-lipped smile that shouldered a lot of meaning. A smile that said *I need you. We need you.* Her gaze bore into me, injecting me with doses of unconditional love. *I'm here for you. Stop worrying, we're all fine. Be with us. Right here. Right now. We're all in this together.*

The sight of the two people I loved more than anything eased some particles of tension inside me, and I mustered a smile back.

The way they looked at me filled my heart and burned it to ashes all at the same time. I had no idea how I should feel. Relieved? Guilty? No, I should not, but yeah, guilty sounded about right because I had messed up, and I lacked the proper word to describe the emotional cyclone killing me inside.

Dahlia walked up to me and grabbed my elbow, stopping me in my tracks as I still debated about my culpability. "Babe, don't. This has to stop. You're making me dizzy."

I tugged at my hair. "Dahlia, Jack is in here because of me," I said, pointing to the room.

Jack waved at me, a curve on his lips, and life shining through his eyes. I returned his wave, and his grin stretched wider.

Peace washed over me, soothing some of my angst.

That boy had a way to connect with my heart in the most raw and powerful way.

"Yeah, because you saved him. You saved my baby's life. He's here, alive, because of you." Dahlia held my hands between hers. Her warmth crept along my arms, reaching my heart and wrapping around it. Like a soft blanket. Like a promise that we'd get through this and a much-needed hug. She lowered her voice, searching my eyes. "Jack is asking for you. They're keeping him for a few more hours, but he's fine. It's just some technicalities. I have to go by the store to drop off the keys, then get his stuff. Can I go to your place afterward? The things he loves the most are all there."

"You should stay here. I'll go."

Dahlia shook her head. "No. He's asking for *you*. I won't be long, and I think you two should spend some time together." She stared at me with trust burning in her eyes.

The thought of staying in that room made nausea reel through me. With a long exhale, I calmed myself down. Yeah, I was stronger than this. No way would I let the last memories of Derek in the hospital haunt me forever. I steeled my back with a new resolve. If required, I could freak out later.

I pulled Dahlia into my arms, filling my nose with her floral scent that made everything better. "Go. And come back. I love you. We'll wait for you, okay? Drive safe."

She nodded, and on her tiptoes, she brushed her lips against mine.

We entered the room hand in hand, and after I fist-bumped with Jack, I lay beside him, stretching my legs before me, crossing them at the ankles. He sank against me, his shoulder pressing into my upper arm.

"Watch dragon with me?" he asked, pointing to the TV mounted on the wall.

"Sure, little guy." I ruffled his hair with my fingers as he settled in closer by my side.

Jack linked our hands, his head resting against my chest as my arm curled around his innocent body, his quiet breathing the only sound reaching my ears.

He's breathing. He's breathing. He. Is. Breathing. Jack will be fine.

The tornado inside me dropped in intensity. Yeah, we'd get through this.

———

DAHLIA

Are you ok? I'm needed at the store. Bridal party just walked in. The girls are overwhelmed.

ME

Jack's napping now. Take your time. Did you know Ross the dragon had magical fire coming out of his mouth? Pretty amazing, if you ask me.

I could hear her snicker in my head.

DAHLIA

You didn't know? It's a shame. Okay, we'll do a dragon marathon. Pizza, ice cream, and us three. That's a date.

ME

Sounds good. Can't wait.

DAHLIA

Forgot to tell you earlier. Carter's on his way. I called him after you contacted me. Took the first flight out. Was north of the border. Should arrive soon. I'll try to come back before he gets there.

ME

Take your time. Don't worry.

DAHLIA

Love you. Hope you know.

ME

I love you too. Do your thing. Talk to you later.

I surfed the channels, Jack wheezing softly in his sleep beside me, now nestled against my chest, his fingers still wrapped around mine.

A knock on the door, and a nurse dressed in colorful scrubs walked in. "Oh, he's sleeping."

I nodded.

"We should be able to discharge him soon. Has Ms. Ellis returned yet?"

"She had an emergency at work. She'll be here as soon as possible. Do you want me to call her?"

The nurse, about my mother's age, smiled and shook her head. "Let the boy sleep. Let us know when she gets here."

She left and seconds later, another knock. Carter Hills walked in, his tall self taking the room hostage with his presence and stealing all the viable oxygen with one breath.

His dark gaze landed on me, and the panic swirling in his melted-steel irises switched to wrath. He didn't even have to say a word. It emanated from every inch of him. Careful not to wake up the child, I swept my legs over the edge of the bed and untangled my body from his, positioning him on the pillow and tucking a blanket around him.

"Hey, Carter," I said, holding out my hand to shake his.

His eyes lowered to where my hand floated between us, but he didn't meet it.

Great. This was going to be fun.

"Let's talk outside," I suggested.

The door hadn't even closed behind me when Carter's

harsh tone broke the silence. "Man, you should go home. I'm here now," he said, his hushed icy tone wakening chills along my spine. "Where is Dah? After what happened, I can't believe she left you here to watch over Jack." He blinked as if to make sure it wasn't a dream. Then shook his head in disbelief.

Without budging, I raised my hands between us. "Whoa, stop right here. I'm not a threat. You're serious now? You can't judge me for what happened this morning. You weren't there. And there's no way I'll let you insult me, my character, or my actions."

Carter looked away. I hoped my voice held more conviction than I did. Not that Carter Hills's presence or anger affected me, but more like I still felt responsible for Jack choking earlier. Even so, Carter wouldn't get the last word.

"You and I started our relationship on the wrong foot, but you know what? I respect you. A lot," I said. "I know what you and Dahlia went through and how painful it was. I've never lost my brother, but I've lost someone as important to me. Grief is fucking hard. I get that. And I know you love them, and they mean a lot to you, but they mean a lot to me too. And I love them. With all my heart. Maybe that's not what you wanna hear, but that's the truth. They're not just yours to care for anymore."

Carter's eyes nearly popped out of their sockets, but he quickly composed himself, drawing in a noisy breath as his jaw flexed and his gaze drifted into the distance.

We both turned our heads to make sure Jack was still asleep. The boy's chest rose and fell under the blanket. Once we were both satisfied, we returned to our heated conversation.

Carter said nothing. He just twisted his lips into a scowl, so I continued.

"Dahlia and I connected from the second we met. We both can't explain it. I have no idea what it's like for you guys, and I don't care. All I want is to be there for her…for them." Carter stayed silent, so I pressed on. "You three are family, and I respect that. I'll never break you apart, but I can be their family too. Eventually." There. I said my piece.

The country music star's gaze stayed fixed on me for a long moment as I tried to decipher the meaning behind his dark stare.

"Listen, you can try to push me away or come between us, but all it'll do is bring us closer together. I have no intention to fight with you. What Dahlia and I share is bigger and stronger than us. I know you love her… It oozes from every bit of your being, and you do a shit job hiding it. And it's okay. I won't play games. I could be jealous and threaten you, but I won't go there. I'm not here to shove our happiness in your face either. What you two have is amazing. The thing is… I won't go away. Dahlia is my soul mate. The one I'm supposed to be with. I'll fight for us. Until I bleed. Because that's what soul mates do. They share the same heart."

Carter cleared his throat, averting his eyes for an instant.

When he brought his attention back to me, the lines around his eyes had softened. "She loves you, you know? I could tell from the moment she talked about you the very first time, that you'd be more than just friends…" He sighed, and his shoulders dropped. He cast a glance down, kicking the linoleum floor with the sole of his shoe. After a beat, he brought his focus back to me. "When Dahlia loves, she loves with all her heart. It's powerful. And I wish I could be on the other end of that love. I would give every-thing I own for a chance…but she doesn't love *love* me the same way." His voice cracked, a contrast to the heavy stare locked on me. "Don't break her heart. This will be my only warning."

"I won't." My eyes drifted to Jack, still asleep, and I sighed. "If you wanna spend some time with him, one-on-one, I'll go home and wait for Dahlia to stop by my place once she's done at the shop. Then I'll drive her back here so she can sign the discharge papers. I know Jack will be excited to see you. He talks about you all the time."

"He does?"

"Carter, Jack's your biggest fan. He looks up to you. He sings your songs and tells me all about what you guys do when you're together. You're his dad. In every way that is important."

Carter pinched the bridge of his nose, glancing down. "Thanks for saying that." His eyes followed Jack's silhouette. "It means a lot. Most times, I'm upset for not being around as much as I should…" His Adam's apple bobbed, and he rubbed the back of his neck. "Thank you for allowing us time together. I freaking miss him. All the time. He's such a huge part of my life…of me…and of my brother. He reminds me so much of him." The fight left him. "Go. We'll be here when you get back."

I nodded and tiptoed inside the room to pick up my stuff. Hovering over the bed, I whispered, "Bye, little guy. You'll have a surprise when you wake up. Sleep for a bit longer. I'll see you later." I laid a kiss on his forehead. "Love you." And left.

Outside, I welcomed the breeze sweeping across my face. My angst returned as I climbed into my truck. All the emotions I'd bottled in for the last few hours reached the surface before I could even shut the door.

With a flat palm, I hit the steering wheel as I pulled out of the hospital parking lot.

"Derek, tell me this is a joke. A stupid prank or a dream I'll wake up from. Please, bro. This day can't be real —" I inhaled a shaky breath, trying to ebb the frustration tinting my words. My anger bled into helplessness. "I can't take it anymore. I wish you could tell me it was the last test…or whatever it was."

My heart sank low in my chest as I pulled into my driveway. It took me a couple of minutes before finding the courage to go inside. My legs weighed like they were made of concrete.

A chill zinged through me.

I stared at the sky. "I know it's not your fault, bro. I'm sorry, you didn't deserve my wrath. I love you." I kissed my fingers and saluted the sky. "I'll be okay. Maybe not today, but I will. I promise. Talk later."

Once inside my home, my eyes landed on the sippy cup on the floor and the half-eaten breakfast still on the table.

Knots I thought had previously loosened tied up my insides.

A weight—something big and heavy—pressed my chest, making it almost impossible for me to breathe.

My entire body shook. Images of Jack's inert body played before my eyes, and I sucked in a breath, trying not to shatter into pieces.

With languid movements and a sluggish mind, as if I were here but also a thousand miles away, I opened the kitchen cabinet to grab a bottle and a glass.

With a drink in hand, I slouched in a chair, elbows resting on the tabletop.

Without overthinking it, I dug my phone out and dialed a number I knew all too well.

The gentle voice, with traces of sleep laced in it, that answered after three rings, soothed the emotional wildfire raging inside me somehow.

"Hey, Nick. It's been a while. Is everything all right?"

"I'm sorry. Did I wake you up?"

"Nick, you can call me anytime. I told you. Whenever you feel the need, no matter how late it is."

I gulped some air but ended up sobbing. The woman on the other end of the line said nothing. We messaged each other once or twice a week, but we hadn't talked to each other in over a month.

She let me empty the tears seeping from my heart, her steady breaths bringing me much-needed comfort.

Once I cooled off, she spoke again. "Having a bad day?"

"Huh…you could say that. God… This is so messed up. You know the boy I told you about?" I asked, my voice unsteady.

Tremors rattled my body, and I placed my phone on the table, pressing the speaker button. With my face buried in my hands, I swallowed, squeezing my eyes shut as if it could prevent the despair to sink in.

"Jack? What about him?"

"He almost died, Murielle. I was watching him, and he choked on a piece of banana. He almost died because of me."

"But he didn't. What happened? Tell me everything."

I gave her a recap of everything that had gone wrong this morning.

"You saved his life. I hope you know that. You saved that boy's life, Nick. Why are you guilt-tripping yourself?"

I tried to speak, but the words got stuck in my throat. My breathing idled in my lungs as my muscles spasmed.

After a minute, I cleared my throat. "It's not…it's… huh, I don't know." My elbows dug further into the wooden tabletop, and I sank my face further into my hands, tears spilling from my burning eyes. "Derek was a child… Jack is a child… They're both too young to have to deal with death. When it all went down, Derek's face kept flashing through my mind. As if…as if it were him I wasn't able to save. As if… Why is this so hard? As if I couldn't do anything to save him. Jack was safe and sound. Still, I kept picturing myself switching Derek's ventilator off. Stealing the…stealing the life from him. Stealing his last breath. Forever."

Sobs tinted Murielle's voice. She blew her nose before speaking again. "You freed Derek, Nick, okay? Don't you ever tell yourself otherwise. Y-you set him free… You were the only one strong enough to grant him his last wish. If Derek were here, he'd tell you himself. Because of you, he…he doesn't suffer anymore. He's not stuck in a hospital bed when he should have been playing outside like kids his own age."

More sobs clogged my throat.

"Nick, for both these boys, you are a hero… A true hero… No, you couldn't save Derek—his fate wasn't in our hands—but you saved Jack. This time, you were allowed to try."

I snorted.

"You really are a true hero, Nick Peterson. Go hug that kid now. You and he both deserve to put this incident behind you and move forward. You…you can't let what happened this morning define your relationship with him, okay?" She paused. "What about his mother? How are things going?"

"Perfect. More than perfect. I love her…like I've never loved anyone before."

"Then be with her too. She needs you right now. Trust me."

We exchanged a few other words, and I promised to call her back the next day to keep her updated. The lining of my throat, raw and itchy, burned. I chugged half my whiskey down, trying to chase the pain away.

A movement by the door caught my eye. I lifted my gaze, and as if pulled by some magnetic force, I found Dahlia standing there, a rivulet drowning her eyes and cheeks.

She watched me with something I couldn't define.

How long had she been here?

How much did she overhear from my conversation with Murielle?

My pulse raced at the idea that she learned things about Derek I hadn't told her yet.

Without a word, she ate the space between us in a few strides. I yanked my chair back and rose to my feet, my body trembling.

Dahlia looped her arms around me, enveloping my body with hers.

I hugged her back. With everything I had.

We stood there in silence for a long time, neither one of us brave enough to talk about what she'd just heard. Our tears mixed. Our breathing blurred together, and our bodies fused.

Time halted.

Once I regained some of my composure, I stepped back and searched for her hands, craving her love and her warmth.

"Why didn't you tell me you were the one who unplugged Derek?" she asked. "I didn't mean to eavesdrop. Carter texted me to tell me you offered him a chance to take over, and I wanted to make sure you were okay. I was worried about you. Nick, you should've told me. Now I understand things I didn't earlier."

A cocktail of hurt, sadness, empathy, and love bled from her glassy moss-green irises.

My throat worked, but I couldn't swallow.

"Nick, I know grief. And how much it can shatter someone. I want to be there for you. For the good parts but also the bad and the ugly," she said, cradling my face and forcing me to look at her.

"Dahlia, I wasn't ready. I'm still struggling. Sometimes… Those last images of him flash back when I'm alone. In my truck… In the shower… Early in the morning…" I shrugged. "They used to haunt me. Th-they don't anymore, but I'm still learning to live with them. And, huh, accept the reality. Jack choking, lying in a hospital bed, wearing that blue gown… Tore open scars I thought were mostly healed… I'm sorry I didn't share the complete story with you before."

I laced our fingers together and led her to the couch. With her body hugging mine and my arms locked around her waist, I told Dahlia all about Derek. We laughed as I narrated incidents of our friendship. We cried together when it came down to the moment I turned off his respirator and how I couldn't say a proper goodbye, since the last night I'd visited him, he'd slept the entire time.

Dahlia sniffled through her tears. "Ohmygod, I'm sorry it happened to you. I can't imagine how hard today must have been." She fastened her grip on me, protecting and loving me. "Nick, I never perceived Derek and you were that close." She pulled my head to her chest, and the beat of her heart was the anchor I needed, the calm in my storm.

"Dahlia, I can't bear to lose another person I love. Derek… Buddy… I couldn't fathom the idea of losing Jack too this morning."

The woman I loved with every chunk of my heart got to her feet and held out her hand for me to grab. Together we made it upstairs. She pushed my shoulders until I sat on the edge of the bed and uncapped the marker she took from the kitchen table on our way up. The one I used this morning while I worked on the construction blueprints.

She clutched it between her teeth, and with both hands, she rummaged through my dresser.

I quirked a brow, wondering what she was looking for. There was nothing but boxer briefs, socks, and sweatpants in those.

Her face lit up when she found it. *Derek's list.*

With the pen still clutched between her teeth, she sat beside me and unfolded the sheet of paper. She struck through the eighth item, with more vigor than required.

Derek's Bucket List - ~~8. Do something deemed impossible~~

Underneath, she wrote:

I saved Jack's life today. It definitely counts as doing something deemed impossible. Only real heroes can do this. I've been giving myself a hard time about it when I should have been celebrating instead. Jack could have choked on anything at any given time, but lucky for him, he did it with me by his side, and I did all the right things. It's worth something. And the woman I love and who loves me back (a lot), says she has no idea how to repay me because what I did today is an act of pure love. And strength. And bravery. She's telling me here and now I'll be her hero for the rest of time.

Dahlia capped the marker, but something caught her eye, and before one of us could say anything, a big tear rolled down her cheek.

She cocked her head until we stared into each other's souls. "You added your last item?"

I nodded.

"You really believe it?"

I rubbed my fists over my eyes, raw and probably swollen by now. "Already told you, Dahlia. I'm in love with you. And I can't see myself feeling any other way. Ever."

She jumped to her knees and crashed her lips on mine. "You're the real deal too, Nick."

I pushed back, my body igniting under her touch. "We have to go. The doctors are waiting for you to sign the discharge papers."

"I know, but I wanna make sure you're okay first."

I breathed in. "I am… I will be."

Dahlia knitted her fingers through mine, and I followed her downstairs. If she'd asked me to, I would've followed her to the end of the world.

Derek's Bucket List — ~~25. Nick. Find the one~~

Derek, I'm pretty sure I've found my person. My soul mate. The one I've been put on this Earth to be with. The one making my days and nights better. I had no clue my heart had been missing one half until she walked into my life. Actually, I walked into hers, but it's just semantics, right? Dahlia completes me. In every way. She's the love of my life. I'll keep you updated. I just hope she feels the same way...

40

NICHOLAS

"Hey, baby. Ready to go home?" Dahlia asked Jack when we entered his hospital room, our hands linked together. The boy nodded, and Dahlia brought her gaze to Carter. "Hey, Cart." She let go of me and jumped into her best friend's arms.

He hugged her tight, and his lips lingered on the top of her head.

My heart trembled in my chest. I'd have to get used to this. Their chemistry. Their proximity. Their love.

"Dah, I was so scared." He stepped back and ran his hands over his face. "I hate it when I'm far away and the distance makes me feel powerless."

Dahlia held his face, her eyes fixed on his. I'd never seen them like this. So close. So... I missed the right word.

Carter pressed his forehead against hers, and for a minute, time stood still. With their eyes shut, they just stayed like that, bringing each other the comfort they both required without even saying a word.

I was amazed as much as I was bothered by this display of affection playing before me.

Jack must have sensed it because he jumped from the bed and came to me, holding his arms above his head until I picked him up.

"Hey, little guy. How are you doing?"

He offered me a *too big for his tiny face* warm smile.

As if he spread magic inside me, the wounds of my heart healed. For good this time.

"Go in the *ambuladalance* again?" he asked.

I shook my head, unable to stop chuckling. "I wish. But we can't. It's only for emergencies. And sick people."

"Like Buddy?"

My insides tightened up. "Yeah. Like Buddy." I squeezed him against my heart. "You wanna get out of here?" I lowered my voice. "Let me tell you a secret. I'm super hungry. I could eat a hippopotamus."

He snickered.

"What about pizza? I'm sure your Mama and Carter would love to join us. I think we should celebrate right now."

"Pizza, pizza, pizza," Jack singsonged, his arms circling my neck.

"Let's go then," Carter added, turning to face us. "I'm starving."

"Gimme a sec, boys. I'll go sign all those papers," Dahlia said, exiting the room.

A silence fell between us. Every breath between us was audible.

After a few seconds, Carter extended his arm. "Thanks, Nick. For saving Jack's life. I'm sorry for giving you shit earlier."

I blinked. Was I dreaming? Carter Hills was thanking me? *Note this day, Derek.* My palm slid into his, but he pulled me into some sort of bro hug instead when our hands connected. That lasted about half a second, but still, maybe we could make it work after all.

Carter blinked what looked like tears away and grabbed Jack's stuff.

Dahlia returned, and we all got going.

In the hallway, I lowered Jack to his feet, and he reached for Carter's hand. After a second, he reached for mine too.

My eyes found Dahlia, and emotions filled hers.

I love you, she mouthed.

I grabbed her hand in mine, and the four of us left together.

Back home, because Dahlia and Jack were spending the night at my place—no way I'd sleep away from them after the day we had—I took Jack aside. We sat cross-legged on the living room floor, facing each other.

"Okay, I have a special someone for you to meet. His name is Rex." I fished out the stuffed dinosaur that used to be Derek's from behind my back. "He used to belong to a friend of mine. A little boy, just like you."

Jack grabbed the toy, kissed his head, and brought it to his heart as if he could feel how important it had been to another child before.

"I want you to have it. Derek would have wanted that too."

Jack glanced at me with his round steel-gray eyes.

"Rex is magic. He'll watch over you at night. To make sure you're safe and sound. You want him?"

He bobbed his head, his eyes still on me. "No cry, Nick. No cry," he said, moving to his feet and brushing my hair.

I wiped my eyes with the back of my hand. I hadn't even noticed the tears pooling there. "You're right, little guy. Let's be happy."

Jack latched onto my neck. "Rex my friend. Rex my best *bestest* friend."

A smile tugged at my lips. "Yes, he is. And this one won't go away. Ever."

I raised my eyes to the ceiling as if Derek could see us in that instant—from his cloud. As if he were here with us. A part of him living through my actions. With my head tilted back, I winked. "Cheers, bro."

I fastened my arms around Jack, and we hugged before joining Dahlia and Carter on the back deck.

Yeah, the country music star had to come over and make sure my house was good enough for his family. *Our* family.

Jack climbed up Carter's long legs to sit on his lap. "Look, *Cattter*," he said, pushing the stuffed animal into his face. "Rex my *bestest* friend. *Nicksaidhemagical.* I love Rex. I love Nick."

An arm snaked around mine. *Dahlia's.*

The way she stared at me…with love and lust. And something more. I got starstruck. Yeah, Dahlia Ellis was the one for me. My person. My soul mate. My everything.

"Derek's?" she asked, her voice soft as a whisper.

I nodded. Because emotions blocked my airways, and I had nothing more to say.

She pressed her head against my shoulder. "I love you, Nicholas Peterson. I'm crazy about you."

I enveloped her in my arms as we watched Carter push Jack on the swing set, both of them laughing their hearts out and goofing around.

Yeah, the four of us were family. For better or for worse.

Kissing my fingers, I saluted the sky.

41

NICHOLAS

Four months later, with a straight back, my hands shoved into my pockets, and my heart having a party inside my chest, I walked toward the lawyer's office. This sounded so official. Hair prickled across my nape at the idea of doing something meaningful. Something big. Something I had never pictured myself doing short-term before moving to Green Mountain.

I breathed out my angst as I pushed the door open. Soft music welcomed me as I entered the office. I glanced around me. Okay, this place looked nothing like the cold and straight-lined law firms did back in Chicago with their over-expensive furniture and interiors. Here the decor was simple and country-chic. A five-chair waiting room, wooden walls, and a latte-beige carpet. It was inviting, almost cozy.

The secretary greeted me with a warm smile. "Mr. Peterson?"

I nodded before finding my voice, my vocal cords sounding rusty as stress took root inside me. I cleared my throat and croaked the words. "Hi, yes, it's me."

She moved to her feet and pointed a finger in the opposite direction of where I stood, showing me the way. "Follow me. They're waiting for you."

I nodded and walked behind her in the corridor toward a closed door at the end. My heart was racing a thousand miles an hour, and I had to press a hand against my chest to calm its hyperactivity.

The woman tapped her knuckles against the wooden door, and I rolled my shoulders back. Yes, I could do this. Everything was coming together, and this last piece would just make it all more real. She exchanged a few words with the people inside the room and motioned me in.

"Thank you," I said, my voice now sounding stronger and steadier.

A man in his early sixties sat behind a desk. "I'm Eduardo Miller, an old friend of Mrs. Jeanine here. It's so nice to meet you, Mr. Peterson. I've heard great things about you."

We exchanged handshakes before I spun and met Mrs. Rutherford.

I offered my hand, but she stepped closer and wrapped her frail body around me in a hug. "Oh, Nicholas, I'm so happy to finally meet you in person. I saw the pictures of the house you sent. It looks absolutely divine. You brought her charm back. I'll never be able to thank you enough."

She patted my forearm before sitting back into the chair she'd vacated seconds ago.

We exchanged small talk, the tension releasing from my back, and my stance becoming less rigid as I learned a few interesting things about the house I'd been living in and the town that had become mine over the last few months.

"Nicholas, I'm so excited you wanna buy the house," Mrs. Rutherford exclaimed, clasping her hands before her, watching me with stars in her eyes. "From the beginning, call me crazy, but I had a feeling you two would be a perfect match."

"It's a beautiful home. I could picture myself living there the moment I stepped inside for the first time. You're right. This house is special. I don't wanna let it go. Well, I'm not ready to let it go."

The storm inside me calmed down when the words exited my mouth. Yeah, putting roots down in Green Mountain felt natural and like the logical next step. And the farmhouse was where I wanted to live.

Last month, Mike had agreed to sell me his business by the end of next spring.

Since that instant, every piece of my life had slotted in its rightful place.

I had a family. Dahlia and Jack were now fully part of my daily life. Soon enough, I'd also be a business owner. The only thing missing, for my life to feel fulfilled—for now—was that house.

In the small amount of time I'd been in town, it had accumulated a lot of memories. Good and bad. Happy and sad. But it was home, and I refused to move and live elsewhere. Everywhere I looked, I could see Jack running into my arms and Dahlia's touches on the walls. Buddy following me around. The night Dahlia and I had realized we could no longer just be friends, and the one when the dog had left us. The bed where we'd made love for the first time, and the yard where we'd exchanged our first *I love yous*. The stargazing nights in the summer, and the swing I'd pushed Jack on countless times. The moments of intimacy when we had confided about our dreams, our heartaches, and our hopes, and the ones that had us holding on to each other or promising each other the world.

This was the house where I aspired to raise my family. Have more kids. Grow old with the woman I loved.

A pinched sensation gripped my heart.

No way would I let this house go. It was my home…*our* home.

"Shall we begin?" I asked, eager to find out if my offer had been accepted so we could proceed with the transaction.

Mr. Miller and Mrs. Rutherford exchanged a glance.

What was that all about? When I spoke to the owner on the phone last week, she had assured me my offer stood and was being taken seriously. The house hadn't been put on the market yet, so I was pretty sure they hadn't received any other offer.

"Something wrong?" I asked, struggling to even my breathing, trying to look—and sound—casual, though I was anything but.

There. They glanced at each other again.

Mr. Miller cleared his throat. "Mr. Peterson…"

"Call me Nick. Please."

"Well, Nick. All the ownership documents were being prepared when Mrs. Rutherford received a call."

I didn't understand. I had spent the past month researching comparable properties currently on the market in Green Mountain, as well as those recently sold. Tucker had helped me with the financial stuff, so I was already pre-qualified for the loan. As my friend had said, my proposition looked sharp and really fucking amazing.

"Someone put up a second offer. I'm sorry, Nicholas," Mrs. Rutherford began. "I just can't ignore it. We'll—"

A soft knock on the door interrupted her.

The secretary peeked in as she opened the door. "Mr. Miller, your next appointment is here."

"Let her in," the lawyer said.

The scene before me unfolded in slow motion.

Mr. Miller moved to his feet to greet the newcomer.

A familiar scent permeated my nostrils, enveloping me. My heart drummed faster. I scratched my nape, unsure what was going on.

My eyes met Mrs. Rutherford's, and she looked at me with an expectant gaze.

The somber look she bore seconds ago had vanished, replaced by a joyful expression.

Mr. Miller exchanged a few words with the visitor, and I pivoted in my chair to see who it was, but well aware of the presence I could distinguish from a million others.

My body recognized her before my eyes saw her.

In the doorway, Dahlia exchanged a handshake with the lawyer, Jack squirming in her arms. She lowered the boy to his feet, and he ran my way, clutching a toy truck in his hand.

"Hey, little guy. What are you doing here?"

Jack said nothing as he held out his arms for me to lift him.

He settled on my lap. "*Nickkk. MissyouNick,*" he finally said as his tiny arms wrapped around my neck, and he dropped a moist kiss on my cheek.

"I've missed you too," I said, hugging him close to my heart. We'd seen each other this morning, but every hour away from the people I loved felt like a lifetime. Since he'd choked almost four months ago, Jack and Dahlia had spent almost every night at my place, and we'd got ourselves into a comfortable routine.

"Surprise. It's surprise. *Shhh,*" he said in a low voice, bringing his forefinger over his lips, as if I were in on what was going on.

"A surprise? You sure?"

He bobbed his head fast.

Mr. Miller shut the door, and Dahlia took the seat next to mine.

"Hey, babe. What are you doing here?" I asked, with my eyebrows probably touching my hairline, reaching for her hand and intertwining our fingers together. I breathed easier. Her touch always brought me peace. I hadn't hinted about my wish to buy the house to Dahlia, but I knew how much it meant to her too. I wanted to make sure it was a done deal before asking her to move in with me.

Shifting in my seat to give Jack more room to roll his toy car all over my legs and torso, I watched her as she angled her upper body my way and grinned at me.

She closed her eyes and shook her head. When she opened them again, she smiled at me. "Here's the thing," she said before taking a big inhale. "I contacted Mrs. Rutherford last week. Call it a hunch, but I was pretty sure you'd make an offer on the house. By now, I know you pretty well, Nicolas Peterson. Anyway, I didn't want you to buy us a house. I wanted *us* to buy *us* a house. Together. Make it official. Build something. A nest. Our family… eventually. You can refuse if you think it's too soon or if you prefer to be the sole owner. It's up to you. No matter what, I will be okay with your decision. No hard feelings. I just hope this is a dream we can share. A beginning to our future. If you will have me as a co-owner… As a partner. As your other half."

Jack had stopped wriggling in my arms and was watching his mother with as much intensity as I did, his widened stare probably matching mine.

"You're already all of these things—"

"I'm all in, Nick. I want everything with you. And I want to start dreaming with you. Not in six months or two years from now. Never will I take anything for granted ever again, already told you. I want us to be a family. From this day on."

I swallowed the lump lodged in my throat and blinked. "Are you serious? You wanna own the house with me?"

Dahlia nodded. "Told you the other night. This house feels like home to me. And you're there. My soul already lives there. It's been for months. This house has a heart, and the man with the biggest heart I know and with whom I'm kinda in love with also happens to live within its walls. How could I wish to live elsewhere? Just so we're on the same wavelength here, I'm not going anywhere. Let's make this home *ours*. The way you see it in your head. The way we picture it together when we go to sleep at night. Those walls already have a story, but just the beginning of ours. Let's give them the entire novel—every chapter—so that one day, they tell our story too."

A whirlwind of thoughts raced through my mind, mixed with all my emotions and so many things I wished I could tell the woman beside me if we were alone in this office.

"Mama crying," Jack said. "No cry, Mama. Surprise. Be happy."

We all laughed at his words. Using the pad of my thumb, I wiped the tears welling up in her eyes and moved closer to kiss her eyelids.

"God, I love you right now. So much. Let's do this," I said. With my free hand, I pulled her in for a kiss. "I want this. With you too."

"Do you wanna think about it first?" she asked.

"No, this is perfect. It feels right. I can't wish for any better scenario than owning the farmhouse together—as a family."

Dahlia sniffled, and I placed my hand on her leg above the knee, unable to resist touching her, and cementing the bond we shared. The leap of faith we were about to take together.

"Mama sad," Jack said.

I shook my head, nuzzling his neck until he burst out laughing, relishing the sound. "No, your Mama is happy, little guy. And so am I."

Jack's gaze drifted between his mother and me.

"Mama happy?"

A smile spread on Dahlia's face when she leaned back and bobbed her head, Jack style. "Yes. Mama is happy," she echoed. "Mama is where she's supposed to be. And Mama loves Nick. And Jack."

Jack clapped his hands, giggling. "Mama loves Nick," he chanted. "Mama always kisses Nick."

"Yes. And we're all moving in together."

———

The next morning, I woke up early, showered, and made coffee while I studied the papers making me a homeowner for the first time in my life. Pride flooded every part of me. Like a complete idiot, I couldn't stop smiling.

Dahlia met me and circled my waist from behind, resting her head against my bare back.

"Did you sleep at all?" she asked.

I swiveled in her embrace. "I did. Because when you're in bed beside me, I sleep like a baby." I planted a kiss on the tip of her nose. "You?"

"Oh, I slept perfectly."

With a quick gesture, she stole the caffeinated beverage from my hand and brought it to her lips with a grimace.

"I can't understand why you'd drink that." A chill ran through her. "It tastes awful. Tea tastes much better."

I twirled a loose strand of her hair around my finger,

my eyes traveling down her body, admiring her naked thighs, the shirt of mine she wore falling just below her bottom.

I was right that night, a while back, when I'd told her my clothes fit her better.

With my free hand, I fished out the mug of tea I had prepared for her and placed it in her hand. "Here."

Her grin widened.

I ventured a hand under her shirt, stroking the soft flesh of her lower back, moving in circles, molding her ass cheek to my greedy hand.

She gasped. "Careful. This thing is scorching hot," she said, gesturing to the mug in her hand.

"It's even better," I said, smoothing her lips with mine. "Are you able to stay put while I explore these delicious curves of you?"

"Nick—" My name sounded more like a whimper coming through her lips. Her eyes turned darker, gleaming in the morning light. "Please…"

"Please what?" I asked, my voice sounding more like a growl.

She sucked in a breath, her eyelids fluttering close. "Nick, I—"

I removed the cup from her hands and discarded it on the counter beside mine.

"Fuck, you're already wet," I grunted as my hand reached between her trembling thighs, tracing the moist seam over the cotton fabric of her panties.

"Take me here," Dahlia ordered. "Now." She wouldn't need to ask me twice. Her tone had lost all playfulness. She had become a puddle of lust, and I hadn't even touched her the way I craved yet. "We gotta christen this house."

"We did just that yesterday before going to bed," I said

with a crooked smile, images of last night coming back to me. Bedroom. Bathroom. Walk-in closet. The staircase.

"Yeah, but we haven't done it here yet."

"What about before?"

She shook her head, her voice a shuddering whisper. Yes, my girl was passionate and irresistible, just the way I liked it. "It doesn't count. We weren't owners back then."

"Gosh, I'll never get tired of listening to your super smart naked ideas."

I skimmed the column of her throat with the tip of my nose, and Dahlia shivered. *Yes, I'd never get tired of this.*

Weighing next to nothing in my arms, I placed her on a stool, yanked her panties down her legs, and let my sweatpants billow at my ankles. With both hands, I flipped her until her back faced my front, and angled her until I could spear into her, my hardened flesh burning for her.

A moan broke the silence, followed by a guttural sound coming from my core. The feel of my steeled length sliding between her velvet lips almost shattered me on the spot.

"Oh, Nick," she said, turning her head and sealing her lips with mine.

I swallowed every sound leaving our hungry mouths.

We waltzed together, our bodies in sync.

Dahlia dug her nails into my skin when I pushed deeper inside her.

I shucked my pants away and peeled her shirt off when she twirled around in my arms. After I repositioned her, I glided back into her warm channel, my home in our home.

With a fistful of her hair, I tugged her to me, kissing the life out of her.

The seconds froze around us.

With my palm, I caressed her flaming cheek, losing myself in the lushness of her irises. "I love you," I murmured, so entranced by her beauty, her wisdom, and her whole being, unable to look away.

She held my gaze for an entire minute as we admired each other, welding our connection for the rest of time.

I pounded a little faster, a little harder. She arched her back in response, and I devoured her neck, supporting her weight with my arms to keep her upright.

In that instant of bliss, my heart broke free. Free from the past. Free from any suffering it had ever endured. Free from all restraint.

Its hasty beats shook the center of me, the cadence intoxicating, hoping to fuse to hers and live in her chest, where I knew it would be safe—and loved. If Dahlia looked closely enough, I bet she could see its hammering through my skin.

Carrying my other half in my arms, I laid her on the floor, careful to place her shirt underneath her head.

Balancing over her, our stares never breaking apart, I rammed into her.

Every expression of pleasure across her face played with the strings of my heart. The display of love on her lips made it swell a little more behind my ribs. The promises dancing in her eyes increased its addictive rhythm.

Dahlia tilted her head back, and together, we inched closer to the edge, nearing the precipice. Holding on. Until it couldn't be contained anymore. Until neither of us was strong enough to resist the pleasure building in our cores. Her walls clenched around me as we unraveled, wringing every last drop out of me. A muffled purr broke the orgasmic silence as our bodies convulsed together, and it took a few minutes for our breathing to go back to normal.

In this time, we lost ourselves in each other, chests heaving, satisfied smirks pasted on our faces.

Dahlia propped herself up on one arm and pressed a kiss to my chin, a soft laugh tumbling out.

I gave her a quizzical look. "What's so funny?"

"You. You have that look. The plenitude of being. Your eyelids are half-closed, and you're so handsome right now."

I kissed the corner of her lips, her eyebrows, and the freckles sprinkling her nose. "You think I'm handsome?"

She snickered. "Don't play dumb, Nicholas Peterson. You know I'm obsessed with you, and I think you're very good-looking."

I winked.

"Oh God, stop. Your level of smugness just multiplied. If I thought you looked vain after what we just did, now it's another game entirely."

"I had no idea you thought I was hot, Dahlia Ellis," I said with a shake of my head, no conviction in my words.

She blushed, pink being my favorite color on her. "Don't be all conceited now."

"Never," I promised, claiming her mouth in the slowest possible kiss, relishing the sensations it awoke inside me like it did every single time our lips touched.

I dropped beside her, and with my arm locked around her waist, we rested like that for a while. Just enjoying being with each other, and the after-sex rapture that enveloped us.

Dahlia, Jack, and I were about to become a family, for real.

A lightness settled in my chest at the idea.

When I'd left Chicago, I was broken and lost. And now I felt better than I ever did. And complete. Positive about my life and the future.

Dahlia went to shower while I attacked breakfast. She came back downstairs a little later, carrying a still half-asleep Jack in her arms.

Picture perfect.

My family. Mine. Mine to love and to protect.

With a satisfied sigh, I let my gaze roam over the space around us.

This house was ours. Because this was where we belonged—together.

The moment he saw me, the boy stretched out his arms, silently asking me to scoop him up. "Nick," he said in his sleepy voice. "*Bakefast* with me?"

My lips found the top of his head. "Yes, I'll have breakfast with you. Hungry?"

He nodded.

"Almost ready, little guy. Will you help me out?"

He nodded again.

With him perched on my hip, we poured orange juice into glasses and set the table together.

"To us," Dahlia said, raising her glass once we sat down to eat.

"To love and family. And to us," I repeated, leaning in to kiss her lips. "I'm happy we're doing this together."

Her gaze found mine. "I wouldn't have it any other way."

She grabbed my hand in hers, kissed my fingers, and I saluted the sky, my eyes trained on her. "Thanks, bro. It's all because of you. Cheers."

42

NICHOLAS

"You're sure he'd want me here? In his house? While he's here too?" I asked Dahlia as she emptied the suitcase and hung our clothes in the wardrobe, a few weeks later.

"Yes. We're together. And I love you both. In different ways, but all the same. You're part of my life, and Carter has to accept it. It's a tradition of ours. If he plays in town, we stay here, all of us. Now just get ready so we can go."

"What about Jack? Are you sure he'll be okay tonight?"

"With Addi? You're kidding, right? She loves him as her own. They will be fine. Stop being a helicopter parent, would you?"

I elbowed her, and she batted her lashes. Now I knew the power of those. The first time I picked her up for our date, she batted them at Carter, and he stopped fighting with her. Now she used them on me too whenever she wished to have the last word—and it worked. I had no idea why. It just did. I just stopped arguing every time Dahlia used her weapon of choice. I was pussy-whipped, as Tucker would say. I kinda liked it, though.

"Whoa, I can't believe you went there," I teased, pulling her against me. "Helicopter parent, really?"

"This new role suits you."

"You think?"

"Ohmygod, stop with the whiskey voice already. You have no idea the effect it has on me."

I blinked. "Whiskey voice? You're still stuck on that one?"

"Yeah. When your voice is half-smooth, half-husky. It's just like you. All calm and in control on the outside, strong and passionate on the inside. Like the liquor. It fits you. And it's the color of your eyes. Whiskey, I mean. It's also a color, so…"

I tipped a brow. "Oh, and my eyes are whiskey too?"

"Yeah. Lucky for me, it's also your drink of choice. I think that should be my name for you from now on."

"Whiskey? You kidding, right? It sounds like a dog's name."

Dahlia shrugged, laughing. She looped her arms around my neck and closed the distance between our bodies. "Okay, you're right. It sounds terrible." She scrunched up her face. "I'll have to find something more fitting, I guess. Anyway, I love both sides of you."

Oh, I owned a weapon of choice too then. "You sure?"

"Babe, I'd get drunk on you every day if I could. You're my new obsession. You look all inoffensive and sweet and hot, but you're addictive, Nicholas Peterson. And I can't live without you."

"Did I ever tell you how much I love you?"

She wrinkled her beautiful face. "Not sure. Tell me once more. Just in case."

"I love you, Dahlia Ellis. I love your heart. Your compassion. Your calm. Your quiet. Your wild." I kissed the bone above her eyebrow. "And I love us together. I love your son. And I'll befriend the man who has been by your side from the moment you were born and took care of you all these years. Because I owe him. A lot. He did it with the selflessness of his heart, never asking for anything in return. He was Derek's idol, and now I can see why."

Dahlia dabbed at her watery eyes with her fingers.

"I have no idea how you ended up in my life, but I promise to love you every day."

She reached for a tissue from the box on the nightstand and and gently dried her eyes. "Shoot, my mascara. Stop being so handsome. It's ruining my makeup." She pushed my chest with a hand in a teasing manner.

My fingers laced through hers over my heart. "For what it's worth, thanks. For all you've just said. It means a lot. I just fell deeper in love with you. Who knew it was even possible?"

We kissed, our mouths rehearsing a languorous dance. I held Dahlia's waist as she dissolved against me. Passion ignited between us. It always escalated quickly every time we were in each other's orbit.

When we broke apart, I chased her away, my hand connecting with her ass as she yelped and flashed me a ten-thousand-buck smile over her shoulder. Trying to tame my aroused self and regain some control over my body, I finished setting up the bedroom that would be ours for the next few days before going to check on Jack who was napping.

He had his own bedroom both at Carter's cabin and his penthouse, here in Nashville. I watched his sleeping form through the ajar door, his tiny fist clutching his favorite blanket to his heart, the sound of his steady breathing bringing me comfort. Since the day he'd choked, I could spend hours just listening to it.

"Hey," Dahlia called from the kitchen, breaking the moment. "I'll prep lunch. Sandwiches?"

I closed the door and went to join her. "Works for me. You need help?"

"Nah, I'm the sandwich queen, remember?" She moved toward the refrigerator, but halted mid-step. "Tell me, I thought Tucker was supposed to fly here for the weekend?"

"He was. Canceled last minute. Said he had a work emergency. I suspect he was afraid we'd force him to come with us tonight."

"It's ridiculous. He could have hung out with Addi and Jack until we got back. Or watched Jack, and Addison could have come with us."

I stopped in my tracks. "Addi and Tuck hanging out together? Nah, it sounds like a recipe for disaster."

Dahlia chuckled. "Oh, you're right. Why didn't I think about it? Luckily for everybody involved, she has a steady boyfriend, so she's off-limits."

I moved behind her and held her hipbones, molding my front to her back. "No woman is off-limits for Tuck, Dahlia."

"Addison can hold her own. Don't worry about her."

I shook my head. "Never underestimate Tucker Philips. You've been warned. But perhaps having them both here would have determined who deserves the craziest friend title. My best friend or yours?"

Dahlia spun between my arms. "Maybe I'm not ready to find out just yet. Let's not force proximity until we're sure we can handle it."

"We have a deal." I held out my hand, and we shook on it.

———

Later that night, we rose from our seats as Carter Hills walked onstage. He had offered us front row tickets, but Tucker had already gotten those seats for me, and they were perfect. Fifth row wasn't bad. As I watched him, I realized something: Carter, the music star, owned the stage. The air in the stadium seemed to hum with his presence. Even my heart raced at the sight of him with a guitar strapped across his chest. Fuck, Tucker had been right, because in that instant, I couldn't help fangirling over him.

"Hi, Nashville. It's good to be home," Carter said as the crowd erupted in cheers and wolf-whistles. "Tonight's show is dedicated to a fan I never got to meet. He fought cancer with all his heart but passed away at just twelve— far too soon to leave this world. Derek, if you can hear me from where you are, this show is all for you. Tonight's net proceeds will go to Chicago Lakeview Children's hospital in your name, supporting research and helping other children in their fight against cancer."

My hands connected in some sort of prayer under my chin. My heart went on break. I tried to breathe, but it came out as a wheeze.

"And because this song was your favorite, here it goes."

Carter waved at the ecstatic crowd before strumming the first chord of "Monkey Business."

That was when my heart dissolved.

"You did this?" I asked Dahlia once some of the shock subsided.

She kissed my lips. "Yes. I thought Derek would like it…and you too. Well, to be honest, I didn't do anything. I just told Carter about Derek. His story touched his heart. He did the rest entirely of his own volition."

Tears filled my eyes. No matter how many times I blinked, I couldn't chase them away. "You told Carter about me and Derek? About his favorite song?"

She nodded. "He may act like a jerk sometimes, but his heart is usually in the right place. He told me he would have visited Derek at the hospital if he had known about him. He respects you, you know."

My jaw almost hit the floor as I glanced at her, speechless.

"You'll be able to thank him yourself after the show. We have VIP tickets."

"As if you need those," I teased.

"They are for you. To give you the ultimate Carter Hills concert experience."

"Don't try to transform me into a fangirl, babe." I grinned. "Well, to be honest, I may be a little bit starstruck right now," I added, pinching my fingers closed together.

Dahlia chuckled. "Not happening. Reel it in. The only person you're allowed to fangirl over, Nick Peterson, is me," she said with a wink.

"And I wouldn't want it any other way." I kissed her forehead, my heart waltzing inside my chest, filled with joy and gratitude—and so much love I believed it could never be contained. I kissed two fingers and raised them above my head. *All for you, Derek. Thank you.*

———

"I can't wait to move into our new place," Dahlia said a few months later as we carried more boxes into her house. After living together for quite some time, we had decided to do all the improvements on the farmhouse we'd talked and dreamed about before moving in together officially. In the meantime, we chose to move my stuff to her place.

In addition to relocating the kitchen, installing a new banister on the staircase, opening walls to let in more sunlight, and building a terrace for the master bedroom, we'd also decided to tear down the old garage and build a barn in its place. A cozy addition with a place for Jack—and hopefully, our other children one day—to play. Some sort of tree house, but not in a tree.

"Dahlia, believe me, I know, but I'm also happy to move in here with you two and be part of the story of this house too. Won't you miss it, though?"

She surveyed the place. "Sure, I will. But I'm ready for something new. With you. To start a new chapter together."

I wrapped my arms around her, brushing my lips against hers. "Will you keep a guitar on the top floor of the barn?"

"Why?"

"Because you'll miss your little secret spot. You won't be able to visit that stable and those horses and play for them as much as you used to do since you'll have to drive there now. So, I figured you could make the top floor yours. We'll bring in haystacks and hang the fairy lights you love so much. We can add anything you want to make the space truly yours"

"Oh, Nick, you serious?"

"Always."

She rose onto her tiptoes to kiss me. "Nick Peterson, you're my person."

We kissed for a little longer.

"Are we still spending Christmas at the farmhouse, as we planned?" I asked after we broke apart.

"Hell, yes."

Later, we picked up takeout and headed home, eager to finish the final Christmas touches before Carter brought Jack back the next morning.

We entered the dark house, and Dahlia flicked the switch, and golden light spilled across the living room. She lowered her hand to grip mine and halted in her tracks. "I was thinking… Can I give you your Christmas present now?"

"Christmas is in two days. I can wait. And you didn't have to get me anything. I have you, and that's all I'll ever need. My biggest wish came true the moment you fell in love with me."

She shook her head, strands of hair brushing her shoulders. "No. I want it to be now. The timing is right. Gimme a sec." She disappeared for a minute and came back with a little, flat, square black box decorated with only a red bow.

"What is it?"

She locked her hands before her, waiting for me to open the lid, chewing on her lower lip.

The sight of her got me nervous. Tingles ran along my spine, and sweat pearled on the nape of my neck. I held my breath as I looked inside.

A small wooden barrel, wrapped in red satin, sat there —just big enough to hang on a keychain.

I lifted it. "What is it?"

"Your own whiskey label."

I blinked. "My what? Huh, are you saying what I think you are?"

Dahlia's grin reached both her ears. "It won't be ready for a while, but I couldn't wait to tell you. I met that expert and we talked about you, your taste, and he came up with a custom recipe. It's been barreled already, so we won't be able to taste it for about three years. See why I couldn't wait to share it with you?"

I rotated the tiny barrel between my fingers and noticed the small inscription engraved on its side.

I watched Dahlia with a raised brow. "Is it?"

She nodded.

"No, you didn't?"

Her smile stretched bigger, and she beamed in the low light of the house. "I did."

"It's you and me?"

"It's us."

Everything in me sizzled with excitement.

Could I be any happier? Could my heart get too big for my chest?

Whiskey and Country.

Whoa, I owned a whiskey label now.

"Thank you. Wow, I'm still speechless. *Whiskey and Country.* It's perfect."

Dahlia inched closer and took my hand in hers. "Nick, there's something else." She paused, inhaled through her mouth, and swiped her tongue across her lips. "Do you want to spend the rest of your life with me?" She kissed my lips before kneeling in front of me.

Time idled.

I was pretty sure air couldn't reach my lungs anymore. The pounding of my heart echoed in my skull.

I blinked, rebooting my confused brain, and dropped to my knees, facing her. "Babe, I was supposed to be the one asking you. I even got you a ring. I was just waiting for the right time. I had it all planned out already."

"Nick, I don't care about the ring. Well, I do, but that's not the point. I don't wanna wait another second to start the rest of our lives together. Here and now, let's promise to love each other until we both shall live. You already own my heart and my present. Let's just make it official, so you'll own my future too."

I dragged a hand over my face, trying to sort out my emotions. "Gosh,I love you so much right now. I can't believe this is happening." I claimed her mouth, wishing I could bask in this state of bliss forever.

Dahlia grinned, and it shook the foundation of me. My heartbeat slowed, matching the rhythm of hers. We were two halves of a soul about to be reunited. About to clash together and shoot stars across the sky.

"I'm lucky I got to ask you first." She wiggled her brows, and I let out a warm chuckle. "If the dark episodes of my life taught me anything, it's to never let love slip through your fingers. Life is too short to have doubts and not aim for what you want when you want it. It can all end too soon. We're already living together. Will you be my husband?"

"I love you, and I'm crazy about you. There's no one else for me in this world. Dahlia Ellis, I know you asked me first, but I'll ask you too. Will you marry me? My life only makes sense when you're in it. When you are beside me. When we plan a life together. When we're in each other's arms. And every time I'm inside you, I'm vibrating to your melody. You're my song. My inspiration. My everything." I paused and cleared my throat. "I'll be your husband. Will you be my wife?"

"Yes."

We kissed on the kitchen floor, unable to unlock our lips as we promised forever to each other.

43

DAHLIA

y heart overflowed with so much love.

I lifted Nick's shirt over his head and kissed his muscled chest, tracing circles all over his flesh with my tongue.

I bit one of his nipples, and he jumped back.

"Easy, woman."

I chuckled as I entangled my fingers in his hair.

Nick fastened his arms around me, trailing his lips down my throat. His hands moved south, greedy to touch me, kneading my skin. "I should go get your ring first."

"Later. Now just love me."

He undressed me, our mouths never breaking apart. On his feet, he carried me in his arms, honeymoon style, and laid me on the kitchen table, the coldness of the wood top contrasting with the warmth of my skin.

"God, I could devour you all day and all night if you'd let me."

"Please do," I said, my voice weird and high-pitched.

He pushed my knees apart and nested his head between my thighs. I shivered as his tongue licked the length of me. He pushed two fingers inside my warmth, and a wave of heat washed over me. A loud gasp tumbled out as my fiancé dived his fingers into my dampness again, spreading it over my most intimate folds. I rocked my hips, trying to set the pace, but he spread a hand across my stomach to hold me in place.

Ache and need rippled through me, and a loud cry parted my lips.

Nick did the thing I could never get enough of with his tongue around my clit, and fireworks shot behind my closed eyelids.

With both hands, I pulled him to me. "Just get inside me. Gotta feel you. To remember forever the first time I made love to my fiancé. The ring can wait."

He thrust his fingers in and out of me faster, and I tilted my head back, unable to contain all the sensations swirling in me any longer. Pleasure built deep in my core. With my eyes closed and my hot fiancé's tongue inside me, I came as if the Earth had shattered beneath me.

Propped up on his arms, Nick hovered over me, and without breaking eye contact, he pushed his throbbing hardness—softness over steel—inside my sheath. Until it molded to my warmth.

Euphoria filled me.

He watched me with so much heat and lust, my brain went blank, all the dirty thoughts swirling in my head seconds ago gone. *Pouf.* Vanished. Nick stole my ability to think and speak.

He rolled his hips at a slow pace. "God, I love you."

I curled my hand around his nape and tugged him closer to my heart. The one that beat only for him.

"I wouldn't want to be anywhere else. You, this place, it's what I wished for so many times. What I'll always want."

Nick rammed into me faster. My body stiffened.

I wasn't part of this world anymore. I floated somewhere in space, ecstasy shooting through me in blissful jolts.

He pulled me into his arms, and still inside me, carried me to the couch and sat.

We kissed, our tongues desperate for each other.

I rocked my hips over his, yearning for the friction of our naked bodies.

My breasts filled his hands as he massaged them. I leaned back, consumed by the rush of sensations he unleashed.

"Dahlia, I won't last long. I'm almost there. Come with me."

I increased the pace as Nick clutched my hipbones as if to anchor himself to the moment and not miss a beat.

With my thighs tight on each side of him, I ground my hips until he let out a chain of curses and emptied himself inside me, the tremors of his sex sending me over the edge.

We stayed like that, our bodies tangled together, unable to break apart, minutes after we both came down from our rush. As if one of us could vanish or we'd wake up from a dream.

Nick peppered kisses across my bare shoulders, leaving shivers behind. "I love you, Dahlia. I'm so fucking gone for you."

Our lips crashed together, hungry and unrelenting, and I deepened the kiss, hoping he'd understand how bad I was gone for him too.

———

"Can I give you your Christmas present?" Nick asked as we dressed after our shower the next morning.

"You don't have to. I can be patient," I said, echoing the words he'd said to me and twisting my ring—a square whiskey quartz gem surrounded by tiny diamonds mounted on a platinum band—around my finger. It was beautiful. And like the whiskey label name I came up with, it told our story. *Princess and whiskey.* Unable to detach my gaze from it, I relished how it reflected the morning light.

Nick continued, "I can't. But you'll have to wait until Carter gets here. Setting it up is a two-man job."

I furrowed my eyebrows. "You'll ask Cart's help? Are you two getting along better than I anticipated?"

Nick flashed me the most beautiful smile. "We have our moments. Our relationship isn't perfect, but we respect each other. We'll get there…I hope so."

I jumped into his arms, unable to contain all the joy and excitement vibrating through my heart. "Nick, you're the best. Thanks for doing this for me. I know Cart doesn't make it easy for you. Give him time, okay? He'll get around. Not today, but one day."

"He's important to you, so he's important to me too. I don't care about his broodiness or his attitude. Eventually, he'll recognize how charming I can be," he said, batting his eyelashes.

I backhanded his chest. "Don't charm him too much, though. I want to keep you all to myself."

Carter and Jack arrived, and once I went inside with my son, the men of my life worked together, fixing something on the front porch. Curious, I stayed upstairs in the room that would be Jack's to avoid spying on them.

I heard laughter. And a few curses. And more laughter.

Yeah, things would settle between them. I loved them both too much to lose either of them. They were both my family, for now and forever. We were in this together, the four of us.

"Dahlia. Jack. Come take a look," Nick hollered from downstairs.

We hurried down and put our jackets and boots on before meeting him by the front door.

"Where's Cart?" I asked when my best friend was nowhere to be found.

"He decided to give us some alone time together. He went to get lunch. Should be back in thirty minutes."

Carter. Always selfless around me—since the day we'd met—even if it broke his own heart in the process. I breathed, my emotions already swirling fast inside me.

"Ready?" Nick asked.

Jack and I bobbed our heads, Jack style.

A large grin broke free on my fiancé's face, and he sucked in a breath.

We stepped outside, and my eyes rounded.

I released Jack's hand, and he rushed toward our gift. *My* gift.

With both hands, I cupped my chest. "Nick, this is… I lack the words. It…it's everything I've ever wished for."

"You like it?"

"You're kidding, right? It's perfect. You made this for me?"

He mirrored my smile.

With his hand in mine, we neared my Christmas present: a wooden swing, big enough for the three of us to sit, with fairy lights dangling from the porch overhang. On a wooden plate, the words "Nick, Dahlia, Jack, and _____ special place."

Moisture gathered at the corners of my eyes, and my heart danced wildly in its cage.

"What's that about?" I asked, pointing to the blank space between my son's name and *special place.*"

"For our other child."

"What if we have a dozen of them?" I asked.

"We'll just make another plate. A bigger one."

"You're really ready for more children?"

"I'll have it all with you, Dahlia. Until we check every one of our dreams on that bucket list we made together."

I ugly cried at his words. "I desire it too. All of it. This is the most wonderful present you could ever give me."

———

On Christmas Eve, Carter entered the farmhouse, his arms overflowing with presents.

"You know we don't need anything, right? I thought I made a deal with Santa this year, asking him not to be overgenerous?" I wiggled my eyebrows, hoping he'd get the message.

He shrugged. "I know, Dah. These are just kids' stuff that Jack and I will use whenever I'm in town. You're too adult to understand." He offered me his renowned panty-melting grin and kissed my cheek, and I forfeited the idea of arguing.

I signed. "I'm not fighting you over this. You're such a big toddler when you're with him. Anyway, I like the two of you together, so I guess it's fine."

I emptied his arms, placing the gifts under the tree.

I stepped back next to him. "This looks charming."

Carter slung an arm around my shoulder and tugged me to him. I lost myself in the safety of his embrace for a minute.

"Cart, I gotta tell you something. Can we talk?"

He leaned back, and his smile vanished. My heart hiccupped in my chest as my best friend stuffed his hands into his pockets.

"Sure. Where's Nick?"

"In the garage. I asked for some time alone with you."

"Are you okay? Is Jack sick?"

I squeezed his arm. "We're both fine." With my fingers intertwined with his, I led him to the kitchen and made tea. We sat beside each other, and I enveloped his hand with mine over the table.

"Dah, what is it? I hate when you do this? Talk to me."

My heart flipped in my chest and leaped into my throat. Pearls of sweat popped on my nape.

"Nick and I are getting married." I swallowed hard and tightened my grip on his hand.

Carter blinked, pushing away the truckload of emotions I knew was searing inside him, and breathed out. It wasn't the time for him to have one of his panic attacks.

"Cart, talk to me," I repeated his own words to him. He looked away and brought his gaze back to mine after a few seconds.

"Don't worry, Dah. I'm okay. I knew this day would come. I had time to get used to the idea."

My eyes rounded. "Wait, you knew?"

My best friend nodded.

"How? When?"

"Nick told me. He actually asked for my blessing. About a month ago."

"He did?"

"Yeah. We had *the* talk, he and I."

"Whoa, I'm speechless. What did you tell him?"

Carter sighed and ran a hand over his face. "The truth. That I love you, but you chose him, and he better take good care of you. And that you are in love with him. Not me." His throat worked. "You found a good one, Dah."

No, he found me, but now was not the time to focus on details.

"You're lucky to have him. All I've ever wished is for

you to be happy, you know that. If you are, then that's all that matters." Unshed tears shone in his eyes, his stormy irises looking brighter than usual. "But I thought he was supposed to wait."

I offered him a small, lopsided smile. "I asked him first." There, I said it.

"You did?"

I nodded. "Yes. We bought the house…together. We're happy. I'm happy. And I know deep inside me we're meant to be. Why wait? We won't get married next month, but I'm not waiting a year either. We still have stuff to figure out. I have no clue what you guys discussed, but anyway, thank you for what you said to him. I know how you must feel right now, and I'm sorry. Even if it's not what you wanna hear. I love you, and I always will. You and I, we'll be fine, I promise. For the record, nothing will change between you and Jack either."

Carter pushed back. I could read all the hurt swimming in his eyes."Dah, I have to ask." He dragged a hand over his face before meeting my gaze again. "Will you let Nick adopt Jack?" He cringed as if the words burned his tongue. And in a way, I was sure they did.

I shook my head. "We talked about it. If Nick does adopt Jack one day, it will be because the three of us— Nick, you, and I—decide it's the right thing for him. You're the only daddy he's ever known, and I don't want to mess things up. He's still yours, Cart. Always will. When he's old enough, and if we haven't decided by then, I will leave it up to him to choose for himself. If he wants to… For now, let's keep loving him, the three of us, and he'll be the most adored child in the entire world."

Carter sniffled. "Thanks, Dah. Thanks for not taking him away from me. I haven't looked at the paternity results yet… I just can't—" His voice cracked and drowned the last word.

"I know. It's okay. I'll never take him away from you, Cart. The three of us, we're family. Until we're all old and gray. But now there will be four of us."

We rose to our feet and hugged, our foreheads pressing together, our hearts whispering unspoken promises that would carve our new reality. We were changed, but our bond remained unbroken—and would last forever.

44

Derek's ~~Bucket List~~ I wish I had experienced in my life list
+ Nick's Bucket List

1. ~~Go to a hockey game with Nick and the guys~~
2. ~~Make 1 new…no, 3 new best friends~~
3. ~~Kiss a girl, until my heart beats fast~~
4. ~~Go camping and sleep under the stars~~
5. ~~Watch the sunrise every morning~~
6. ~~Dip my toes into the ocean, even if jellyfish are gross~~
7. ~~Go to a Carter Hills concert, because duh, he's the best~~
8. ~~Do something deemed impossible~~
9. ~~Build something with my own hands that I'll keep forever or gift someone~~
10. ~~Nick. Go on an adventure (now you must pick one)~~

11. Nick. Knowing I can always count on my friends
12. Nick. Be a knight to a damsel in distress, not that the damsel truly needed me.
13. Nick. Work on a ranch (why not?)
14. Nick. Having a meaningful encounter and finding something that makes you truly feel alive
15. Nick. Do something that's right even if it doesn't feel like it at first
16. Nick. Feeling like my life is moving forward and I am floating
17. Nick. Being speechless (in a good way)
18. Nick. Having a soul-connecting experience
19. Nick. Share something with someone I cared about that can't be described with words
20. Nick. Go on a different kind of date
21. Nick. Make someone smile my newfound mission
22. Nick. Share parts of my life with the person who means the most
23. Nick. Feeling like the cracks in my world are healing
24. Nick. Being brave even when it scares me
25. Nick. Find the one

45

Nick and Dahlia's Bucket List
(or the things we want the most from this life)

1. Have a house full of kids
2. Fill our house with love
3. Adopt a bloodhound
4. Sleep under the star once a month
5. Name Dahlia president of the interior design department of Nick's construction business
6. Go see the ocean as often as possible
7. End each day telling people we care about how much we love them
8. Grow old together
9. Keep dreaming together
10. (This place is reserved for all our other dreams that will come along the way)

EPILOGUE
NICHOLAS

Three years later

"Dah, are you sure it's supposed to look like this?" I asked, trying to block the smell by breathing through the fabric of my long-sleeved charcoal sweatshirt. "This is disgusting."

My wife traipsed our way with a warm grin plastered across her face. "Don't worry. It'll be gross for a while." She neared us. "But you're doing great. Look at her smile. She only has eyes for her daddy."

"Yeah, I suppose it's worth every diaper," I said with a wink.

I leaned forward and kissed Violet's chubby cheek. She looked at me with her big golden eyes as if she'd never seen something so amazing, and my heart flip-flopped inside my chest. Our daughter looked like a tiny replica of Dahlia with her fiery copper hair and porcelain skin, but she had my honey-colored eyes—or whiskey-colored as Dahlia called them.

Violet babbled as I picked her up and brushed her soft baby hair with my fingers. "Are you coming to the park with Daddy and Jack?"

She smiled, and I took it as a "Yes, Daddy. Please. I wanna play too."

I grabbed the knitted blanket Barb had gifted me all those years ago and wrapped it around my daughter, exiting her room.

"Hey, son. Get your mitt ready. We're leaving in five," I said as I knocked on Jack's bedroom door.

"Come in, Daddy. I'm almost ready." I opened the door and peeked inside. Royal-blue walls, white trims and ceiling. Carter Hills's album covers, enlarged and framed were next to Derek's signed jersey, above his bed. A large picture of his daddy, Jeff—Carter's older brother, the one Jack never got to know—was set on the opposite wall. Next to it was another one of Dahlia with the Hills brothers when they were teenagers on prom night. Jack's guitar, the one Carter had gifted him on his birthday, stood in a corner, next to a giant stuffed hippopotamus Jeff had gotten for him before he was born, and Jack-the-Bear, the stuffed animal that used to belong to his dad when he was a kid. Rex, the dinosaur, was probably hiding in its usual spot under his pillow.

On his white-painted chest of drawers was a picture of us—him and me—taken the day we hiked to see the waterfall, and another from when he was three, on Dahlia's and my wedding day, when he had become my son in every way that truly mattered. Beside it was a third one of our entire family after Violet was born.

It was a beautiful collage of everyone who cared about him.

Jack had more parent figures at his young age than most people had in their lifetime.

I helped him fix his baseball jersey and held out my hand for him to take.

Baseball was something we bonded over. During the summer months, I was the assistant coach to his Little League team, the Black Bears.

"Is Mama coming?" my son asked.

"Not today. She has to go to the store for a few hours. Violet is coming with us, though."

"Cool."

My heart beat faster.

I had everything I'd ever wished for.

Who knew I would have found it in the middle of Green Mountain, Tennessee, all those years ago?

I watched my kids, my heart full, still thankful to Derek for pushing me to leave my old life behind in Chicago, and go on this journey. To this day, I still kept his bucket list tucked in my drawer, alongside the last letter he had written me and Kelly's card with the pancake recipe. Once in a while, I re-read them, remembering how lucky I was and all the progress I'd made since I chose to turn my life around and start afresh. Reminders of how far I'd come after my world had shattered.

"Can we take Spencer?" Jack asked. Spencer was our bloodhound puppy, the latest addition to our family. "If he stays here by himself, he'll whine all day from his playpen." As if he'd heard his name, the dog rushed to Jack's legs, and the boy squatted to pat his head. "See? He really wants to come with us to the park."

"Sure. Get his stuff and meet me in the car."

My son pumped his fist. "See, Spencer? I told you it would work," I heard him whisper in his new best *bestest* friend's ear as he used to say when he was a toddler.

The memory of him and Buddy, inseparable, flashed through my mind. My lips turned upward. For some reason, it seemed like a lifetime ago. So many things had happened in our lives since.

I stepped outside with a giggling Violet tucked in my arms, her tiny fingers tugging at my ear.

My gaze lingered on the mailbox with the inscription, *The Petersons,* carved on the side. A moving-in-together gift Dahlia had ordered from Stud the day we had visited the lawyer's office and I had found out she had put in an offer on the house so that we could buy it together.

When we had come back to our new home that afternoon, Greta and Brett had hung a *Welcome Home* sign over the front door, where they, along with Mike and a few guys from work, had joined in to celebrate that life-changing event with us.

Dahlia met me after I buckled our daughter in her car seat, cutting my trip down memory lane short. She kissed our baby's rosy cheek and turned her attention to me. "Next time, I'll join you guys," she said as she wound her arms around me. "I'll call you when I'm done. I'm having lunch with April later."

I pulled her into my arms and kissed her with all the love pouring out of my heart.

My wife moaned into my mouth, and my entire body woke up.

I grabbed a handful of her ass, and she gasped. "I promise to love you and take my sweet time tonight."

Dahlia ground her hips against mine. "I can't wait."

She deepened the kiss for a long minute before letting go of me when Jack walked out of the house with the puppy on a leash.

"Have fun with your friend. Tell her I'll give Carter pointers on how to get that baby out of her if she wants. Lessons free of charge." I winked, and Dahlia kissed me again.

"Is he meeting you there?" she asked.

"Yep. Can you believe it took us years to get there?"

Dahlia's grin widened. "April is good for him. He's happy now. We all are. It was about time we chased that storm away and we all found our place in this world."

"I agree. And you were right. All this time. Carter and I, we're good. Derek would be ecstatic."

"Derek would be proud of you… I'm sure he is from wherever he's watching over you." Yeah, that cloud. A wrinkle crossed Dahlia's forehead. "Have you heard about Tucker lately?"

I paused to think for a moment. "No. Why?"

She shrugged. "I don't know. A feeling. The last time I talked to our friends was almost a month ago. When they're distant for a while, it is usually an unmistakable sign they did something wild. You know, like the last time we were vacationing together without the kids. We should invite them over. To make sure they're okay. And it could be fun. I miss our friends."

"Don't worry. I'm sure they are fine. They have so much on their plate right now. We'd be overwhelmed too if we were in their shoes. Anyway, I'll call him later. I'm sure he won't refuse a weekend in the mountains. Fresh air… and some much-needed help. Anyway, we're scheduled to taste *Whiskey and Country* for the first time two weekends from now. They could come to town early and spend a few days here beforehand. With us. And the kids."

Dahlia clapped her hand. "I like how you think. I can't wait for all our friends to join us. We've been waiting three years for this moment. Riley, June, Stud, and Belle are coming to town in a few days and will be staying all week at one of Cart's cabins."

We exchanged a grin.

"To this day, that private whiskey label is still my

favorite Christmas present." I kissed her lips. "About Tuck, don't worry. Let me deal with it, okay? I'm sure everything's fine."

Dahlia nodded, pressing her body against mine. "Is Jace coming too? For the tasting?"

I sighed and shook my head. "Nah. Not that I know of. It's like the wedding all over again."

"I'm sorry," Dahlia said.

"It's fine. He's supposed to be a no-show, but he might surprise us—let's hope so."

"We could visit him next month. We haven't been to Chicago in a long time."

"Dahlia, I love you. So much. And a whole lot more every day," I said. "I'd like that. Thank you."

"I love you more. Now go play with our kids because I want you all to myself tonight."

I kissed her cheek, adjusted the crotch of my pants, and climbed behind the wheel.

My wife waved at us as I drove away.

I eyed the kids through the rearview mirror. Jack was tickling a giggling Violet.

Every piece of my heart belonged here in Green Mountain with my family.

Now.

And forever.

———

Thank you for reading Nick and Dahlia's
emotional and beautiful love story.

Want more? Grab an invite to Nick and Dahlia's nuptials
in ***Wild Encounter***, Tucker and Addison's story.

Read Wild Encounter now
emmanuellesnow.com/products/wild-encounter

————

FREE bonus chapter
Want even more? Your bonus chapter awaits here:
emmanuellesnow.com/collections/bonus-chapters

WANT MORE EMOTIONAL LOVE STORIES?

WHICH COUPLE WILL YOU PICK NEXT?

False Promises

★★★★★ "The angst, the utter heartbreak, and protectiveness I felt for Carter during this book is unreal!"

★★★★★ "Emmanuelle Snow really knows how to tug at all of your emotions and does such a great job of bringing her characters to life!"

***False Promises* is a gripping story of sizzling passion, lust, and the price of fame.**

Start Carter Hills' story now

———

Sweet Agony

★★★★★ "If I could give more than 5 stars, I would."

★★★★★ "This is not a romance, it is a story about first love, first heartbreak and growing up. It is a story that helps to build foundation upon who someone is at their core, and what makes them strong, vulnerable, loving, caring and heartbroken but willing to take chances and learn to love again."

***Sweet Agony* is a compelling tale of love, friendship, and self-discovery that will tug at your heartstrings and leave you questioning the true nature of happiness and fulfillment.**

Read Dahlia and Jeff's love story now

————

Cruel Destiny

★★★★★ "Wow. Just wow. If that could be my review, that is all I would write."

★★★★★ "Emmanuelle has done it yet again. She found a way to slip into my mind and heart with her words and the creation of characters you can't help but fall in love with."

★★★★★ "This book broke my heart in the first twenty five percent and sewed it back together."

A story of healing, second chances, and the risks of opening your heart to someone new. Can they trust each other with their hearts, or will their pasts keep them apart?

Read Nick and Dahlia's love story now

————

Wild Encounter

★★★★★ "This is by far one of the most well-written

book I've read this month. It is dynamic, intriguing, interesting, unafraid to go there and most of all touching."

★★★★★ "I personally wouldn't call this book JUST a romance novel because it's so much more. I 100% recommend it no doubt in mind."

In a world where love is tested by life's obstacles, *Wild Encounter* captures the essence of trust, hope, and resilience as two souls navigate the tumultuous journey of fate together. A tale of passion and perseverance that will leave your heart racing and your spirit soaring.

Read Tucker and Addison's love story now

––––––––

<u>Last Hope</u>

★★★★★ "This book was not only about the darkness but it was about pure love, hope, spice, family, and friendships on point with just the right amount without overpowering the storyline at all."

★★★★★ "Devon and Riley's story is a beautiful one with a lot of emotions. The subject matter is intense but it is handled very gently."

A tale of resilience and second chances in a world where love and danger intertwine.

Read Riley and Devon's love story now

––––––––

Midnight Sparks

★★★★★ "The characters, the love, the humor, the steaminess, the emotions… it's everything I hoped and more."

★★★★★ "I think that is one Emmanuelle Snow's sexiest novels yet."

Escape to the island where Holiday magic meets unexpected romance and a chance at a fresh start.

Read Gavin and Aisha's love story now

————

Fallen Legend

★★★★★ ""The love that grows, not only through tough angst but through unconditional moments had my heart. This is a spicy and riveting book"

★★★★★ "Emmanuelle Snow doesn't just tell a story, she creates an entire world."

***Fallen Legend* is a poignant and uplifting journey of hope, love, and the power of second chances.**

Read Sam and Madison's love story now

SnowBound

★★★★★ "5 big stars from me for this amazing story. Absolutely loved it!"

★★★★★ "Emmanuelle Snow's stories are always full of angst, and Snowbound is no exception."

***SnowBound* is a captivating tale of love, serendip-**

ity, resilience, and the enduring power of the heart that will leave you riveted until the very last page.

Read Anderson and Abigail's love story now

———

All available at emmanuellesnow.com

ACKNOWLEDGMENTS

Oh. My. God. Where do I even begin? Wow, I can't believe *Second Tear* (previously titled *Whiskey and Country)* is finally published. What a ride. First draft. Rewrites. Tears. Sleepless nights. Edits. Joys. Smiles. Pride. Seriously, this book has been a tough one to write. It's so emotionally charged that I had a hard time capturing the complexity of the journey. Those big emotions were needed to get the importance of where Nick's journey started and where it ended, and how and why he became the guy he is today. But… Wow. I'm lacking a better word. My characters are usually pretty straightforward with me, but for some reason, Nicholas Peterson gave me a hard time. Now I get why. He was stuck in his own grief and was trying to find ways to heal. To soothe the scars of his heart. But we're good now.

Yes, I have that kind of relationship with my characters (haha!) Countless times I wish to invite them over to have a talk or ask them out for a drink.

Nick's journey became mine through each page. Our souls fused for a moment, healing and being brave together.
In this adventure, I have people to be thankful for.

My husband and kids. Okay, I know I wasn't available sometimes, and you found it hard, but you were always there cheering me up, even when tears were rolling down my cheeks and my vision was so blurry I couldn't type anymore (Yes, this is an emotional book, even for me as an author). We're a team, the six of us, and you mean the world to me.

Shalini. Let's be honest. How many times did I actually have to rewrite scenes to translate in words the poignancy of the story or seek emotions from deep inside me to give Nick the voice he deserved? This was our Everest, as you told me, but we climbed it, never backing down, and now we can look back and high-five. Because, girl, we did it! I'm so proud of the story. But mostly, I'm proud of us. Once again, your book fairy godmother's talent and love are priceless, and I'm lucky to have you in my life, as an editor and a friend. To many more books together!

Virginie. Your words of encouragement and your faith in me are invaluable. Yes, Nick's the story of my life. I was just too close to it to notice it.

Jacynthe. Your optimism is priceless. Thank you for being my friend through it all.

Steph. Thank you for giving me the opportunity to share what I was born to do with your students. Two decades ago, you made me fall in love with the language, the words, and the storytelling. Your passion is contagious. And if all teachers were as enthusiastic as you, school would be a place where dreams are supported and nurtured. When I look back, I realize I've come a long way. And it is partly due to you.

Readers. Without you, I wouldn't be calling myself an author. Your love for my books and my characters means the world to me. Carter Hills Band wouldn't be half the universe it is today without your unconditional support and enjoyment of my stories. And yes, the real-life Carter Hills Band Fan Club is something I have never seen coming! Thank you.

Bloggers. Bookstagrammers. YouTubers. TikTokers. Every one of your reviews and early reviews/publicity gave me goose bumps and brought happy tears to my eyes. Thank you for giving my books a chance and for sharing the love.

Second Tear is a wrap, as my editor and I would say, but I'm super emotional at the idea it's over. Sure, every time I type the word "The End" I'm tearful, but for some reason, this one made me super extra-emotional.

Nick and Dahlia, I love you from the bottom of my heart. And you both deserve your happy ending. And so much love.

To all y'all, cheers!

Emmanuelle

ABOUT THE AUTHOR

Soulfully Beautiful Love Stories

USA Today Bestselling Author Emmanuelle Snow is an author of contemporary YA and women's fiction love stories, who gives life to strong characters who'll fight with all they have to reach their life goals and find their own happiness. She loves her characters to be relatable and realistic.

Emmanuelle is in love with love. Especially complicated, deep, and passionate feelings that make a relationship extraordinary and complex all at the same time.

In her spare time, when she's not writing or reading, she likes to go on road trips—with her four kids and her own soulmate—watch movies, paint, or do some DIY, always with a cup of green tea in her hand and listening to country music.

She splits her time between beautiful Canada and the small US towns she adores.

Find all of Emmanuelle's books here:
emmanuellesnow.com

––––––

Want to connect with Emmanuelle online?

You can find her here:

Website
Author's bookstore and merch store

Snow's VIP newsletter

emmanuellesnow.com

Readers' VIP group Snow's Soulmates

facebook.com/groups/snowvip

amazon.com/author/emmanuellesnow

goodreads.com/emmanuellesnow

bookbub.com/authors/emmanuelle-snow

facebook.com/esnowauthor

instagram.com/snowemmanuelle

x.com/snowemmanuelle

pinterest.com/snowemmanuelle

tiktok.com/@snowemmanuelle

ALSO BY THE AUTHOR

CARTER HILLS BAND UNIVERSE

(suggested reading order)

Carter Hills Band series

False Promises

HEART SONG DUET

Blindsided

Forevermore

Whiskey Melody series

Sweet Agony

SECOND TEAR DUET

Cruel Destiny

Beautiful Salvation

BREATHLESS DUET

Wild Encounter

Brittle Scars

Upon A Star Series

Last Hope

Midnight Sparks

Love Song For Two Series

<u>Lonesome Heart Duet</u>

Fallen Legend

Rising Star

<u>Two of Us Duet</u>

Snowbound

Wicked Love

MEDORA BEACH UNIVERSE

Wrecked series

Cast Away

Ride for a Fall

Touchdown series

Kickoff

Read them all

emmanuellesnow.com

All available on author's bookshop

EMMANUELLE
USA TODAY BESTSELLING AUTHOR
SNOW
WILD
ENCOUNTER
a love story
Whiskey Melody series - book four
HOCKEY
HOCKEY
SAVE THE DATE
LOVE
HLIA & NICK

WILD ENCOUNTER

ADDISON

I slumped down on the couch of the posh hotel we were staying at all weekend and huffed, a wine bottle hanging from my fingers by its neck. Glasses were overrated, anyway. "That's it. I'm over men. I'm done."

My childhood best friend snickered.

"I'm serious, Dah. This time I mean it. You know I do."

I scanned the space around me. Large windows with a direct view of Nashville's busy streets below, high wooden beam ceilings, dark flooring, and handcrafted wood furniture. Chic and tasteful, with an unmistakable country vibe.

"Yeah, right. I'm sure you won't last a week. Two at the most," Dahlia teased.

My friend, and the bride-to-be, inched closer, and I zipped her up. Her cut-out mermaid gown was a gray-lavender hue and looked both sexy and demure, showing just enough skin without being indecent. Perfectly Dahlia Ellis.

Before I could sink back into my lazy position on the couch, she beckoned me to follow her with a finger. Sitting on the edge of the bathtub, I glugged the wine straight from the bottle while I watched her apply mascara.

"Addi, there are good men out there who would appreciate your light. Don't punish all of them because you dated a few who were total dickheads." She grinned at her reflection, but it was meant for me. It warmed my heart as she continued, "I'm confident you won't last in your quest to ignore them all when they turn on the charm."

"Laugh all you want, girlfriend. You'll see. Be prepared to be shocked. This time, I'm not backing down. Anyway, remember Felicia from college? She messaged me last week. It's destiny."

"The one you 'experimented' with?" my friend asked, curving her fingers into elaborate air quotes, her gaze fixed on her eyelashes in the mirror, not sparing me a look.

Another sip. "The same. We could have been in love and lived happily ever after. The timing was just not right back then."

"Huh, you said the same thing about Carter once. Besides, I thought women weren't your thing," Dahlia added with a quirked brow.

"It's not the same. And perhaps I changed my mind. Who knows? I might be into women more than men after all. Think about it, we should have been a couple, you and I. Everything would have been much simpler."

"You think?"

I shrugged. "We get along fine. And we're friends, so our relationship would have had a solid foundation. Look at you and Nick. Friends, then lovers. I believe that's the secret to long-lasting love. Back to business..." I sighed. "Felicia and I experienced some pretty memorable moments together. It's just Shawn happened to cross my path, and I couldn't resist him. Stupid me. Stupid men. I'm telling you their species is old news. You're lucky you found two awesome ones in your lifetime. What are the odds? God knows I've tried. I usually don't back down easily, but hey, maybe it's time I try something else. That I understand once and for all what life has been trying to tell me all these years…"

Dahlia shook her head, focusing her attention on me for the first time since I started the conversation about my disastrous love life. "Addi, you know how much I love it when you're not being overdramatic, right?"

I poked my tongue out, and we both burst out laughing. A sense of peace washed over me. Dahlia Ellis had that effect on me. Her presence was always enough to ease all my doubts and bring a curve to my lips, even when I didn't feel like expressing joy. "That's why you love me. I'm entertaining…despite myself. Anyway, where are the bridal shower festivities taking place? I can't wait to party all weekend. The distraction will do me good."

My best friend reached over and landed a kiss on my cheek, her eyes searching mine. Worry shimmered in them. "You okay?"

I nodded.

"You'd tell me if it wasn't the case, right?" I sensed the apprehension in her question.

"Always. You're the only one I willingly confide in."

With a warm smile that promised everything would turn out just fine, she went back to applying her makeup. "All over town. Tonight, we're having dinner with only the people closest to us. Tomorrow, we'll have a get-together with some friends and the guys on a yacht before splitting up and maybe meeting again later."

"Rewind for a sec. We're having your bridal shower with your future husband and his friends?"

"Yep. His best friend. Guys from work. That's the idea."

"Yeah, I should've been the one organizing the whole thing." Dahlia raised a hand, ready to argue, but I kept going. "For what it's worth, I'm sorry I let you down. I was really looking forward to throwing you the bachelorette party of the century."

A new weight grew heavy on my shoulders. In the fog of my latest relationship blowing up, I had lost focus on what really mattered. This time, my tears had knocked me out more than ever. But I was back now, and no way was I failing the girl I considered a sister again.

Dahlia pulled me into a hug. "It's okay. Don't chastise yourself. It'll still be fun. And you did plan most of the wedding already. You deserve a night off…to enjoy yourself… You, me, booze, music. And the man I love and his friends."

I leaned back, studying her for a moment. Dahlia had no ounce of evilness in her. She really meant everything she'd just said.

"What is it?" she asked, a frown marring her forehead.

"Real sweet, Dah. After I told you I was done with men, you're going to make me spend hours with a bunch of Nick's buddies. And alcohol. If I didn't know your heart, I'd think this was a test. To check my newfound determination." One more sip of wine. *Be strong, Addi*, I repeated in my head. I flicked my hand and pasted a smile on my lips. "Know what? It doesn't matter. I won't back down. I'm done with men, and I'll prove it to you. Tonight. I won't flirt, and I won't kiss. Nope. Nada. D.O.N.E. Just watch and learn, girlfriend."

I held out my hand, and we shook on it.

Read Tucker and Addison's story,
Wild Encounter, now

emmanuellesnow.com/products/wild-encounter

Author's bookstore at emmanuellesnow.com

"Tucker freaking Philips!!! Wow! Emmanuelle Snow has written another beautiful, rollercoaster, sneakily emotional romance." *(Goodreads)*

"This is without a doubt Emmanuelle's best work yet!" (Goodreads)

Wild Encounter is book one in the ***Breathless*** duet. Read the first part or the complete duet now

www.ingramcontent.com/pod-product-compliance
Lightning Source LLC
Chambersburg PA
CBHW050841210726
48290CB00004B/1036